Anne Baker trained as a nurse at Birkenhead General Hospital, but after her marriage went to live first in Libya and then in Nigeria. She eventually returned to her native Birkenhead where she worked as a Health Visitor for over ten years before taking up writing. She now lives with her husband in Merseyside. Anne Baker's other Merseyside sagas are all available from Headline and have been highly praised:

'A heartwarming saga' *Woman's Weekly*

'A stirring tale of romance and passion, poverty and ambition' *Liverpool Echo*

'A fast-moving and entertaining novel, with a fascinating location and warm, friendly characters' *Bradford Telegraph and Argus*

'A wartime Merseyside saga so full of Scouse wit and warmth that it is bound to melt the hardest heart' *Northern Echo*

'Baker's understanding and compassion for very human dilemmas makes her one of romantic fiction's most popular authors' *Lancashire Evening Post*

'A gentle tale with all the right ingredients for a heartwarming novel' *Huddersfield Daily Examiner*

'A well-written enjoyable book that legions of saga fans will love' *Historical Novels Review*

D1363217

By Anne Baker and available from Headline

Like Father, Like Daughter
Paradise Parade
Legacy of Sins
Nobody's Child
Merseyside Girls
Moonlight on the Mersey
A Mersey Duet
Mersey Maids
A Liverpool Lullaby
With a Little Luck
The Price of Love
Liverpool Lies
Echoes Across the Mersey
A Glimpse of the Mersey
Goodbye Liverpool
So Many Children
A Mansion by the Mersey
A Pocketful of Silver
Keep The Home Fires Burning
Let The Bells Ring
Carousel of Secrets
The Wild Child
A Labour of Love
The Best of Fathers
All That Glistens
Through Rose-Coloured Glasses
Nancy's War
Liverpool Love Song
Love is Blind
Daughters of the Mersey
A Liverpool Legacy

Anne Baker

A LIVERPOOL LEGACY

headline

First published in 2013
by HEADLINE PUBLISHING GROUP

First published in paperback in 2014
by HEADLINE PUBLISHING GROUP

10

Cataloguing in Publication Data is available from the British Library

ISBN 978 0 7553 9960 4

Typeset in Bembo by Avon DataSet Ltd, Bidford-on-Avon, Warwickshire

Printed and bound in Great Britain by Clays Ltd, St Ives plc

Headline's policy is to use papers that are natural, renewable and
recyclable products and made from wood grown in sustainable
forests. The logging and manufacturing processes are expected
to conform to the environmental regulations of the country of origin.

HEADLINE PUBLISHING GROUP
An Hachette UK Company
338 Euston Road
London NW1 3BH

www.headline.co.uk
www.hachette.co.uk

A LIVERPOOL LEGACY

Chapter One

Late March, 1947

Emily Maynard, known to the family as Millie, leaned back on her hard seat, enjoying the bright spring sun on her face. The heavy old-fashioned yacht was slicing through the water at a good pace and the only sounds were the ripple of water against the hull and the rush of wind in the sails. This was sheer bliss after the pressure of work and the hard, bleak winter.

It was Saturday and her husband Peter's sixty-fourth birthday. He'd taken a long weekend away from his business and brought the family with him to celebrate. He very much needed a break because he'd been working overtime, but this morning with his head thrown back and his chin thrusting forward, Pete looked at least a decade younger than his age.

'You keep me young,' he'd told Millie often. She was his second wife and at thirty-four was only two years older than his elder daughter from his first marriage. But Millie thought it was Pete's personality that kept him young, he always threw himself into what he was doing and brimmed with enthusiasm and contentment.

Almost everybody else in Britain was in a lacklustre mood. They had just endured a bitter winter, Britain's coldest and longest spell of heavy snow and severe frost for fifty years.

Many schools and factories had had to close for lack of heating, but theirs had not, they'd all carried on working wearing their outdoor coats and scarves.

'Sylvie, Sylvie,' Pete called, 'be a good girl and get my sunglasses for me. They're in my bag in the cabin.'

Millie watched Sylvie, her seventeen-year-old daughter, come round from the bow to oblige. She'd said she wanted to sunbathe but hadn't yet stripped down to the swimsuit she was wearing under her blouse and shorts.

'Not much warmth in this sun yet,' she said to her mother as she passed.

'It's only the end of March,' Millie said.

'And only a couple of weeks since the big thaw,' Pete told her. 'But it's lovely to see the sun again.'

The whole family loved Sylvie, as an infant in her pram, as a charming little girl, her eyes alight with mischief, and now as a young lady trying to appear more grown up than she was. Sylvie had not done all that well at school and had wanted to leave and work in the business. After a year at commercial college, Pete, and James his brother and partner in the business, had taken her on.

Pete said that Sylvie looked very like her, but Millie knew she'd never had stunning beauty like her daughter's. Both were petite and slightly built, but inevitably Millie's figure had filled out a little with childbirth and maturity.

Sylvie had a childlike face, a neat small nose and rosebud mouth. They both had fair colouring but while Millie thought of her hair as being pale fawn, Sylvie's hair shone golden in the sun, while her eyes were a very beautiful soft golden-brown – unusual with such blond hair. Her looks never failed to work their charm on Pete and her two much older half-sisters and she always got what she wanted. Millie thought Sylvie had been indulged all her life, possibly they'd over-indulged her, but she'd always been a happy and loving girl.

2

Millie and Pete also had two young sons, Simon was eleven and Kenneth nine, but they'd not taken them out of school to bring them. This was just a short break, primarily for her and Pete to rest and recover from their grinding workload.

It was no great novelty for them to come to Hafod, the holiday home in Anglesey that had been bought by Pete's father. James, his elder brother had used it in his youth but had long since lost interest. Other members of the wider Maynard clan occasionally visited but it was only Pete and his family who came regularly. They counted themselves lucky to be able to get away from Liverpool fairly often. The boat had also belonged to his father and the family all enjoyed sailing and fishing trips in it when they were down here, though they rarely went far.

In summer, the locals ran boat trips to Puffin Island for holiday visitors to see the seals, but it was some distance off and they knew a nearer place where more wildlife could be seen. Today they were heading to a tiny island, really just an outcrop of rock from the seabed, a mile or so off the coast. As far as they knew it didn't have a name though the family had always called it Seal Island because it was inhabited only by seals and seabirds which they could watch from the boat.

Pete remembered his parents taking him to Seal Island once and landing there to enjoy a picnic. He'd decided they'd do that too, it would be something different to celebrate his birthday. Now wearing his sunglasses, he was at the tiller and in a very upbeat mood. He loved messing around in the boat. He could handle *Sea Sprite*'s thirty-four feet single-handed and sometimes did. His eyes were like the ocean, bluish green, and they challenged the world and sparked with confidence in his own ability. They'd been planning this trip and looking forward to it over the freezing winter months.

Winning the war had put Britain on the breadline. The population was exhausted, all its reserves had been spent. It had run up huge debts and everything was in short supply. The country had had to switch its efforts from fighting a war to earning a living again, and it was now facing an uphill struggle for survival. Austerity Britain, the newspapers called it.

Bread had been rationed for the first time last year. Heavy manual workers were allowed more than clerical workers and housewives. The wheat content had been reduced to the 1942 level so the bread was darker and was known sarcastically as Victory Bread. Worse, to save grain, the amount of brewing was cut and then cut again more drastically, so there was little beer to be had. Butter, margarine and fat rations were cut, and no rice was imported because it was sent to starving Europe.

The politicians were making huge plans to provide a free health service, better housing and a decent education for all, but they had no money to do it. Businesses were being harried to produce and export more to pay for a better life. William C. Maynard and Sons was working flat out, struggling to do this.

'Dad, Dad.' Sylvie was sitting on the cabin roof and shouting excitedly. 'I can see the seals – over there.'

Millie straightened up to look. They were nearing the island, an inhospitable rocky cliff rising from the sea, with almost every ledge occupied by squawking seabirds.

'We'll have to go round to the other side to land,' Pete said.

The cliffs soon gave way to lower land and more seals could be seen now. Pete started the auxiliary engine and gave the order to collapse the sails. Sylvie leapt to do it, she called it crewing for Dad.

'I can see the inlet,' she said. Pete nosed the *Sea Sprite* slowly into it. It was very sheltered and the water was calm. Millie kept checking the depth of the water to make sure they didn't run aground. A quarter of a mile or so in, Pete said he could see a place where it would be possible to tie up. The bank overhung the sea loch and a scrub of tangled brushes grew along the water's edge. He put out the old tyres he'd brought to act as fenders and said to Sylvie, 'Here's the painter, get ready to jump.'

'What do I tie it to, Dad?'

'There aren't many decent trees, are there? I'm looking for a few feet of clear space where you can get a foothold, but with a strong bush nearby. How about this place coming up?'

'Fine, how did you know about it?'

'Put it down to experience.' He edged the yacht closer until Sylvie could jump ashore to make the boat fast.

'Will this do, Dad?'

He climbed out to test the holding power of the bush. Millie knew he wouldn't be satisfied.

'Throw me a line from the stern,' he called. Millie did so and he tied the other end fast to a different bush. 'Now let's have the anchor.' Millie heaved it up and he swung that into the bank too. 'There, that should hold us. We'll be safe enough now.'

'I can't wait to see what's here,' Sylvie said, climbing across the short wiry turf that covered this part of the island. Millie and Pete followed more slowly.

'There won't be much of anything,' Millie said, 'if it's uninhabited.'

'I think we saw the ruins of a house when I came with my father, so somebody must have tried to scratch a living here once.'

They climbed higher until they could see the whole of the island laid out before them. There were seals in plenty swimming in the surf but one half of the island had been taken over by a large colony of seabirds. Pete had brought his binoculars and they tried to pick out different species.

Millie found it fascinating. 'I do wish we could take photographs,' she lamented, but film was almost impossible to obtain. They found the ruins of the cottage, now reduced to a few stones shaped from the local rock.

They retraced their steps back to the boat because Sylvie said she wanted to have her first swim of the year, but dipping in her toe made her decide the water was too cold. 'Too early in the season.' Pete smiled and clambered on board. 'I'm not going in.'

'What about lunch then? I'm hungry.'

'Already?'

'It's gone one o'clock, Dad.'

Millie opened up the hamper that Valerie and Helen had packed for them. Pete loved his daughters and wanted to keep them close, he always included them in family celebrations. Esme, their mother, had died of leukaemia after a long illness when they'd been teenagers, but Pete had managed to be father and mother to his girls for several years.

'I'm afraid they'll think of me as a wicked stepmother,' Millie had confessed nervously to him when she was first married. 'I can't be a mother to them.' She'd been barely eighteen herself at the time and couldn't imagine it.

Pete had laughed. 'Sweetheart, you won't have to be.' He'd dominated them all, she didn't doubt he'd dominated Esme, but with him they'd coalesced into a happy family unit.

'We aren't going to eat on the boat, are we?' Sylvie asked now.

'Why not?'

'This is a celebration birthday picnic, and it won't be a picnic at all if we stay here.' The cabin was small and cramped and didn't have a table. 'We've got to eat in style today.'

6

'All right, you find us a more stylish place, but don't forget we'll have to carry everything.' Peter filled the kettle with the water they'd brought and picked up the Primus so they could make tea.

'If it's to be a proper picnic we should light a fire,' Sylvie said.

'There aren't any trees here so where would we find wood?'

Millie brought the car rugs, and she and Sylvie carried the hamper between them. 'We shouldn't go too high,' Millie said. 'The wind is still cold up there.'

Sylvie chose the first level spot and shook out the rugs to sit on while Millie unpacked the hamper. Yesterday afternoon, Pete's older daughters had baked a sponge cake and a Scotch egg each to provide what luxury they could for the picnic. There was salad and bread to go with it.

Valerie and Helen were staying in the house with them. Both were married, Valerie had twin toddlers and Helen had a four-month-old baby to care for. They'd decided against the boat trip, it would not be suitable for the babies.

'Valerie's given us a tablecloth,' Sylvie enthused, 'so we can sit round it and make it a bit special.'

Pete lit the Primus and settled the kettle to boil. 'It would be more special if she'd given us chairs,' he said, lowering himself stiffly to the rug. Millie knew he found it more comfortable to eat on the boat where at least he had a seat, but it was a jolly meal. They all had hearty appetites and agreed the lunch was excellent.

When they returned to the boat, Sylvie stripped down to her two-piece swimsuit and settled down in the bow with some cushions and her book. 'I'm hoping to get a tan,' she said.

Pete baited some fish hooks and cast them over the side. 'Wouldn't it be great if we could catch enough fish to take home to feed us all?' he said. But he was yawning and before long he had stretched out on one of the bunks in the cabin.

Millie was left to sit in the sun and keep an eye on the fish hooks. Helen had lent her a book and she was enjoying it. She glanced up and saw one of the lines twitch and leapt to pull it in, but it was only a three-inch tiddler so she threw it back into the water and rebaited the hook. It was soporific in the sun and she could feel herself dozing off too. She woke up to find Sylvie wearing her pullover again, helping Pete to pull in another of the lines with a silver fish jerking on the hook.

'It's quite big, isn't it? What sort is it, Dad?'

'Codling, I think.'

'There's another on this line,' Sylvie screamed with excitement. 'Gosh, Dad, I can see a whole lot of them in the water down below.' Millie jumped up to help.

'A fish this size would make a good dinner,' Pete chortled. 'So we need five, and if we could get six we could feed the twins too.' Within half an hour they'd caught six. 'The best afternoon's fishing I've ever had,' he said happily. 'That was a real treat. Have we got some paper or a towel or something to wrap them in?'

Millie found a clean tea towel for him and for the first time realised it was much cooler, the sun had gone and the sky was grey and darkening. She looked about her and felt a moment of disquiet. Her husband and daughter were still admiring their gleaming catch. 'Just look at this one, it must weigh over a pound.'

'Pete, I think there's a storm brewing,' Millie said. The wind had got up and could be heard whistling through the inlet.

Sylvie shivered. 'The sun went a long time ago.'

'Goodness!' Pete was frowning, clearly troubled. 'This is a surprise! It wasn't forecast.'

8

'We'll be all right, won't we?' Sylvie asked.

'I'm going to walk a little way down the inlet until I can see what the sea looks like,' he said and set off scrambling over the rocks. They both followed him.

When it came in sight Millie couldn't stop her gasp of horror. 'What a change since this morning!' The sea was pewter grey like the sky and was hurling itself at the rocky shoreline in thunderous crashes, resulting in lots of seething white foam. Beyond that they could see the huge swell and the white-crested waves, but they couldn't see far, the weather was closing in. 'It's raining over there,' Sylvie said.

'Let's go back to the boat,' Peter sounded shocked, 'before it starts raining here.' They went as quickly as they could and threw everything possible into the cabin to keep dry.

'What are we going to do now?' Millie asked. 'It looks pretty bad out there.'

She could see Pete was pondering the problem. 'Do we go now before the weather worsens, or do we stay here until the storm has passed?' he asked.

'How long will it take to pass over?' Sylvie wanted to know.

'That's in the lap of the gods, but we'd be all right in this inlet, it's very sheltered. We could stay all night if necessary.'

'What? Spend the night here?' Sylvie was shocked.

'We have enough food,' Millie said. 'We have the fish and just enough butter left over from lunch to fry it. There's a little bread too and half that cake.'

'But it's Dad's birthday and he's booked a table at the Buckley Arms for dinner,' Sylvie objected. 'I was looking forward to that. Valerie's arranged a babysitter . . .'

Millie froze. 'There's no way of letting them know we're staying the night,' she said slowly. 'Won't they be worried?'

'They'll imagine we're lost at sea,' Sylvie added. 'I vote we go.'

'It's twenty to five,' Millie said. 'We have to go now if we're going to have time to change and get to Beaumaris by half seven.'

'All right, we'll go,' Pete said. 'Really we have to. The girls will be worried stiff if we don't turn up.'

'They'd call out the coastguard,' Sylvie said with a laugh.

'*Sea Sprite* is a heavy boat and it's stood a few storms in its time. We'll be fine. Let's stow everything shipshape and get ready to leave.'

Millie could feel a heavy ball of anxiety growing in her stomach. She had faith in Peter's judgement and knew he was an experienced sailor but he rarely went out in the boat unless the weather was fine.

Chapter Two

Pete hoisted the sails and got the engine running before they cast off. He tied a lifeline to Millie, securing her to the boat, and as soon as Sylvie jumped back on board he did the same for her.

'You too,' Millie reminded him.

'You bet, there'll be some big waves out there.'

When they came in sight of the raging sea, Sylvie asked fearfully, 'Had we better wear our lifebelts too?'

'You're tethered to the boat,' Pete said, 'but it wouldn't do any harm.' They were at the mouth of the inlet and could feel the spray being thrown up. 'They'll keep you warm and dry.'

He had remarked on the size of the swell this morning but by comparison it was enormous now, and the rain had reached them so visibility was down to a few yards. No life jacket would keep them dry in this downpour. He turned to smile at Millie. 'You two shelter in the cabin. You'll be safer there.'

They did as he suggested. Sylvie threw herself on one of the bunks, shouting, 'This is awful!'

She looked frightened and Millie didn't blame her but she pinned the cabin door open and stayed in the opening watching Pete, in case he needed her to help in some way. He was gripping the tiller with a look of intense concentration on his face and pointing *Sea Sprite*'s bow directly at the huge wave sweeping towards them. She'd been out with him often enough to know that if a wave like that caught the boat sideways on it could swamp it and turn it over, and that could mean curtains for them all.

Millie's heart was in her mouth but she couldn't drag her eyes away from the next green curling wall that was advancing towards them. Suddenly, she felt the bow being tossed up and all she could see to the front of them was the dark sky. Then just as suddenly the boat plunged in the opposite direction and seemed to be diving to the bottom of the sea. As she grabbed the door for a handhold she heard Sylvie scream, 'Mum, what's happening?'

The boat smacked on the water with a thump, and there were ominous creaks and cracks in *Sprite*'s old timbers but behind the wave the boat popped up level again like a cork, and travelled on at breakneck speed.

'We're all right, love,' she tried to comfort her daughter, 'just a wave.'

'A big one.' Pete's voice was snatched by the wind which was now a howling gale and she had to watch his lips. 'Don't worry, we can manage them.' It helped to ease her panic that he still seemed quietly confident but the waves kept coming and her mouth had gone dry.

She couldn't help but think of all the ships that had been lost along the east coast of Anglesey. The place was notorious for shipwrecks. Not far from their house an obelisk had been erected to commemorate the loss of an ocean-going passenger ship. It had been heading for Liverpool and had foundered on its return from its first voyage to Australia. It had been newly built and state of the art for its time, but many people on it had lost their lives. She told herself that was a long time ago in the last century, though she couldn't recall exactly when. It didn't help to remember that *Sea Sprite* had been built in the eighteen nineties.

Millie couldn't stop herself leaning out of the cabin doorway to take another look. The wind felt strong enough to blow her head off, but suddenly it shifted direction, the boat shuddered and the boom thundered across with its heavy sail. The bangs, cracks and creaks from the mast sounded even more sinister.

'Mum, don't leave me,' Sylvie screamed, lifting her head from the bunk.

'No, love, I won't,' she said as calmly as she could. 'There's nothing wrong.' Her daughter's face was paper-white. 'Are you feeling seasick?'

'No,' Sylvie said and staggered to join her at the cabin door. She was shaking.

'We'll be all right, love,' Millie told her, giving her a hug. 'Try to relax.'

'What's making that noise? It sounds as though the boat's breaking up.'

That was exactly what it did sound like but it wouldn't help Sylvie if she admitted it. 'No, the *Sprite* is solidly built. You know it is.'

She saw then that Pete was beckoning to her. 'I'm going to see what Dad wants. You stay here where it's safe.' She ducked low and moved to sit on the seat that ran along the side of the boat, slithering along towards him. As soon as she left the shelter of the cabin the wind buffeted her and tore at her hair.

Pete put a hand on her arm but his eyes didn't lift from the sea. The next wave, a beautiful deep green cliff, was rearing up in front of them. Millie held on until they were over it and it was breaking up all around them in huge torrents of white foam.

He put his head down close to hers so she could hear him. 'It wasn't as big as the last,' he said. 'I'm worried about the mast, it's never made noises like this before. There it goes

13

again, almost like a gunshot. This wind could break it off.' Millie felt a stab of sheer terror as he went on. 'I want the mainsail down, it's wet now and the weight is making things worse. We don't need it anyway and the boat would be easier to control if we weren't going so fast.'

'You want me to put it down?' Millie closed her eyes and shuddered. She'd acted as crew for Pete on other holiday trips and knew what had to be done, but today the *Sprite* was tossing about so much she could hardly stand up against the force of the gale.

Pete said, 'I'll do it if you like. This wind is gusting. Every so often it gives an extra powerful blast from a different quarter and that puts more pressure on the mast.'

Millie was watching the mast in awful fascination. 'It's doing it again,' she screeched, grabbing for his arm. The sail slackened for a moment as the wind turned and when the powerful blast hit it, the boom flew across as though propelled by an engine. All the time, the mast was protesting with creaks as loud as pistol shots and the yacht heeled over in an additional burst of speed.

'Oh my God!' Millie breathed as she hung on for dear life.

Pete's voice was in her ear. 'If I collapse the sail you'll have to hold the tiller.'

She felt another stab of fear. She'd steered the boat many times but never in conditions like these.

'Keep it on this course unless you see a big wave coming at you from a different quarter. If you do, aim the bow straight into it. That's the important thing. If the wind gusts and changes again, you could find it pulls you broadside on but you must keep the bow heading straight into the waves.'

'Yes, I know.'

'It's better now we're away from the island.'

'Right,' she said, and moved to take his position in the stern. 'Be careful.'

Sylvie was still watching them from the cabin door. He grinned and said, 'Aren't I always?'

The tiller felt like a wild thing, it wasn't easy to keep the boat on course. Millie only dared take quick glances to see what Pete was doing. He looked quite stiff, poor dear.

Then she realised the wind was gusting again. It took all her strength to hang on to the tiller and keep the boat straight. She heard the mast protest ominously yet again and felt the slight lull followed immediately by the boom beginning to swing. 'Going about,' she yelled to warn Pete.

She heard another thud and the boat jerked so violently the tiller was snatched from her grasp. She heard an almighty splash and screamed at exactly the same moment Sylvie did.

This was disaster. Nobody was controlling the boat; they were at the mercy of the wind and the sea. Sylvie was continuing to scream.

Millie saw another wave bearing down on them on the starboard side and lunged for the tiller. In the nick of time, she managed to bring the bow round so that they rode the wave safely. On her right, a rope had whipped taut straight across the stern.

She glanced round to see what Pete was doing because the main sail was still up. She couldn't see him. He wasn't here. Everything went black in a moment of sheer panic. Sylvie crashed on to the stern seat beside her to yank at her arm.

'Dad's gone overboard,' she screamed. 'Turn back. We've got to look for him.'

'Oh my God!' Millie felt she couldn't deal with this, she was terrified, but just as quickly she realised that if she didn't do something, all would be lost. The taut rope pulled tighter, it was made fast to the seat supports, and it dawned on her in

15

that instant. 'That's his lifeline,' she screamed. Sylvie stared blankly back at her. 'He's secured to the boat. It's that rope, next to you. Quick, pull on it. Let's get him back on board.'

Sylvie knelt on her knees and tried. 'I can't,' she sobbed. 'I can't. It's impossible.'

'Why not?'

'It's too tight. I can't pull him in any closer.' She gave a scream of frustration. 'He's drowning. He must be.'

Though still struggling to control the steering, Millie glanced behind her and she knew another moment of panic. She could see they were towing Pete in their foaming wake, but the speed of the boat meant they'd never be able to pull his weight out of the water and get him on board. They needed to turn back to make the rope slack, but another wave was roaring towards them. They coasted that in the nick of time but already another wave was coming, it wouldn't do to let one catch them broadside on. She couldn't turn in this sea. The boat shuddered, the mast cracked and every other timber seemed in its death throes.

'We've got to get the sail down.' That should make it easier to turn. She had to grip Sylvie's arm to get her attention. 'That'll slow us.'

'But what about Dad? Can he breathe like that?'

'I hope so. You'll have to steer while I do it.' She saw Sylvie's mouth drop open in horror. 'You've done it before, Dad taught you.'

'Not now, I can't,' she whined. 'Dad could be drowning.'

Millie screamed with frustration. 'Pull yourself together. You've got to help him or he will drown. We'll all drown.' Sylvie's white face was awash with tears and rain, and her wet hair was blowing about her head. 'Please don't go to pieces on me,' she implored.

Obediently, Sylvie sat down and took the tiller. 'What course am I to steer?'

Millie no longer had the faintest idea. 'Just keep the bow nose on to the waves and the swell.'

Keeping low, she crept forward as quickly as she could to the bottom of the mast. She could see no sign of any cracks in it. The rope was wet and her fingers stiff with cold but eventually the knot gave and the sail came down.

She felt the boat slowing as she scrambled back. She had to help Pete. Crying with fear and frustration, she hauled with all her might on his lifeline and managed to twist a little of the spare round a cleat, but his body was acting like a sea anchor. They were travelling at a controllable pace but unless they stopped, she knew they'd never get him aboard. Should she stop the engine? What if she couldn't restart it? Without the mainsail they'd not get home without the engine. She knew very little about engines.

'Mum.' Sylvie's voice was excited. 'I can see land. We're heading straight for it. Where are we?'

Millie gave the lifeline one last turn round the cleat before collapsing on the seat beside her daughter to take a look. The rain and mist were clearing but it was almost dark. Yes, she could see a light and perhaps another one further over. They were fast approaching the coast of Anglesey, but she didn't recognise this part. Her stomach lurched and seemed to turn over. She knew just how treacherous this coast was for shipping. There were outcrops of rock all along here, some just beneath the water.

'Change places with me, Sylvie,' she said urgently. 'Keep pulling Dad's lifeline in. It's easier now.'

She took over the tiller, scared stiff by this new emergency. Where were they? Pete would have planned their course carefully but clearly they hadn't kept to it. If she continued on like this she'd drive them straight up on to the long stretch of beach she could now see ahead. But there was no sign of life there and she'd need immediate help for Pete. The beaches were always deserted except in the holiday season. They could be miles from anywhere.

In another flash of panic she realised that if she went aground on the beach, she'd never get the boat off again; heaven knows what it would do to the keel and the engine.

She had to make up her mind quickly whether to turn north or south and she couldn't think. Where were they? Pete never travelled without charts but there was no time to get them out. The currents and the tide would have carried them but where? Her mind stayed blank.

If she went north she could sail off into the Irish Sea and keep going until the engine ran out of petrol. South was her best guess. The population was greater to the south. Beside her, Sylvie grunted with effort.

'How are you doing?' she asked.

'I can't . . . It's not easy but Dad's closer,' Sylvie gasped. 'He gives no sign . . . But his face is sometimes free of the water, do you think he can breathe?'

'Oh God!' Millie felt sick. 'Yes, perhaps.'

'Do you know where we are?'

'Not really . . . But . . . that wouldn't be the lighthouse at Point Lynas, would it?' She felt a first spark of joy. Of course it was! Why hadn't she thought to look for it sooner?

'It is,' Sylvie said. 'It is. It must be. Thank goodness this murk is lifting. It's stopped raining over there so we can see it.'

'Going about,' Millie said to warn her as she turned south. The boom swung slowly across, dragging the sail. Pete insisted they kept all the tackle shipshape and ready for use and she certainly hadn't today. She looked back at the Point Lynas light. How far away from it were they? Could that long stretch of sand be Dulas Beach? If so, they might not be all that far away from home. She kept her eyes peeled as they chugged along the coast, hoping to recognise her whereabouts.

Fifteen minutes later she heard Sylvie's shout above the roar of the gale. 'That's Hafod.' Her voice was full of heartfelt relief. 'Mum, we're home, you've done it.'

Millie slowed the engine. Sylvie was leaping about and waving madly. The lights gleamed out of Hafod. Never had any sight been more welcome. In the gathering dusk she could make out two figures wearing yellow sou'westers running down to the jetty to meet them. The storm must have made Valerie and Helen anxious. Help was at hand.

Millie took a deep breath, she felt completely drained of energy but she slowed the engine right down as she brought the yacht in closer, and cut it at just the right moment so they slid alongside the jetty.

Chapter Three

Millie could hear the rain splattering against the window as she woke up in the double bed. Her head was swimming and she felt drugged to the eyeballs. The first thing she always did was to reach across for Pete. To feel only cold empty space shocked her. He wasn't there. It brought the events of the day before slamming back to her mind.

She remembered climbing stiffly off *Sea Sprite* and virtually collapsing, unable to do another thing. Valerie and Helen had taken over. She knew they'd pulled Pete out of the water and sent for the local doctor. He'd prescribed sedatives for her and Sylvie, and the girls had made them take hot baths and get into bed.

She felt across her bedside table for her watch. It told her it was half past four but she knew from the light it wasn't morning. She pulled herself across the bed to see Pete's alarm clock, but that agreed with her watch. She felt she'd been asleep for a long time but surely not for the best part of twenty-four hours?

She struggled out of bed, found her dressing gown and slippers and crept downstairs. The house was quiet but she could hear a voice and it drew her to the living room. Helen was swinging gently back and forth in the old rocking chair and cooing to her baby Jenny as she gave her a bottle. Helen had long dark hair with an auburn tinge and was said to have her mother's pretty upturned nose. Valerie was nothing like her to look at, she took after her father.

Pete's birthday cards were still spread along the mantelpiece. 'Pete,' she blurted out. 'Where is he? Is he all right?'

She knew she'd alarmed Helen. 'No, no, I'm afraid he isn't,' there were tears in her dark eyes. She got to her feet and hurried the baby out to her pram on the terrace. Millie followed. The storm had passed but the day was grey and dull. She saw her settle Jenny in her pram without much ceremony. Predictably, the baby began to protest, but her mother dropped a kiss on the child's forehead. 'Off you go to sleep, love.'

'What's happened to Pete?' Millie demanded. She felt she was peering through swirling mist and could feel herself swaying. She groped to a chair for support. 'Tell me.'

Helen took her hand and led her back to the rocking chair in the living room. 'There's no easy way to tell you, Millie. Dad was dead when we got him out of the water.'

'Oh God! He drowned?'

'No, they did a post-mortem on him this morning and found there was very little water in his lungs.' She mopped at her eyes and blew her nose. 'You told us he'd been swept overboard by the boom . . .'

'That's what Sylvie said.'

'Well, it cracked him on the head; we could see a big wound. They say it fractured his skull and that he was probably unconscious when he went into the water. That would be why he didn't help himself.'

Millie felt tears burning her eyes. 'It all happened so quickly, I wasn't able to take it in.'

'You did marvellously well, bringing the boat back safely. Val and I are very impressed with that. It could have been much worse.'

'Where is Val?'

21

'She took the twins out walking to tire them out. She thought she'd better ring Uncle James to let him know about Dad. He sent his deepest sympathy to you.'

Millie sniffed into her handkerchief. James and Pete had not got on well, but Pete had been two years older and head of the family. Because James was a virtual invalid and had hardly come to the office in recent years, Pete had run the business and they'd all relied on it to earn them a living.

'He's quite worried, Millie, about how the firm is going to manage without Dad.'

That thought was like a kick in the stomach to Millie. Pete was going to be missed both at home and at work. She was reminded that it was very much a family business. This was a total calamity, she couldn't face it. 'How's Sylvie?'

'Her hands were raw and bleeding from pulling on the rope. The doctor dressed them.'

'Where is she?'

'She hasn't woken up from the sedative yet.'

'Yes I have, well, I've half woken anyway.' Sylvie staggered in and slumped down on the sofa. 'I know Dad isn't all right,' she choked, 'but what's happening?'

Helen started to repeat the sad tale. Millie couldn't bear to hear it all again and went out to the terrace. Jenny's sobs were quieter, she was settling, but Millie picked her up as much to comfort herself as the baby.

Back in the living room Sylvie was sobbing noisily. Millie joined her on the sofa and sat as near to her as she could. She put one arm round her shoulders and pulled her closer. 'I can't believe this has happened to Pete. He was so careful with everything.'

'I'm sorry, I'm sorry, Mum,' Sylvie wept, burying her face on Millie's shoulder. 'I didn't mean to hurt Dad, please forgive me.'

'There's nothing to forgive, love . . .' It was a disaster that

22

would change her life and those of all the family for ever, and it had happened so quickly.

'It's all my fault. I persuaded Dad to come back yesterday through that awful storm.'

'I know it's a terrible shock, love, but you mustn't blame yourself.'

'He wanted to stay there until the storm passed over, he was ready to stay all night. But I wanted to go to the Buckley Arms for dinner, I had a new dress to wear and I told him how much I was looking forward to it.'

Millie said firmly, 'Sylvie, it's not your fault, you mustn't think like that. Dad decided to come home because he knew Helen and Valerie would be worried if we didn't turn up.'

'Worried?' Helen sobbed too. 'What would that matter? Being worried is nothing compared to losing him like this.'

'See what I mean?' Sylvie lifted a face ravaged by tears. 'I didn't realise how bad that storm was, and I thought having a meal out was more important than his life.'

'You didn't *know*.' Millie held her tight. 'We none of us knew what would happen.'

'What are we going to do now?' Sylvie sobbed. 'How are we going to manage without him?'

'I don't know, love, I've been asking myself that, but it wasn't your fault.'

'It's utterly terrible,' Helen said, 'but you mustn't blame yourself, Sylvie. Dad wouldn't want that.'

Millie was worried about Sylvie, her beautiful eyes were puffy and red-rimmed. She kept breaking down in floods of tears if any of them spoke to her, even when they were trying to be kind. The accident cast a black cloud over everything and they talked endlessly of Pete.

They all wanted to get away from Hafod and its raw memories, and the next day Millie and Sylvie, with Helen and her baby, took the train home to Liverpool. Valerie elected to stay because she felt somebody needed to as there were a hundred and one things to be arranged and ends to be tied up. She said her husband Roger would join her at the weekend to keep her company.

Millie was glad to be back in her own home but it had been Pete's home for longer than it had been hers. He'd been born here and so had his father before him. His clothes and books were everywhere. She sat in his favourite armchair, fingered his favourite records and started to read the book he hadn't finished. She could sense his presence in every room and it drove home to her that he'd never be coming back.

She put off going to bed, knowing she wouldn't sleep. To be alone in their double bed would make her weep with grief and loneliness. She didn't know how she was going to break the news to their two sons, Simon aged eleven and Kenneth aged nine, that their father had died, so she put off thinking about that too. Sylvie was inconsolable and though she appeared to be sleeping when Millie looked in on her, she was woken by her daughter's screams at three in the morning.

Sylvie was having a nightmare, reliving her ordeal on *Sea Sprite*. She clung to Millie. 'I wish we'd never gone on that boat trip,' she wept. 'Why didn't we go up Snowdon instead?'

It took Millie half an hour to calm her. She made them both cups of tea, and took hers back to her own lonely bed. She was cold and couldn't sleep, she tossed and turned for another hour, thinking of Pete.

Years ago, when she'd been in trouble and couldn't have survived without help, Pete had come to her aid. He'd been her saviour, her mainstay and prop, and he'd taken care of her ever since. She needed him now desperately. Pete had been kind and generous to everybody but particularly to her and Sylvie. They'd wanted for nothing. He'd been a loving husband, always smoothing out any little problems or difficulties she had.

When finally Millie went to sleep she, too, had a nightmare in which she relived the storm that had caused Pete's death; she woke up sweating and agitated.

She was frightened and worried that she wouldn't be able to keep his business running. Who was going to run it now? Millie had been thrown out of the cosy niche she'd lived in and was floundering. She couldn't imagine how she'd cope without him.

She couldn't lie still any longer, she got out of bed and went down to the kitchen but she didn't want any more tea. She stared out of the window feeling lost, but finally went back to bed, cold and miserable. However impossible it seemed, she would have to cope.

Chapter Four

Millie's mind went back to 1928, to the days before she'd married Pete. She'd been Millie Hathaway then and those had been tough times, very tough, but she'd managed to survive. She'd faced an acute shortage of money through the years of her youth and there'd been nobody better at making one shilling do the work of two, but it was as though juggling with the pennies had scarred her mind and she now needed affluence to feel secure.

Her early childhood had been happy though she'd never known her father except in the photograph her mother Miriam had kept on her dressing table. He'd been killed in the Great War. Her mother had always worked in Bunnies, one of the big Liverpool department stores, and loved her job, but they'd never had much money.

When Millie was reaching her fourteenth birthday and was due to leave school, Mum had asked Bunnies if they would employ her daughter. They'd agreed, although business was not good at that time. Thereafter, they'd both set off to work in the mornings wearing their best clothes and looking smarter than those who lived in similar rooms nearby. But her mother was no longer feeling well. Her health was beginning to fail, and though she went to the doctor, he didn't seem to help much.

Millie had not been able to settle at Bunnies. Although employed as a junior sales assistant, most of her time was spent unpacking new stock and pressing the clothes before they were put out for sale. She was not allowed to work anywhere near her mother and was at the beck and call of other more senior staff. She ran errands, wrapped purchases and made the staff tea.

'You have to start at the bottom,' her mother told her. 'I did. You'll soon start serving customers, just be patient. At least you've got a job.' She had, and many of the girls she'd left school with had not.

Then she met Ryan McCarthy who lived nearby and worked for William C. Maynard and Sons who owned a factory down in the dock area. He brought her little gifts of luxury soap and tins of talcum powder that smelled heavenly, and beguiled her with stories about his job. He was seventeen now and working for the sales manager; he told her he was learning how to run the sales department. They were sending him to night school and he'd have to take exams but in a few years he'd have a job that paid a decent wage. He meant to go up in the world.

'If you don't like what you're doing,' he said, 'why don't you apply for a job with the company I'm with? They're a very good firm to work for.' He showed her a copy of the *Evening Echo* where they were advertising an opening for a school leaver to help in the laboratory attached to their perfume department.

Her mother hadn't been too pleased but she knew Millie wasn't happy at Bunnies. She'd done well at school and wanted a job with better prospects. 'Lab work appeals to me,' she'd said. She'd applied for the job and was delighted when she got it. They gave her a white coat to wear over her own clothes and she went home in the evenings with the scent of exotic perfumes in her hair.

Millie was fifteen when she started working for William C. Maynard and Sons. It was a small family firm with premises

27

near Liverpool's Brunswick Dock and an enviable reputation for its luxury products. She had always loved its scented soaps and talcum powders, as had half of England. The firm found its customers amongst the wealthy.

Pete called it a one-horse firm because they made nothing from scratch. Instead they bought in the best quality half-prepared materials from companies that manufactured in bulk. Their soap was bought in pure shreds from a firm in Widnes and their raw material for talc was a rock-like lumpy powder from France.

What Maynard's did so well was to add exotic perfumes and colour, and shape the soap into large luxurious tablets finished to the highest possible standard. They were wrapped to look elegant and were advertised in the ladies' magazines that were gaining popularity in the late years of Queen Victoria's reign.

Millie found she'd been hired to keep the equipment clean and be a general dogsbody. She was expected to follow Arthur Knowles, the chemist in charge, round the lab as he worked on the perfumes, helping where she could. As they moved along, he explained what he was doing and why, and he was happy to answer her questions. He recognised her interest and did his best to encourage her. She felt she'd entered a new world that was truly absorbing and was soon very content in her new job. Mr Knowles was gentle and kind and treated her like a fond child.

She felt she had everything she could possibly want. The other young girls working near her in the office admired her handsome boyfriend, they thought Ryan McCarthy quite a catch. The only flaw was that her mother's health continued to deteriorate and she didn't approve of Ryan. 'He's wild,' she said, 'but perhaps he'll quieten down and grow out of it.'

Most of the working day Millie spent in the laboratory with Mr Knowles, and he was friendly with other members of staff who came into the department to chat from time to time. In the lunch break one or two would drop in to eat their sandwiches round his desk. Millie made the tea and pulled up a chair to listen to their conversation. Soon she was joining in.

She discovered that the boss, Peter Maynard, took a great interest in the perfumes they made, coming occasionally to work with them. It was he who decided which of the scents would be used in the products the company made.

She learned that every lunchtime many of the senior staff went to a small dockland café called Parker's Refreshment Rooms in the next street. They spoke approvingly of the food there. One day Mr Maynard asked if she knew the place.

'Yes,' she said. 'I walk past it twice a day, delicious scents drift out but I've never been inside.' She'd never had a hot meal anywhere but at home.

There was white lettering across the Refreshment Rooms' window: 'Large Helpings, Good Hot Meals Served Every Day, at Everyday Prices'. Millie was fascinated by the blackboard standing outside displaying the day's menu: Irish hotpot, beef stew and dumplings, casseroled mutton chops, apple pie and custard, rice pudding with rhubarb. It made Millie's mouth water just to read it.

In the week before Christmas, Millie was thrilled when Mr Maynard brought round two of the fancy boxes of soap and talc made in the factory to catch the Christmas gift trade, and swept her and Mr Knowles out to lunch in Parker's Refreshment Rooms. That day, there was roast pork with stuffing and roast potatoes followed by Christmas pudding.

'I've got two daughters pretty much your age,' Peter Maynard told Millie. He had a way of looking at her and teasing her gently. She liked him, he was popular with all his staff. They said he was a fair and considerate boss.

Her mother no longer had the energy to do housework when she came home from Bunnies, so Millie took it on bit by bit. She got up early to do it and make breakfast for her mother. On two evenings each week, she went to night school with Ryan, and he took her to the pictures and to dances at the weekend. Millie was in love and enjoying life.

Ryan had a friend whose family earned their living as greengrocers, making a series of weekly rounds through the residential streets of Liverpool selling fruit and vegetables from a horse and cart. Ryan earned a little extra pocket money mucking out the stable and giving the horse food and water on Sundays. Millie loved going with him to help. He had a key to the stable and considered it a valuable asset because there they could have peace and privacy.

For the last year, her mother had been taking the odd day off work because she didn't feel well enough to go, but Millie only realised how seriously ill she was when the doctor came to visit and told them she had breast cancer. The diagnosis seemed to knock the stuffing out of her mother and she went downhill quickly. Soon she had to give up work completely and spend much of her day in bed. She was able to do little for herself.

Millie looked after her with the help of the neighbours. She continued to go to work because her small wage was the only income they had. Ryan was very generous, he did their shopping when she was pressed for time, bought little extras for them, and sometimes put in money of his own. He also cleaned out the grate and laid the fire so Millie could concentrate on caring for her mother. She didn't know what she would have done without Ryan. With his help she was just about able to manage.

She continued to go to the stable with him on Sundays and by way of repayment he asked for favours. She was scared and held back but not for long. 'Why should I do all this for you when you won't do anything for me?' he asked. 'Anyway, you'll find it fun.'

Perhaps it was over the following six months, but that all changed the morning Millie woke up feeling that all was not as it should be with her body. She'd been fearful that she might become pregnant but Ryan had said no, he'd take good care that she didn't.

Today, she was horribly afraid he could be wrong. With sinking heart and full of dread she got up and rushed through her early morning routine. She said nothing to anybody, hoping against hope she was mistaken. At work, she did her best to forget it and immerse herself in her work.

The passing days brought worry and growing certainty, until Millie had to accept she was going to have a baby. It was a calamity. She was sixteen and knew there was no way she could possibly carry on in this way for more than another few months. She knew only one person who could help her but she was unable to screw up her nerve to tell Ryan. He lived for the good times, she was frightened of telling him, frightened he'd not respond in the way she needed. A baby would be a huge complication in his life too.

It was getting colder so she took to wearing her mother's larger bulky pullovers to hide her changing shape and blessed the fact that she was required to wear a shapeless white coat at work.

One Saturday night Ryan took her to the Odeon to see Humphrey Bogart and Lauren Bacall in *The Big Sleep*. He was keen to see it as he'd enjoyed many of the Philip Marlowe books. A neighbour was sitting with her mother and for Millie it was a rare break. In the semi-dark she held his hand, her eyes were on him more than on the film and she was taking in little of the story.

In the interval, she forced herself to say, 'Ryan, there's something I have to . . .' but he was intent on kissing her.

She turned her head away to avoid his lips and felt tears of fear and frustration burn her eyes. Ryan rubbed his cheek against hers and seemed not to notice.

Before going home, Millie knew Ryan would want to take her, as he usually did, to what he called 'our special place'. She would tell him there, she had to. She walked through the dark back streets with his arm round her; it didn't comfort her. He unlocked the door, took her by the hand and led her into the warm dark stable smelling strongly of horse. They always took time to pat and stroke Orlando before they threw themselves down on his meagre supply of hay and straw. Ryan was already unbuttoning her coat when she made herself say, 'There's something I have to tell you but I'm scared . . .'

He laughed and his lips came down on hers. 'No need to be scared of anything,' he whispered, 'not with me.'

He was unfastening the buttons on her blouse when she got the words out. 'I think I'm pregnant.' She heard his intake of breath as he drew away from her. It was too dark to see his face. 'Ryan?'

'You can't be! I mean, I've been using French letters. Well, most of the time.'

Terror had her in its grip. 'I'm afraid I am,' she choked.

'When? When will it be born?'

'I'm not sure.' It had taken her a long time to accept that she really was pregnant.

'You haven't been to the doctor?'

'No!' It was an agonised cry, tears stung her eyes again. 'He knows me, he comes to see Mum, he'd tell her. I can't pay the bills he sends for her, I can't add to them.'

'Oh God!' he said. 'Perhaps you're making a mistake. Perhaps you're not having a baby at all. Perhaps it's all in your mind.'

Millie shuddered. This was what she'd feared most. 'I can

feel it move inside me,' she said quietly. 'Sometimes it kicks me. There's no mistake.'

He was sitting up, putting distance between them. 'What are you going to do?'

Millie was horrified. He hadn't said, what are *we* going to do. She could see only one way out of her difficulties and made herself say, 'Couldn't we get married?' She held her breath waiting for his answer while tears ran down her cheeks.

'I'm still on a learner's wage,' he protested. 'What would we live on?'

Millie began to do up her buttons, there would be no love-making tonight. 'You could move in with me.' She desperately wanted his ring on her finger and his assurance that they'd face this together, but she hated begging for it. 'It wouldn't cost any more.'

'You've only got two basement rooms,' he said, 'and your mother's there.'

She scrambled to her feet and made herself say, 'She won't be with me for much longer. I'd better get back to her.' Normally, Millie couldn't bear to think of it but her mother now spoke of death in matter-of-fact tones.

'I hate the thought of dying and leaving you on your own when you're so young,' she'd said, 'but the McCarthys will look after you.' Now even that looked unlikely.

They walked home in silence, though Millie held on to his arm as she always had. She knew now that he wouldn't willingly marry her. She had ignored the disquietening rumours she'd heard at work about Ryan – that he was frequently late for work and not so highly thought of by management as he'd led her to believe. He'd given up going to night school though she had not.

He usually came round on Sundays to see her and chat, but the next day he did not. And he usually called for her in the mornings, but on the following Monday he didn't, though she saw him at work. They would wait for each other so they could walk home together but that evening there was no sign of him and she eventually gave up and went home alone with a heavy heart. She knew he was avoiding her and that filled her with dread.

On Tuesday she looked for him in the office but his colleagues said they hadn't seen him since yesterday morning, that he'd disappeared at lunchtime and hadn't turned up for work today. Millie had to hold on to the door for a moment, the room had begun to eddy around her. She felt sick with fear. Surely Ryan wouldn't abandon her when he knew she really needed him? She'd never felt more alone and had no idea how she would cope.

When she got home, Ryan's mother was waiting there for her. She was distraught. 'Have you seen our Ryan? He went to work yesterday and he hasn't been home since.'

Millie burst into tears. Mum was grey-faced and anxious and hardly able to pull herself up the bed. This would be another major worry for her. It took Millie a long time to get the facts out but there was no avoiding it now. Mrs McCarthy was furious and said a lot of hurtful things. Millie sat on the bed and her mother wept with her.

When at last they were alone, she said, 'Millie, you've made the same . . . stupid mistake . . . that I made . . . I wanted you to have a better life . . . than I've had.' There was agony on her face and she couldn't get her breath. 'But now look at the mess you're in.'

It had never occurred to Millie that her mother wasn't married. She called herself Mrs Hathaway and had always worn a wedding ring. Millie's eyes went to the photograph in the silver frame beside the bed. 'I believed you when you said my father died in the trenches,' she choked.

'He did. He was posted to France . . . That was the trouble.'

Millie mopped at her eyes and blew her nose. 'At least you knew that if he could, he would have come back to marry you.' She understood only too well that to have no husband and be with child was the worst sin any girl could commit. Society looked down on women who did that.

Ryan had no reason to leave, except that he didn't love her enough to stay and help her. It was cold, heartless rejection and if he'd slashed her with a knife it couldn't have been more hurtful. Millie was too upset to cook supper, she felt sick, and neither of them wanted to eat. She went to her bed in the alcove off her mother's room but hardly slept all night.

When her alarm went the next morning Millie got up as usual and made breakfast for her mum though she felt terrible. Her mother was listless and red-eyed, she hadn't slept much either.

In the cloakroom, before she reached the perfume department, Millie heard the rumours that were flying round. Ryan had disappeared and his account books had been examined; the sales he said he'd made did not add up. Somebody told her they'd heard he'd signed on as crew on a ship going deep sea. He wouldn't return to England for two years.

Millie climbed the stairs to the perfume laboratory in a state of despair, put on her white coat and tried to follow her usual morning routine. Within five minutes, she'd dropped and broken one of the glass flasks she was cleaning.

'What's the matter, Millie?' Mr Knowles asked. She didn't want to tell him. She was too ashamed, it was all too raw and painful and she was afraid she'd be thrown out of her job. She couldn't risk that. She needed to go on working for as long as she possibly could.

When she didn't answer he went on in his slow, gentle drawl, 'You've been crying and you don't look well. In fact you look positively ill.'

She couldn't explain. She couldn't even raise her eyes to look at him.

'Something's happened to upset you, but not here. All is well here, so it must be at home. How is your mother?'

Some time ago she'd told him Mum was ill, but he didn't know how much worse she was now. The memory of the anguish she'd caused her mother brought tears coursing down Millie's cheeks again and she broke down and began to tell him. Once started, it all came flooding out, even the name of her baby's father.

'Ryan McCarthy?' He was shaking his head. 'Well, that explains one thing that was puzzling us. You're better off without him, lass, I doubt he'd be much good to you. It seems your Mr McCarthy has been stealing and selling the company's soap for his own benefit. The books show he's been altering the figures over the last year.' He thought for a moment and then said, 'I'm going to tell Peter Maynard.'

Millie started to protest but he held his hand up. 'You aren't well enough to work and he'll have to know why.'

'I'm all right,' she insisted and made to go back to the sink where she'd been working, but suddenly she felt dizzy, the shelves with their many bottles were swirling round her. She would have fallen if he hadn't caught her and backed her into the chair.

'When will your baby be born?'

'I don't know,' she had to admit. 'I haven't told the doctor, he'd have said something to Mum, you see.'

'Oh my goodness!'

At that moment Peter Maynard walked in. 'Is something the matter, Millie?'

She could feel her cheeks burning but Mr Knowles said, 'Millie's in a bit of bother,' and went on to explain while her toes curled up with embarrassment.

'Why haven't you been to see a doctor?' her boss asked. 'You must know you need to.'

She felt petulant. 'It costs three shillings and sixpence to see him in his surgery, and he'd have told my mum. I didn't want her to know.'

'Oh dear, dear, dear,' he sighed. Then he said gently, 'I'm afraid you'll have to tell her. You can't go on hiding this for ever.'

'She knows,' Millie said. 'Ryan's mother came round to see us last night, and it all came out.'

Peter Maynard picked up the phone on Mr Knowles's desk and asked the operator for Dr Fellows. 'Right, young lady,' he told her, 'you can see the company doctor right away. You know Dr Fellows, he gave you a medical before you started work with us. His surgery is on the corner of the street just down there.'

'Yes, I know,' she said. 'Thank you.' Millie really needed to know how much longer she had before the baby would be born. She'd have to get things ready.

'You're all right to go that far?' Mr Knowles asked.

'Yes, I'm fine now.'

'Come back here afterwards and tell us what he says. When you can't work we'll have to find someone else to take your place.'

'Poor kid,' she heard him say as she closed the door behind her. So they felt sorry for her. Millie wanted to die with humiliation. Telling them had been awful, but it was a relief that they knew and were offering to help.

The doctor gave Millie a date for the birth that was only eight weeks off and confirmed that her baby was developing normally. He prescribed iron tablets and vitamins and told her she must eat more if the baby was to continue to grow, recommending milk, eggs and cheese. 'You'll need to book a hospital bed for the delivery.' He explained how to go about that but not how she'd be able to pay for it.

She returned to the laboratory feeling reassured in one sense but overawed at the short time that was left before she had to take care of a baby as well.

She told Mr Knowles and was reaching for her white coat to return to work when he said, 'Go along to the boss's office, he wants a word. Go on, he told me to send you.'

Millie was swamped with the fear that he'd sack her. If he did she'd be without money for food or medicines for her mum. Since she'd given up work at Bunnies, she knew her mother had worried about having nowhere to turn but the workhouse. Millie had heard fearsome tales about the place from her neighbours, and she knew it would finish Mum if she had to apply. She tapped nervously on the boss's door, dreading what might be coming.

'Come in,' he called and looked up as she did so. 'Come and sit down, Millie. Did you get a date for when you can expect this baby?'

'Yes, the doctor says November the tenth.'

He frowned. 'That's not long.'

She was suffused with panic. 'Eight weeks but I feel fine. I can carry on working for another month or six weeks.' She had to struggle to get her breath.

'Millie, you can't. I'll have to advertise for another school leaver to help Mr Knowles.'

She was going to lose her job! 'I have to earn …' she was saying but everything was going black, the room was spinning and she was sliding off the chair.

She knew he'd stood up and was coming round his desk towards her. 'Be careful,' he called but he seemed a long way away.

She came round to find she was lying flat on the floor

and Mr Maynard was standing over her. 'You fainted,' he told her. 'It proves my point, you can't go on working now. You're not eating enough, are you? Lie there for a minute until you feel better and I'll run you home in my car.'

'I'm all right, really I am.' She insisted on getting to her feet by herself although he offered her a hand to help her up. 'I can't trouble you to drive me home.'

'It's no trouble. How d'you get here, by bus?'

'No, I walk, it isn't far. I feel much better now, I'll be fine.'

'I'd be afraid you'll faint again and fall under a bus. Come on, let's go. Where is Wilbraham Street? Is that the Scotland Road area?'

'Yes.' Millie had never ridden in a car before and would have enjoyed it if she hadn't been so worried about the future. He drew up outside the house where she and her mother had rooms and she got out.

A flight of five steps rose to the peeling front door, and the stout figure of Mrs Croft, her landlady, came bustling down to greet her. 'About your rent,' she said in ringing tones so half the street could hear.

Millie cringed. 'I'm sorry . . .'

'Sorry isn't enough. I'm tired of having to ask for it. You owe five weeks now. You said you'd pay something on account but you're making no effort. I know your mother's sick but I have to live too. I'm sorry, but it's now a question of pay up or get out.'

Millie was struggling not to burst into tears, she couldn't take any more humiliation. She felt searing indignity that her landlady had said that in front of her boss, and had to hold on to the railings that fenced off the steps to the basement.

She heard him say, 'How much is owed?' but couldn't

listen to any more of that. 'Millie, have you got your rent book?'

He had to ask twice before she took in that he meant to pay off her debt. 'I can't let you—'

'I don't think you have much choice,' he said.

He was right, she hadn't. She crashed down the steps to the basement, pushed her key into the door and called, 'It's only me, Mum,' so she wouldn't be scared. She rummaged in the sideboard drawer for her rent book and was back up on the pavement with it in moments.

'It's twelve shillings a week,' Mrs Croft demanded, 'and five weeks is owed.'

Millie was mortified to see Mr Maynard getting out his wallet. He handed over three pound notes and Mrs Croft scribbled in the rent book.

'I don't know how to thank you.' Millie wanted the pavement to swallow her up. She went down to the basement door which she'd left open.

He followed her. 'I can't believe you're battling against all this,' he said. 'You're so full of smiles and bubbling high spirits in the lab. It never occurred to me you were in a situation like this.'

They were in the dark living room, the door to the bedroom was open and her mother was lying on the bed. Millie went to see her as she always did when she came home. 'Hello, Mum, how are you feeling?'

Her eyes opened, she was sweating and listless, her skin was a greyish yellow, but she tried to smile. 'A little better, I've dozed all day.'

'Good.' It wasn't yet lunchtime, Mum had no idea what the time was, she'd lost track. 'This is Mr Maynard my boss, Mum. He brought me home.'

Miriam Hathaway tried to lift her head from the pillow but it required too great an effort. 'Hello,' she said. 'Pleased to meet you.' The bedclothes moved and it seemed she was about to put out her hand but that also needed more strength than she could find.

'I'm sorry to see you so poorly, Mrs Hathaway,' he said but her eyes were closing again. 'Who looks after you?'

It was Millie who answered. 'I do.'

He took her by the arm and steered her back to the living room, closing the door softly behind them. 'Do you have anyone to help you?'

'The neighbours do and Ryan McCarthy did. He was very good to us.'

'He got you into this mess. If you weren't having this baby, you might have managed.'

'Yes, but it's no good blaming him, is it?'

He smiled and gave her a look that spoke of affection. 'That's the only way to look at it now. Your mother needs proper nursing, she's really ill. You can't possibly cope with an invalid as well as a job and everything else.'

'I still have a job?' Millie sniffed into her damp handkerchief. 'I thought you'd said you were going to replace me.'

'I am. Millie, I'm going to find a nursing home for your mother where she'll be more comfortable. You're not well enough to cope with all this.'

'Mum will be fine here with me now, really she will. You've done such a lot for me, paid out so much money.'

'You've managed marvellously well until now. You're very brave and tougher than you look, but neither Arthur Knowles nor I saw you struggling, and we should have done. You must be worn out.' He was taking out his wallet again and put two more pound notes on the table. 'Buy some food, you both need to eat. And get some rest. I'll see what I can fix up for your mother and come back to let you know.' He patted her on the shoulder and walked briskly out.

Looking round her unchanged living room, Millie found

41

it hard to believe. Mr Maynard had come in like a fairy godfather, waved his wand and made everything seem almost rosy. She was not battling this alone any more. She went back to tell her mother, but she wasn't sure whether she understood. She sat by her bed for an hour holding her hand.

Pete Maynard went back to his car and sat in the driving seat for a few minutes to think. He'd rarely seen such raw poverty yet all was orderly and neat and clean. Her mother seemed close to death, but she was loved and cared for. He couldn't help but admire the girl being able to cope with all that as well as an unwanted pregnancy and a boyfriend who had deserted her in her hour of need.

He would have anticipated that from Ryan McCarthy. He'd had his fingers in the till for a long time. He should have had the guts to sack him when Sam West first voiced his misgivings about him. He hadn't deserved the second chance he'd been given. Yet it had not soured Millie, she hadn't blamed him for her predicament. She might be only seventeen but she had a real inner strength that he had to admire. She was only a couple of years older than his eldest daughter Valerie and to think of her in a similar position was heartbreaking. And Valerie would never have coped in the way Millie had.

That evening, he told his daughters that he felt sorry for the girl but the truth was he felt guilty. How could Millie take care of her mother, look after herself and run a home on the pittance he paid her? All she needed was more money and she'd have managed it. Except her pregnancy meant she couldn't work and that would cut off what little income she had and give her another mouth to feed.

Millie had caught his eye as she'd flitted about the laboratory like an exotic butterfly, beautiful and intelligent and always jolly as if she hadn't a care in the world. Arthur had taken to her and said, 'She's really interested in perfumes, always asking questions. She's a lovely girl, a very attractive girl.'

She was too attractive for her own good. He couldn't let her sink.

It was about six o'clock that evening when Millie answered a knock on her door to find Mr Maynard with two young girls on her step.

'These are my daughters,' he told her. 'Valerie is only two years younger than you and Helen is almost four years younger.' They each put out a hand to shake hers.

Millie's first impression was that they were still children and years younger than her. They were strong, healthy look-ing girls, Valerie resembled her father and Helen was especially pretty. Both were innocent, fresh-faced and beautifully dressed and she could see the Maynard family was on close terms. That he'd brought them to her house embarrassed Millie all over again, but she felt she had to ask them into her dismal living room.

'I want you to start packing,' Mr Maynard said. 'I've booked your mother into the St Winifred's Nursing Home and they'll send an ambulance to pick her up at ten o'clock tomorrow morning. I really do think that's the best thing for her.'

Millie nodded with gratitude. She couldn't fight him over this, couldn't fight any longer. 'You're very kind, but I don't know where St Winifred's is.'

'It's in Mossley Hill, a short walk from where I live. It might be difficult for you to reach from here. Probably it would mean taking a couple of buses in each direction. I thought perhaps I could find you better rooms nearby, but there's such a shortage of accommodation after the bombing that it looks impossible. When I asked my daughters what I could do about it, they suggested we give you a room in our house while your mother's there, so you can walk down and spend time with her whenever you want to.'

Millie could hardly take it in. 'We'll look after you,' Valerie said. 'Dad said I must be sure to tell you that.'

'We have a biggish house,' Helen added, 'with several guest rooms. You won't be any trouble.'

'I don't know what to say,' Millie faltered. She could hardly take it in, that all her difficulties were being eased so rapidly.

'You don't have to say anything. It'll do you good to have a change and a rest from here. I suggest you pack a bag for yourself as well as your mother and go in the ambulance with her. It's Saturday tomorrow so the girls won't be at school, they can pick you up from St Winifred's after your mother has been made comfortable.'

Everything turned out as Mr Maynard had said it would, and Millie felt there was no kinder man in the world. She had never felt so grateful and wished he was her father. There was an aura of peace about St Winifred's and her mother settled almost at once. Millie sat in the bright airy room with her until her eyes were closing.

Then it seemed the nuns had telephoned the Maynard house and Valerie and Helen came to collect her. Mossley Hill was an old, well-established and genteel suburb of Liverpool. They walked along two residential roads with large houses half hidden by walls and trees.

'This is ours,' Helen said and led the way through a high wrought-iron gate with the name Beechwood on it. The garden was vast with manicured lawns and lovely flowers, and the house looked as though it had been home to several generations of the Maynard family. It was large and had been freshly painted and had gleaming brasses on the front door.

'Our great-grandfather had this built in eighteen eighty-seven,' Valerie said. 'There's the date over the front door.'

Once inside, Millie was led from one enormous room to another. Everywhere sparkled with cleanliness and order. 'This is our sitting room,' Helen told her, 'and this is the drawing room but we don't use it much. This is our dining room,' a large table took up much of the room, 'we all have our meals here together, including Mrs Brunt and the gardener if they're here working.'

'Later you'll meet Mrs Brunt, she comes on weekday mornings to do the heavy work and Mungo is a nice old man who takes care of the garden,' Valerie explained, as she hurried her on. 'The kitchen is this way,' it seemed to be a whole suite of rooms, 'this is the pantry, this is the cold room and the storeroom, and here is the laundry and the ironing room.'

'What are those?' Millie paused under a row of bells along one wall.

'In the olden days they were for summoning the servants,' Helen told her, 'but Dad has had them disconnected as we don't have proper servants any more.'

'There's only Hattie now. Come and say hello to her, she'll be in the library.' Millie followed them in, and a slim, elegant lady in late middle age got up from the desk where she'd been writing. 'I do hope you'll be able to rest here,' she said, 'and that you'll soon feel better. The girls will look after you, but if there's anything more you need, just let me know.'

'Hattie is a sort of relative, she was married to Dad's cousin but was widowed when she was quite young,' Valerie said when they were out of earshot. 'When our mother was ill, she came to live here to look after her and us too. She takes care of the housekeeping. Both she and Dad are very family-minded and think we should take care of each other.'

'Come upstairs,' Helen said, 'and see our playroom and Dad's study.'

Millie was dazzled. 'You have a room just to play in?'

'Yes, and then we have to go up to the second floor to our bedrooms.' Valerie was throwing open the doors as she walked along the corridor. 'Dad thought this would be the best room for you, it's next to mine and Helen's.'

Millie found herself installed in a bedroom with a floor space greater than that of the whole flat she'd left. It had a lovely view over their garden and seemed luxurious, but it took her some time to feel at ease in her new surroundings. She found Hattie was kindness itself and took her under her wing, making sure she'd booked a hospital bed for her delivery and that she also saw a nearby doctor.

Millie was able to rest more and still spend many hours with her mother. The nuns were very kind and attentive to her needs, but Millie could see she was fading and found it agonising to watch her strength ebbing away. She eventually lapsed into a coma and died three weeks after the move to St Winifred's. Millie was heartbroken at losing her but knew how much her mother had suffered and that she hadn't feared the end.

Hattie arranged a simple funeral for her and Peter Maynard paid for it. Mungo helped her pick flowers from the garden to put on her coffin. Millie ached with her loss and was overwhelmed with gratitude. The Maynard household attended the funeral service at the church with her, but apart from Mr Knowles, there was nobody else.

It left Millie feeling in an emotional turmoil and she knew she'd reached another crossroads. She was alone in the world and frightened of what the future would bring. She was dreading going back to the flat but at the same time she was embarrassed by the never-ending kindness of the Maynards and was half expecting them to say, 'Enough is enough, you can't expect to stay here for ever.'

At dinner the next day she thanked them for their hospitality and all the help they'd given her but said she felt she should go home and not be a further burden to them.

'You've come through a very difficult time,' Peter Maynard said, his eyes kindly and full of concern, 'that can't be just shrugged off. You need peace to grieve and time to rest to get over it. I think you should stay another week or two at least.'

'So do I,' Hattie said. 'You don't look well, how could you? You need building up.'

'Anyway,' Valerie said, 'it's your birthday on Friday, you can't go before then, Hattie is planning a special dinner that night.'

Millie let them persuade her to stay. She was going to be eighteen but on the morning of her birthday, while the girls were at school and their father at work, she felt her first pains. She was panic-stricken and doubling up as she ran to find Hattie. 'I think the baby's coming,' she wept, 'but it's three weeks early.'

'What a good job you stayed with us,' Hattie told her and took charge. 'This is no time to be on your own.'

Millie's pains were getting worse and she could think of nothing else. She was scared stiff of giving birth but thanked her lucky stars that help was at hand. It was Hattie who called a taxi and took her to the hospital. Her baby girl was born that night, weighing six pounds four ounces. She named her Sylvie and was delighted to hear the doctors say her baby was healthy and normal in every way.

Millie knew all newly delivered mothers had a two-week stay in hospital to ensure the baby was thriving and they had sufficient rest. The hospital almoner came to see her to ask how she would pay, and feeling humiliated all over again Millie had to explain her circumstances and say she'd been living on the charity of others for the last few weeks.

The almoner told her she would put her down as a charity case and the hospital would provide free treatment. She was relieved that Peter Maynard would not be asked to put his hand in his pocket for her yet again, but found having to rely on the charity of others very hard. She had to get back to work as soon as she could, but how could she do it when she had a baby to care for? She was in an impossible situation and it terrified her. She could think of little else.

The following day, a vicar came round to talk to the patients. She didn't know him but he seemed to know something of her circumstances. He was kind and sympathetic and suggested she think seriously about having her baby adopted.

'I have thought about it but I feel it would be wrong,' she said through her tears. 'I want to keep her and bring her up myself.' It was what her mother had done for her, wasn't it?

'You should think of the baby's needs not your own,' he told her gently. 'Would your baby have a better life with an older married couple who can't have children of their own? They would be able to give her a good home, a settled home, and they would love her as much as you do.' He left her a card giving his name and telephone number and told her to get in touch if she changed her mind and needed his help.

Millie spent two terrible hours with her head buried in her pillows, torn to shreds in indecision. Should she keep her baby or give her up for adoption? If only her mother had lived long enough to see Sylvie, she would have been such a help and comfort.

She was no nearer to making up her mind when Sylvie woke up. She was due for a feed and began to whimper. Millie picked her out of her cot and hugged her. Sylvie opened her big round eyes and stared up into her face and Millie made her decision. She couldn't possibly give her up.

An hour later, the almoner came back to the ward to give her a parcel of baby clothes and a dozen napkins. They were not new but there was still plenty of wear in them. Millie accepted them with yet more gratitude. She'd made the right decision and was pleased her baby would have some clothes to wear when she went out. She'd cope somehow.

Hospital visiting was strictly limited to two hours on Wednesday and Sunday afternoons, and for new fathers half an hour between seven and seven thirty on the other evenings. Hattie came on Wednesday afternoons and the girls on Sundays, bringing little gifts for the baby.

'What a way to spend your birthday,' Valerie laughed. 'We've brought your presents as you'd gone before we gave them to you.'

Millie unwrapped them with a lump in her throat, feeling she didn't deserve such affection. There was a book from Valerie and chocolate from Helen. 'Thank you,' she choked, 'you're both very kind.'

Helen said, 'Although you weren't there we had the special dinner to celebrate, it was roast chicken. Hattie had it all prepared and we wished you a happy birthday.'

Millie couldn't stem her tears when they'd gone. She longed for her mother, and she couldn't begin to imagine how she was going to manage when she went back to their flat. She didn't expect to have any visitors in the evenings and felt very alone and uncomfortable at those times. She tried to read her book, it did interest her but it wasn't enough to shut out the cooing of new fathers and the delighted chatter from all the other beds.

But one night when visiting was already in full swing she looked up to see Peter Maynard advancing towards her bed with a great armful of big bronze chrysanthemums. Her heart turned over and she felt reduced to an emotional tangle of nerves.

'I've come to see the new baby,' he said, peering into the cot that swung on the foot of her bed. 'Very pretty. I hear you've called her Sylvie.' He put the flowers down on the end of her bed. 'Mungo picked these for you from the greenhouse.' He sounded like a fond father as he pulled out a chair to sit down. 'How are you, Millie?'

'I'm glad it's over but thrilled with my baby. She's lovely.'

'You look surprisingly well. Nice rosy cheeks.'

Millie's cheeks were burning. She was blushing and knew it was bashfulness at his unexpected visit.

'You must come back to my house when you're discharged from here,' he went on. 'You'll need to get your strength back and you'll have this new baby to look after. Better if you have Hattie around to start you off.'

His thoughtfulness brought the ever ready tears rushing to Millie's eyes again. How many wakeful nights had she spent wondering how she'd manage when she went home to Wilbraham Street without any income. 'I'm afraid I'm going to overstay my welcome with you,' she choked. She couldn't look at him.

'Millie, you'll never do that.' Her hand was on the counterpane and he covered it with his. 'You're welcome to stay. The girls love having you. They talk of nothing else but your baby and they're knitting bootees and bonnets for her.'

The sister came to the ward door and rang a bell. 'Time's up, fathers, time to go.'

Millie said, 'You're very kind. You're all very kind.'

He stood up and she felt him give her a fatherly peck on the cheek, then he paused to look down at her sleeping baby. 'She'll be a real beauty when she grows up, you mark my words.'

'Thank you for coming.' Millie thought she was being daring. 'But aren't you afraid you'll be thought to be Sylvie's father?'

He laughed. 'James, my brother, already believes I am, but everybody else knows that's not the case. Hattie says to tell you she'll come tomorrow.'

Millie watched him join the stream of men who were leaving, and buried her face in the flowers he'd brought. He looked so much older than all the others, but he was wonderful, absolutely wonderful. She wished he was Sylvie's father.

She spent the next half hour imagining how marvellous it would be if she could rely on Peter Maynard's support for ever. But real life wasn't like that.

Chapter Five

Peter Maynard drove home telling himself he was an old fool. He couldn't get Millie out of his mind. How could she overstay her welcome? He'd feel bereft if she left. She was a fiercely proud girl and seemed not to expect anybody to give her anything.

He'd been telling himself for weeks that he was not falling in love with her. What could be more ridiculous at his age? He'd thought he'd finished with all that when Esme died. For goodness sake, where was the sense in it when Millie was just eighteen? He was twenty-nine years older than she was, more than old enough to be her father.

When the time came for Millie to be discharged from hospital, he took Helen with him when he went to collect her. He had to give her and everybody else the impression that his feelings for her were fatherly.

Once back at the house, Millie found Helen and Valerie ever ready to pick up the baby to nurse and play with her. They'd brought down a cot they'd found in the attic and made it up in Millie's room. Mrs Brunt, their daily, brought her a pram that she said had been her grandson's but he was walking now and had grown out of it. Millie couldn't believe how kind everybody was being to her, and she could hardly credit their generosity.

She had not so far seen the old nursery on the attic floor

that had been used for Valerie and Helen. Hattie took her to see it. 'I asked Mrs Brunt to give it a spring-clean, it hasn't been used for years.' Millie was amazed at the child-size furniture, the playpen, the rocking horse and other toys as well as chairs and a sofa large enough for adults. 'Use it if you want to, it'll give you a quiet place where you can attend to Sylvie.'

Millie settled into the comfort of the Maynard household, her baby thrived and the weeks began to pass. One night, she was in the playroom having just given Sylvie her last feed and was winding her before she took her to her cot. Hattie and the girls had gone to bed but had run up to say goodnight to her. Helen had left the door ajar.

She looked up to find Peter in the doorway holding his nightcap, a glass of whisky. He smiled and said, 'You look tired, Millie.'

'I am.' She yawned. 'Sylvie wakes me at the crack of dawn, but at least she's sleeping through the night now. Hattie reckons that's pretty good for a babe of two months.'

He came in, sat down in the chair opposite and took a sip of his whisky. 'Millie, I don't think you should go back to live in that flat,' he said. 'I've been wondering if you should tell your landlady you want to end the tenancy.' That was enough to bring scalding tears to Millie's eyes again. 'Why don't you go there and decide which of your things you want to keep? We could arrange for them to be brought here and finish with that place.'

Millie was biting her lip. 'If I did that you'd have no way of getting shut of me. I'd have nowhere to go.'

'I don't want to get shut of you, Millie. I don't like to think of you and Sylvie alone in that flat.'

Millie stifled a sob. 'I've been worried about you paying the rent for me for all these weeks. I've let you do far too much . . .'

Sylvie had gone to sleep, she put her down in the opposite

corner of the sofa, so she could give her mind to what Peter was saying.

'It doesn't add up to any great sum and anyway, I've a proposition to put to you that will solve things.'

Millie had thought of little else for months but how to earn a living and look after her baby, and could see no way round it, but she was glad he was trying to help her.

He was looking at her intently. 'Hattie has been with us since my wife died and she feels ready for a change. Her sister Mary has just nursed her husband through a long illness, and now she's alone she wants Hattie to go and live with her in West Kirby. It seems a good idea. They're relatives on my mother's side and Hattie has been very good to me but now the girls are older, she feels I don't need her as much as Mary does. The only problem is the housekeeping. Would you like to take that over and act as housekeeper? I would pay you.'

'You don't have to pay me.' Millie was touched and almost overwhelmed by emotion. She brushed away a surreptitious tear. 'You've already paid out a small fortune on my behalf.'

'Of course I must pay you.' He looked serious and intent.

'I'd be happy to do it for nothing. It's just that I don't know whether I could do all the things Hattie does.' Another tear rolled down her cheek.

'Hattie is happy to stay on for a while to explain what needs to be done, and we'll give you time to get the hang of things. She says you're a great help about the house and already quite a good cook.'

'Well, I don't know. I used to cook for my mother of course, but plain stuff.' She thought of the complicated four-course meals Hattie put on the table and her confidence deserted her. 'She cooks delicious food and seems so efficient.'

He laughed. 'You will be too, with a little practice. Arthur Knowles was full of praise for the work you did in the lab and you're coping well with the baby, so perhaps you could find time to do a little more about the house.'

Millie suddenly realised what a gift he was offering. 'Yes, yes, thank you. You're giving me a wonderful chance. Where else would I get a job and a home and be able to keep my baby?' She looked at him suspiciously. 'Are you sure? It sounds so suited to my needs that it's almost as though . . . Well, it sounds as though you are trying to help me rather than provide yourself and the girls with a well-run home.'

He jerked to his feet. 'What if it is? We would miss you if you left us.'

Millie leapt to her feet too, flooding with relief. At last she could see her future beyond the next week or two. 'Thank you,' she said, standing on tiptoe to plant a grateful kiss his cheek. 'From the bottom of my heart, thank you.'

It came as a surprise to feel his arms tighten round her and his lips descend on hers in a passionate kiss. Tingling all over she responded, full of exuberant joy, but just as suddenly he released her and pushed her away from him.

'I'm sorry.' His face was the picture of embarrassment. 'I shouldn't have done that. It was taking advantage . . .'

'No, it wasn't,' she protested earnestly. 'You've done so much for me that nothing would be taking advantage. I'd do anything for you.'

He stood looking down at her for a moment. 'It would, Millie, that's the trouble.' He shot out of the nursery and she heard him hurrying downstairs to his bedroom on the floor below. He'd forgotten to say goodnight and usually he was punctilious about such pleasantries.

For her part she felt swept away by her feelings. Peter was a lovely, kind person and she felt full of gratitude and relief, but she'd been wrapped up with her baby and so full of her own problems that it had taken that tingling thrill when he kissed her to make her realise what she felt for him.

Of course she'd known he'd liked her. He wouldn't have done so much to help her if he hadn't, but that one kiss had changed everything, she was now overwhelmed with joy. She laughed out loud. She had something to thank Ryan McCarthy for after all. She was no longer an innocent young girl. She understood that all men needed love and sought it in this way.

She doubted now that Ryan had ever been truly in love with her. He'd been uncaring and had thought only of himself, but Peter Maynard? His first thoughts had been for her welfare, but in that one unguarded moment he'd betrayed his feelings for her and been mightily embarrassed. She'd seen love in his eyes. Love for her.

She felt warmth spreading through her, she was thrilled. She found it hard to believe that a man in Peter Maynard's position could fall in love with her, but why else would he go out of his way to be this generous to a girl who used to work in his business?

Now she thought about it, she had sensed that his attitude towards her was changing. He'd told her not to keep calling him Mr Maynard. 'I can't do with that sort of formality at home.' The way she thought of him was changing too, but she was living in his house and they were seeing more of each other, so it was bound to change in one way or another.

Millie picked up her sleeping daughter and went slowly to her bedroom. She'd been delighted, excited even at the thought of being his housekeeper and part of his household. That would have allowed her to keep her dignity and bring Sylvie up in pleasant and happy surroundings, but if she was right, this was a total miracle. She needed to discuss all this quietly with him. Millie could see why he wanted to fight his own feelings; nobody would see her as likely to make him a good wife.

Over the next few days Hattie took up most of her day as

she taught her how to run the house. It took Millie some time to realise that Peter was avoiding her. She began to think that perhaps, after all, it was a housekeeper he wanted.

Another month passed, and while Millie believed she was growing closer to the rest of the family, she felt she was being sidelined by Peter and this upset her.

The conversation at mealtimes tended to centre on Valerie and Helen, as they had both decided they wanted to have careers as teachers. Valerie was the more academic and wanted to go to university and teach history to teenagers, while Helen liked young children and wanted to teach in a primary school.

Peter smiled at Hattie. 'Teachers, would you believe it?' Esme had been a teacher. 'They're following in their mother's footsteps.'

'Don't you think it's a good idea?' Helen demanded.

'Yes, if that's what you want. You've both got time to change your minds a dozen times if you need to, but it's as well to have something to aim for.'

'It's essential,' Valerie retorted. 'You'd sweep us into the family business if we weren't set on something else. You'd better watch it, Hattie, or you'll end up there.'

'I'm looking for less work not more,' Hattie said. Recently, she'd spoken a lot about her plans and had set a date for leaving. 'Anyway, it's too far to come from West Kirby.'

'No it isn't,' Peter said. 'There's a fast train service.'

'See what I mean?' Valerie giggled.

'I'm too old and I know what a hard taskmaster your father can be,' Hattie teased. 'Now Millie's showing her mettle and can cope with you all, I look forward to a life of leisure with not a teenager in sight.'

They laughed together but Millie felt left out. Peter had hardly looked at her throughout the meal. It had been the same at other recent meals. There had been so much passion in that one kiss, it should have shown him that they loved each other, but it had made him less friendly. It had spoilt everything. Of course, she should have realised straight away that marrying a girl like her with an illegitimate baby was a step too far for a Maynard. They were an important family and he was her boss.

But it didn't have to be marriage, she'd settle for less. After all, she'd done that with Ryan McCarthy though she sensed that Peter would never treat her as he had done. She loved Peter Maynard and wanted as much of his love as he could give. She spent some time wondering what she could do about it, but this was bringing it to a head. She would have to make an opportunity to talk to him and tell him what was in her mind. Never mind the awkwardness and embarrassment; she'd have to get over that.

That evening, she fed and put Sylvie to bed a little earlier than usual. Nowadays she made preparations for breakfast before she went upstairs, so she busied herself in the kitchen until she knew the family had gone to bed and Peter was alone in the sitting room. At the last minute her resolve weakened, she felt shy of what she would have to say. Don't be a coward, she told herself, if he couldn't do it and she wanted it, then she would have to, so taking a deep breath she forced herself to join him.

He was slumped in his favourite armchair enjoying a nightcap of whisky. 'Hello,' he said. 'I'm going to miss Hattie and so will the girls, she's been a real friend to the family.'

Millie made herself sit down. 'Nobody will miss her more than me, I'm not at all sure I can fill her place. I'm going to need her, but I don't want to talk about Hattie.'

His eyes came up to meet hers and she knew she had his full attention. 'What is it?'

Millie forced herself to say, 'You're avoiding me and it's

the last thing I want. You showed your feelings and now you're sorry.'

He pulled himself upright in the chair, 'Yes,' he said stiffly. She waited but he didn't go on. She couldn't look at him.

'Why are you sorry? Have you changed your mind about me?'

She'd rehearsed these questions and thought it would pin him down, but though she waited, he said no more.

'I haven't changed my mind about you,' she added, and realised she'd never spoken of her own feelings. 'I love you,' she stammered. 'You've made me love you.'

She stole a glance at him to find his gaze was on her face. She felt he was looking into her soul. 'Millie,' he said at last, 'you're a young girl and you have all your life in front of you. I'm nearly thirty years older. More than old enough to be your father.'

'I know that.'

'You haven't thought through what it would mean. Youth leaps into things. I've grown more cautious, I've learned to consider things carefully first. You have so much more energy than I have, you'll want to be out doing things. There's so much of the world that's new to you, whereas I've had years of it and now need my armchair and slippers. I won't want to take you out dancing very often.'

Millie's mouth had gone dry, how could he believe such things should stop them? That first kiss had left her longing for more. 'I can live without dancing,' she said. 'You do a lot of things I've never even thought of. How do you know that I won't enjoy them too?'

He didn't answer for a long time. 'I'm not sure it's a good thing for you to tie yourself to an old man like me. I'm very staid and set in my habits. I know what I like and what I don't.'

She smiled. 'I think it would be a marvellous thing.' Again he didn't answer and she was forced to go on. 'Why are you afraid of getting married again?'

She saw the shock on his face. 'Married?'

Millie had misgivings but made herself go on. 'Wasn't that what we were talking about?' He finished off his whisky in a gulp and got up to refill his glass. It seemed he didn't want to discuss marriage. 'I know you like Hattie. She's much the same age as you and she likes the same things as you do. I see you laughing and talking together, she's everything you seem to be looking for.'

'Hattie? Yes, she's good company.'

'So why are you letting her leave? Is that down to your caution too?'

He was silent for some moments. 'No, not caution – it's a long story. She came to help us when we needed it. She sorted us out. Hattie and I have got to know each other pretty well over the years. But I thought you didn't want to talk about Hattie.'

'You've got me interested in her now. What you say makes it even less likely that she'd want to leave. Go on.'

He smiled. 'You know how to dig. You're better at it than the girls.'

Millie said, 'Aren't you going to tell me?'

'Well, many years ago, when we were both in our twenties, Hattie and I were very fond of each other. She had a friend called Esme and she introduced us. Somehow I turned to Esme and married her instead.'

Millie had to smile. 'Didn't that upset Hattie?'

'She married someone else soon after and went on to have three children. But we are related so we didn't lose touch. Her husband died of cancer about the same time as Esme died. I thought … and I think perhaps she did too, that we might get together again.'

'But you haven't.'

His smile was tremulous. 'The spark was no longer there – if it ever had been. Without that, marriage wouldn't have worked, would it?'

'Oh, the spark!' Millie felt her heart somersault. 'I think you've decided you like me,' she said shyly. 'Does that mean I have the spark for you?'

The question hung between them for what seemed an age. 'I suppose you must have,' he finally admitted.

'Well,' Millie said with utter conviction, 'you certainly hold the spark for me.'

'I do?'

'Absolutely. That makes two sparks.' Her confidence was growing. 'Couldn't we have a blaze?'

'Possibly, except that you're so painfully young.'

'It doesn't have to be marriage,' she said, daring again. 'Not with me. You must know I'd settle for less.'

'Millie!' He jerked upright in his chair. 'Do you think I would allow you to do that?'

The silence stretched between them endlessly while Millie tried to think. At last she said, 'So the problem is my age? Don't I seem a lot older than Valerie? Hasn't my life made me grow up more quickly?'

'Yes,' he said, 'you seem very much older than Valerie, but not old enough to get entangled with an old man like me.'

Pete felt no less embarrassed than he had the last time. He had to get away from her before he committed himself too far. Of course he was in love with her but how stupid could he get? James would laugh at him and so would all his friends. He daren't touch her, because once started he'd never stop. Yet it was taking more strength than he had to keep his hands away from her. The law would say he'd enslaved a girl too young to resist his persuasion. She was already cooking for him and handling his laundry; if he took her into his arms and showed his love, they'd call her Lolita.

He'd seen her breast-feeding her baby with a tranquil Madonna-like smile on her face and that would set any man's emotions on fire. He wanted to marry her, make it all legal and above board, but she was a minor. She'd need permission from a parent or guardian before she could marry. She'd told him when and how she'd discovered she'd been an illegitimate baby. Millie had said she knew of no other relatives and sobbed that she was afraid her mother had been turned out of the family home when her pregnancy became noticeable, and how she wished she'd been able to talk about that with her. But by the time she knew about it her mother had been too ill to open her mind to her. That had wrung his heart.

It seemed Millie's mother had brought her up single-handed and he'd seen the close relationship they had, but now when Millie needed her permission to marry, she was no longer alive. She'd said she knew of no other relatives. Pete had no official status as her guardian though he'd inferred to Hattie and the girls that he was acting in that capacity, but that wouldn't give him any legal rights and as he was thinking of marrying her himself he'd be laughed at. Perhaps also he'd be seen as taking advantage of a vulnerable young girl who had no one else to turn to.

Pete told himself he was several sorts of an old fool, but yes, it was what he wanted. He wasn't sure how it could be done or even if it could be done, but there must be some way. Millie seemed very sure of her feelings and he was too old to waste the years waiting until she was twenty-one.

He gave the matter a good deal of thought over the next few days, and then in the office where Millie could not possibly overhear him he telephoned Alec Douglas, the solicitor who had acted for his family for years, and to whom he paid a fee to help with any legal problems that might arise in his business.

'Alec,' he said, 'I need your advice on a personal matter.' He outlined his problem.

'Not a common problem,' he was told. 'More people have difficulties breaking up a marriage than putting one together. Well, I can't deal with that myself, it's not my field, but I can recommend somebody who can.'

Peter rang the person whose name he'd been given. 'Yes, it's perfectly possible. The young lady will need to apply to the Court of Summary Jurisdiction for permission. I can handle that for her if you would make an appointment for her to come in, and she gives me the details.'

'Is this permission easy to get?'

'They're unlikely to withhold it unless there's good reason.'

Pete sank back in his office chair. Now that the difficulties seemed surmountable, he felt he could seriously consider marrying for a second time. It was seven years since Esme had died and he'd been in emotional turmoil for several years after that, but it had been a happy marriage and once he was able to think of the future he'd wanted another wife. Hattie had sorted out his house and his family and was eminently suitable but they'd eventually decided not to settle for a marriage based on friendship.

He was now forty-six and many would consider eighteen-year-old Millie to be less than suitable. He didn't care, he loved her and she'd had enough guts to tell him she loved him. He'd been surprised at how tenaciously she'd talked about their feelings, it hadn't seemed to embarrass her. She was his best chance of happiness now and he decided to grasp it. He'd talk to her tonight when he'd got the girls off to bed.

Chapter Six

It was Hattie's last night with them and Pete had wanted an especially good dinner of four courses to say farewell. Millie had pushed Sylvie round the shops trying to buy extra food and had helped Hattie with the cooking. Pete opened a bottle of wine and gave the girls half a glass each as a taster. Millie knew he was in high good humour but put it down to the party spirit on Hattie's last night.

During most evenings while they ate, Sylvie dozed or kicked happily in her pram in the hallway but tonight the louder sounds of merriment made her howl to join them. It was Helen who picked her up and brought her to the table where she was passed round, wide-eyed and playful, smiling at them all.

It was later than usual when they finished eating, and Millie then had to give Sylvie her last feed of the night. She carried her up to the nursery to do it and was surprised to find Pete was following her. She started by changing her napkin because Sylvie was usually half asleep when she'd had her feed.

When she was ready to start she found Pete was standing at the door but making no move to go. She hesitated. 'You don't usually like watching me feed her, do you?'

'I do, Millie, very much, too much. I'm staying because I have something to ask you.'

'Oh, what is that?' Breast-feeding had become a matter of routine to her, she got on with it.

'Will you marry me, Millie?'

She felt the blood rush up to her cheeks and jerked up so suddenly that the baby lost her grip on her breast and wailed in protest. 'Marry you?' She stared at him open-mouthed while she fumbled to settle her baby again. 'I'd love to, you must know it would be a dream come true for me. Beyond my dreams really, but I thought you said I was too young. And there's Sylvie, she's another man's child.'

'I love you and I can love Sylvie because she's yours. She's a beautiful baby and less demanding of attention than my two ever were. I want you both close to me for the rest of my life. It can be arranged. Anything can be arranged so long as you love me.'

'I do,' she said. 'How could I not love you? You've done so much for me.'

'It's not your gratitude I want, Millie, that's not the same thing. It's full-grown love I'm looking for.'

'I love you very much. You know I do. Heart and soul.' He came over to sit beside her on the sofa and tried to kiss her, but the feeding baby got in the way.

It was after midnight when Pete and Millie went downstairs again and found that Hattie and the girls had washed up, reset the table for the morning and gone to bed. Millie had never felt less like sleep, she was excited and it seemed Pete felt the same. He found the unfinished bottle of wine and poured what remained into two glasses.

'We've made the big decision,' he said, 'but there's a lot of practicalities to decide. I want you to know that I'll legally adopt Sylvie. I'll be her adoptive father if not her natural one, so you'll know I'll always have her interests at heart. She'll know no different.'

Millie nodded. 'She'll have a much better life, here with you.'

'I want you to have a better life with me too. I want to do the right thing for you. I want you to be happy. I want our love to last. Hattie has shown you how she thinks this house should run, but as my wife I'll expect you to change things you think might make it easier or better.'

'Pete, the more I see of you, the more I trust you. You always do the right thing for other people.'

'You'll need a year or so to settle down as a wife and mother, but you also made a good start in our perfume lab, and if you decide later that you'd prefer that to being a full-time homemaker, that would be fine by me. Is there anything else?'

She couldn't suppress a giggle. 'The thought of becoming stepmother to Valerie and Helen scares me.'

'It needn't. They're good girls,' he said, 'they've got their feet on the ground and we're all getting along very well together already. I shall make it a prime aim to see that things continue in the same way.'

Millie got up early the next morning to feed Sylvie and set about making tea and frying bacon for breakfast and very soon the family was all round her chattering like birds.

Pete smiled his understanding across the table to her as he announced, 'Millie and I have some news for you. We are going to be married.'

Valerie and Helen screamed with excitement. 'How marvellous! Can we be bridesmaids?'

'No,' Pete said. 'Due to my advanced years, it isn't going to be a wedding like that. It'll be a very quiet wedding.'

Valerie gasped. 'Millie, you mustn't let Dad talk you out of a white bridal gown and veil.'

'He hasn't. I've grown up too fast, left all that behind.'

'You must.'

'No, a white gown and a big celebration is not what we want. I've got Sylvie, you see. It'll be in church, but just for the family.'

'Millie, you'll be our stepmother!' Helen pulled a face.

'I'll try not to be a wicked stepmother to you.' Millie tried to smile.

'They aren't scared, Millie, they already know you. And they know you aren't going to change.'

Hattie laughed. 'I could see this was about to happen.'

The wedding took place at ten o'clock one morning just as Pete had planned, in the nearby church the Maynard family had traditionally attended. Only Hattie and his two daughters were present to witness it. Millie carried a bunch of flowers from the garden and they went home to lunch afterwards. There was no music, no marriage pageantry, but it was legal, and Millie set about being a wife and a homemaker. She'd never been happier and knew Pete felt the same, though it took her a while to feel at ease housekeeping on the scale he required for his family. He doted on his daughters, and Millie learned to love them as much as he did and miraculously they seemed to meld into a happy family.

'We Maynards were brought up to believe that the family was very important,' Pete had explained to her. 'We support each other and stick together. William, my grandfather, started the business in eighteen forty-nine and it proved profitable. He had ten children and as his family grew he expanded his company, with the intention of giving all his progeny and kinsmen a means of supporting themselves in perpetuity. Every boy born to the family after that has been given the name William to honour him. My father was William Alfred, I'm William Peter, and my brother is William James. Grandfather took a long-term view and we heirs should all show our appreciation of that.'

* * *

The years passed, Sylvie started school and Valerie and Helen grew up and went to college. Millie decided that she'd like to go back to work and do the training course Arthur Knowles had once recommended. She took time off to have her babies, and worked part time while Simon and Kenny were young. Pete encouraged her, saying she needed to reach her full potential to be truly happy.

Arthur Knowles was still running the perfume department when she returned. He'd worked there all his life and told her she needed to learn more about the science behind the making of perfumes. He lent her books and recommended others, and she went regularly to night school classes for years. Pete took her to Grasse to see the fields filled with flowers grown entirely for the production of perfume. Then he'd taken her to the French perfume houses where the flowers were distilled for their scent and from whom they bought it to use to manufacture their soaps and talcum powder.

Maynards had made little profit during the Depression of the 1930s and even less during the war, though they'd kept the factory working using the employees who were too old to fight. Their products had been reduced to utility standard; much plainer with minimum packaging.

Sadly, Arthur Knowles was killed early on in the war, and Millie had had to run the laboratory on her own after that. When at last peace came, the firm had used up its financial resources. The same could be said of Britain as a whole.

The population was exhausted but factories had to change immediately from making munitions to earning a living again. With so many of the ingredients in short supply, it had taken superhuman effort on Pete's part to recommence making the luxurious soaps and talcum powders they'd once found so profitable. But he had turned the company round, the profits were increasing.

★ ★ ★

The first morning she was back home in Liverpool, Millie slept late and felt she was jerked violently back to the loss and grief of the present, and the dreadful prospect of telling Simon and Kenneth that they would never see their father again.

The boys were weekly boarders at Heathfield, a preparatory school in Woolton. She couldn't bear to tell them the news over the telephone, so she waited. On Friday, she tried to ring the headmaster because she thought he ought to know, but he was teaching. His secretary made an appointment for her to see him before she picked the boys up at the end of the school day. She drove over to collect them that afternoon as she usually did, and had a quiet word with the headmaster first.

She took away two small boys with happy, innocent faces wearing their smart school uniforms. Simon was very like his father to look at, and the first thing he said was, 'How did Dad's birthday trip go?' That threw her a little, but she was non-committal and soon the boys were telling her about a sports match at the school.

Millie had spent days trying to think of the best way to tell them, but like Helen she'd come to the conclusion there was no best way. She'd made up her mind to say nothing in the car where her attention had to be on driving; instead she planned to get them home first and had set out an afternoon tea of sponge cake and scones on the dining-room table in readiness. Sylvie met them at the front door with a face ravaged by tears.

Simon could see there was something wrong and said, 'What's happened? What's the matter?'

They sat on hard dining chairs, one on each side of her, and she put an arm across each of their shoulders to pull them close. They all wept for Pete, Sylvie too, though in truth she'd never stopped. Millie had never missed him more, he was so much better at explaining away their problems than she was.

Later that evening when she'd quietened them down a little, the phone rang. She was glad to hear Valerie's voice. 'I'm arranging for Dad's body to be brought to Liverpool,' she said. 'The police haven't officially released it yet though they say there will be no trouble about that. I'm told there'll have to be an inquest but it was described to me as routine. All the same, Millie, you'll be called to give evidence because you were with Dad at the time.'

Millie had been expecting it, but the prospect made her shudder all the same.

'Don't worry about it. The police tell me that the findings at the post-mortem mean Dad's death will almost certainly be found to be an accident. There won't be any difficulty.'

'What about Sylvie? Will they want her to give evidence too?'

'I'm afraid they might. I've given them your home address, you'll hear direct about that. How is Sylvie?'

'Taking it badly, she can't stop crying. The boys are coping better with the bad news. I'm going to take them all out for the day tomorrow to try and take their minds off it.'

'By the way, I've rung Uncle James again and he says he'll make the funeral arrangements, and would you let him know what hymns you would like in the service, and whether there's anything special you want.'

'I must go and see him,' Millie said. 'Pete and I should have gone back to work on Wednesday.'

'Uncle James won't expect you yet,' Valerie tried to soothe. 'Don't go back until after the funeral.'

'You're probably right, I'll leave it a bit longer but it's my responsibility to make sure there's enough perfume on hand to keep the factory working, and I'm sure the sooner Sylvie has something to occupy her, the sooner she'll feel better and more her normal self.'

Millie was worried about her changed financial position. She was suddenly head of her household and responsible for three children, though Sylvie considered herself grown-up now that she had started to earn. The problem as Millie saw it was that she wouldn't have Pete's salary.

He'd always spoken freely about their income, but he'd believed in enjoying life and she knew they'd lived up to the hilt on it. He'd encouraged her and Sylvie to spend their earnings on themselves. She knew he had life assurance and had made a will in her favour when they were married. He'd shown her a copy at the time but it was so long ago she'd forgotten the details. She knew where he kept important personal documents so she looked it out.

The sum assured on his life now seemed quite small. His will gave a legacy of three thousand pounds to Sylvie and to each of his older daughters, and a codicil added at a later date left the same to each of his sons. Millie could see that he'd left her the residue of his estate, comprising the family home on which there was no mortgage, all his goods and chattels as well as his half share of the business. It was more or less what she'd expected.

Pete had been a good provider and had taken his responsibilities seriously. She was comforted. She'd have her own salary and a share of the business profits and it all seemed manageable, she had no reason to worry. She rang Pete's solicitor to tell him about the accident and his words of condolence made her weep again after she'd put the phone down.

William James Cornelius Maynard had been in bed when his niece Valerie had telephoned; he rarely felt able to get up before eleven o'clock these days. His man Dando had had to help him into his dressing gown and slippers so he could speak to her, as his phone was downstairs in the hall. It had given him a nasty shock to hear of Peter's terrible accident. He'd felt quite faint and had had to go back to lie on his bed for half an hour.

He was sorry about Peter, of course he was. He'd not had a lot in common with his brother, but Peter had stood by him and supported him in his periods of illness. It was unfortunate that he couldn't run the business in his brother's place, but he was afraid his bad back would no longer allow him to spend long days in that office.

Lilian his wife and the eldest of his three sons, Roderick, had been killed in a freak daylight air raid in 1941. They had been visiting Lilian's mother and sister when the house had received a direct hit, wiping out all that side of the family. Roderick had been the son most interested in working in the business and the most able. Peter had praised him and said he always pulled his weight. He'd been the designated heir for the job of managing it.

Marcus, his youngest son, had started work in the office too, but both Pete and Roderick had thought his heart wasn't in it, that it didn't suit him. It had been his own wish to leave and he'd tried several other careers afterwards, some with more success than others.

Marcus had married in 1938 and James had expected that to settle him down, but the following year he'd been off again. He'd volunteered to join the King's Own Regiment where his public school education had been sufficient to ensure that he'd been sent for officer training and offered a commission. His rather aggressive manner seemed to suit the army and though he saw little actual fighting throughout the war, he'd achieved promotion to the rank of captain.

Always in the past he'd become dissatisfied in a year or two and moved on to another job, but the army didn't allow for personal choice, especially not in wartime. Now it was over, Marcus had written to say he couldn't wait to get out and that he felt he ought to do his duty by the family business and try to restore it to its pre-war profitability.

James was not sure Marcus had the ability to do that, but he would have to earn his living. At least he'd married well. Elvira had been an eminently suitable choice, being the daughter of a small but long-established firm of soap makers. Surely he'd settle down once he came home.

Nigel was older by two years and a totally different personality. He'd gone haring off to India in 1936 and James had heard little from him since. But Nigel had a better brain than Marcus, he was more academic and had achieved a degree in archaeology from Liverpool University, though he'd been unable to see that there were subjects that might be more useful to him in business than that.

He'd played around on archaeological digs in Crete and Syria for a few years, before joining the Colonial Service and going out to India, and once war had been declared he'd been trapped there for the duration. Now at last he had written to say he'd given in his notice and hoped to get a passage home. He, too, felt it was his duty to join the family firm.

He'd married two years after arriving in India. His wife Clarissa had been born there, and it seemed her father was a senior official in the Indian Railway Service. Her only experience of life in England had been seven years in boarding school, and James had misgivings about how she was going to get on without servants in austerity Britain.

He'd meant to talk to Peter about both his sons joining the firm but he'd not got round to it. Peter would surely have been happy to train them both. All would have gone well except for this terrible accident. But what really worried him was Peter's will. He'd have made a new one when he married for the second time, but in James's opinion Millie had been an unfortunate choice of wife. The best he could hope for was that Peter had left his half share in trust for his two young sons. As James saw it, if it was going to Millie it could give them problems. She could turn difficult. He didn't trust that girl.

All the misgivings he'd had when Roderick had died returned to plague him. His back had been troubling him from long before that but it was his profound grief at the death of his wife that had given him insomnia. He'd never recovered his health since then. He'd do his best for his two remaining sons by trying to return to work and take Peter's place to help them ease in.

He rang the vicar about Peter's funeral. He was sympathetic and James couldn't halt his words of comfort, but he promised to take over most of the funeral arrangements on his behalf. James rang their solicitor to tell him of Peter's death; he was full of sympathy too, and said he'd already been notified of his death by his wife and had looked out the will. The news couldn't have been worse and was very worrying: Millie would inherit Peter's half share of the business. It meant that half of the profit would be going her way and they'd never ease her out of the door while she owned half. It made James feel so sick that he had to go and lie down again. His brother's death was giving him so much extra work and worry.

Chapter Seven

Millie was dreading the funeral. There was something frighteningly final about that, it was the end of everything she'd known. And every time she closed her eyes, Pete's face was before her, seeming to urge her on as he often had, 'Come on, love, you'll get through it,' the corners of his mouth turning up in their habitual half-smile. He only left her thoughts when she had to concentrate on something else.

Pete had been brought to Liverpool by the undertakers and was lying in their chapel of rest. Millie went to see him the evening before the funeral and tried to persuade Sylvie to go with her. She was still very much troubled by what had happened and refused. Millie was afraid she was still blaming herself for the accident.

Pete had been laid in his coffin but it was open. She sat with him for more than an hour, thinking of all he'd meant to her. A white cloth had been used to hide the wound on the side of his head but she lifted it away to see for herself. She'd been told the swinging boom had fractured his skull and caused his death. She shuddered to see the wound but it settled her mind once and for all: there never had been any hope of saving his life.

She went home to explain this to Sylvie, believing it would help quieten her fears. 'I'll take you to see that wound for yourself,' she said.

But Sylvie shook her head at the thought. 'I couldn't! I've never seen a dead person.'

'There's nothing to be frightened of,' Millie said. 'Pete loved you, he'd never have done anything to harm you. Looking at him, I could almost believe he'd just fallen asleep.'

'That's what you want to believe,' Sylvie said.

Her insight surprised her mother. 'I think you should come and see him. You'll be able to say goodbye to him.'

Sylvie leapt to her feet. 'I've told you, Mum,' she flared, 'I'm not going. I don't want to,' and she went banging up the stairs to her bedroom before Millie could stop her.

The state allowed the bereaved an additional issue of clothing coupons and Valerie had applied for them on behalf of them all, but Millie was not in the mood to look for new clothes. She had a grey suit and thought that would do well enough. Pete would not think black clothes a necessity.

Sylvie had been fascinated with Dior's New Look which was said to be taking the women of the country by storm. She'd made cuttings of pictures from newspapers and magazines showing the longer more glamorous clothes, but very few had reached the shops in Liverpool. The government was campaigning against the new style, saying it was a waste of cloth and the country couldn't afford it at this time. Usually Sylvie needed no encouragement to add to her wardrobe, but though Helen took her when she went to buy her own outfit, they could find no black clothes in the New Look and so Sylvie bought nothing. She borrowed a navy coat and hat from Valerie.

James had been kind enough to make all the funeral arrangements. William Charles, Pete's grandfather, had bought a large family grave in a churchyard in Mossley Hill, and Pete was to join his forebears there. Helen had volunteered to provide the refreshments for the mourners in her house, which happened to be conveniently near the church.

Millie had given much thought as to whether their sons should attend and had come to the conclusion that it might help them cope with their grief if they did. The point of the funeral was to give family and friends an opportunity to say their last farewells. Both Simon and Kenneth had been close to their father.

The morning of the funeral was wet and overcast. Millie collected the two small boys from school wearing their school uniforms, their faces white and anxious. The church was full because the service was being held at lunchtime so the company staff could attend without taking much time off. Millie and Sylvie were in tears throughout the service. The sight of Pete's coffin standing on its bier at the front of the church and the organ music made it impossible to hold them back.

Out in the churchyard afterwards it was worse. Floral tributes were laid out along the grassy edges of the graveyard paths. Millie could see the family grave had been opened up in readiness to receive Pete and the ornate black marble superstructure lifted off on one side. She read again the list of names outlined in gold.

William Charles Maynard 1817–1895. His wife Isabel Louise Haskins Maynard 1826–1857, and nine of their children, five sons and four daughters.

Pete had told her his grandmother had died of a haemorrhage during her last childbirth, though her baby daughter had survived. Millie could understand why the Maynards considered William Charles to be the founding father of their family. He was said to have been kindly and paternalistic to his employees, and had meant to leave the world a better place than he'd found it.

He should have had an enormous family of descendants by now but fate had decreed otherwise. To help immigrants coming over during the Irish potato famine, he gave some of them work in the factory but they were half starved and ill, and brought disease to both his employees and his family.

Of his ten children, only Pete's father William Alfred 1851–1896 had survived long enough to provide strong sons to carry on the family business. He had married Eleanor Mary Willis Maynard 1860–1932 and now their son William Peter was about to join them.

Valerie and Helen paused with the boys to remember their forebears, and Millie felt the bonds tightening between her and their families, but Uncle James stood apart and said little beyond, 'Heartfelt condolences, my dear. A great loss, I shall miss Peter too.'

She had always felt that James hadn't bonded with the rest of the family. Their kinsmen the Willises were there in force, several elderly aunts, uncles and cousins. Millie knew most of them because Pete had kept in touch. In his youth, Pete had been close to his cousin Jeffrey Willis, a giant of a man, whom he'd seen as something of a war hero because he'd spent months fleeing from the Japanese advance across Asia. He came over to kiss Millie and tell her how sorry he was. She was especially glad to see Hattie Willis and gravitated to her for the final part of the ceremony.

It was thinking of Pete that gave her the strength to control her tears while she used the brass shovel to throw the first soil down on his coffin. 'You can do it,' he was saying. 'You always knew I'd have to leave you one day, I was so much older than you.'

Millie let most of her family leave the graveyard before her and spent a few moments seeking her mother's grave. Pete had marked it with a simple stone that read: Miriam Hathaway 1890–1928. These were the two people she'd loved most and they were lying not very far apart.

She had put flowers on her mother's grave fairly regularly at first but now the vase lying on its side and the few dried stalks caught up against the headstone made her feel guilty.

She retraced her steps to pick up one of Pete's many wreaths to put on her grave and found this time that Hattie had followed her. She caught at Millie's hand and said, 'We none of us forget our mothers.'

Hattie's was a face from the past and once they reached Helen's house she spoke kindly of Pete. 'You made the last seventeen years of his life happy,' she told Millie. 'I'm glad of that, he deserved to be happy.'

'How are you?' Millie asked. She'd been fond of Hattie who had been kind and motherly towards her when she'd needed it most. Valerie and Helen were making a fuss of her, they were glad to see her too.

Sylvie wouldn't leave Millie's side. 'Who is this old lady?' she whispered.

Hattie heard her. 'You won't remember me,' she smiled, 'but I remember you very well. You were a tiny baby when I saw you last. The prettiest baby I'd ever seen, I knew you'd grow up to be beautiful. Pete must have been proud of you.'

'No.' Sylvie burst into tears again, and started to gabble about being on the boat. Millie drew her away and it was left to Helen to explain Sylvie's problem.

'If there's anything I can do to help, you must let me know,' Hattie said as she kissed Millie goodbye.

James was woken every morning at nine o'clock when his man, Jasper Dando, came to his room to open his curtains and plump up his pillows. This morning when he set his breakfast tray across his legs, James saw there was a letter propped against the teapot.

'From my younger son,' he said, recognising the writing, but he liked to eat his boiled egg and toast before they grew cold so he put it aside until he had poured his second cup of tea.

Dear Father,

Thank you for your assurance that the firm will welcome me back. It has been frustrating waiting so long for my turn to be demobbed. I'm very much looking forward to returning to civvie street and getting down to the job of putting the old firm back on its feet.

I shall be free of the army by Wednesday next and expect to be in Liverpool on Thursday. Would you be willing to put me and Elvira up until we can find a house of our own? I hope we won't be a burden on you for too long.

The shock gave James such a jolt that he spilled tea on his eiderdown. Irritably, he tossed the letter aside and mopped at the stain with his serviette. It hadn't occurred to him that Marcus would want to come and live with him. The lad hadn't been able to get away quickly enough when he'd been twenty years of age, and he'd only been back for two or three days at a time since.

Thursday next? And bringing his wife too? James felt quite agitated. He'd lived alone with Dando since Lilian and Roderick had been killed, and he'd reached the time of life when he needed peace and privacy. He'd already been upset by Peter's death and the worry about his will, but now in addition it seemed his domestic life would have to change.

For years he'd organised it to suit himself. Almost every evening Dando drove him to the Connaught Club by seven o'clock where he ate a light dinner. He let it be known that it was a private club for gentlemen but it was actually a gaming club. In his youth he'd played roulette and blackjack and stayed until the early hours of the morning, but now his ill health prevented that and he had Dando bring the car to the door at ten thirty.

He knew many of the members and met them in the bar where he enjoyed a pre-dinner drink. Like him, many were widowers; mostly they were retired and had run Liverpool's largest businesses in their working life. They provided interesting conversation over dinner and James counted it his social life.

But as Marcus was being demobbed and had decided to return to Liverpool to work in the business, he really should . . . Yes, he felt obliged to provide a roof over his head. Perhaps it wouldn't be for long, although he couldn't count the number of times he'd discussed with his friends the acute shortage of residential property in the city in the wake of the bombing. Perhaps Elvira's family could help. Anyway, they must have enough money to buy a place of their own. It would just be a question of them buying a house when a suitable one came on the market.

When Dando came to take his tray away, he asked him to tell Mrs Trotter, who came in to clean on three mornings a week, to prepare a room for his son and his wife.

'Which room did you have in mind, sir?' Jasper Dando was a small and slightly built man, with a thin ferrety face and a deferential manner.

'The big one overlooking the back garden.' It was at the other side of the house and well away from his own. Dando slept in the old servants' quarters in the attic. He'd taken over two bedrooms and turned one into a little sitting room for himself.

'And how long will they be staying, sir?'

'Not too long, I hope.'

The following Thursday, James was having his lunch when he heard the doorbell ring. He listened when Dando went to answer it, and as soon as he heard Marcus's voice he put down his knife and fork and went out to greet him. A car with gleaming paintwork and sparkling chrome, brand new, a rare sight these days, was pulled up at his front steps and his son was unloading suitcase after suitcase on to the gravel.

'Marcus, my dear. Hello.' He hadn't seen him for some time and he seemed almost a stranger, though like him he wore thick bottle-glass spectacles in heavy dark frames. He was a big burly man, both tall and broad. He was also beginning to develop something of a paunch, and as for Elvira, he hardly recognised her.

He'd seen little of her since their wedding day when he'd thought her quite a handsome girl and a catch for Marcus, but she'd put on more weight than any woman should and now she looked matronly. Her cheeks were flushed and there was an aura of pent-up anger about her. She reached up to kiss him. It was an impatient peck on his cheek.

'How are your parents? Well, I hope,' James said. 'Do come in. Dando will show you up to your room.'

'This way, madam.' Dando was heading for the stairs.

'Would you kindly help with our cases?' Her tone was frosty.

'Sorry.' He turned back immediately to scoop up two suitcases.

'You've brought a lot of luggage,' James said.

Marcus gave him a quick hug. 'I've had to arrange for two more trunks to come by train, Pa.'

It looked as though they were planning to stay for months. 'You can use the bedroom next to yours as a storeroom.'

Mrs Trotter came from the kitchen to help with the baggage, wiping her hands on her apron. He'd asked her to work a few extra hours today.

Marcus looked at her vacantly. 'Hello, it's Mrs Trotter, isn't it?' He too seemed to be struggling to hide his anger. 'And Dando, how are you? Nothing has changed here.'

'No, little changes.' James went back to finish his meal wondering if they'd had an argument in the car. His omelette had gone cold and was tasteless.

Five minutes later, Marcus appeared at the dining-room door and asked apologetically, 'Do you have any lunch for us, Pa?'

'You didn't tell me what time you'd arrive. I'll have to ask Mrs Trotter.' He rang the bell for her.

'I have some soup I can heat up in a few minutes for you, sir, and I can make you a sandwich.'

'I'll have some soup too,' James said, pushing his empty plate away.

She picked it up. 'Sorry, sir, there's only enough soup for two. Shall I ask Dando to bring your pudding?'

Elvira sailed in looking like the lady of the manor. She was a big, tall woman who held herself well, with her large bosom thrust out before her. In her youth she'd had a pretty face and an hourglass figure but neither had lasted. Now she was getting older she was developing deep lines of discontent running from her nose to her mouth, but both she and Marcus looked very prosperous. 'Thank you for taking us in,' she said. 'I hope we won't have to trouble you for long.'

James hoped so too but he said, 'You're welcome to stay as long as you need, my dear.'

Dando appeared with the inevitable fruit salad which James's doctor had advised to help his constipation. He looked at it with disfavour, today it was mostly stewed apple. Dando was setting two more places at the table.

'We'll go round the local estate agents this afternoon,' Elvira said.

'There's Markham's in the village, isn't there?' Marcus asked. 'And Stanley Jones's in Woolton. We'll start there.'

'I think they may have closed,' James said slowly. He knew they had; many estates agents had closed their premises during the war as their trade shrank. The news caused a few moments of uncomfortable silence.

'We've brought our ration books.' Elvira pushed them

across the table to him and snapped shut her crocodile handbag.

'Oh dear, I know nothing about rationing.' James pushed them back. 'Dando deals with all that for me but I can't ask him to buy for you too. Why don't you cater for yourselves, Elvira?'

'Good, I will.' She sounded short. 'Marcus can show me where the local shops are.'

There was another silence and then Marcus asked as their soup arrived, 'What about dinner tonight?'

'In the evenings I mostly eat out, except for the weekends,' James said. The soup smelled delicious, he'd have preferred that to the omelette. 'With a few friends,' he added hastily. 'Old fogies really, I don't think you and Elvira would have much in common with them. It might suit you better if you found your own places to eat.'

'Yes.' There was no mistaking the relief on Elvira's plump face.

'And you can use your ration books to buy food for your other meals. I don't get up for my breakfast so it's just lunch I eat here, possibly more on Saturday and Sundays, but possibly not.'

James hoped he'd see John Maddox this evening at the Connaught Club. He'd spent his working life running an estate agent business and his son was carrying on, with offices in several suburban areas of the city. He would ask him to find a house for Marcus to buy. Or rent. A house of any sort, a flat, or rooms, furnished or unfurnished, anything. And there was Nigel to think of too. He was due to dock in Southampton in the next few weeks and it was no good expecting him to have fixed himself up with somewhere to live.

'You'd think now the war is over things would be getting easier,' Elvira said, biting into her sandwich.

'They will soon,' James said but she was soon into her conversational stride, going on about shortages. He got to his feet. 'It's time for my rest now. Why don't you ask Mrs Trotter to show you round the kitchen? She comes only three mornings a week and would normally be gone before now. Perhaps I'll see you at teatime. Dando usually makes a pot between four and five. Good luck with your search.'

Marcus held his breath as he waited for the door to click shut behind his father. He knew Elvira was seething and had held back until they were alone. 'I can see we aren't going to be made too comfortable here,' she said. 'You didn't tell me we'd have to share a bathroom with your father and he's not exactly welcoming, considering he hasn't seen us for two years or more.'

'He's an invalid; we can't expect much from him. We'll have to look after ourselves.'

'You mean I'll have to look after you.'

'We'll find a place of our own just as soon as we can.'

'And should anything decent ever come on the market, what are we supposed to use for money? You're a damn fool, Marcus. You should have stayed put until you'd earned enough to buy us a house. It was ridiculous to get up and go on the spur of the moment as you did.'

'You know why I had to,' he said through clenched lips. 'Don't start on that again.'

It didn't stop Elvira. 'It was a stupid thing to do. Hamish said there was nothing to worry about.'

'I thought there was. I don't want to end up in jail and—'

'Shush,' Elvira hissed, as the door opened and Mrs Trotter came in.

'If you've finished,' she said, 'I'll take your plates. Shall I make you a cup of tea before I go, madam?'

'Is there any coffee?'

'No, I'm sorry.'

'Tea will have to do then, thank you.'

As soon as they were alone again, Elvira went on, 'For heaven's sake don't let anybody hear you saying things like that or you really will end up there. Don't forget, our story is that we came straight from Catterick and that the army dispensed with your services yesterday.'

'As if I could,' he said angrily. 'You have your cup of tea, and when you're ready we'll go out. I'm going upstairs to start unpacking.'

But once up in the bedroom, he viewed the mountain of luggage and couldn't decide where to start. He eased off his shoes and threw himself on the bed to consider his position. It was the perennial problem that had dogged him all his life, a shortage of money.

In 1938 he'd started married life feeling he was the luckiest man alive. He'd been very much in love with his pretty new wife, who came from a well-heeled and generous family. He'd been working for a London insurance company at the time and her parents had given them a house in Streatham as a wedding present.

They'd both enjoyed a wonderful first year of marriage in London, their only problem being that his job hadn't paid very well. Elvira had thought he could do better; she and the growing fear of war and of conscription had persuaded him to join the army. She'd been sure he'd be offered a commission if he volunteered, and she'd been right about that. To start with he'd enjoyed his time in barracks and he'd liked his officer's uniform. Elvira visited his mess as often as ladies were invited, and sometimes when they were not. She got on very well with his fellow officers and their wives and said she enjoyed being an army wife, but almost all his pay went to settle his mess bill. Elvira turned out to be a lavish spender.

His first posting had been to Aldershot and Elvira had moved into a nearby hotel to be near him, but she'd left her friends behind and said she had nothing to do but wait for him to come off duty. To relieve the monotony she made frequent trips to London where she enjoyed shopping, restaurant meals with her friends and visits to the theatre.

'Wouldn't you feel more settled if you rented a flat or a cottage nearby?' Marcus had suggested.

'No point in getting settled there,' she'd said, 'you could be posted somewhere else at a moment's notice. There's a war on, you know,' but gradually Elvira built up another circle of friends.

A year later, Marcus had been sent to Catterick and Elvira had booked into another hotel there. It was the blitz that ended her trips to London and she put the house in Streatham on the market. Marcus assumed they'd always have enough money behind them to buy another house, but unfortunately while the blitz was on nobody had been keen to buy, and their first house had sold for less than it had originally cost.

When the war ended, the army began discharging personnel on the principle that those who had joined first were demobbed first, especially if their years of short service commission had expired. When Marcus was given a date in February 1946 and began thinking of a new career, he'd taken his first careful look at their finances and had the shock of his life. Elvira had run up a staggering debt in his name. He was more than shocked, he was frightened.

'I'll never be able to find a job that will let us live and pay interest on a debt like that,' he'd said. 'It'll cripple us. It isn't possible for me to earn that sort of money. You must ask your family for help, it'll have to be paid off.'

Marcus insisted she went home immediately to do it, but he couldn't bring himself to face her family while she did. He tried to close their joint bank accounts to stop her spending any more but he was summoned to an embarrassingly painful interview with his bank manager who told him he must start repaying the debt immediately.

When Elvira returned, he wished he'd gone with her and helped her plead for help, because she said, 'Daddy says he can't afford to give me any more money, I have three brothers and they need to keep every penny in their business because it suffered during the war.'

Marcus felt desperate. 'We've got to get money from somewhere,' he said, 'absolutely got to.'

Chapter Eight

Elvira had had ideas about how it could be done, which she talked over at length with her army friends. As soon as the war ended, the government had begun to dispose of the weapons, vehicles, uniforms and a long list of general goods that the fighting forces no longer needed. Elvira told him her friends were applying themselves to the lucrative market of war surplus and Marcus felt he'd been drawn into the ring almost without being aware of it. He knew several of the other members, he'd served with some, and he was soon introduced to the civilian members.

Marcus spent the next fifteen months travelling the country to attend auctions of army surplus materials, mostly vehicles, but he'd been advised to say nothing about it. 'It would be safer for us all if your family and friends at home think you are still in the army,' he was told and he'd been sworn to secrecy.

The ring he'd joined often went to auctions twelve or fifteen strong. They aimed to buy as cheaply as possible by bidding only against strangers, never against each other. This could have a dramatic effect on the prices on which the auctioneer brought his hammer down.

Sometimes the ring held an unofficial auction between themselves afterwards, and the difference between the price the article had been bought for and the price it achieved now was their profit which they shared.

The members had also learned to sell on the goods. Armoured cars were sometimes knocked down to the ring for as little as £45, and Marcus had taken his turn at delivering them to several docks on the east coast, where he understood they were being shipped to Russia. The civilian market had a voracious appetite for cars, vans and lorries of every description. The ring learned to re-spray and re-register them and they sold like hot cakes.

Marcus had heard what they were doing described as collusion and it made him nervous but, even worse, he was afraid that sometimes the vehicles were stolen. He counted himself honest and hated the thought of theft, but he couldn't control what the other members did.

It had become common knowledge amongst those who were interested that the government had sold off sixty operational bombers and a number of fighter bombers. Then Marcus heard from other members of the ring that first two Beaufighters and then two Mosquito fighter bombers had taken off from an airfield in Oxfordshire and neither the pilots nor the aircraft had been seen again.

It was rumoured that Special Branch had established they'd been sold to the Israelis and that had started an international hunt for those responsible. A week or two later he heard that two pilots had been arrested and further arrests of those running the scheme were expected shortly. Marcus knew that a member of his ring was involved and felt sure that the activities of other members would be investigated.

He was worried stiff. He'd thrown in his lot with them for long enough to pay off his debt, and now felt he had to stop and cut himself off from activities like that. Elvira wanted him to continue. 'We need a house and a thousand other things. We need capital behind us. You'd be a fool to stop now.'

'That's easy for you to say,' he objected. 'The police won't be after you. You'll be in the clear whatever happens.'

'Don't be so silly,' she said. 'You didn't steal anything. You didn't sell armaments to other nations. All you did was odd jobs, running around at the beck and call of others who were doing those things.'

'It was fraud and collusion,' he said.

'Nobody was hurt, it was only government money.'

'That won't stop me being charged.' Marcus felt he'd been forced into doing it. Nothing else would have paid off the debt Elvira had run up. She tried to persuade him to carry on, but once he'd told the men running the ring that he wanted to stop there was nothing Elvira could do about it. They were not pleased, and he had to swear over again that he'd never mention the ring or anything about it to anybody. Fortunately, Greg Livingstone had been a good friend of Elvira's family so Marcus had been allowed to drop out.

After that Elvira was keen for him to find a job. 'I think you should either work for your family or mine,' she'd said. 'You'll earn more that way than trying to work for someone who doesn't know you.'

Marcus hadn't liked that, it sounded as though she no longer trusted him to do well in the world. Elvira's father was a formidable man and she had inherited many of his traits – both were dictatorial, self-opinionated and demanding. Marcus decided that working with his own family would be the better option, especially after he heard about Uncle Peter's accident.

Elvira agreed, though for different reasons. 'Your family will need you,' she said. 'Who else is there to run their business? This could be a good thing for you, and it's the right time to start.'

For Marcus, once they reached Pa's house everything

seemed to go wrong. Elvira had forgotten what the house was like and said it was uncomfortable, and Pa dropped two bombshells at teatime that first afternoon. He said, 'I'm expecting Nigel and his wife to come home from India within the next few weeks. He wants to work in the business too.'

That really upset Marcus, the last thing he wanted to do was to work with his brother. He'd never got on with him. Nigel had made it quite obvious that he thought him a dimwit. He'd looked down his nose at him. At school, the teachers had held Nigel up as a good example to him, whether it was for class work or on the games field. Nigel had acquitted himself well at Cambridge and landed a job he'd wanted in the Colonial Service, while he had struggled all his life to keep his head above water. Everybody seemed to like Nigel better. Marcus had had to accept that his brother outclassed him.

'Where will they live?' Elvira wanted to know.

'Here with me – until they find a home of their own. Where else can they go?'

That shocked Marcus too and he could see Elvira wasn't pleased, but Pa had even worse news for them. 'Millie is going to inherit Uncle Peter's half share in the business.'

'Millie will?' Elvira's face fell.

Marcus swallowed hard, that was a setback. 'Is Uncle Peter allowed to do that?' he asked. 'After all, it is a family business and should be kept in the family, not given to a girl like that. What about me and Nigel?'

'I don't like it either but according to Alec Douglas, Peter's will is legal and there's nothing we can do about it. He says he's applied for probate.'

'But who is this Alec Douglas? Is he right?'

'Of course he's right. The business has been paying him a retainer to handle its legal problems for years. We've had one or two difficulties and he's dealt with them satisfactorily, but Peter always liaised with him and I think they became quite friendly.'

'So we can't contest it?'

His father lost his patience. 'There are no grounds on which we can.'

'But that means we own a half share of the business between the three of us and the other half is owned by *her*.'

'No, Marcus, it means I own the other half. You don't own any shares.'

Marcus felt he'd been choked off and said no more, but Elvira said plenty to him as soon as they were alone. It rankled that Millie was going to own half the business. He hadn't seen her for a few years but he remembered her well. A small, slight but friendly girl, of about his own age; he'd quite liked her when he was young, but she'd made her fortune by marrying his uncle. Over the next few days he and Elvira could think of little else.

When he next took afternoon tea with his father he said, 'It isn't fair that Nigel and I are going to run the business and own none of it. Millie is going to gain by our efforts, isn't she?'

'Yes, it means she will be entitled to a half share of the profits.'

'Well, I don't think that's on. We won't be able to earn enough to live on.'

'If you and Nigel are running the business, you will both be earning a salary from it.'

'But the same applies to her, and that doesn't make me any happier.' Pa didn't realise how extravagant Elvira was. 'Isn't there some way we can ease her out of the picture?'

James sighed. 'You and Nigel could offer to buy her share from her. In fact, I think you should.'

'How much would that cost?' Elvira's voice was harsh.

'We'd have to agree a price with her. Between you, you could surely rake together what is needed. You could try anyway. More than likely she won't have the slightest idea what the shares are worth. It could be a good investment for you. Yes, it makes economic sense to buy her share.'

Marcus had a moment of panic. No amount of raking would find his share of the money needed to buy Millie out, and Elvira looked as though she was about to have a fit. He said, 'We could make things generally difficult for Millie so she'll want to get out. Without Uncle Peter she'll back down if we put on a united front. She won't know much about business, not coming from where she did.'

His father said slowly, 'I've never really got to know Millie and what I've seen of her I don't like. She's a very good-looking woman but an obvious gold digger and a bit of a floozy. To produce a baby in the way she did makes her disreputable. I don't know what Peter was thinking of, he should have had more sense than to accept her bastard and marry a girl like that. Still, Marcus, you should be able to handle her. By all accounts you controlled the other ranks in your regiment, largely called up from the same back streets of Liverpool Millie came from. At least you'll be able to start work straight away.'

Now the funeral was over, Millie thought she ought to be getting on with her life, but she felt at sixes and sevens and hardly knew what she was doing.

On Thursday evening, Valerie rang up to ask how she was. 'I ought to go back to work.' She really needed to check that all was well in the lab. It was her responsibility to make sure there was enough perfume on hand to keep the factory working. 'And Sylvie would be better off at work. Unless I make an effort to occupy her, she spends her time in tears in her bedroom.'

'You've both had a terrible shock. Try and rest . . .'

'But the house needs cleaning and I feel such a mess. I'm just drifting, spending too much time staring into space, thinking of Pete.'

'Millie, I'll come round in the morning to help you clean up. Helen will look after the twins for me and we'll fix something up for the weekend to keep you and Sylvie occupied. Monday is plenty soon enough for you to go back to work.'

Millie was very grateful. Valerie came and pressed Sylvie into helping her clean and polish. When Millie mentioned that her hair needed washing, Valerie had her upstairs to the bathroom and her head in a bowl of warm water five minutes later. Valerie knew how to set hair and did a good job for her. In the afternoon, she sent her and Sylvie off to collect the boys from school with instructions to take them straight to Helen's house. She had invited them all to have supper there.

It was the same over the weekend, and Millie was grateful that she and her children were kept occupied by Pete's older daughters. She got up early on Monday morning to take the boys back to school and get herself and Sylvie down to the works by nine o'clock. It was a dark, wet morning and there was little traffic about because petrol was very scarce. Pete had been given a rationed allowance in order to run the business but they had to use it sparingly. It was rumoured that a modest ration for pleasure purposes might soon be restored.

She drove down to the factory and office of William C. Maynard and Sons. The building was upriver from the Pier Head in the heart of the industrial area near the docks. Good views could be had up and down the Mersey from the front windows, though some had been covered with grimy mesh to prevent break-ins.

They'd had the building extended in 1934 when business was seen to be picking up after the depression of the twenties and early thirties. Their own building had suffered some bomb damage which Pete had had repaired under the government emergency scheme, which covered the minimum to keep it safe, but nothing had been done since. It looked shabby and down-at-heel, but then so did most of the buildings in Liverpool. Paint had been unobtainable during the war. Millie made up her mind to do something about it as soon as she could.

As they entered the building the strong scent of many perfumes immediately enveloped them, and they could hear the machine stamping out tablets of soap as they climbed the stairs to the offices on the upper floor. Millie paused outside the door to the typing pool. 'Come and collect me when you're ready to go to lunch,' she said to Sylvie. They often went to Parker's Refreshment Rooms in the dinner hour as it saved the rations for other meals.

Sylvie didn't look well but she was dry-eyed and seemed more composed than she had for days. Millie dropped a kiss on her cheek before walking along the corridor to the rather grandly named Perfume Laboratory, which was at the back of the building overlooking desolate ruins, buildings that had been bombed in the blitz and were still waiting for redevelopment. Pete had bought for the company a cleared bomb site next to the building to provide added space to load and unload goods and materials, and also to use as a car park.

Millie ran the lab with the help of Denis who had joined the firm three and a half years ago at the age of sixteen to learn the trade as an apprentice. He was proving very competent and she was able to leave a lot of the routine work to him now.

Arthur Knowles had fired her own interest and taught her most of what she knew. Denis's mother was Arthur

Knowles's daughter and as Arthur had run the lab for years and been very friendly with Pete, they'd both taken a keen interest in Denis. Millie was grateful for the help Arthur had given her and wanted to hand on her knowledge to his grandson. Not that Denis resembled Arthur. He had a round, youthful face, inquiring brown eyes and dark curly hair that fell all over his forehead.

Millie opened the door and caught the powerful waft of fragrance, a potpourri of the many scents she blended. It was a large room set up as a basic laboratory where dyes could be mixed and perfumes blended. Almost all the wall space was covered with shelving holding bottles and jars of every size filled with essences and essential oils, all carefully labelled and dated.

There were huge copper containers holding the concentrates she produced, and big stands held more jars, bell jars and aluminium drums, making avenues up and down the room so it was impossible to see across it. There were two sinks and benches at which she could work. She had her desk in the furthest corner, while Denis had taken over what had been her workstation when she'd started – a small table with a bookcase and chair in a corner near the door.

As she closed it behind her Millie heard an exasperated voice say, 'Well, come on, I want to know what this is for.'

She pulled up short when she saw James's younger son leaning over her equipment. A nervous looking Denis stood at attention beside him. 'Hello, Marcus,' she said coldly. 'What are you doing here? Has something gone wrong?'

Denis looked relieved to see her. 'Morning, Mrs Maynard,' he said and scurried out of sight to the other end of the room.

She could see that Marcus was ill at ease. 'We didn't expect you to come in, Millie. How are you?'

She gulped. 'As well as can be expected. I thought I'd left enough essentials to keep the factory working, but of course I expected to be back on Wednesday.' She could think of no other reason why he should be here. 'Is the factory running out of perfume?'

'No,' he said awkwardly. 'Father thought you might not want to work here any more. He asked me to familiarise myself with what needed to be done.'

'Heavens! The last thing I want is to stop working. From now on, I shall need something to fill my day.'

Marcus looked embarrassed. He was Pete's younger nephew, and was some two years older than Millie. He was balding a little now but that was only visible from the back. He had a rather lordly attitude and Pete had said he was inclined to throw his weight about. His father spoke proudly of him, though he'd spent most of the war years behind a desk in Catterick.

Millie asked slowly, 'Are you saying that you're coming to work in the firm?' She didn't like the idea.

'Father wants me to.' His eyes wouldn't meet hers. 'Now Uncle Peter has . . . gone, everything will have to be reorganised, won't it?'

'Yes, but . . .' Millie felt she should have been consulted; after all, they must realise she'd inherit Pete's share and she'd worked here for years. 'Is he in today? Your father?'

'Yes,' he mumbled.

'I'd better go along and see him,' she said, 'to tell him you won't be needed to do my job. I'll continue to take care of the dyes and perfumes.' She could hear him blustering as he followed her along the corridor but she took no notice.

Some years ago, Pete had given up the largest office in the building to James because he complained of difficulty in getting up another flight of stairs to his smaller one. A large mahogany table took up some of the space as it was also used as their boardroom. Its several windows provided good views of the Mersey.

She rapped sharply on the door and went in, closely followed by Marcus. James lowered the newspaper he'd been reading and pushed himself back from his grand mahogany desk. He was three years younger than Pete but had developed heart trouble in his forties and had suffered two small strokes. He'd had considerable ill health since and was absent from work a good deal of the time.

It had been Pete's opinion that he'd slowed down to the point of doing next to nothing and should have retired years ago. But James needed to believe he was still capable of doing a day's work so Pete had taken over all responsibility for running the business while encouraging his brother to think he was still playing an important part.

'Emily!' He was struggling to pull his bulk from the chair and come to greet her. He had a florid complexion and very little hair left, his pink scalp was shiny and he was seriously overweight. 'There was absolutely no need for you to come in, my dear. How are you?'

'A bit shocked, James, to find Marcus in the lab trying to familiarise himself with my job so he can take it over.'

James looked taken aback. 'Oh my dear, that was not the intention, not at all. You mustn't think like that. We were afraid you'd be needing help now.'

'Not with a job I've been doing for years.' She stood resolute before him. 'He was trying to pick Denis's brains on lab work but I'd prefer him to deal with me.'

'He didn't want to bother you at this difficult time. Come and sit down.' James pulled out a chair in front of his desk and urged her to it. 'How are the children? They must be very upset.'

'They are but—'

'Peter's death affects all of us. It also affects the business. I

99

meant to have a word with Pete, but events have overtaken me there. To be honest, I'm thinking of retiring. There doesn't seem much point in carrying on now Marcus has been demobbed.'

She stared at him. 'What?'

'Now the war's over I need to find another career,' Marcus told her.

Millie turned back to his father. 'Are you telling me Marcus is going to take over from you?'

'Millie, it's been on my mind since poor Peter . . . well, since he died,' James took off his heavy spectacles and mopped at his eyes, 'that you might like to sell his share of the business to another member of the family.'

Millie was astounded. 'Why?' she demanded.

'Well, we thought you might prefer to move on now Peter's gone.'

'Sell to Marcus, you mean?'

'Well, yes, Marcus and Nigel.' James was struggling. 'They need to earn a living and the business won't support us all, not like it used to. They work well together and both want to find a new direction in life.'

'But they know nothing about the business,' Millie protested. 'We need somebody who does.' Most of their senior managers had been working for them since before the war. Pete had believed them to be totally reliable but they were all close to retirement age now, and there wasn't one who would want to run the company. 'Wouldn't it be better to bring in an experienced professional manager from a similar trade?'

'I don't believe that will be necessary. Both my sons are adaptable and quick to learn.'

'But Marcus has spent years in the army and Nigel in the Colonial Service in India. They can't run the company without an understanding of—'

'These are hard times, Millie,' Marcus came to his father's aid, 'and there's no point in hiding the fact that we're disappointed with the way the business is performing. It isn't making the profit we'd hoped for. The war drove it almost out of existence, but it should be pulling up now. It needs more vigorous management, a different approach, a tougher hand with the staff.'

Millie was horrified. 'It's doing well, Pete was a good manager.'

James was waving his plump hands about and his large nose was developing a purplish tinge. 'We need to watch our expenses, increase our sales, cut out the dead wood . . .'

Millie's mouth had gone dry. 'You count me as dead wood?'

'No, Emily, not you. Not you at all. You mustn't take everything we say personally.'

Marcus asked, 'Didn't Peter tell you we were worried about the business?'

'No, quite the opposite. I thought—'

'Peter was worried too.' James was trying to support his son.

'No,' she was shocked, 'no, he wasn't.'

'I don't suppose he wanted to talk about it when he was home with his family. We're all upset about it. It's depressing to see the family firm go down like this.'

'James, what are you talking about?' Millie was aghast. 'I can't understand where you get that idea. You must know the war almost brought the company to a standstill because all our young staff were away fighting and soap was rationed. It still is because the politicians have decided scarce fats are needed for food.

'We could sell every tablet of soap we make but although we're able to get more of what we need, the lack of essential ingredients is still holding us up. All the same, both turnover and profit were up in last year's accounts.' Pete had said they were continuing to climb slowly. 'He was delighted and thought the company was getting back on its feet.'

They were looking at each other somewhat disconcerted. James said, 'Oh, I think you're mistaken, my dear.'

Millie could feel a wall of anger building up inside her. For years, James had been leaving almost every decision to Pete. It offended her that they were running down what he'd achieved. She took a deep breath, she needed to keep her temper now.

'What you say isn't true,' she said, looking Marcus in the eye. 'Pete has already pulled the firm out of the doldrums. He's turned it round. Of course it still has a long way to climb before it's making the profit it once did, but it is making a profit and everything is on course for that to continue. Pete worked very hard . . .'

James put up his hands to stop her. 'We know how hard Peter worked. Please don't think we don't appreciate all he did, but with new blood in the company, Marcus feels he can pull it together and make it achieve more.'

Marcus added for good measure, 'There's been no growth for years and very little profit.'

Millie was so furious she could hardly get the words out. 'I'm telling you there has. Have you looked at last year's accounts?' She turned to his bookcase in which the latest figures had always had a slot. Today the folder wasn't there. 'If you look at them, you'll see that both profit and growth have increased. I think he worked marvels.'

'The point is,' Marcus said at his most lordly, 'do you wish to sell Uncle Peter's share so that you, too, can make a fresh start and get on with your life?'

Millie could feel tears prickling her eyes but she was determined not to let them fall. 'I haven't had time to think much about the business since the accident, but I'll give it some thought now. I'll need to work and managing the perfume laboratory is all I know. Without Pete's salary, I'll need to maximise my income to support the children.'

James said disparagingly, 'Peter always had expensive tastes. You may have to live more economically in the future. Selling your share would give you a little money for your new life. You think about it, my dear, and let us know what you decide.'

Millie got up from the chair so quickly that it rocked. She made it back to her desk before her tears began to fall.

She felt sick with worry. It had never occurred to her that Marcus would want to buy her out of the business. That had come as a shock, especially as she'd never needed her job more. She'd thought she was good at it but perhaps . . . She leapt out of her chair and strode to the window to stare down into the shabby dockland street. Oh goodness! She must not let them get her down.

Pete had always shielded her from arguments with his brother, she wasn't used to it and it had infuriated her to hear him say they were worried about the way he'd been running the company. Marcus had been dogmatic about last year's results being bad, but she was almost sure he was wrong. She felt confused and could no longer trust her memory. It was many months since the accounts had been drawn up and she and Pete had talked about them. She didn't have a copy of them here in her office, though there'd be one in Pete's desk.

She needed to see for herself exactly what the figures were but the office Pete had used was up another flight of stairs in a turret at the end of the building, and she was afraid Marcus had already taken it over.

Chapter Nine

Millie decided to run along the corridor to see their accountant Andrew Worthington. He'd been working for them for only four months, since their previous accountant had retired. He'd been recommended to them by a relative and Pete had been pleased at the way he'd settled in. He'd thought him efficient and had told her they'd made a good choice. When she went in she was glad to see he was working on the new comptometer that they'd had to apply for a government permit to buy. He jerked to his feet when he saw her.

Pete had thought him a young man but he was actually six weeks older than Millie. Thin and rather gaunt, he'd spent months evading capture by the Japanese forces when Singapore had fallen. That he'd succeeded had made Pete see him as a war hero, but he was self-effacing and all they could get out of him was that he'd been lucky enough to have Pete's cousin who could speak Malay as a companion, and that he'd organised everything.

'You want to see a copy of last year's accounts?' Andrew pulled a chair up to his desk for her and slid a file in front of her. Millie opened it but was looking at the figures through a haze of angry tears. 'I was so sorry to hear about your husband,' he went on awkwardly. 'It must have come as a terrible shock to you. An accident like that alters everything in a moment. I liked Pete. He was a good boss to work for.'

That didn't help her tears. Neither did the sympathy she saw in his deep green eyes. 'Shall I ask for some tea for you, Mrs Maynard?'

'Yes, ring for some tea please.' She mopped unashamedly at her eyes. 'James has just told me he's going to retire and Marcus and his brother are going to take over the running of the company.'

'Oh!' He went back to his seat on the other side of the desk. 'I can see why that upsets you,' he said gently, 'but there will have to be changes.'

'I know that, but Marcus is saying Pete didn't run the company efficiently, and I know he tried very hard. They're trying to tell me we made no profit last year.'

'That isn't true.' Andrew Worthington was on his feet again. He turned to the last page of the document in front of her. His finger prodded at it. 'Here you are, you can see the figures set out in black and white. Your husband lifted the company out of the doldrums of the war years, got it producing again. You can be proud of what he achieved.'

Millie was frowning. 'That's what I thought. Well, it's what Pete told me. We've just completed another year, haven't we? Has the improvement continued?'

'Yes, the year ended on April the fifth. I've started to work on the accounts. I can't give you any figures yet but it all seems fine. I think the profit will have increased.' He supported his chin on his hands in thought. 'Why would Marcus say such a thing when you'd probably know the exact figures? Anyway, it would be easy for you to check.'

Two cups of tea arrived. Millie sipped hers gratefully and tapped at the documents she'd been given. 'I knew all this because Pete was always talking about the business. He was very involved in it. I couldn't help picking up basic facts. Marcus must think I'm a fool.'

'It makes him look a fool. Hang on.' Andrew Worthington

sat back in his chair and thought for a moment. 'He does know the position is good. His father brought him in to introduce him a few days ago, and we talked about the annual accounts. He knows what the position is.'

'What? Both he and his father say the company needs stronger management, that progress is slow.'

'Whatever they are saying, they both understand the current position. Mr Maynard senior would have received a copy of these accounts from my predecessor. Look at the bottom, there's a list of the managers who received it.'

Millie studied the printed name William James Cornelius Maynard in disbelief. 'Then why are they saying such things?' She blew her nose. 'I know James used to think of me as Pete's child–wife playing around in the lab, but that was years ago. Surely they'd give me credit for learning something since?'

The accountant was shaking his head.

'They've offered to buy me out.' She was so upset she felt her head wasn't working as it should.

'How much did they offer you?'

'No figure was mentioned. It was just the suggestion that I'd need money for my new life without Pete.' Millie stopped and tried again to think. 'What reason could they possibly have to talk of the business being run down when they know very well it is not? Would that make it cheaper to buy me out?'

His emerald eyes were searching hers. 'Wouldn't they expect you to ask for an independent assessment of the value?'

'They think I'm too stupid to do that. They think I'll jump at any offer of money. And I think they want to get rid of me, so they talk about the business as if it's too run down to be worth very much.'

'How could they expect you to believe that when you work here and can check on the profit being made at any time?'

'I don't know, but I want to stay. I'm not going to be bought out.' She spoke with more feeling than she'd intended. 'I need to work. I've got children to support and making perfumes is all I know.'

'Good for you. Your husband told me you'd developed quite a "nose", he was proud of you. Scent is very important in this trade.'

That made Millie feel better, she smiled at him for the first time. 'It is, but Marcus doesn't know much about the business and even less about perfumes. It'll all be new to him.'

'Then he'll find that you're important to the running of this business.'

'Am I?' That perked her up.

'Yes, could anybody else take your place?'

'Pete would have been able to. He had a good "nose" too, but as general manager he had too much other work. Denis would be able to make a good attempt at it but he'll be called up to do his National Service as soon as he's twenty-one, so it's no good thinking of him.' She got to her feet. 'I'm not going to let them put me out. I need to work. I'll carry on.'

'That's the spirit,' he said.

She went back to her own desk feeling a nervous wreck. She found it hard to believe James and Marcus were saying things to her they knew were false. She must treat it as a warning and not trust anything they told her. She could only surmise that they wanted her out of the business and were prepared to go to any lengths to achieve it.

It pleased her that she had an ally working here, Andy Worthington had made her realise she was in quite a strong position. He was on her side. She wouldn't be fighting the Maynard clan without support.

★ ★ ★

A few days later an official envelope was pushed through Millie's front door while she and Sylvie were having breakfast. It seemed the consequences of Pete's terrible accident would never be over. It advised her that the inquest would be held the following week in Holyhead at ten thirty in the morning, and that both were required to attend.

She rang Valerie, who said, 'I've been told to attend too and so has Helen, because we got Dad out of the water. Helen's husband will lend us his car so we can all go together. He's going to find the petrol from somewhere.'

'I have Pete's car here,' she choked.

'Eric's would give us more room and we'll need it because we'll have to take the children.' Eric had been lucky enough to buy a big new car just before the war started.

'Thank you, I'm glad Sylvie and I don't have to go on our own.'

'Shall we stay at Hafod the night before to make sure we get there on time? With the children it will make it easier.'

'Yes, whatever suits you, Val.'

When she told Sylvie, she said, 'I don't want to go. I couldn't.'

Millie put her arms round her and gave her a hug. 'I'm afraid you'll have to, love,' she said. 'It's the law of the land.'

They packed their funeral clothes to wear to the inquest and, as arranged, Helen drew up at their gate in mid-afternoon on the day before. Millie had always enjoyed the journey, with the lovely scenery of mountains and small hill farms on one side and the seascape on the other, but today nothing would ease her troubled mind. She and Sylvie sat on the back seat with the twins between them.

Since their hurried departure from Hafod, the house had been cleaned and tidied as it always was by Mrs Olwen Jones who lived in a nearby cottage. When they arrived, there was a jug of fresh milk in the larder and a vase of fresh flowers picked from the garden on the living-room table. Valerie had brought most of the food they'd need for dinner tonight and breakfast and lunch tomorrow.

She said to Millie, 'Why don't you and Sylvie take the twins for a walk along the lane while Helen and I unpack and get the dinner on the table?'

'We could give baby Jenny an airing in her pram at the same time,' Millie said. They set off in the late evening sunshine. Millie was glad to stretch her legs after the long car journey but it bothered her that Sylvie wouldn't even look towards the jetty and the sea. Tonight it was calm, benign and beautiful. She could almost feel Pete's presence in the lane with them. *Oh Pete, Pete, if only you were with us, it would seem like a normal holiday break.*

Helen got them to Holyhead in good time the next morning, and the officials in charge were relaxed and polite. Millie had the impression they saw it as a low-key affair. They started on time and she was the first witness to be called to the stand. Then it was Sylvie's turn. Everybody was very gentle with her and she managed to give her evidence clearly though tears were streaming down her face. When she came back to her seat, Millie put an arm round her shoulders and pulled her closer.

The proceedings were conducted at a fairly brisk pace. The children were very good and were passed over to other family members while their mothers gave evidence. They heard from the doctor who had been called to the jetty, then came the evidence found at the post-mortem and the coroner gave the verdict as accidental death.

'Thank goodness that's over,' Helen said as she led the way out to the car.

'It's all very well for them to call it routine,' Sylvie sniffed, 'but it was about my dad and it didn't seem like routine to me.'

'It's all over now,' Valerie tried to comfort her. 'All we have to do is learn to manage without Dad.'

'That's going to be the hardest part,' Helen said with a little sniff.

After they'd eaten lunch at Hafod, she drove back to Liverpool and dropped Millie and Sylvie at home. 'Would you like to come in for a cup of tea?' Millie asked, feeling much in need of one.

'No thanks,' Valerie said. 'The twins are beginning to get stroppy after being confined in the car for so long. Better if I get them home.'

Millie nodded. 'Thank you both,' she said as she kissed them goodbye. 'You made it all bearable for me and Sylvie.'

Millie had found the inquest easier to get through than she had expected and afterwards the days began to pass quietly. She'd been in touch with Pete's life assurance company, filled in the forms they'd sent her and complied with their requests. They'd confirmed that all was in order and they would pay out but explained that the money would be sent to his executor to be included in Pete's estate.

His will had named his solicitor, Alec Douglas, as his executor and Millie had spoken to him two or three times about the will. He'd told her that James had questioned its validity.

'I did suggest to Peter that he might consider putting the half share of the business in a trust fund for his sons, but he said, "I don't need to do that. I trust Millie, she's their mother and she'll know how to manage things. They're her sons too, she'll look after them." '

Millie could feel the tears burning her eyes again. Any mention of Pete brought back the terrible feelings of loss. She hoped after this she'd completed all the formalities associated with his death and could put them behind her.

What she needed was to get used to her new life and learn to stand on her own feet. She craved peace to enable her to get on with it. When Mr Douglas rang her again and said he'd like her to come in and see him, she thought he'd completed the task.

'No, I'm sorry, I'm a long way off that. I've applied for probate but I'm afraid there's a difficulty I need to discuss with you.'

When three days later she was ushered into his office, he looked grave and she knew immediately that something was wrong.

'I'm afraid I have some bad news for you, Mrs Maynard. I've been trying to collate your husband's investments and bank account monies. You gave me a list.' He riffled through the papers on his large desk. 'Yes, here it is, but I'm afraid the total doesn't amount to a great deal, probably not as much as you or he anticipated.' His solemn eyes behind rimless glasses surveyed her face. 'Does he have any other bank accounts or investments? Money that you've forgotten, that should be included in this list?'

Millie could feel herself going cold. 'No, I don't think so. Pete wasn't much concerned about money. He hardly ever spoke of investments or savings.'

'I see.' He sighed. 'Well, the problem is that he has left legacies to his five children totalling fifteen thousand pounds and there would seem to be insufficient monies accruing to his estate to meet that sum.'

'What about his life insurance?'

'Yes, I have the two thousand seven hundred sixty-nine pounds from that. It was taken out a long time ago. Yes, almost forty-six years and unfortunately the war altered the value of money out of all recognition. I also have statements of the three bank accounts.' A sheet of paper came across the desk to her. 'Here are the figures. You'll see that another

111

seven thousand three hundred pounds is needed to cover payment of the legacies.'

'Oh dear, so the children won't get as much?'

'Yes, they will, but it will have to come from the residue of the estate which he has left to you.'

'What?' She was shocked and stared at him open-mouthed.

'The residue includes his house, his half share of the family business and all his goods and chattels. The house, I understand, is free of mortgage.'

'Yes.' She'd understood that to mean she'd always have a home for herself and her children. 'It belonged to his grandfather and it was handed down the family to Pete.'

'I'm afraid the law requires that your husband's wishes are carried out to the letter. What remains of his estate, the residue, cannot be calculated until that is done. In other words, in order to pay the legacies he's gifted to his children, money will have to be raised from his estate.'

Millie felt suddenly cold. 'That seems—'

He held up a plump hand. 'It can be done, you mustn't worry. For instance, it would be possible to raise money against the value of the house, a mortgage in reverse so to speak.'

'Yes, but we'll need the house, it's our home. The children will need a home.'

'I realise that, but it doesn't mean you'll have to sell it. You'll still be able to live there. It's a substantial house, I understand.'

'Yes, but wouldn't the mortgage in reverse mean monthly repayments?'

'Yes, or it could be sold and a smaller house bought for your use.'

Millie felt paralysed. She'd spent all her married life in that house. It was spacious and comfortable and the only permanent home she'd ever known. She forced the words out at last. 'I don't want to sell it.'

'There are other ways, of course. Perhaps sell some of the goods and chattels such as the car?'

'Not the car, I need that. Anyway, it wouldn't be possible to raise enough on that.' She thought for a moment, 'But there's Hafod, I could sell that, and I'd be glad to see the back of the boat.'

He sighed, 'Well, there is a difficulty there. I'm afraid Hafod didn't belong entirely to your husband. That house and its contents were left to Peter and James jointly by their father. I understand they enjoyed holidays there as children. When probate is granted you will inherit half of it, so you would need to ask James if he would be willing to buy your share and advance you the money to meet the cost of the legacies.'

Millie felt near to panic. 'James hasn't been near the place for years. He's not in good health and I don't think he ever leaves home. I'd be afraid to mention Hafod to him in case he asks me to buy his share.'

'Oh dear. You could raise money against your share of the business.' That really sent shivers down her spine. Millie had made up her mind to refuse James's offer to buy her out but would she be able to now?

'No, I want to keep that.'

He seemed to lose patience. 'I think you should discuss this as soon as possible with someone who can advise you on financial matters,' he said. 'Possibly your husband's bank manager will be able to help.'

Millie felt dazed. 'The legacies will have to be paid before the will can be settled?'

'Yes, I'm afraid so.' He stood up as if to indicate he'd explained it all, so she stood up too.

She'd not anticipated anything like this but she didn't doubt the truth of what she'd been told. Pete had enjoyed the good things in life, he'd looked upon money as a commodity to be used, and he'd always been very generous to his friends and family. She was not going to have anything like as much money to live on as she'd first thought. Would she have enough to continue to live as they had?

As she walked up the wide leafy road, Millie assessed the home she expected to inherit. Pete's grandfather had had it designed by an architect and built to his own requirements in 1887. It had many bay windows both rounded and square and lots of ornamental brickwork. She'd thought it enormous the first time she'd seen it, but somehow Pete's family seemed to spread through its many rooms. It didn't bother them that some were rarely used. Somebody would go in and dust them sooner or later. Once there had been an enormous garden too, but when the shortage of domestic labour began to bite during the Great War, Pete's father had sold off some of it as housing plots.

Millie was not the sort of person who could keep her troubles to herself and as soon as she saw Sylvie, she poured her worries out to her.

'Dad's left me three thousand pounds?' Sylvie was pleased and didn't seem to take in the downside.

Millie rang Valerie and talked it through with her. 'That's just like Dad,' she said. 'He was always over-generous to everybody. I'll be very glad of the money.'

That made Millie worry all over again about her income and it drove her back to the accountant, Andrew Worthington. She went along to his office the next morning and poured out her financial troubles to him, showing him the figures Mr Douglas had given her.

'What is the best thing for me to do?' she asked. 'I don't want to raise money on the house and then find I have to pay interest on it every month. What would you advise?'

'Better if it's not my thoughts straight off the cuff,' he said. 'I'll need a while to think about that.'

'Can we talk about it at lunchtime? Will that give you long enough?'

'Yes, I'll try.'

'One o'clock then? What do you do for lunch?'

'I bring a sandwich.'

'Good, I've done the same today.' In the interests of economy she had to stop taking Sylvie out to lunch every day, even if it was only to Parker's Refreshment Rooms. Pete had taken them both there on a more or less regular basis. 'I'll come here, shall I? You've more space than I have.'

'Yes, Mrs Maynard,' he said. 'Please come here.'

'Look, this office is overfull of Maynards and we're talking personal issues now. Call me Millie.'

'Right, in that case I'm Andrew.'

She managed a wavering smile. 'I know,' she said and fled back to the lab.

Chapter Ten

When Millie took her sandwich to the accountant's office at lunchtime, he was working on his calculating machine again.

'Come and sit down.' He pushed the comptometer and the business files to the end of his desk and took the documents she'd left with him from his desk drawer. 'I've looked at your figures,' he said, 'but there's not much I can suggest. You'll have to raise the money from somewhere.'

'I got that far by myself,' Millie said, her unexpected problem making her short, 'and I know I need to do it quickly, because everything stands still until it's done.'

'I'm afraid that's it exactly.'

She sighed. 'I've no money of my own so it will have to come from the residue of Pete's estate. What in your opinion would be the best way for me to raise it?'

She thought Andrew Worthington looked switched off. 'I'm afraid that's for you to decide. It's a matter of personal choice, isn't it?'

Millie felt hurt. It seemed he didn't want to help her. His dark green eyes appeared to look through her. Suddenly he shook his head. 'If you want to go on working here, I'd advise that you keep the half share of this business. To sell that to his relatives would weaken your position and strengthen theirs.'

'I have to go on working here.' Her voice grated harshly though she didn't mean it to. 'It's my only income.'

'Well, that's not entirely true.' His eyes came to rest more squarely on her face. 'Your half share of the company entitles you to half the profits and it could be a growing income. My advice would be to hang on to that at any price.'

She took her sandwich from a creased paper bag and took a savage bite. 'Yes, I do realise that, but I need to raise seven thousand three hundred pounds.'

'You say you want to keep the house but it would be sensible to sell it and buy a smaller place to live in.'

'That would take ages,' she said impatiently. 'I want to get all this settled.' She had half a dozen other reasons why she didn't want to do that. She loved the house and, anyway, it would be unsettling for them all when they needed peace. 'There'll be the boys' school fees and a hundred other things I'll have to pay.'

'You don't have to spend money on school fees. You could give up the idea of sending them on to public school.'

Millie felt her back go up at that. 'It was Pete's choice,' she said. 'He wanted them to have the same advantages he's had.'

'The world is changing. Who is to say it will be an advantage to them? The grammar schools are free now.'

'For some.' Millie paused for a moment. 'Did you go to a grammar school?'

'Yes, to the Institute. Your boys would get a good education there.'

Millie didn't answer. For herself she'd have seen a grammar school the chance of a lifetime, but she couldn't think of it for Pete's sons because he'd wanted them to go to his old school, the school where all the Maynard boys had been educated.

'I'm sorry,' he sounded off-hand, 'there really isn't much else I can suggest.'

'No, I was clutching at straws.' She must think seriously about selling the house.

Andrew Worthington took his lunch from a drawer and unwrapped the table napkin to reveal cheese sandwiches.

'That's a good idea,' she said. 'I should have thought of table napkins myself.'

'There's no greaseproof paper to be had anywhere.'

'I know. This paper bag held half a pound of Marie biscuits originally. It was all I could find.'

That relaxed the tension somewhat. He smiled. 'Sorry, but the only way to raise any money is from what you've been left. Did your husband have anything of value that you won't need? A watch, for instance?'

Millie was wearing Pete's watch on her wrist. She found it a comfort to have his belongings near her. His fountain pen was in her handbag too, but selling both wouldn't help to raise the sum she needed.

Ten minutes later, she went back to her desk and sank slowly into her chair. Had she been a fool to see Andrew Worthington as an ally? He hadn't been very friendly today. In fact, he'd seemed cold and standoffish. They'd not been on the same wavelength.

When the door closed behind Millie, Andrew Worthington sat back to think. The figures she'd shown him were easy enough but it had been an effort to get his head round what she wanted from him. She was an attractive woman and newly widowed, and one glance at these documents showed that really she was in a comfortable financial position. She had a fairly high-powered job here too and was a member of the owning family.

He was used to handling professional difficulties but it was a long time since he'd tried to see personal problems other than his own and he didn't think Millie Maynard had too much to be worried about.

Andrew had been very sorry to hear of Pete's death, he'd

liked him and he was a good manager, whatever the rest of the family told Millie. He knew James had recently started coming to the office more regularly, which he'd expected because Pete's death would have left a vacuum at the top.

He'd thought James was coming in to run the company until he heard his colleagues discussing him. They said James didn't know what was going on, that he'd been left high and dry decades ago, and he wasn't actually doing anything. He was leaving them to get on with things as they always had.

One possible explanation he could think of was that James was fighting for his own side of the family and could it really be that they wanted Millie out of the business? They seemed to resent her inheriting such a large share of it and possibly were also afraid she would take a greater share in the running of it. She had long experience of its perfume needs and perhaps Pete had talked through its management problems with her over the years. Andrew had heard Albert Lancaster say she was better equipped to run it than Marcus. He was beginning to get a better grasp of the situation.

And he was beginning to feel sorry for Millie, she was trying to come to terms with her loss and do the best for her children. She had a good brain and talked sense and was popular with the staff. All the other managers would be glad to help her. Perhaps it would be better if he let them get on with it.

That evening, Millie went home to make a scratch dinner of bubble and squeak with a fried egg on top for herself and Sylvie. They were washing up together afterwards when they heard the front-door bell ring. Millie went to see who it was, still clutching the tea towel.

Helen was on the step with the late evening sun glinting on her dark auburn curls. She was lifting her baby out of the pram. 'Can I come in for a few minutes? How are you, Millie?'

'All right, I suppose.' She opened the door wider. 'Yes, come on in, we could do with cheering up. How's Jenny?'

'She's fine.' Helen followed her to the sitting room. 'Have you finished eating?'

'Yes. Hi, Helen.' Sylvie came to take the tea towel from her mother's hand. 'I've got the kettle on for tea, do you want a cup?'

'Yes please.' Helen sank down on the sofa with the babe in her arms. 'I was afraid you'd be worried. Valerie told me that Dad has left each of us offspring a legacy, with no thought as to where the money is to come from.'

Millie leapt to his defence. 'He was only sixty-four and in good health. He didn't know he was likely to—'

'No, of course not,' Helen said hurriedly.

'Besides, it was the war that drove the business down and made him spend his capital.'

Helen's face was concerned. 'Millie, I've come round to tell you that you don't have to raise money to pay me. Eric agrees. We aren't short, we don't need it and I'm afraid you might. Eric is doing very well.'

Millie caught her breath. 'I know that, but . . . Your father wanted you to have it.'

'I don't need it, Millie.'

'Are you sure? It's very generous of you.'

'Of course I'm sure.' She was smiling tremulously.

'Still, to give up what's legally yours . . . Thank you, I'm . . . I'm touched.'

'Will it solve the problem?'

Millie was biting her lip. 'It will help of course. Ease things. I'll only have to find four thousand three hundred pounds instead of seven thousand three hundred pounds but I don't know how to do that.'

'Have you had a proper look round this house? There's a

lot of stuff here that used to belong to Grandpa. It's all old. Some of it could be worth something.'

'Antiques, you mean? I don't know much about that sort of thing.'

'Neither do I but Eric does, that's his job. He's out tonight, but why don't I bring him round here tomorrow night to see if there's anything of value?' Her eyes were full of compassion.

'Yes please, Helen, I'd be glad if you would. I wouldn't mind selling off some of the old-fashioned stuff.'

Sylvie came in with the tea, but they didn't stay to drink it, Millie was keen to have a preliminary look to see if she could identify any treasures. They all trooped upstairs.

Most of the hard furniture Pete's grandfather had chosen for the house was still in use. Over the years they'd bought new sofas and armchairs because modern ones were thought to be more comfortable.

'What about the attics?' Helen said. 'We used to play up there when we were kids. There's lots of old furniture and household stuff up there.'

Millie was amazed at the vast number of Maynard belongings that had been dumped in their attic and forgotten. When she'd first moved here the big house had excited her, and she'd made several exploratory trips through the rooms, but the contents hadn't seemed important at the time and she remembered little of what she'd seen. Here were Victorian sofas and easy chairs stuffed with horsehair and embellished with carved mahogany, and there were other household odds and ends of every sort.

'What is this?' Sylvie held up a strange sort of cup and giggled.

Helen giggled too. 'That extra ridge of china is supposed to keep a gentleman's moustache dry. It's a moustache cup.'

Millie laughed. 'There's loads of things here and I have no idea what most of them are for.'

When Helen was leaving half an hour later, Millie put her arms round her and gave her a big hug. 'Thank you for giving up your legacy and for coming to help me.'

'It's what Dad would want,' she said simply. 'He didn't mean to drop you in it.'

That night Millie slept better, at last she could see an acceptable way out of her financial difficulties. What a fool she'd been not to take a good look round the house before she worried herself sick like that. The following day she was better able to cope at work and that evening Eric came round as arranged. The baby was asleep in her pram when Helen ran it into the vestibule.

'I'll take Eric upstairs,' she said, 'so he can get started.'

Valerie had come with them. 'I'm not staying,' she said. 'I've just come to tell you that I'm going to give up my legacy too.'

'Val – you don't have to,' Millie protested. 'I don't expect—'

'I do have to,' she said. 'Helen wanted to do it. That made me see it would be greedy and selfish of me to accept when you're struggling to bring up Father's second family.'

'You are truly Pete's daughters,' Millie choked. She felt swamped with love and gratitude; she was aware, too, of Sylvie's heightened interest. 'But I'm hoping Eric will be able to find enough of value amongst the goods and chattels to raise what I need. I know you aren't as well placed as Helen, and you have the twins to bring up.'

Valerie had her father's sea-blue eyes; like his, they were full of compassion. 'Roger and I will manage.' Roger was a schoolteacher.

'Yes, but if Eric finds another way, you may not have to.'

'I'd feel guilty if I took money from you.'

'Mum.' Sylvie was tugging at her arm, her face scarlet. 'I'm going to give up my legacy too. I feel guilty now. If I took the money, I'd feel terrible. I'd have twice the guilt.'

'No,' Millie said firmly. 'Darling, you can't.'

'I want to. I know I'll feel better if I do.'

'I'm afraid what you feel and what you want doesn't enter into it.'

'It does,' Sylvie screamed at the top of her voice, suddenly in a state of near hysteria. 'It does.' Millie tried to put her arms round her but Sylvie elbowed her out of the way, all self-control gone. 'I don't want Dad's money.'

Valerie caught her in her arms. 'Stop screaming, be quiet, and listen to me,' she said firmly. 'Millie is right.' Sylvie was struggling and she had to give her a little shake. 'It's a question of satisfying legal requirements. Val and I have to ask Mr Douglas, Dad's solicitor, to draw up a deed of variation that we then have to sign before the will can be changed. But you are under age and you can't. Your legacy and those for Simon and Kenny will have to go into trust funds until you've turned twenty-one, and there's nothing you or your mum or Mr Douglas can do about it.'

Sylvie was silent, the colour in her face had drained, leaving it paper-white. Valerie led her to the sofa and pulled her down to sit beside her. 'You don't need to worry,' she went on more gently. 'Eric may well find enough of value to sell amongst the junk upstairs so none of us need go short.'

Millie sank down on Sylvie's other side and took her hand between her own. She was worried about her daughter. Pete's death had left her more traumatised than she'd realised.

'I've got to go.' Valerie looked at her over Sylvie's head. 'I've left Roger putting the twins to bed and he's usually exhausted by this time of day.' She got up, 'Bye, Sylvie.' She patted her shoulder.

Millie got up to see her to the door. 'Poor Sylvie,' Valerie whispered. 'She's really upset.'

'She thinks it's her fault Pete died,' Millie said. 'It's playing on her mind.'

Millie returned to her daughter and pulled at her hand. 'Come upstairs and see if Helen and Eric have found anything saleable,' she said.

'I don't want to. I'll stay here and keep an eye on Jenny.'

'She's fast asleep in her pram. Come on,' Millie insisted, 'you used to love playing up there.'

Reluctantly she came but dragged her feet more as they passed the bathroom on the first floor. 'Go on then,' Millie said, 'give your face a quick rinse. It'll make you feel better. I'm dying to see if Eric has found anything of interest.'

Eric had made quite a collection of broken furniture and chairs with worn upholstery on the landing. 'I'm afraid there's nothing here that's worth a lot,' he said. 'It was not top of the range when it was new. Your grandparents, Helen love, went for machine-made furniture. But so much was lost in the air raids and so very little furniture has been made since that there's a shortage of everything. Almost any furniture sells like hot cakes and for good prices. I'll get a carpenter to mend these things and I'll have the old armchairs re-upholstered. Some of them are quite elegant and well worth the trouble.'

'Won't that cost a lot?' Millie asked anxiously.

'There will be a cost, yes, but when they're sold you'll recoup all that. We find it pays better than selling them worn and broken.' Eric was an auctioneer and owned a share of a company that held sales all over the north of England. 'Don't worry. I'll do it through the firm.'

'Will it take long?' Millie wanted everything settled as soon as possible.

'It won't be quick,' he admitted.

'Then I'll have to be patient.'

'Dad and Grandpa thought this was just rubbish,' Helen said. 'It's doing no good up here, just taking up space. You might as well get what money you can from it.'

When they started looking through the bedrooms that were no longer used, Millie was surprised and delighted to find they were unearthing articles of real value. Helen had opened the drawers of what had once been her grandmother's dressing table.

'Look at all this jewellery!' Even Sylvie's interest was captured. They began to open up the small leather cases and boxes.

'I think your grandfather paid good prices for most of this,' Eric said. 'This gold Boucheron brooch is top quality.' It was in the form of a feather, studded with diamonds, sapphires, emeralds and rubies. He took out his eyeglass to look at the hallmarks. 'Yes, it's eighteen carat and dated eighteen eighty-nine. Still in its original leather box too.'

'It's gorgeous,' Sylvie said. They found pearl necklaces, bracelets, rings and earrings.

'You won't need to sell all this,' Eric told Millie. 'You can raise all you're likely to need on just half a dozen or so of these items.'

'I'd like you and Valerie to have some of it,' Millie said. 'It's quite a hoard. You must choose what you like most. What about this pendant?'

Sylvie took it from her to hold up to her neck. 'I love this.'

'Hang on a moment,' Eric cautioned. 'It's one thing to sell off some of the goods and chattels to raise money for legacies to be paid, but it's not OK to start distributing stuff until the will is settled. It isn't legally yours yet.'

Millie said. 'Thank goodness you know something about wills, Eric.'

He smiled. 'A lot of stuff comes to our salerooms following probate.'

Sylvie was putting all the jewellery back in the drawers. 'When this is yours, Mum, I'd like to have that pendant.'

'Then you shall,' she said.

Eric said, 'I think your grandparents were interested in china too. There's a pair of Royal Doulton candlesticks here, and over there a pair of Doulton figures. Your best plan, Millie, is to let me take just enough to raise the one thousand three hundred pounds you still need to pay the legacies. Let's pick out things you don't want to keep, and I'll put them in the first sale I can. I think it'll be a week tomorrow.'

'That would be marvellous,' Millie said. 'And how soon will I get the money?'

'Just a day or two later.'

'I rang Mr Douglas this afternoon about drawing up a deed of variation,' Helen said, 'and he asked me to come in to sign it next week. Val said she'd ring him tomorrow morning to do one for her, so there need be no delay.'

'And I'll send a van round tomorrow to pick up the stuff from the attic,' Eric said, 'and put that in hand. It's no use to you and it'll give you a bit of cash to get you started on your own.'

Millie was filled with relief; she took a deep breath. 'I'm so grateful to all of you. It's a real weight off my shoulders, I can tell you. You've sorted my financial problems.'

'That's what families are for,' Eric said. 'To help each other out of the holes we find ourselves in.'

Millie felt much better as she went to bed that night. She hadn't expected ever again to find the sort of loving support Pete had given her, but she had. Val and Helen had the Maynard genes and she should have known they'd do their best to help her. Pete had brought them up to be like him. Never again would she feel overwhelmed by a shortage of money.

Chapter Eleven

Millie had barely settled at her desk the next morning when the internal phone buzzed. It was Marcus's voice. 'Where did Pete keep the keys to his desk?' he barked. 'I can't get into it.'

'Let me think. Yes, on his key ring.'

'Well, where is that?'

'I might have it here, I'm not sure.' She felt for her handbag. 'Just a minute while I look.' She'd driven his car in this morning but had she used his keys? He'd given her a set of her own. She found two sets. 'Yes, Marcus, I have them here.'

'For goodness sake! How can I take over if his desk is locked up? Send them up right away with that lad that works for you.' She heard his phone crash down.

She felt her cheeks blaze with anger all over again. Marcus was treating her like a junior employee who had made a stupid mistake. She was not going to put up with that from him. She would soon own half this business, and Marcus owned no part of it. She was a major shareholder and the only one with much experience of working in it.

She put Pete's key ring in her pocket and got Denis to find an empty cardboard box for her. Pete's office had been up in the turret that jutted up at one end of the roof and he'd liked it because it was quiet. She'd often climbed these stairs in the past and had to steel herself today not to think of those happier times.

Marcus had a tray of tea and biscuits on his desk and was splayed out in Pete's chair in a position of exaggerated relaxation. 'You've come yourself,' he scowled.

'I'd like to keep Pete's personal possessions,' she said icily. 'If you'd be good enough to move out of the way, I'll put his things together.'

'I thought I'd done that.' He lowered his feet to the floor and stood up. 'I put them on top of the bookcase in case you thought they were worth keeping.'

The little heap of belongings did look pathetic but Pete had valued them. She put the photograph in a silver frame of herself with all his children, the couple of pens and one or two books into the box she'd brought. The agate clock that Valerie had given him last Christmas was still on his desk, and so were a set of cut-glass inkwells. She swept those into her box too.

She unlocked the drawers and opened them one by one to add Pete's leather gloves, his silver propelling pencil, his desk diary, a street guide and his favourite dictionary to her box. She was conscious of Marcus watching every movement she made.

'You can clear all those papers out,' he told her. 'I'll get the cleaner to dust the drawers out.'

Millie was taking every document she saw that referred to the perfumes and dyes that they used, though she knew she probably had copies. 'There are a few files here to do with running the business, you'll need them,' she said, replacing them in the drawer.

He peered down at them. 'They look pretty scruffy, are they very old?'

'We still have an acute shortage of stationery so we've had to make do. These are the current files on matters Pete handled personally. You'll need to read them through if you're going to do his job.'

Marcus glared at them with distaste.

'Ah, now here is something else.' Millie pushed it towards him. 'A copy of last year's accounts, including the balance sheet. I gather you haven't seen it.'

'I have now,' he mumbled.

'It'll be well worth your while to study it. It'll put your mind at rest and show you just how wrong you were about the current trading position. You'll be able to give the good news to Uncle James and settle his mind too.'

He was tight-lipped and scarlet-faced. She was twisting the desk keys off the key ring. 'Here are the keys to your desk.'

'What about the rest of those keys. I want them too.'

'Sorry, Marcus, this was Pete's key ring and these are the keys to our house and car. I'm sure you'll understand why I don't want to give them to you.'

His colour deepened to crimson. 'What about the office door? How do I lock that?'

Millie shrugged. 'Why would you want to? Pete never did. He liked the staff to come in during the day and talk to him so he knew what was going on, and it has to be open at night so the cleaners can get in.' She couldn't stop herself adding sarcastically, 'I know you intend to turn over a new leaf and do things differently but you're not thinking of doing your own cleaning, are you?'

She heard his gasp of indignation as she carried her box out. Pete would say she was wasting her energy battling Marcus when she should be spending it on solving her other problems. With hindsight she knew it was a mistake to get his back up. She went back to her desk feeling drained after that spat.

James Maynard was delighted when his friend John Maddox approached him in the bar of the Connaught Club to tell him that his agency had a furnished flat coming vacant at the end of next week. 'It's in Woolton and one of our better flats,' he said. 'Ground floor, two bedrooms and in reasonable condition. It would suit your son until he finds a house where he wants to live permanently.'

'We'll take it,' James said without hesitation. 'I'll give you a cheque for the first month's rent.'

'Don't you want to see it first? I expect they'd let you in to have a quick look round tomorrow.'

'No, it sounds fine,' he was pleased that he'd succeeded so quickly.

He was finding Elvira difficult to live with. She spent hours in the bathroom, ran out all the hot water and the lock was always on when he wanted to use the place. She rubbed everybody up the wrong way and both Dando and Mrs Trotter had complained about her. She'd altered the atmosphere in his house and he could get no peace in his own home. James couldn't wait to get her out.

The next morning he had his breakfast in bed as usual but instead of opening his newspaper, he put on his dressing gown and went down to the dining room to see Marcus to tell him the good news.

'A furnished flat?' Elvira looked up from her porridge, her face creasing with disdain. 'We were hoping for a house, we need a bit of space.'

'I'm told it's one of their better flats.' James was defensive. 'It's in a good area and has two bedrooms.'

'Only two? Is there a good bathroom?'

'I don't know what the bathroom's like.' James was getting cross. 'I haven't seen it.'

'You haven't?' Elvira was suspicious.

'There is a bathroom, I know that. I've paid the first month's rent. I had to, before somebody else stepped in. You'll have to pay a deposit against damages as well.'

'Good gracious,' she said, 'we won't cause any damage.'

'We'll go and check it out this morning,' Marcus said hurriedly.

'Is it worth moving there if we are shortly to move somewhere better?' Elvira asked with her nose in the air.

James could feel his anger growing. The woman was insufferable. 'There'll be no question of you moving on quickly,' he said, 'you'll have to sign a six-month lease.'

'Oh. Well, Redwood's are quite hopeful about finding us a house,' she said.

'You're expecting a gentleman's residence, I presume?' James was scathing. 'Well, there's absolutely no reason why you can't wait for a house if you prefer. Nigel will need a roof over his head too.'

'We'll go and look at it today,' Marcus said again, trying to save the situation.

'I wouldn't want to put Elvira to any trouble,' his father said. 'She clearly knows what she wants. My friend John Maddox thought it would be suitable for you and offered it as a favour to me, and I was trying to help, but I'm sure Nigel will be glad of it. Maddox knows all there is to know about the present housing market.'

James rushed for the stairs in a fury. The wretched woman had taken over his house, his staff and caused endless disruption. Now when he'd gone out of his way to help her and found her a place to live, she'd refused to go. A flat wasn't good enough for her. After that, he was going to make quite sure Nigel got it and not her.

It was only when he calmed down he realised Elvira would still be living in his house if he did that.

A few days later, James was having his afternoon tea when the phone rang. He recognised Nigel's voice. After a lot of preliminaries he said, 'We've arrived in Southampton. We've got a hotel for the night and we'll catch a train up to Liverpool

131

tomorrow. I've made enquiries and it'll get us to Lime Street at five o'clock.'

'I'll ask Marcus to come and meet you,' he said and went back to do it.

It was only after James had poured himself another cup of tea and sat down that he noticed the black thunder on Marcus's face. 'He's coming to stay here too?'

'Yes, the flat isn't quite ready. The cleaners will be going in tomorrow.' There were six bedrooms in James's house but the congestion would be in the bathroom; he hoped Clarissa would not spend as long there as Elvira.

'And he's going to work in the business too?'

'I told you he was.' Clearly Marcus had hoped Nigel would get a better offer somewhere else. 'He'll probably need a few days to sort himself out before he starts.' James recollected that Marcus had always felt overshadowed by his older brother. Well, all that childish jealousy was a long way behind them now. No doubt they'd learn to get on and work together, they'd have to.

When Dando came to take away the tea tray, James asked him to prepare a room for Nigel and his wife. Dando's eyebrows rose in silent protest.

'They'll only be staying for one night,' he said. 'I've found other accommodation for them.'

'I'm glad to hear that, sir,' he replied but James didn't miss the reproachful look he directed at Elvira. Her lips were compressed into a hard straight line.

'Have you heard any more from Redwood's about your gentleman's residence?' James asked pointedly.

'Not yet.'

'You need to hurry them up, Elvira. You know as far as I'm concerned you're welcome to stay here, but it gives Dando and Mrs Trotter more work. She's asking if a washer-woman could come once a week.'

'We'll pay for that,' Marcus choked out.

'Wouldn't the laundry be easier?' Elvira asked haughtily.

It pleased James to be able to say, 'It works out cheaper to have a washerwoman.'

At four thirty the following afternoon, Marcus stood up. 'Are you coming with me to meet my brother, Elvira?' he asked.

'No,' she said coldly. 'I'll say hello to him when you get him here.' Marcus went off without another word, and Elvira returned to her book. At teatime she usually read and ignored both of them.

James was still in the sitting room when Marcus ushered Nigel and his wife in an hour later. James swept him into a hug that showed real warmth. 'Welcome home,' he said, and turned to study his daughter-in-law. 'Lovely to meet you at last.'

Clarissa was slim and elegant. She smiled and kissed his cheek. He thought she had a very gracious manner; the years she'd spent at Cheltenham Ladies College had given her real polish. Nigel looked very well, he'd kept an eye on his weight, and though he was two years older than Marcus, he looked younger.

'It's just dinner, bed and breakfast here,' James told them. 'I've found a flat for you and today the cleaners are going in. I wasn't sure whether the beds would be made up in time for you to sleep there. Anyway, you can go along tomorrow morning and make sure all is as you want it.' He couldn't resist baiting Elvira. 'Perhaps you could go with them to give them a hand? They'll have a lot of unpacking to do.'

Elvira rewarded him with a scowl but agreed to do it. James went on giving them details of the flat. 'I hope you find it adequate.'

'I'm sure we will,' Clarissa said sweetly. 'We're very grateful for your help.'

When James took Nigel and Clarissa upstairs to see their bedroom, Marcus turned to his wife. 'You stupid fool,' he burst out. 'You never stop complaining about living here but when Pa finds us a place you tell him it's not good enough.'

She looked down her nose at him. 'Do you really think you'd be happy living in a furnished flat?'

'We'd both like it better than living here with Pa. And it would stop you finding fault with Dando and Mrs Trotter. You're getting up everybody's nose here, the sooner we get out the better. You've got all day to go round the estate agents while I'm at work. For heaven's sake badger them and find us somewhere.'

'Your father loves Nigel more than you,' Elvira hissed spitefully. 'He's putting on a big dinner tonight to welcome him home. He did nothing like that for us.'

Marcus was very much on edge and he blamed it on having to live in his father's house. Pa and Elvira had taken a dislike to each other and were at daggers drawn. He kept sniping at her and Elvira had a shrewish tongue and could make Pa feel acutely uncomfortable. He was making it very clear that they'd overstayed their welcome.

Redwood's, the local estate agent, had sent them particulars of two very desirable houses that had come up for sale, but Marcus knew he couldn't afford them. Elvira insisted they went to look over them and, once seen, she was very keen. The larger, more expensive one was for sale or rent. 'If you can't afford to buy, at least let us rent it,' she said as they walked out to their car. 'We've got to find somewhere else to live. Staying with your father is getting desperate.'

Ever since Elvira had chained him to a huge debt, he'd been scared of being overdrawn. It was debt that had driven him into the hands of those fraudsters because there had been no other way he could pay off a debt of that size.

'The rent would take most of my salary,' Marcus protested, 'and we've sold off most of our furniture. It would be almost impossible to get more.' Elvira's extravagant ways were giving him sleepless nights and he couldn't risk running up another debt.

'It's a lovely house. It's what we've been waiting for,' she insisted.

'It's too big. We don't need six bedrooms and a huge garden, we can't afford it. We need something smaller and cheaper.'

Elvira flared up. 'It always boils down to lack of money. You'll never earn enough to buy us a house of our own. You're wasting your time here. Your father's a skinflint, he pays you a pittance and we live like paupers in his house, but the real problem is that you're a yellow-bellied coward.'

Marcus drove faster, wanting to put distance between them and that tempting house. She went on, 'When you were earning enough to accumulate a bit of capital, you got so frightened you gave it up.'

He found that hurtful. 'It wasn't exactly earning, was it? It was cheating and stealing. I wanted an honest job.'

'You were scared of being caught.'

He could see she was fulminating, and clashes of this sort turned him into a nervous wreck. He shot up Pa's drive to the front door, jammed on the brakes, causing a spray of gravel, and escaped for a lonely tramp to the nearest pub.

James had had a bad back over the last few days. He'd had his usual breakfast tray in his room and slept a little afterwards. He got dressed and had a little lunch downstairs, but returned to his bed for a nap afterwards. By half past three, he was feeling a little better and in need of his tea. As he went downstairs, Elvira came in, slamming the front door behind her and divesting herself of her coat and hat. At the same

135

time, Dando sailed across the hall in his stately manner, carrying the tea tray to the sitting room.

James rubbed his hands with satisfaction. 'Ah Dando, you've found us a cherry cake, very nice.'

Elvira shot into the sitting room ahead of him as though there was a tornado behind her. 'You can pour, Dando,' she said; sometimes he left it to her.

'I'll have two pieces of that cake while you're at it,' James told him.

Dando turned to Elvira. 'Madam?'

'Thank you no, I don't care for cherry cake.' She looked angry.

'Have you been shopping?' That seemed to be her usual pastime.

'No, Redwood's sent us particulars of a very nice house,' she said. 'We've been to see it.' She put a sheet of paper in front of him.

'Splendid, when are you moving in?'

That seemed to upset her. 'Marcus says we can't afford it.'

'I'm not surprised.' James liked to goad her.

'No, your firm doesn't pay him enough.'

'I doubt he'll get more anywhere else. I told the accountant his salary was to be ten per cent more than the going rate for a manager. Nigel thinks it generous.'

'But it isn't enough to afford a house of our own. Could I make a suggestion?

'Of course, my dear.' He was beginning to feel riled but was still acting the gracious father-in-law.

'Would you consider giving Marcus a few shares in the business? I mean, he's working in it and it seems only right and fair to hand them on down the family. A share of the profit might give us enough to pay a mortgage.'

James almost choked on his cake. 'No,' he barked, 'I wouldn't. Marcus isn't worth what he's paid now. He's doing damn all as far as I can see. I'll hand on my shares when I'm good and ready.' He gulped at his tea, feeling affronted. 'You've had free board and lodging here in my house for weeks, and you've got the cheek to ask for more.'

Elvira leapt to her feet and left the room, leaving most of her tea in the cup.

Marcus returned that evening feeling low. He met his father in the hall on his way to the Connaught Club for his dinner. 'My shares are mine,' James said to him belligerently, 'and they're going to stay mine. I'd like to retire when you and Nigel are capable of taking over and I'll need the payout from them to survive on my pension.'

Marcus was at a loss. 'Has Elvira said—'

'Yes, and I don't want that wife of yours putting her oar in. It's none of her business. You must keep her out of it.'

Marcus felt like groaning. He found Elvira waiting for him upstairs ready to do battle.

'To stay here and carry on like this is pointless,' she said angrily. 'It's getting us nowhere and your father wants us out. He told me so very rudely this afternoon. Come on, I'm hungry. Do you want to get changed before we go out?'

The current arrangement was that if they wished to eat an evening meal at home Elvira would buy something and cook it. Today, she'd done nothing. Marcus didn't care whether he ate or not but she was insisting on going out. At the restaurant they usually patronised they consumed their soup in sullen silence.

When the plates had been taken away she said, 'Well, we've got to do something. What is it to be?'

Marcus wanted to go to bed, he felt at the end of his tether. 'What do you suggest?'

'There's nothing to stop you rejoining that auction ring. I

137

told you I'd seen Greg Livingstone the other day. He was doing a job in Liverpool.'

Marcus was tempted but he'd been clean since coming home and working for the business, and he wanted to stay that way.

'You're scared,' Elvira said disparagingly. 'There's nothing to worry about. You gave up nine months ago and nothing has happened since. You'd have earned enough to buy us that house if you'd carried on and we'd be in a much better position now.' She pushed a piece of paper across to him. 'Greg gave me this phone number. You can contact him there.'

Without a word he pushed it into the breast pocket of his suit and went on toying with his fish. It was presented on the menu as white fish which suggested nobody could name the species; it was overcooked and tasteless.

'Will you do that?'

'I don't want to, it's against the law.'

'You're being stupid about this,' she said scornfully. 'Are you enjoying working in your family's business?' She knew he wasn't, he'd complained often enough about Nigel being high-handed and Millie treating him like a fool.

'There's only one reason to go into business and that is to make money. If it isn't doing that for you and you don't like working there, where is the logic in staying?' Elvira laid down her knife and fork.

Marcus was suspicious about Elvira's relationship with Captain Livingstone although she said he was a friend of her family. He had known him too, they'd been members of the same mess, but it was Elvira who had made the original arrangements that had allowed him to pay off his debts.

'Where did you see Greg Livingstone?' he asked.

'In the Bon Marche, a department store. I was buying gloves on the ground floor and he was walking through to the lift. I went up to the men's department with him, if you must know, and helped him buy a new dress shirt. He said he'd be glad to have you back in the ring and would find other jobs for you.'

'I don't want that. There must be another way.'

'There isn't,' she said shortly.

Chapter Twelve

It was six o'clock on Friday when Marcus got home from work. Nigel had given him an uncomfortable afternoon in the office and he'd called in at the Sailor's Return to help ease him into the evening. When he opened the front door, he was shocked to find a mound of Elvira's suitcases piled up in the hall.

He rushed to the sitting room where his wife had her feet up on a footstool and was deep in a book. 'All that luggage!' he choked. 'Where are you going?'

She gave him a withering look. 'I told you last night, I've had enough of you and your father. I'm going home.'

Marcus stared at her with his mouth open. Last night they'd had a real set to about the discomforts of living with his father, and in a fit of temper he'd told her that it was her spendthrift ways that kept them here. If she'd saved the money from the Streatham house they'd be able to buy another now when they needed it. In return, she'd told him a few home truths about his lack of ability, but he hadn't registered that she'd intended to leave.

'You're going home to your family for a short break?'

'Don't you ever listen? I've had enough of this place, I'm going for good.'

'Elvira, no, I love you, I want you here. Just take a short break, have a rest and come back.'

'That won't help. I've ordered a taxi for half eight tomorrow morning, there's a train at five past nine.'

'I could run you to the station if that's what you want, but say you'll come back.'

'No, Marcus, I hate this place, you do nothing but argue and complain, and your father is worse. I've had enough.'

He slumped into an armchair, feeling cold with horror. 'If I can find us somewhere else to live, will you come back? This isn't final is it?'

'Yes it is. We're neither of us happy. I'm on my own all day and bored out of my mind. I'm ready to call it a day.'

Marcus wasn't bored, he felt pushed to the limit and a bag of nerves. 'We should have accepted that flat instead of letting Nigel have it.'

'It's more than that, we've had enough of each other and we both know it.'

He felt sick, his life was a misery.

When they went to bed, he couldn't sleep, while Elvira snored for most of the night. He was awake again when her alarm went off and aware she was dressing quickly. He sat up and tried once again to persuade her to come back after a short stay.

'No, my mind is made up,' she told him. 'Either you join the ring again and earn enough for our needs, or we're finished. If you won't then I will join Greg's ring, and you and your family can stew in your own juice. Have you got that? Goodbye then.' She collected up some small bags and he heard her clattering downstairs.

Marcus rushed after her in his pyjamas and caught her as she opened the front door. 'All right, I'll do it,' he said. 'I'll join the ring again and do a few jobs for Greg until we have enough to buy a house.'

She looked up with a triumphant smile. 'A decent house?'

'Yes, you can choose it, have what you want. Come back and unpack your cases.'

'No, I've told Father I'm coming, so I better had.' She was pushing her cases out on to the step. 'But I'll come back in a week or so if you ring the number I gave you and tell Greg you want to do a few more jobs. Bye.'

Marcus went slowly back to his bedroom and threw himself on the bed. Elvira was blackmailing him but he'd have to do as she demanded or stay here with Pa. He felt exhausted and closed his eyes, and was so lacking in energy he didn't feel he could get dressed and go to work, not today. He'd made a life-changing decision to please Elvira but it terrified him. It was the last thing he wanted to do.

It seemed only minutes later that Elvira came bustling back into the room again. 'Marcus, my taxi hasn't come. I'm going to take the car, where are the keys?'

He sat up with a jerk. 'No,' he protested, 'you can't take it. I earned the money for that car.'

'If I hadn't made all the arrangements with Greg, you'd have done nothing.'

'I'll run you to the station, I said I would.'

'You aren't dressed yet. I'll miss the train if I don't go now.'

Marcus pushed his feet to the floor. 'What does it matter? The trains to Rochdale run every hour.'

'I'm fed up with waiting around for taxis while you breeze off every morning in the car. I'm taking it. You can try taxis for a change.'

He'd left his keys on the tallboy. He heard them rattle as she picked them up. 'I want my car back. I'll come and get it at the weekend.'

'It's my turn to have it. I haven't had a look in up to now. Just ring that number and get started with Greg and soon we'll have two cars.' The door slammed behind her.

Marcus felt ready to weep. Elvira had run a little MG of her own before they'd been married. She'd written one off in a nasty accident and when the basic petrol ration for everybody was cut off completely, she'd been charged with buying petrol on the black market and her MG had been mothballed for the rest of the war. Unfortunately, Elvira had sold it before the petrol ration was restored.

Later that morning, Marcus rang for a taxi to take him to work and arranged to be collected every morning at a quarter to nine for the next week. Once in his office he found the slip of paper Elvira had given him in the top pocket of his jacket and laid it on the desk in front of him. It took him ten minutes to screw up his nerve to ask the operator to connect him.

He was scared stiff, there was no point in pretending otherwise. He was afraid they'd all be caught. Greg Livingstone couldn't go on running a racket like this forever. Sooner or later he or one of the other dozen or so members of the ring would be caught. It was a miracle the fraud had lasted this long.

Greg was friendly enough. 'I'll meet you in Manchester tomorrow morning at about eleven.' He dictated an address where an auction of surplus military vehicles was to be held. 'There'll be plenty of jobs to keep you busy, mostly ferrying cars from one part of the country to another.'

'Excellent.'

'Give me some telephone numbers so I can contact you.'

Marcus dictated his office number. 'Be sure to ring me here,' he said. 'I can't talk on the phone at home without being overheard.'

Chapter Thirteen

Elvira had been growing increasingly impatient with Marcus for the last year or so. He'd caused great concern for the others in the ring by wanting to opt out and work in that hopeless business for his father. She'd had a hard job convincing Greg that he had no intention of pulling the plug on them, and as proof she'd had to agree to doing a few jobs for him herself. She'd very quickly been drawn into the ring and found she enjoyed working for Greg. Soon she was sleeping with him too. Her life suddenly became much more interesting. She felt she was in the thick of things.

Marcus was a drag on her, a hanger-on dithering over everything, and he was scared of his own shadow. Also, he hadn't the nerve or ability to play a major part in the work of the ring, while she could. He was stuck with the menial jobs, but what had really got her down was living with his father, he was a real pain in the neck.

She'd got to know Greg and the other members of the team during the years she'd spent as an army wife. She didn't see her relationship with Greg as anything more than a bit of fun. He would take any woman he could get and would never be a faithful partner. What they shared was the thrill of organising the ring and making big money, and it was giving her money of her own. She had no intention of buying a house to share with Marcus. She'd had enough of marriage and had decided she'd be better off on her own. She was preparing to ditch Marcus. From now on she was going to take care of herself.

Greg was very safety conscious. 'Marcus could be a problem,' he told her. 'He's the sort that'll collapse under pressure. He'll tell all, land us all in trouble, if the police get hold of him.'

'I'll see he doesn't,' Elvira said.

Greg had made careful plans to ensure not only his own safety but that of the other members of the ring. He encouraged them all to send money to Spain; he meant them all to get out with as much cash as they could before any net closed round them. Mostly what they earned came in cash, and he preached to every member of the gang about taking care of it. They must not let a huge balance build up in their personal bank account, as that could attract attention to them. That would never be a problem for her and Marcus, and neither would unusually heavy spending, another thing he warned against, as that would be normal for them.

Greg had accounts in several different banks and several deposit boxes too, and he didn't settle anywhere; he rented and moved every six months or so. He always rented at least two flats in different towns, and he changed his telephone numbers regularly. Above all, he did his best to impress on members of the team that they must not keep written records. Any instructions they had to write down must be destroyed as soon as the job was done.

Millie was fascinated by what she and the family had turned up in the unused rooms of her house. She'd learned a lot about Pete's parents from sorting through their possessions and she found Sylvie was equally intrigued. They went back to it again at the weekend and Simon and Kenny were more than happy to join them.

The boys unearthed a box of toys in the attic and brought

it down to the playroom. Soon the floor was covered with lead soldiers and the boys were setting up a battle scene.

'These must have belonged to Dad.' Simon was thrilled at the thought.

'Or possibly Uncle James,' Sylvie reminded them.

Millie sat back on her haunches. 'You still like the same things. Children don't change much, do they?'

'Would Dad have looked like me when he was my age?' Simon wanted to know.

'Quite possibly, yes.'

That sent the children scurrying back upstairs to look for old photographs. Millie went to the kitchen to organise lunch. They were gone for some time, and she thought the hunt through old family possessions not only interested them but eased their grief. There was comfort in the thought that Pete had played with these toys. It showed them the stability of the family.

They came down when she was about to call them to eat. 'Not many photos there,' Sylvie said, but she produced a framed sepia print of two small boys with their parents.

'There you are,' Millie was delighted with it, 'your father and Uncle James with Grandpa and Grandma.'

'I don't see much family likeness,' Simon said.

'That's because their clothes are so different. This must have been taken ... Let me think.'

'It was taken in eighteen ninety,' Kenny said. 'The date is on the back.'

She turned it over; the date had been pencilled there. 'That would make Dad about seven years old and Uncle James about four.'

Kenny said, 'It was taken in the back garden. You can see it's our house.'

'The Maynard family as it was in eighteen ninety,' Millie said.

'They had servants then.' Sylvie produced some postcard-size photographs. 'Look at these people ranged behind the family. They had a housekeeper and two maids, and these two men who I think must be gardeners.'

'The Maynards must once have been an important family,' Simon said.

'We still are,' Kenny said, 'we've got a factory. But why don't we have servants?'

'We have Mrs Brunt to do the heavy work, and Mungo to do the garden.'

'But they aren't proper servants, are they?' Kenny said. 'Are we poor now?'

'Not as rich as we were,' Simon said sadly.

'Times change,' Millie told them. 'Nobody has servants these days because there are plenty of better jobs about.'

'I still can't see much family resemblance.' Simon was once again studying the framed print.

'Good,' Kenny said. 'We don't want to look like Uncle James when we grow up, do we?'

Millie wanted to learn more about Pete's family, and when the children were in bed that night she returned to his parents' bedroom, but she kept turning over the things she'd already seen. She gave up and went to the study instead. She'd hardly ever come here when Pete was alive and she hadn't used it much since. It was a darkish masculine room furnished in high Victorian style, and must have been used by his father and grandfather before him. The scent of cigar smoke still seemed to hang there though Pete had never smoked.

There was a large and heavy roll-top desk, and several cupboards in which old business files were packed tight. She blew the dust off one dated 1900 and opened it on the desk. Her interest was gripped in moments, here was the balance sheet for that year, showing a handsome profit. She took out more. Year after year, good profits had been made. She was particularly interested in the years of the Great War, and found as she'd expected that turnover fell away, but less so than in the war they'd just had. She was pleased to see it had recovered quite quickly in the years that followed.

Tiring of balance sheets, she started opening the drawers in the desk and came upon some large leather-covered notebooks. She opened one and found the pages were closely covered with writing that was small and crabbed and hard to read. It took her a few moments to realise it was a diary. The writer had not made entries every day but had recorded his or her thoughts and deeds and dated them, filling several pages at one sitting.

Millie was thrilled with her find, this was exactly what she needed; she couldn't have asked for a better way of finding out more about Pete's family. But whose diary was it? She knew Pete had never kept one, but it wasn't his father's either. She'd just seen examples of his handwriting in the business files, and he wrote in large, strong script.

On one of the flyleaves she saw the name Eleanor Mary Willis Maynard. So the diary had belonged to Pete's mother, the mother-in-law she had never met. Millie counted the diaries, there were twelve in all and they completely filled the large bottom drawer of the desk. They were all dated. She looked through them until she found the earliest one, it was for the year 1878.

She took it, but before going to bed she went to the playroom where the children had left the albums of photographs they'd been looking at. She wanted to see what her mother-in-law had looked like.

A good-looking woman was smiling out of the sepia prints. She wore her hair piled on top of her head with a few wisps of fringe and was stiffly corseted into a wasp waist. Her wedding pictures were here. She'd been married in the family church as Millie had, but her dress had been much more ornate. Pete's father looked young and elegant in full morning dress and he had a moustache. It had been high summer and the overdressed guests were pictured in the back garden, there was even a photograph of a five-tier wedding cake. Life, Millie mused, had been very different then.

She went to her room intending to have a long read, but she was tired and once she'd settled against her pillows she soon gave up, the writing was too squashed and tiny to decipher easily. But over the following days and weeks she dipped into them every night before she went to sleep, and found them absolutely riveting. She'd discovered that Pete's mother Eleanor had married William Frederick Maynard in 1877 when she'd been seventeen and he twenty-six. Eleanor had written:

It is not easy starting married life under the eyes of Freddie's father but he insisted that we live with him. It wasn't our choice, we were looking for a small house for ourselves, but Freddie said, 'I'm afraid we have to give in on this, poor Pa is lost without Mum and he needs you to take care of the house.'

That terrified me at the time, as I knew little about housekeeping, and he is very fussy and often finds fault with what I do. But then he doesn't like me.

The trouble is that Freddie's father, William Charles Maynard is a disappointed man. He wanted Freddie to marry his cousin Margaret Haskins. They grew up together and were great friends, she was the cousin whose company he enjoyed most, but he knew she was in love with someone else and he wanted to marry me.

Freddie had his way over that, but my father-in-law doesn't approve of my family, he thinks the Willises are not in the same class as the Haskins and the Maynards. My family have been watch and clock makers for generations but modern industrial methods have put them out of business. The watches that my family designed and made by hand, piece by careful piece, and then fitted together, are now stamped out on machines and made to sell at half the price. My family are reduced to repairing the new timepieces when they go wrong. Watch repairers, Charles calls us with such a note of disdain in his voice.

His father had this dream of earning a fortune and building a great family dynasty to enjoy it. It was his aim to build up and manage a profitable business on which his family and their progeny could live in comfort for the rest of their lives, but now his life's work is almost in tatters. He has the business and the house, but his big family has been decimated, and he is looking to me and Freddie to produce a big family and replace the generation of Maynards that has been lost.

I want babies, I would love to have a family and so would Freddie. He wants sons to follow him in the business and he wants to please his father. I come from a large family and the Willises are, to say the least, prolific. Within three months we had happy news for Freddie's father, his first grandchild was on the way. There was such rejoicing and he started to look on me with more favour.

When Millie discovered that Eleanor was Freddie's second wife she felt they had much in common. She could see things from her point of view and it brought the mother-in-law she'd never met closer to her. It seemed Freddie's first wife had died of tuberculosis at twenty-three years of age without having any children.

But that night Millie read that Eleanor's hopes were dashed.

We are all sick at heart, I have had my second miscarriage, but Freddie said, 'Don't give up hope, we'll wait until you are stronger and then try again. You are still very young.'

But his father was in tears when he came to my room see me. Seeing such a proud man in tears and knowing I am the cause of it is very upsetting.

Millie knew all had eventually come right for Eleanor when she'd had Peter, and was glad she'd been able to put her miscarriages behind her.

Back in the present, things did not seem to be coming right for Sylvie. She'd always been rather shy and introverted but she'd seemed to enjoy her job in the firm's typing pool. This was run by Miss Franklin, a spinster who looked older than her years, and who also acted as James's secretary when he came to work. The firm started young girls there straight from commercial college, so they could gain experience before being promoted to secretary to a senior member of staff.

Sylvie had made friends among her colleagues, and went out occasionally with Louise Lambert and also Connie Grey and her brother, who worked in the production department. But she'd never had a special boyfriend and had always seemed content to spend most of her leisure time with the family.

Now suddenly she was moody and rebellious and dissatisfied with everything. Millie knew that she was grieving for Pete, and that the manner of his sudden death had been horrifyingly traumatic for her. She was hoping that in time Sylvie would get over it. She filled her weekends with trips out with Simon and Kenny, and visits to either Valerie's home or Helen's.

Eric had sold off some of the jewellery and both girls had done exactly what they'd said they'd do. When Millie knew there was sufficient money in Pete's account to pay the legacies he'd willed to those of his children who had not reached their majority, she rang Mr Douglas to ask if she could expect Pete's will to be settled now.

'Yes, my dear, all is in order. I'll arrange for a trust fund to be drawn up for the children and their legacies to be paid in. But the law is notoriously slow and the Probate Registry will take its time to settle your husband's affairs as it does for everybody else. I'm afraid you'll have to be patient for a few more weeks.'

Now her financial difficulties had been solved, Millie felt she could wait. She enjoyed her job but thought Uncle James and his sons were being difficult. They were spending a lot of time together in James's office. James told her they were assessing the present set-up of the company and making plans, but when she'd asked him later about the plans, he evaded the question, and he never came to the lab to discuss any changes.

Pete had called a meeting of the department heads once a month so everybody knew what was being planned and what progress had been made. Apart from Andrew, all of them had worked for the firm for twenty to thirty years and had kept the place running during the war. Tom Bedford ran the soap production, while Albert Lancaster was responsible for talcum powder. She dreaded the time when they'd want to retire and was grateful it was still a year or two off. Dan Quentin their sales manager was a little younger, very efficient and always smartly dressed, and their buyer was Billy Sankey. He was a bit of a maverick but they were all fond of him.

Pete had trusted the senior managers and they'd always done their best for him. They were continuing to work hard now and everything was running smoothly, but it was nearly four months since Pete had died.

Yesterday, she'd had a word with Tom Bedford. 'James brought Marcus to the factory floor the other day,' he told her. 'When I approached them and asked if I could be of any help, they said no. They didn't speak to anybody but they were taking notes as they walked round and peered into everything.' Albert Lancaster told her much the same thing.

Millie had no idea how they spent their time in the office. As far as she could see, they were doing precious little.

Millie continued to find the diaries fascinating and was trying to read more of them, but the pages were so crammed with tiny writing which was hard to decipher that it was taking her a long time. There were little anecdotes about Pete and his brother, snippets of information about the Maynard business and information about the garden and their favourite recipes. Millie was totally hooked.

She'd decided it would take years to read them from beginning to end, and she was dipping first in one diary and then another in her search for facts about the family. She knew she must be more methodical, and began marking the passages she'd read.

She thought of giving one of the books to Sylvie and getting her help, but Sylvie was at last acting like a normal teenager wanting to be out and about all the time. What she needed was more sleep.

The diaries were heavy on her stomach in bed and Millie took to reading them at the roll-top desk on Sunday afternoons as well, and asked herself how much of his mother's life Pete had known.

The diaries were in his desk drawers so it seemed likely he'd read them, but he'd been very open, talked about everything and he'd never mentioned them to her. She thought he'd have encouraged her to read them if he'd known what was in them. He'd been proud of what his father had achieved, and talked of him from time to time. Tonight Millie had come to bed early and was feeling drowsy until she read:

Freddie and I were invited by a business connection to a pheasant shoot on an estate in Wales. It was a clear sunny day but cold and we wives were taken up to the moor to join them for a picnic lunch in a specially erected tent. Our vehicle was pulled by four horses and also carried the food and the servants to serve it.

It was a substantial meal with hot soup and a casserole taken up in hay boxes and as the men had had a successful morning, they were in a jolly mood and spent rather too much time over it. The beaters were sent off promptly to drive the birds into position for the first afternoon shoot and when reminded, the men rather hurriedly picked up their guns to resume their sport. We ladies went for a short walk in the opposite direction to allow the servants time to repack the dishes and tidy up the brake for our return.

We heard a few shots and then agitated cries and calls, and knew something had gone wrong. We rushed back to the tent but the shooting brake had already gone racing past us and we heard that a serving woman had been accidently shot and was being taken to the doctor.

It was only when I saw Freddie sagging against a tent pole in great distress that I realised he was the one who had shot her. Everybody was kind to him, offering support, condolences and brandy, and agreeing that the woman had caused the accident. She had no reason to be in the place where it had happened. It made them lose interest in pheasant shooting and we all went back to the house.

Mrs Trott was a woman from the village, not one of our host's servants, and had been hired for a few days to help with the shooting party. When the news reached us at dinner that she had died, poor Freddie was in a fever of remorse, made worse when we learned she was a widow of only a few months, her husband having been killed in a threshing accident at harvest time. Even worse was the news that she

154

had a two-month-old son being cared for by a neighbour.

I have never seen Freddie so stricken. Some of the house guests left the next morning but we couldn't go home. Freddie wished to make amends. Our host sought other relatives of the Trott family but none were to be found and the neighbour to whom the child had been entrusted already had seven children of her own and no wish for more.

As the child was an orphan, Freddie could see only one solution: we would add him to our family, a brother for our darling Peter. Both Freddie and I had been longing for another baby. What I really wanted was a little girl, but Freddie wanted sons to run his business when they were grown up. This baby boy, although dressed in rags, was quite handsome, and appeared well fed and healthy. Peter was now coming up to two and a half years old, so this baby would fit into our family very well.

We will bring him up in greater comfort than his mother could ever have done. He will receive a good education and will have a better life than he would otherwise have done, and at two months of age, he need never know that we are not his natural parents. Neither need Peter, he is not old enough to understand. The child had been named Sidney, but we had him christened William James.

Millie sat back feeling shocked. The Maynard family had secrets she'd never even suspected. Had Pete known about this? She was quite sure James did not, he'd been proud to say that he and his sons were of the Maynard bloodline, and superior to her who had only married into the family. Well, she could certainly put them in their place now, and wouldn't it serve them right? She positively itched to do it.

They'd been more than rude to her, shown their dislike and their wish to put her out of the business. Next time they came to the lab trying to make trouble for her she would have all the ammunition she needed to silence them.

It was only when she'd thought it over that she asked herself if Pete would do that. He was a much kinder, more generous person than she was; she'd heard him say several times that he must not be unkind to James. James was his brother and allowances must be made if he did not feel up to coming to work.

Perhaps Pete had known and that was why he'd not told her about his mother's diaries. It had been his parents' secret too, and on further consideration she decided she must respect their wishes. She could not tell James or his sons that they'd been born into a background as lowly as hers. Pete wouldn't want her to do that.

She was glad now that she hadn't told Sylvie about the diaries. Goodness, she'd even thought of asking Valerie and Helen to read some of them, and would have done had they not always seemed so busy with their own families.

Millie was wide awake now and continued to read. Eleanor was comparing her two boys.

Peter is much the brighter. He's more alert, into everything while James is quite bucolic and doesn't seem to have Peter's energy. Freddie believes nurture plays a greater part in a child's development than nature and quotes the Jesuit saying, 'Give me a child until he is seven and I will show you the man.'

They'd both wanted to believe the upbringing he'd have would enable James to play a useful part in running the business.

Well, there would be no argument now. Pete had definitely turned out to be the more able person.

Chapter Fourteen

A few days later, Millie found a typed memo on her desk calling a staff meeting at ten o'clock that morning in James's office, which was also used as their boardroom. 'About time,' she said aloud to Denis.

She set out promptly and met Andrew Worthington heading in the same direction. She'd hoped she could count on him as an ally against Marcus, but she'd been disappointed by his lack of interest in her problems. Except to say an occasional good morning, he'd barely spoken to her since that lunchtime when she'd asked for his help.

There was no one else within hearing and today his dark green eyes looked into hers as he asked diffidently, 'How are you getting on? Did you decide how you were going to raise the money you needed for those legacies?'

'Yes, it's all sorted,' she said cheerfully. 'The family stepped in to handle it.'

'Good, good,' he said, with a look of surprise on his thin face.

Millie led the way to James's office where Miss Franklin was placing a typed agenda in front of each chair. The heads of the departments were already assembling round the boardroom table. James was fussing around and she found that as well as Marcus, his elder son Nigel was here.

'Hello, Nigel,' she said, 'I haven't seen you for years.

Welcome home.' He'd really changed. He was more elegant than Marcus, with a pencil moustache and a deep tan.

'Thanks. I'm glad to be back.'

'When was it you went to India?' she asked. 'Nineteen thirty-six?' He was wearing a well-cut suit with his pocket handkerchief showing just the right amount of corner protruding from his breast pocket. He'd taken great pains with his appearance.

'Yes,' he said. 'I was very sorry to hear about Uncle Peter. How are you?'

'I'm managing, thank you.' Millie saw Marcus was closing the door so she sat down and Andrew took the seat next to her.

Andrew Worthington opened the file he'd brought and said to Millie, 'I've got the figures worked out for last year. I think you'll be pleased, there's a further increase in profits.'

He'd regularly attended Pete's monthly staff meetings where they'd been greeted with cups of tea and if possible biscuits. He could see there would be no such comforts this morning.

James rapped on the table and called the meeting to attention. 'I'd like to start by introducing my elder son Nigel to you,' he said.

Nigel beamed round the table, looking fit and much slimmer than the rest of his family.

'I've been waiting for him to be demobbed,' James went on, 'before I felt I could—'

The door opened and Dan Quentin and Albert Lancaster came noisily in to join them. 'Are we late? Sorry, Mr Maynard.'

Into the silence that followed, Andrew heard Millie say, 'Demobbed, Nigel? I didn't know you were in the army, I understood you were working in the Colonial Service.'

'I was,' he said in the same rather lordly manner his brother had. 'Everybody is being demobbed at the moment; that was a slip of Father's tongue. I knew it was my duty to come home and join the forces but, try as I might, I couldn't get a passage. But I was needed there in the Colonial Service.'

James rapped impatiently on the table. 'As I was saying, I've been waiting for my sons to return home before I retired. I want you to know that I've decided to go at the end of the year. And starting in the New Year, Nigel and Marcus will take over from me and run the company.'

Millie straightened in her seat. Andrew could see she didn't like that but he thought under the circumstances she should have expected that Peter and James would be replaced by younger family members.

James went on in a strong, dictatorial voice, 'Nigel and Marcus will bring new energy into the company. They have a great many plans and they're going to reorganise everything to take the business into the future. As you know, it's a changing world and if this company is to be as successful as we all hope, then we will all have to change with it. It's going to take a lot of hard work but I know you'll all be behind the fourth generation of Maynards, helping them to achieve it.'

That seemed to Andrew like a lot of hot air meant to motivate them to work harder, but a not unusual way to open the meeting. The men were all nodding their agreement.

Millie asked with frigid politeness, 'Do we need new plans?'

'Of course we do, Millie, we have to progress. A business can never stand still. Either it drives forward or it starts to fall back.'

Andrew rustled his documents. He believed James knew exactly how good their progress had been since the war ended.

Millie spoke up again. 'May we know what new plans Nigel and Marcus have?' There was a moment's silence. James's antipathy was evident, Millie's interruption was unwelcome.

Marcus took over from his father. 'I'm sure you'll all agree we need new lines. The company has launched nothing new on the market since before the war and we have only light floral perfumes.'

'We three have discussed it,' Nigel said, 'and we believe a stronger perfume might be more attractive to today's customers.'

James took over again. 'We need a change of emphasis on what we produce, a perfume with more general appeal so we can increase our customer base. I'm sure you all agree with that.'

'No,' Millie said firmly. 'I'm not sure that I do.'

But James took no notice. His face was glowing with enthusiasm. 'Look how popular "Evening in Paris" is proving to be. The sales have grown overnight. We need to get away from flowers and use something stronger, woodland spices perhaps. If we forge ahead with the work now we could get it launched on the market in time for the Christmas trade.'

'That would be quite impossible,' she said quietly.

Andrew heard a snigger that was quickly changed to a cough. He could see that the three experienced department chiefs were taken aback by James's announcement. Since Millie would own half the company once probate was granted, he thought she was right to speak up.

Marcus rounded on her to demand, 'Why not, if we're all prepared to put our backs into it?'

'I can't believe that you and your father know so little about the business your company is in,' she said. Andrew could see that the men were ready to applaud that. 'There are two very definite reasons. Firstly, we are slowly growing

160

our customer base, but it takes time because we make luxury products that sell at high prices that not everybody can afford.'

'Of course.' Marcus was getting angry. 'We all understand that.'

'We can't compete in the mass market for toiletries. Lever Brothers make a superb range which they can sell at very reasonable prices because they operate on a huge scale. What our customers are looking for is something that is different, more top of the market. Their tastes are different.

'Secondly, it takes at least one year and sometimes much longer to develop a new scent and put it into soap and talc. The perfume has to be stabilised so the soap we make today smells exactly like the soap we made last month, or last year come to that.'

'Obviously,' James growled. 'That's common sense.'

'The finer the perfume, the longer it takes to develop,' Millie went on furiously, 'and we also have to be sure that the soap still holds the scent while it is being used. Don't forget it can be in the soap dish on the side of the bath for a month or longer.

'And thirdly, Billy Sankey has to make sure he can obtain a steady supply of the essential oils and fixatives and anything else we put into a new perfume.' She paused for breath. 'Where is Billy? Is he not in this morning?'

'Yes, he is,' several voices assured her. Billy Sankey was their buyer.

'Why isn't he here?' She looked from James to Marcus. 'Did you ask him to come?'

'Er . . .' Father and son were looking at each other. Andrew smiled behind his hand, he guessed they hadn't rated Billy highly enough to ask him to a senior staff meeting. He was a bit of a rough diamond but he was reputed to be very efficient at his job.

'We can't do anything without Billy,' Millie said firmly. 'Not while so many things are in short supply. He draws up the contracts with our suppliers. There's also the new wrappers for the soap to be printed and the tins for the talc to be made and contracts drawn up for them to ensure we don't run—'

'Hold on, Millie,' James interrupted. 'We've heard enough of your opinions.'

She carried straight on. 'There's another very important thing I haven't said yet. We don't need new lines at this time as we can sell everything we make ten times over. Isn't that so, Mr Quentin?'

'It is.' Dan Quentin was their sales manager who had fought in the war and returned when it finished. He looked like a polished country gentleman and exuded charm. 'It's never been easier to sell because the country has been starved of everything for six years. A good deal of our production is going for export and we could sell twice the volume being made.'

'There you are,' Millie said. 'Those of us who have been involved in running this company are agreed that our strategy must be to increase production over the next year or two. We can take our time over preparing new lines. They aren't needed at this time. Ask any of the staff here.' Andrew noticed that the men's smiles disappeared at that invitation.

James rapped on the table and said in icy tones, 'We need to keep to the agenda or this meeting will drag on all day.'

'I quite agree,' Millie said, picking up her notebook and pencil and getting to her feet. 'James, you haven't really made plans at all, those were just vague ideas from the top of your head.' She looked from Marcus to Nigel. 'You both need to learn something about this business and how the company functions before you can run it successfully.' Then she strode out, closing the door quietly behind her.

162

Andrew's jaw dropped. Millie had more guts than he'd given her credit for but she'd lost her temper with them. That had been a mistake and it had really got their backs up. That was not the way he'd have done it.

There were a few moments of silent embarrassment; both Nigel and Marcus looked more than a little put out by Millie's outburst. It was left to James to pick up the agenda and carry on. The meeting broke up some ten minutes later, having floundered and run out of impetus.

Andrew went back to his office, slumped into his chair and absent-mindedly took a sip from the cup he'd left on his desk. The tea had long since gone cold; he crashed it back on its saucer and considered what he'd learned at the meeting.

It had been very noticeable that the other side of the family had talked brashly about their big plans for the perfume department without ever discussing them with Millie. As she owned half the company he could understand why she'd been a bit miffed, but she'd shown up their incompetence in front of all the senior staff. Nobody likes to have their mistakes pointed out to them in public and James and his sons seemed particularly needy about being thought to be in control. They would have hated that.

Nobody had taken to Marcus. He might be Pete's nephew but he didn't have his charisma. The general opinion was that he was snooty, that he treated everybody as though they were inferior beings and, worse, that he was quite sure he could help them do their jobs more effectively. Andrew knew they laughed about Marcus behind their hands and said he had an overblown ego. They would have enjoyed seeing Millie lay into them. None of them knew anything about Nigel.

But the joint owners of this company had had a very public fight. James and his sons looked set to do their utmost to force Millie out. Andrew reckoned she'd be lucky to hold out against them. He was afraid she might have a big fight on her hands.

Millie was livid as she went back to the laboratory to busy herself with routine tasks, hoping the work would calm her down. Half an hour later the phone on her desk rang. Denis answered it and called, 'It's for you. It's Mr Douglas, your solicitor.'

Millie hurried to talk to him. 'I've received probate for your husband's will,' he told her. 'I can now settle his estate. Could you come in and see me this week?'

'What about tomorrow?' Millie made the appointment feeling glad it would soon be settled.

Moments later the door flew open, and James followed by Marcus stormed in. 'Out,' James he said to Denis, waving him towards the door. 'Take an early lunch.'

'No,' Millie protested, 'he's helping me. Why are you ordering my staff about?' But Denis had disappeared. 'What's the matter?'

James was angry. 'To take that confrontational attitude to us in front of the staff was totally uncalled for.'

'Yes, I know, I'm sorry.'

'It was unforgivable, Millie,' James blustered. 'I'm glad you realise you mustn't say things like that. It lets the side down, does the firm no good, and it's very bad manners.'

'I apologise. I should have chosen my words more carefully.'

'You tried to make a fool of Marcus.'

Millie was not going to have that. 'Oh no, Marcus made a fool of himself.' She swung round to him. 'You made yourself look a complete ass.'

'Millie, you can't—'

'Just for once hear me out.' Millie was getting angry. 'Pete got this company going again after the doldrums of the war

164

years. Now it's being run by the senior staff without Pete, but they're doing all right. And today, without knowing the first thing about it, you burst in and give them a wake-up homily about working harder and getting new products out by Christmas. I had to point out why it wouldn't be possible. They'd have thought me pathetic if I'd gone along with that.'

James looked fit to burst, his face was puce.

'All right, Father,' Marcus said, 'let me handle this.' He turned to Millie. 'Obviously we're not going to find it easy to work together. We seem to be temperamentally unsuited.'

She said as patiently as she could, 'Perhaps if we tried, we could find a way.'

'You'll have to find a way,' James thundered. 'You've got to work together.'

Marcus said in a more amicable tone, 'I understand you're going to inherit Uncle Peter's half share of the company. Father says you're considering selling it back to the family.'

'No,' Millie said.

'You haven't made up your mind yet, have you?' James's furious gaze levelled with hers. 'You said you wanted time to think it over.'

'I did not. I thought I'd made it clear at the time that I meant to keep it. Without Pete, I need to go on working. Making perfumes is what I know and there aren't many jobs about like this. I want to stay.'

'Well, of course,' James began more diplomatically, 'we could keep you on as an employee after we'd bought your share.'

'No thank you,' Millie said. 'I'll not agree to that.'

James was holding up his hand. 'Don't dismiss it like that. Maynards started this business, they've always owned it and you aren't family.'

Millie's blood was coming to the boil. 'I married into it.'

James said vindictively, 'It isn't right that you, a stranger, will hold so many of our shares. Nigel and Marcus are true Maynards.'

Millie was ready to burst with fury. She wanted to let fly and tell him how mistaken he was and that he and his sons were not of the Maynard bloodline. She wanted to tell him that Eleanor's diaries said he was the son of a village woman who had wandered in front of the guns at a pheasant shoot. That Frederick and Eleanor Maynard had brought him up out of the kindness of their hearts because he had no living relative left to do it.

Millie had to bite her lips. It took real effort to choke back the words. She wanted to put him in his place, use the knowledge which she knew would do it. Instead, she made herself say as calmly as she could, 'Pete decided it was right and that is the legal situation.'

James lost his temper. 'You're a girl from the wrong side of the tracks who got her hooks into Peter. You thought you'd made your fortune, didn't you? He must have been out of his mind to marry a girl like you, a junior employee heavily pregnant with the child of a fraudster and a thief.'

Millie felt that like a slap in the face. It took her breath away. She'd thought all that was long since forgotten. Never had she been so tempted to get her own back, but it was a Maynard family secret that had been kept for over six decades and not hers to tell.

She managed to grind out, 'You might remember that Pete and I have two small sons. You can't deny that they are of the Maynard bloodline. In time, Pete hoped that one or both might work in the business.'

'But they are no use to us at this time, and may never be.'

Millie took a deep breath. The words to destroy James hovered on her tongue, but it might also destroy the family and their company. It was in her interests, and those of Simon and Kenny, to maintain the peace and keep the business growing. She said, 'James, I've spent most of my life working in this business. I know ill health has kept you out of it, but you left everything to Pete and you've lost touch with what is going on here. You know nothing about how this business is trying to recover from the war. You remember only how it used to be run twenty years ago.

'And as for you,' she fumed, turning to Marcus, 'you must accept the heads of departments know more about running it than you do. All your experience has been elsewhere. It's no good sitting in your father's office pontificating about it, he can't help you. You need to start at the bottom, talk *to* the staff not *at* them. Treat them as intelligent human beings. You've got to find out what's possible and what's not. Above all, talk to the accountant and find out where the money is made.'

'We've done that,' James thundered.

'Then why are you running down what Pete has achieved? Why all this nonsense about you three turning the company's fortunes round?'

'We have to,' James insisted. 'The object now is to make more money.'

'I suppose, Millie, you think you could make a much better job of it.' Marcus was flushed and haughty. 'You see yourself as general manager, do you?'

She was furious. 'No, I do not. As I told you, I want to stay here in charge of perfumes, which is just as well as you won't find it easy to replace me. I own half this company, that's as much as you three own together. If you have any plans, you need to consult me first. If you want to change the way Pete has set things up then we'll have to discuss it.'

'You have a very high opinion of your own ability,' Marcus sneered. 'I do hope it's justified. That illegitimate daughter of yours has certainly not inherited much brain, but why would she, when her father was a fraud and a thief? She's quite useless. I dictated some letters to her the other day and she made a complete hash of them. They had to wait until Miss Franklin came back from holiday to sort them out.'

Millie was truly shocked by that and it took all the wind out of her sails. She hadn't expected that; both Tom and Albert had praised Sylvie's work, but that was before Pete had died. She should have guessed her work would suffer.

'Please be patient with her,' she choked. 'Pete's death has upset her dreadfully. She was with him when it happened and found it traumatic. She's really quite competent.'

'She deserves the sack,' Marcus said belligerently. 'If she was anybody else she'd get it.'

A movement caught Millie's eye and she looked up to see that Sylvie had come in behind him. Her face was white and her mouth open in horror. It was obvious she'd overheard. Her glazed eyes were on Marcus. 'Is that true?'

Millie threw her arms round her daughter and pulled her close. 'Everybody's work suffers when they're upset,' she tried to comfort. 'Don't let it worry you. You'll be all right once you're over this. It's a bad patch for us all.'

'Not that.' Sylvie pushed her away angrily. 'About me being illegitimate and Dad not being my real father? Who is this fraudster and thief?'

Millie felt suffused with horror. Sylvie had been listening for some time.

'Didn't you know?' Marcus asked her contemptuously. 'I thought it was common knowledge.'

Sylvie burst into tears and Millie turned on Marcus. 'Please go,' she said angrily.

Chapter Fifteen

As the door banged behind them, Sylvie wailed, 'It is true, isn't it? Dad wasn't my father! Why didn't you tell me, Mum?' Sylvie felt the world as she knew it had turned upside down. 'Why didn't he?'

'We should have done, I'm sorry.'

'But you didn't,' she cried through a storm of tears. 'Why not?'

'It wasn't that we meant to keep it from you, Sylvie.' Millie was almost in tears too. 'By the time you were growing up we all saw you as part of the family. You'd been accepted into it.'

'But I thought we were a family. I didn't know that Dad wasn't my father.'

'He thought of himself as your father. Legally he was because he'd adopted you. He was a doting father to you.'

'But he wasn't my natural father. Marcus said everybody else knew. Did you think I'd never find out?'

'To start with we were waiting for you to grow up so you could understand. I didn't think enough about telling you and I'm kicking myself now.'

'Well, you left it too late. It's important to know who your father is. He's part of who I am.'

'Yes, and I'm very sorry. There were always so many other things going on. I should have told you long ago.'

'Do Valerie and Helen know?'

'Yes, they knew me before you were born. Pete explained it all to them and they accepted you as part and parcel of me. They had no need to talk about it or even think about it. You were absorbed into the family.'

'But I'm the cuckoo in the nest. It isn't my family at all. Who was my father?'

'Look, it's nearly lunchtime. Why don't you fetch your sandwiches and we'll eat them here and I'll tell you all about it now.'

'I couldn't eat anything, I'm churning inside. I feel sick. Connie and I were going to walk down to the river at lunchtime but I don't want her to see me looking like this. She'd want to know what's happened and I couldn't possibly tell her, could I?'

'No, but you'll feel better if you eat. Get your sandwiches and—'

'I don't want anyone to see me like this,' Sylvie screamed. 'I look a mess, and my eyes feel terrible.' They always looked red and puffy if she cried.

'Give me the key to your desk. I'll ask Denis to get your handbag and sandwiches.'

'Mum! He's heard it all. I know he has. He tried to stop me coming in, to divert my attention.' Sylvie was appalled at the thought. Soon it would be all round the office.

'No, James sent him out and he's only just come back and he's been crashing bottles about at the other end of the lab, hasn't he?' She knew her mother was trying to comfort her.

Millie handed Denis the key. 'Sylvie, why don't you bathe your eyes at that sink while I put the kettle on for tea?' The cold water eased them but it didn't really help, how could it?

'You weren't married when you had me?' Sylvie asked. 'I can't believe you'd do such a thing.' This was a real shock, everybody knew it was the greatest sin a girl could commit, and it would ruin her whole life.

170

'Wait until Denis comes back with your sandwiches, then I'll explain everything.'

Sylvie couldn't look at him when he returned to slide her things on to Millie's desk. 'I'll go to lunch now, shall I, Mrs Maynard?'

Millie nodded. She opened her sandwiches, her face anguished and her lips tight. 'Eat,' she urged, 'and I'll tell you.'

What she had to say came out like a confession. Sylvie listened avidly to her mother's story, it horrified her. 'I was your age and I loved your natural father. His name was Ryan McCarthy . . .'

'Was he Irish?'

'Well, Liverpool Irish. His family had come here in the years before he was born. I believed him to be a decent person. We'd grown up together in the same street and he had a job here with Maynard's as a salesman. He said they were a good firm to work for and persuaded me to apply for a job, that's how I first came here.'

Sylvie's head reeled. 'So Dad knew him? Everybody here knew him? Was Dan Quentin working here then?' Quentin was their present sales manager.

'Yes, no, I can't remember.'

'And is it true that he was a thief and a fraud?'

'I'm afraid it is. He treated company stock as though it was his personal property.'

'That's awful! And to think he's my real father. What did Dad do about him? He must have been furious.'

'He didn't have to do anything because Ryan went away. He left Liverpool, disappeared.'

Sylvie could see her mother's face twisting in remembered pain. He'd deserted her when she found she was pregnant. 'You've heard nothing of him since?'

Millie shook her head. 'Even worse, I wasn't the only one to find myself with a baby before I had a husband. My mother did the same thing. My mother's family threw her out and didn't want to know her or me. She'd had to bring me up single-handed and it was only when she was dying that I understood why we had no other relatives. We were poor, really poor, but Pete came to our rescue and gave us a good life.'

It was a lot to take in but Sylvie understood now just how much she owed him. 'And I caused his death,' she said bitterly.

'No you did not.' Millie rounded on her. 'Haven't I told you half a dozen times it was Dad's decision to sail home in that storm?'

But to Sylvie, it was only too obvious that, but for her, Pete would still be alive today. She'd persuaded him to sail back because she'd wanted to have dinner at that posh hotel, the Buckley Arms.

'Whatever you do,' Millie gripped her wrist, her eyes burning with intensity, 'make sure you don't make our mistake. It can land you in terrible trouble.'

Sylvie let out a long, slow breath. 'Ugh! A baby is the very last thing I'd want. But if it happened, I know you'd help me,' she said.

'Of course I would, and I understand how you must feel now suddenly hearing all this, but it's better if you take life's big milestones in the right order.' She sighed. 'Do you feel better now you've eaten?'

'Yes.' She did a bit. 'The girls in the typing pool said I was lucky to come from a rich middle-class family like the Maynards and I was proud of it. Now I find I'm Liverpool Irish,' she knew she sounded bitter, 'and my father was a scoundrel.'

'It all happened years ago, it's ancient history. It changes nothing in your present circumstances.'

'It does, Mum. It's not just me who knows, everybody else does too and they're talking about me.' Sylvie shuddered at the thought, it scared her. And on top of that, there was Marcus, she'd never be able to take shorthand from him again, not after hearing him say she was rubbish and should get the sack. And she knew she'd been making mistakes for others and her typing was messy. She'd done a bit for Mr Lancaster recently and most likely he thought the same way about her.

'Right,' Millie said, 'perhaps you'd better take the rest of the day off.'

Sylvie was relieved. She couldn't have faced working this afternoon. She listened when her mother rang the typing pool and thought it was Connie Grey who picked up the phone. Millie left a message for the supervisor. Then she rang Helen but she wasn't at home, so she tried Valerie's number. Sylvie heard her answer, and thought she said, 'Poor kid, send her to me.'

'I'd rather go home,' she said mutinously, getting to her feet.

'No,' Millie said. 'You'll feel worse if you go home and spend the afternoon alone. I'm afraid you'll cry on your bed. Come on, get your coat, I'm coming with you.'

They'd come to work on the bus this morning because of the shortage of petrol, so they had to wait in the drizzle at the bus stop to go to Valerie's, but Sylvie found the cool damp air calming although the name Ryan McCarthy was going round in her head on a loop like Kenny's toy train.

Millie felt ready to weep, she ached in sympathy for Sylvie. She was furious with Marcus for throwing all that in her daughter's face. She had come very near to enlightening him and his father about their own origins.

Valerie was very understanding. She said to Sylvie in matter-of-fact tones, 'Dad fell head over heels in love with your mother. He couldn't wait to marry her and you came

173

as part of the package. You were the prettiest, most engaging baby ever, and we all loved you. In fact, the whole household fussed over you and continued to do so until Simon arrived. Dad adopted you legally, and always treated you as one of us. So what is there about that to bother you?'

'Uncle James was nasty about it,' Sylvie still had a sob in her voice, 'he called us names.'

'He said I was a slut who hooked your dad to make my fortune,' Millie said.

'It wasn't like that at all.' Valerie was indignant. 'The truth is, Dad was making all the running and we encouraged him because we liked playing with you.'

'But Dad wasn't my real father. Uncle James said he was a fraudster and a thief.'

'We never knew him,' Valerie told her. 'But he deserted your mother when he'd got her in a mess and when she really needed his help. He wasn't a kind man so he wouldn't have looked after you as well as Dad. You were far better off with us,' she looked up and smiled at Millie, 'and so was your mother. So it all turned out for the best, didn't it?'

Millie could hear the twins waking from their after-lunch nap upstairs. 'There they go,' Valerie said to Sylvie. 'Come and help me sort them out and bring them down.'

Millie lay back on the sofa, closing her eyes in gratitude and relief. As they were coming downstairs, she heard Valerie say, 'Have you heard the news? Princess Elizabeth has become engaged to Prince Philip of Greece, isn't it exciting? Where did I put the newspaper?'

It was produced and Sylvie's interest was captured by the pictures and the article about the royal wedding plans. It said it would take place in November and provide a welcome touch of romance for the country, struggling as it was with austerity and shortages of every sort.

It was said that Princess Elizabeth would not be able to have a trousseau because she hadn't enough clothing coupons, although other members of the royal family were said to be giving her theirs. There was speculation about her wedding gown and where she and Prince Philip might go for their honeymoon.

The long summer school holidays were about to start and Simon and Kenny would be home at the end of the week. Valerie and her husband had planned to spend the next week at Hafod and some time ago had offered to take the boys with them. They had been keen to go.

'Why don't you come with us?' she suggested now to Sylvie.

'A good idea,' Millie said. 'You might feel better if you had some time away from work.' She'd tell James she thought it advisable for her to start her two weeks summer holiday straight away. As a family they'd always taken their holidays together and Millie had booked them to start in another week's time.

'I don't want to go to Hafod,' Sylvie was alarmed, 'I never want to go there again.'

Valerie took hold of her hand. 'You need to go back,' she said seriously. 'It'll lay your ghosts. When you see the house, the mountains and the beautiful beaches again, common sense will tell you they had nothing to do with Dad's death. It was the storm ...'

'And the boat.'

'It was just a terrible accident, Sylvie. You must see it as that. Yes, it happened on the boat but a lot of other things caused it. We haven't had the boat out since, but Roger has always loved it and it will need to be checked over anyway. He'll be happy to take Simon and Kenny out if they want to go.'

Sylvie blew her nose in her wet handkerchief. Millie offered her a drier one from her own pocket. 'Hafod is a lovely place for a holiday, you used to enjoy it.'

'We'd all like to go somewhere different for a change,' Valerie said, 'somewhere warmer and more exotic. But right now that's impossible. There's rationing and austerity in Britain and we are allowed to take only twenty-five pounds in foreign currency. Anyway, half Europe is in ruins. I think we're lucky to have Hafod. At least we can get away from home once in a while. Why don't you come with us?'

'There'll be plenty for you to do,' Millie tried to persuade her. 'You know what Simon's like, he always wants to be out doing things.'

She was rewarded by Sylvie's snuffle, 'All right.'

As they left the laboratory, Marcus felt his father take his arm and hurry him up to the privacy of his office in the turret. Nigel was there, still brooding over what had happened at the meeting. All three of them were furious at what Millie had said.

'That was humiliating, she made me look a fool,' Marcus complained. 'She flew at me.'

'Losing your temper with her and shouting and waving your arms around is not the way to go about getting what we want,' Nigel said firmly. 'You're all aggression. What could be more stupid than to say Pete wasn't running the business properly and deny it was making a profit?'

'That was Father's idea.' Marcus was ready to scream with temper. 'He was hoping to buy Millie's share for less than it was worth.'

'We thought we could get rid of her quickly by offering to buy her out,' James said, trying to calm his sons. 'That is the fair way of doing it.'

'But we don't have any money, Father. Do you?'

'No, I haven't. You know doctors' bills have taken a huge bite out of my income. And ill luck and the war have dogged our efforts.'

'You shouldn't have told her the firm was losing money and tried to get it on the cheap,' Nigel said. 'That was the wrong way to go about it. She knew it was a lie and so did the rest of the staff. She's no fool, you know, and she was married to Uncle Peter for eighteen years, she's bound to have picked up a few pointers from him.'

'This business was started by our grandfather and it's all wrong that half of it has been given to her.'

'But it has and she's refused our offer to buy her out.'

Nigel was losing his temper too. 'Perhaps that's just as well.'

'Don't be silly, Nigel, we could have taken a loan from the bank, but anyway, she's not going to budge on that.'

'All right, as Millie has refused to let us buy her out, we'll have to find some other way to get rid of her.'

'I'm going to demand an apology.' Marcus was belligerent. 'The nerve of her, telling me what I should do.'

'Don't go near her until you calm down,' Nigel advised. 'In fact, it might be better if it was the other way round. You apologise to her.'

'I couldn't. I wouldn't. I feel more like kicking her into the middle of next week.'

'Leave her to me,' James said. 'I could try and talk her round. We'll get nowhere if we descend to shouting at each other. We can make things difficult for her, can't we? Two can play at that game.'

'We'll have to think of something,' Nigel agreed.

'Yes.' James nodded. 'She makes out she knows a lot about the business but I find that hard to believe.'

'Don't underestimate her,' Nigel said. 'That's been your problem from the start. The staff seem to think she knows more than we do, they turn to her.'

'Why don't you do something then?' Marcus snapped. 'You're supposed to have the brains.'

'Right, I'll make a friend of her, disarm her and think of some way to loosen her control of this company.'

'Particularly financial control,' his father said. 'It gives her too much power.'

After she'd seen Sylvie settling down with Valerie, Millie felt she really had to return to work. As usual, Tom Bedford had sent her a copy of the factory schedule and for the next two weeks they'd be making soap with the wild rose perfume. She needed to check through her aluminium drums and arrange for a sufficient amount of that perfume to go down to the factory floor.

That done, she rang James's office meaning to tell him Sylvie was upset and needed to start her holiday straight away, but there was no answer. She rang Miss Franklin to tell her about Sylvie, and it was she who told her James had gone home because he didn't feel well. Then she set about working through the other drums of wild rose perfume and marking those that should be ready for use in another month or so.

Later that afternoon, Nigel came into the lab alone. 'I'm sorry about what happened this morning,' he said, sounding calm and reasonable. 'Is Sylvie all right?'

Millie sighed. 'No, I'm afraid she's still very troubled over Pete's death, and what she overheard Marcus say made matters worse. Much worse, I'm afraid.'

'I know, Millie, I'm sorry.'

She tried to explain why Sylvie felt so guilty about the part she'd played in Pete's accident. 'Valerie is looking after her. She's going to take her back to Hafod on Saturday for a week's rest.'

'The accident must have been terrible for you too, terrible for everybody, but I'm afraid you upset Father, he's had to go home to rest.'

'We're all upset,' Millie said. 'Marcus was extremely rude about me as well as Sylvie, and he raked up things from the past that Sylvie didn't know about.'

'I have apologised but I—'

'I know that's not your fault but the truth is we didn't see much of your father at work while Pete was running things. He'd turn up once or twice a month when he felt like it, and he's only coming in now to make sure you two take Pete's place. He thinks he's easing you in but he has no idea what goes on here and he's giving you the wrong slant on things.'

'I can see that.' Nigel looked contrite. 'You'll have to make allowances, Millie. I've been in India for nine years. I've lost touch with everything.'

Millie was relieved Nigel was trying to make peace. Years ago the family had always met up at Christmas and for birthdays. She could remember holidays when Marcus and Nigel had spent time with them at Hafod. Marcus had always been prickly while Nigel had got on better with Pete and his daughters, but really, she hadn't known him well nine years ago.

'It's going to be you, me and Marcus who will be running this place in future,' he said. 'Father doesn't have the energy and anyway, as he said, he wants to retire. I'd like to think we could do it without fighting like this.'

Millie managed a wry smile. 'So would I, I'm delighted to hear you say that. The staff must be beginning to think . . . Well, Marcus is getting their backs up. We're going to have to get on together. We can't waste our energy fighting.'

'No, we'll need all our push to run this firm. I know I've a lot to learn, and I probably know less about perfume than any other part of it.'

'If you've got time now I could start showing you round. Uncle James spoke of getting a new fragrance out by Christmas. Come and take a sniff at some of these. I've got seven new fragrances started up, but they'll need months if not years of work before we can use them. What do you think of this one?'

He took a long sniff. 'Yes, I like it. It's a strong woody scent. Is it what Father was thinking of?'

'Yes, it's sandalwood. Try this one, it has an oriental scent, and this one is fruity.'

'Mm, refreshing, it smells of citrus and blackcurrant. I like that too.'

'It's not difficult to find a fragrance that people like, but I often turn up problems that make it unusable.'

'What sort of problems?'

'When we put it in the soap we might find the scent fades too quickly. It could bring customers out in a rash, or it's impossible to find a sustainable source of an essential ingredient. Sometimes it's just plain too expensive.'

'I see.' His dark eyes smiled into hers and she decided he was quite a charmer, not like Marcus at all. 'There's more to perfumes than I thought.'

'Yes, I'm afraid there is.'

'Can you explain the basics of what you do?'

'Well, let's go back to the strong woody scent that you liked.'

'The sandalwood?'

'Yes. I showed you the concentrate and I made that by mixing raw oils and essences. These have to be left for several weeks until they've blended and matured. Then before it can be used, I need to dilute the concentrate in alcohol to the required strength to scent the soaps and talcum powders. Then I leave it again for a further few weeks in these great copper containers to blend again. After that it needs a fixative to ensure the scent remains for as long as the tablet of soap is being used. There are many fixatives but the best are expensive.

'My job is to make sufficient volume in lavender, wild rose and verbena to ensure there's always enough ready to use to keep the factory working. I also produce the dyes to colour the white soap with faintest tinges of pink, lavender and honey-yellow to match the scents, and I have to ensure a uniform quality each time I do it.'

Millie knew she was giving him more detail than he'd be able to take in but she went on showing him round her lab.

'Thank you,' he said at last. 'It'll take me years to understand all this. Look, Millie, we need to get to know each other too. Why don't you and Sylvie come to my place for supper on Saturday night?'

She was surprised but pleased. This was a complete turnround. 'Valerie is taking Sylvie to Hafod on Saturday.'

'Oh yes, so you said. Well, no reason why you can't come by yourself. I'd like you to meet Clarissa, my wife. It'll be a quiet meal, just the three of us.'

'Thank you, I'd like that,' Millie said.

Chapter Sixteen

Millie was glad to go, the house felt empty without Sylvie, and it gave her less time to worry about her. Nigel's house seemed not unlike hers, Victorian with large rooms. When she rang the front-door bell, he came to let her in. She'd thought him elegant in the office, but tonight he shone. He was wearing an immaculate white shirt, silk tie and smartly cut grey lounge suit that looked new.

'You found the place all right?' he asked as he took her coat.

Removing her lacy apron, Clarissa came out of the kitchen to say hello and lead her into the lounge. She was very slim and ultra-sophisticated with her dark hair done up in a French pleat and a rather haughty expression on her handsome face. Her finery surpassed Nigel's. She was wearing a blue silk two-piece, with a nipped-in waist and flared peplum over a generously full and long skirt, and she carried it on high heels with magnificent elegance.

Millie couldn't hold back her gasp of admiration. 'My goodness, you do look grand,' she said. She'd seen very few people actually wearing the New Look; people just didn't have the clothing coupons to buy it. She recognised what it was from newspaper and magazine pictures.

'We stocked up on clothes in India before we came home,' Clarissa said disarmingly. 'The local tailors there aren't bad.'

Pete hadn't done much dressing up, he'd always worn pullovers when he was at home or visiting his family. Millie had washed and ironed her best summer dress for this occasion, but it was of the vaguely military style popular two years ago. It was of cotton and a rather more faded shade of blue than Clarissa's. She had never felt more dowdy.

She sat down and accepted a glass of dry sherry, trying to pull her skimpy skirt further down her legs. 'You look very settled,' she said, looking round the comfortable room and knowing they'd only recently moved in.

'Heaven forbid,' Clarissa said in indignant tones. 'I do hope we don't have to settle here. We have only the ground floor of this house and the neighbours upstairs come tramping through the hall at all times. It's awful, but after the blitz there's nothing much available.'

'Father found this for us,' Nigel said, 'or we'd have had to push into his place alongside Marcus and Elvira. He knows an estate agent and it was as a favour we were allowed to rent it.'

'Do you have somewhere decent to live, Millie?' Clarissa asked.

'Yes.' It was Nigel who answered. 'Uncle Peter took over Grandpa's house when he died, so Millie does have comfort.' There was no resentment in his voice.

But Clarissa was complaining. 'We feel very cramped here after the house we had in India, we really could do with more space. We'd like to start a family, but I couldn't contemplate having a child here, it just isn't suitable.' She sighed. 'Though really, we can't put it off much longer.' Millie knew they'd been married for four years.

They did have a separate dining room and the supper table was very stylishly set with flowers, starched damask, sparkling silver and cut glass. Despite rationing, Clarissa managed to serve very good food.

'I love cooking,' she said. Tonight she produced duck with a raspberry sauce. 'Oranges would go better with duck, but I couldn't get any.'

'I believe they are importing them again,' Nigel said, 'but they're only available on the blue ration books for the under-fives.'

'It's absolutely gorgeous with raspberries, I'm enjoying it,' Millie told her. 'It's a real treat.' She knew ducks were not bred in large enough numbers to make rationing feasible but were available on the black market. They cost a small fortune.

'Clarissa went to haute cuisine cookery classes,' Nigel told her proudly. 'It's her hobby.'

'Do you like cooking?' she asked Millie.

'I used to, Pete enjoyed meals like this. But once rationing started, our meals had to become simpler.'

'I'm probably very lucky to have married a cook like Clarissa.' Nigel smiled across the table at her.

'Lucky tonight anyway, I've made a summer pudding for you,' Clarissa's hand nudged the small silver bell placed near her wine glass and made it tinkle. 'Nigel,' she asked, 'what makes you keep putting this on the table?'

He shrugged. 'Habit, I suppose.'

Clarissa laughed, and said to Millie, 'He set the table for me tonight. Back home the bell was always set at my place so I could ring when we were ready for the next course. Here it's pretty pointless.' She got up to clear the plates and take them to the kitchen.

'Clarissa was brought up in India,' Nigel said. 'She's finding the lack of help in the house difficult.'

'I'll manage better when rationing finishes and we get a better house,' Clarissa sighed as she returned with the pudding.

Millie drove home thinking that although Nigel was

showing no envy for her house, his wife certainly was. The evening had not eased her worries, it made her wonder if Nigel was good at hiding his true feelings and if he might be playing some deeper game.

Valerie and Roger returned from Hafod the following week-end and brought Millie's children home. They all looked tanned and well, even Sylvie. Millie had arranged to take her own annual holiday over the next two weeks so she could spend time with them.

At Simon's suggestion she'd arranged a few days' camping in the Lake District which they stretched to a week because they hit a spell of good weather. Millie found the break from work restful and was glad to be able to give her full attention to her children. The boys talked all the time about their father, asking many times about exactly how the accident had happened, but she thought they were coping with it better than Sylvie.

Simon was twelve now and would be returning to his prep school for his last year and was facing examinations to get into Liverpool College. He said, 'I would quite like to be a day boy, Mum, and I think Kenny would too. We could get there on the bus.' It was quite close.

'Your father was a boarder and he wanted you to have that advantage.'

'I'm not sure it is an advantage,' he said, which made Millie think about it in a new light, but they were going to finish this school year as weekly boarders at Heathfield.

Sylvie had pink cheeks and looked rested, her suntan made her more beautiful than ever. She'd seemed more her normal self until Millie talked about her returning to work as she'd already had two weeks' holiday.

'I don't want to go back, Mum, not yet, please.' She pulled a face. 'You've still got another week. I don't want to be at work on my own. Couldn't I take another week with you and the boys?'

That made Millie anxious, Sylvie used to enjoy her work, but she rang Miss Franklin who was supervising the typing pool to tell her Sylvie would be away for another week.

During that week, Millie had drawn up a programme of visits to the seaside and the museums in Liverpool and Chester, but the weather turned wet, so mostly it was the museums. Simon had invited a school friend to stay with them so Millie had quite a busy time. Sylvie's friend Connie had a birthday, and she was invited to her party on the Saturday night. Millie took the boys to the cinema to see Charlie Chaplin in *Monsieur Verdoux* and they all laughed till their sides ached.

'I had a lovely time, Mum,' Sylvie said the next day. 'Connie's brother Graham brought me home on the back of his scooter, it was quite exciting. He works for Mr Lancaster and he's very nice.'

Millie wished her friendship with him would develop. A boyfriend might be Sylvie's salvation. She needed something to take her mind off her troubles.

The following week, Simon went to stay with his school friend and Kenny went to stay with Helen because Millie and Sylvie had to go back to work. Millie hoped Sylvie would now settle back into her normal working life and for the first few days it seemed she would.

Denis had kept everything in the laboratory functioning smoothly. He was showing a real interest in his work and proving reliable. She was pleased with him, and because he was doing more, it made her life easier.

Over the weeks that followed, Millie kept telling herself things were manageable and she could cope. Valerie and Helen made sure that when she was at home her time was filled as pleasantly as possible with family activities.

Uncle James came to the office only on odd occasions, but Marcus and Nigel were always trying to make changes to the way the staff worked, and when she asked him to explain what the advantages would be, Marcus would turn aggressive. Millie was aware that it was ruining the usual harmonious atmosphere, though the senior staff continued to come to the lab to chat and show their support.

Since Andrew had confirmed that the profits were slowly increasing at that staff meeting, Millie felt they were becoming friends and he was on her side after all. From time to time she'd taken her lunchtime sandwiches to eat in his office to mull over work-related problems.

Last week, he'd taken her to Parker's Refreshment Rooms to have a hot meal and said he'd enjoyed it. But all the same, something of the stiffness between them remained. Today, he'd invited her to have another lunch at Parker's, and when they'd eaten cottage pie and plum duff and the need to pay for it arrived, she'd said, 'Let me settle it this time,' and put out her hand to take the bill.

'No,' he'd said with such firm politeness that she knew he felt offended. She could see that Andrew was proud and believed the man should pay when he invited a woman out. But Millie knew to the penny what his salary was and that she had more. It was a delicate situation. He said little as they walked back to the office. They were going upstairs to the office and at the top would go their separate ways, but she didn't want to part from him while this discomfort hung between them.

'I enjoyed the meal', she said to him. 'It was a lovely break to get out of the office.' Behind them, other people were returning from their lunch break and they had to draw aside against the corridor wall out of the way. 'I'd like to do it again. What about next week, say Friday?'

'A week today?' His eyes lit up, a smile was tugging at his lips. 'I'd like that very much.'

'But only on my terms, that we pay turn and turn about. Your way makes me feel I'm sponging on you. Agreed?'

'Of course. Put like that, what else can I say?' His smile broadened.

'It's better to know where we stand,' she said and turned towards the lab. She liked Andrew, and now she no longer had Pete she felt she needed friends.

In her twenties when she'd gone to college, Millie had made close friends with some of the girls on the same course, and they'd vowed to keep in touch. To start with, they'd met every few weeks to have a sandwich and a cup of tea at lunchtime, either in Parker's or some other small café. But eventually most had found jobs in different towns and now only Lizzie Green remained in Liverpool.

Millie continued to meet her occasionally. Lizzie had married and had had a son who was almost the same age as Simon. They'd spent more time together when they both had babies, but Lizzie had gone back to work when war was declared. Recently, she'd been having marriage problems and their meetings since Pete's accident had not been such happy occasions because they'd each poured out their anguish to the other and that left Millie feeling low. Though she was full of sympathy and continued to meet Lizzie occasionally at lunchtime, she found Andrew, despite the occasional embarrassments, more congenial company.

At mid-afternoon that same day, Millie was working with Denis when Sylvie, in torrents of tears again, came running through the lab to find her. Millie's heart sank. 'What's the matter?'

She ushered her to a chair near her desk and Denis asked, 'Shall I make you some tea?'

Millie nodded gratefully while Sylvie wailed, 'It's Marcus, I can't stand him. He asked me to come and take dictation and when I told him Betty Jackson had been designated to work for him, he said he was trying to catch up and he'd already overloaded her with work. He was horrible.' She was shaking with sobs. 'He dictated letter after letter in great bursts he knew I'd never get down. I think he was doing it on purpose.'

'No, love, that's probably just the way his thoughts come out.' It upset Millie to find Sylvie now felt she wasn't good at her job. 'I think others find him difficult too.'

'No, he keeps asking me, "Have you got that? It's important and I don't want it messed up." His letters are really long and complicated and I think he's deliberately getting at me.'

'What are these letters about?' As far as Millie could see, Marcus wasn't doing any real work. Tom Bedford and Albert Lancaster had come to the lab to talk to her and they both said Marcus was keeping out of their way.

'I don't know. Something about soap but they don't make real sense to me.'

'Who is he writing to?'

'He dictates a name and address, garbles it and never gives me a file with other letters from which I can copy it. I have to ask him to repeat it, sometimes more than once, and he looks at me as though I'm an idiot. When I'd finished the letters and took them back, he didn't sign them like everybody else and hand them back to me to post. "Just leave them with me," he said. "I'll need to make sure you haven't typed a lot of nonsense again." '

Millie swallowed hard. 'You're saying he's bullying you?' She considered asking Sylvie to take an extra carbon copy next time so she could see what he was writing about, but she was afraid Marcus would find out and be furious with Sylvie.

'Mum, he's trying to drive me mad. I know he is. In fact, he's succeeding. I don't think he ever posts the letters.

They're just a way to get at me. Sometimes he looks at me with real hate in his eyes. I know it's me he doesn't like.'

Millie's felt cold with horror, what Sylvie was saying frightened her. Surely she couldn't be right. It made her worry more about her daughter. 'When you get more used to taking letters from him—'

'Mum, I'll never get used to him.' Sylvie's big golden eyes blazed. 'I can't do it, and there'll be more and more work from him because Betty Jackson is leaving to get married.'

Millie knew that because Betty Jackson had sent her letter of resignation to her. She'd been Pete's secretary and they'd all got on well for years, but her fiancé had a job in London so she wanted to leave.

Sylvie was very upset and seemed obsessed with the idea that Marcus was out to harm her. If so, she was in an even worse state than Millie had supposed.

'Shall I have a word with Marcus?' she suggested. 'Tell him to go easier on you?'

'No! No, don't do that.' Sylvie was growing agitated. 'It'll tell him he's getting to me and make him put more pressure on.'

Millie felt Sylvie should not back off if she truly believed Marcus was bullying her. Had she also lost the ability to stand up for herself? She said, 'I'll ask Miss Franklin not to send you to take letters from Marcus.'

'Mum,' she cried, 'I've already done that.'

'Well, hopefully you've solved the problem,' she said. 'Come on, drink your tea and we'll knock off early today. We need to collect Kenny from Helen's house on the way home.'

Kenny came running to open the front door to them in high good humour and threw himself into Millie's arms. 'I've had a lovely time this week. Eric took me to work yesterday. There was an auction sale on, and the stewards let me hold up the goods for the buyers to see. It was good fun. I think I'll be an auctioneer when I grow up. Valerie is here too but I'm not to tell you anything about—'

'Come on in,' Valerie called. 'Helen's got some news for you.' Millie could feel ripples of excitement in the atmosphere as soon as she entered the sitting room. A sandwich cake was set out on the tea trolley with the cups and saucers.

'To celebrate,' Helen said, waving her hand towards the cake. 'I'm going to have another baby. We wanted to have two and I'm thrilled.'

'They'll be close together in age,' Valerie said, 'and she doesn't realise how much work that will give her.'

'Eric is over the moon.'

'Congratulations to both of you.' Millie kissed her cheek.

Sylvie was managing to smile again. She asked, 'Do you want a boy this time or another girl?'

'Eric would like a son, but I don't mind.' Helen's dark eyes shone with happy anticipation. 'All I want is a fit and healthy baby.'

On the bus going home Millie shared a seat with her daughter and said, 'Isn't Helen happy? I'm delighted for her and I'm glad you've seen how she welcomes another baby into the family.'

Sylvie was staring out of the window. Millie felt it her duty as a mother to point out, 'Helen has timed everything right. She studied for a career in her teens and waited until her twenties to marry and have babies. I didn't feel that burst of joy when I first realised I was expecting you. I was too young and had no husband. It all came right in the end for us, but I was worried stiff at the time. And after I had you I had to find time to study for a career. It isn't the easiest way to do things. You will be happier if you get your timing right.'

Sylvie made no sign that she'd even heard her little homily. They had a quiet weekend and by Monday morning

Sylvie seemed better and able to accept that she'd have to go in to work. Millie was anxious about her all day but over supper Sylvie told her that she'd been sent to take letters from the accountant and found them manageable because they'd all been short and to the point.

'So you've had a good day?' Millie asked.

Sylvie pulled a face. 'Denis has let the story out, just as I said he would. Everybody knows,' she said, 'they're all talking about me, I'm sure, but they've been kind.'

'You don't know it was Denis who spread the gossip,' Millie pointed out. 'It could have been anybody.'

Sylvie snorted in disbelief. 'Somebody has certainly opened his mouth but everybody's on my side. Mr Lancaster said it doesn't matter what sort of a family you come from, it's what you make of yourself that matters.'

Millie smiled, so all had gone well. 'And Mr Worthington treated you well?'

'He was sort of normal, but kind too,' she said. 'Marcus has commandeered his secretary and left him high and dry without one.'

'Frances Somerton?' Frances had been employed for several years and was one of their senior secretaries. She'd worked for their previous accountant. Obviously Marcus considered her senior enough to please him.

'They're saying he's increased her salary and told her it's promotion, so she's happy about it. He'll probably be kind to her.'

Millie thought that high-handed of Marcus but let it pass. She thought it important to settle Sylvie and now she could see how she could help her. The next morning she went to have a word with Andrew in his office. As usual, he was busy working when she went in.

'Do you have a minute?' she asked. 'I've a favour to ask of you.'

'Of course.' He pushed the comptometer to one side.

Millie sat down. 'You know my daughter? She took dictation from you yesterday.'

'Sylvie, yes, a charming girl.'

'Did you find her work adequate?'

He was frowning. 'Perfectly adequate, yes.'

'Marcus has complained that she's useless.'

'Good lord! He must have got out of bed on the wrong side. No, Sylvie's all right.'

'She tells me Marcus has commandeered your secretary's services.'

'So I gather. He didn't ask how I would feel about that.'

'No, he's not the most thoughtful.' Millie hesitated for moment. 'I'd like you to ask Miss Franklin to promote Sylvie in her place. Will you do that?'

His dark green eyes were staring into hers. 'Why – yes, if that's what Sylvie wants. Usually the girls aren't keen to work for me. They don't like typing figures and at certain times I produce page after page of them.'

'I think she'd be very happy to work permanently for you.' Millie went on to tell him something of Pete's accident and the terrible effect it had had on Sylvie. 'She thinks Marcus is bullying her, but she won't stand up to him so he'll do it again if he gets half a chance.'

He hesitated. 'Are you worrying too much about your daughter? She seems to be coping well enough. She spent a week helping Frances Somerton to reorganise my files so I've seen something of her. She gets on well with people.'

'She did ask Miss Franklin not to send her to work for Marcus again, but that's the easy way out, she isn't standing up for herself.'

He smiled. 'But isn't it the sensible way? She doesn't come out with her fists up spoiling for a fight. I'd say she's perfectly capable of looking after herself.'

'You think I'm always spoiling for a fight?'

'Oh dear, forgive me, I didn't mean . . .' His eyes came up to meet hers. 'If I'm speaking out of turn, I'm sorry, but you don't let Marcus and Nigel get away with anything.'

'I can't,' she choked. 'Pete would have kept them in order but I have to do it now.'

'Well, tackling James and Marcus and telling them in the strongest possible language exactly where they're going wrong was, I think, unwise. And you did it in front of the senior staff so it's no secret that the owners of this company are battling it out. It got their backs up, Millie, so they're looking for revenge. It guarantees they'll do their best to deliver as much hurt as they can, but for Marcus to turn his ire against your daughter is despicable. She's just a kid and less able to punch back, but he knows you won't like it, so he targets her.'

'You think it was my fault?' Millie was horrified, that hadn't occurred to her.

'Yes, but what I'm trying to say is that I think she handled Marcus the right way. He's a powerful man and has had a lifetime to hone his sarcasm. In a battle of words Sylvie knows she can't beat him, but it doesn't mean that in the future she won't find some other way to give him a dig.'

'Perhaps.'

'She's the sort who thinks before she speaks, and with due respect, you instantly leap in to lock horns.'

Millie jerked to her feet. This wasn't what she'd wanted to hear. 'I'd appreciate it if you'd ask for Sylvie's services, and let both her and Miss Franklin believe it was your idea.'

'Millie, please don't take umbrage! I'll be glad to help Sylvie in any way I can. I'm on your side. I know you're finding things hard at the moment. I'm doing my best to help you.'

Millie felt somewhat mollified. 'I suppose you think I'm

an over-protective mother but Sylvie was very upset. Please be patient with her.'

'I will.'

She stood for a moment, trying to think of a way of saying Sylvie's self-confidence needed boosting, but she failed to find the right words and in the end said, 'Thank you,' and fled back to the lab.

Chapter Seventeen

Andrew Worthington stood up when Millie did, and went to open the door for her but she whisked out before he reached it. He collapsed back on his seat in surprise. Millie Maynard had revealed quite a lot of herself and her difficulties. He'd intended to ask Miss Franklin to appoint another girl as his secretary and had in mind to ask for Louise Lambert. She'd filled in for a few days when Frances had been off sick and they'd got on well together, but he was happy to do what Millie Maynard wanted. He picked up the phone and spoke to Miss Franklin before she could come up with some idea of her own.

The more he saw of Millie, the more he liked her. She'd been friendly and sociable to him and had real guts and a quick brain, but she was trying to fight Sylvie's battles as well as her own and she needed to think more before she responded to Marcus's attacks.

Millie was an attractive woman but Sylvie was a real stunner. He'd watched her scribbling down her shorthand on the other side of his desk with her blond hair falling forward, half hiding her face. When he stopped dictating her head would come up and her big golden-brown eyes would look up, waiting for more.

She'd turned all the boys' heads on the factory floor. They talked about her, why wouldn't they? She was the boss's daughter, or so they'd thought. Like everybody else in the firm, he found the recent gossip about the Maynard family totally fascinating. Knowing more had made him sympathetic towards Millie. The staff agreed she had a tough fight on her hands and were all on her side but Marcus was out to retaliate now. The general feeling was that he'd get her down in the end and she'd give up.

Millie didn't look like a fighter, she was small and slight. He'd heard the men say Pete had doted on her and denied her nothing; she was generally popular and said to be a soft touch for anybody in trouble.

He liked Sylvie too, there was nothing the matter with her work, what she'd done for him was fine, but she was shy and not outgoing like her mother. What she needed was experience to give her more confidence. If she felt guilty about the part she'd played in Pete's accident he could see that it would make her very vulnerable to Marcus's jibes. He felt sorry for them both.

Andrew had had family troubles of his own and they'd left him feeling raw for years. He understood only too well how painful and upsetting they could be, he'd wanted to bite off people's heads. He'd married Annabel three years before the war broke out and believed they were both very happy and had the sort of marriage that would last for ever.

He'd wanted a family, but once married Annabel had said, 'Don't let's rush into responsibilities like that. Let's have a good time while we're young. I'm not ready for babies yet.' She'd been twenty-six then. When his call-up papers came he didn't want to join the Pay Corps, which was where many accountants ended up.

'But the Pay Corps is the best place for you,' Annabel insisted. 'You're a fool if you can't see that. Look at Agnes's husband, he volunteered and asked to serve in the Pay Corps.' Andrew had known Malcolm well, they'd been work colleagues. 'He's doing his bit for the war effort, and they both know he'll be safe. He's stationed at Aldershot and unlikely to leave England. Agnes has found a cottage to rent nearby so she can see him when he's off duty. They're having a good time and they're happy about it. Why can't we do the same?'

Andrew had been younger than Agnes's husband, and he'd aimed to be part of the fighting force though he didn't achieve that. With hindsight, it had proved a big mistake. He should have done his best to stay with Annabel.

Shortly after he had completed his training in 1940, he'd received a posting to the Far East. Annabel had been envious, she'd always wanted to travel and now he was doing it without her. She accused him of abandoning her in war-torn Liverpool, and when the Germans started bombing the city she'd written angry letters describing her hurt.

Andrew was stationed at battalion headquarters in Singapore and put in charge of the battalion's finances. That was hardly a full-time job and he was given additional duties, often the job of organising social events. He'd had a thoroughly good time of it and felt guilty that he'd left Annabel in greater danger than he supposed himself to be. He'd worried about her and her letters left him agonised.

All that changed after Pearl Harbor, when the Japanese entered the war and set out to capture all of South-East Asia. They advanced very quickly and rumours began to circulate that Singapore could fall, but it was the largest British base in the Far East and there were said to be 85,000 British and Australian troops stationed there, so it was hard to believe.

Andrew and his friend Graham Brown watched anxiously as the enemy advanced but assumed the generals in charge were making plans to hold so important a base. They could see large numbers of European civilians were leaving and the harbour had never been so busy. Women and children were packing large passenger liners to capacity. Australian freighters took the maximum number of passengers they could squeeze on board. People were even crowding on to the local native craft trading round other Asian ports.

More and more Pacific islands were falling to the Japanese. It began to look as though Singapore really was in danger. If the worst happened, the advice Andrew heard was that British soldiers would be treated as prisoners of war if they surrendered but gunned down if they tried to escape.

Over drinks in the mess, Andrew began discussing what they could do should Singapore fall, though nobody treated that seriously because they couldn't believe it would happen. One glance at the map showed them that once captured it would be almost impossible to escape as virtually the only ways out of Singapore were by sea or air. There were other rumours about the enemy, that they were treating their prisoners with far more brutality than the Germans did, and ignoring the Geneva Convention. The consensus of opinion in the mess was that it might be wiser to avoid being caught.

The Japanese began bombing the city. They brought up big guns to add shells to the savage bombardment. Andrew and his friends drew money out of their bank accounts, collected together any small valuables they might exchange for necessities and packed a few basic essentials.

On 14 February 1942 the Japanese entered Singapore in a storm of gunfire. Out of the blue, the British and Australian forces suddenly surrendered, taking everybody by surprise. Large numbers of British troops surrendered and became prisoners. Others were rounded up by the Japanese, of whom some were taken prisoner but many were beaten and gunned down.

The next day, the 15th, was even worse. Law and order had completely broken down. The disaster they'd discussed over beer in the mess was now a reality. Andrew and his friend Graham shed their uniforms and raced for the harbour.

Ear-splitting bursts of gunfire close by and fires breaking

out in many parts of the city meant that most of the ships had hurriedly put to sea to avoid danger. Andrew was afraid they were too late.

They spent that night sheltering in a warehouse, kept awake by gunfire and the ever present fear that the enemy would burst in and capture them. At two in the morning the door creaked open. They were wide awake in a moment but able to breathe again when Andrew recognised the newcomer as Sergeant Willis, a military policeman who had worked with him once or twice on crowd control for the social events he'd organised.

Andrew had found him a likeable fellow. He was a few years older, and a professional soldier who had seen more of the world. He discovered Willis spoke a little of the local Malay language. He had been a reassuring presence, and had become a good friend. Andrew pulled a ledger towards him and sighed. He needed to get on with the job instead of day-dreaming about the past.

Millie craved normal routine and a quiet life. She wanted to see her children happy and everyone pulling their weight in the business so that it grew in profitability.

Things were quieter because Simon and Kenny had gone back to school for the autumn term. Marcus and Nigel seemed to be keeping out of her way, for which she was grateful, and although James's official retirement date wasn't until the end of December, he only came to the office for a few hours once in a while.

Sylvie was not rushing to the lab to see her quite so often, which Millie thought was a sign she didn't need as much support. Until Sylvie said, 'I don't like the way Denis hangs around when I come to talk to you. It's as though he's waiting to hear more gossip he can pass on to his friends.'

'Sylvie! Denis isn't like that. I thought you liked him.'

'But he does spread what he hears in the lab. How else would my life story have got round the factory? Besides, he gives me funny looks.'

Millie tried to smile. 'I think you're imagining that.'

'I'm not, Mum.'

At least Sylvie said she was pleased with her promotion and liked working for Andrew Worthington. She seemed happier now she'd moved out of the typing pool and into a room with three other secretaries. Things were settling down, and routine was more like it had been in Pete's time. He had always held a party on Guy Fawkes' night.

'Can we do it this year,' Kenny asked, 'and ask all our friends round?'

Because they went to boarding school, the boys didn't have many local friends. Kenny meant the family and all their friends, including many who worked for the firm. They'd always built a big bonfire in the garden and baked potatoes in their jackets in the embers. Millie wanted to keep up Pete's traditions but couldn't make up her mind whether it was a good idea or not. They'd had fireworks last year but Pete would not be here to let them off.

Nevertheless Simon and Kenny began collecting firewood and constructing a guy in the garden shed.

'I'd like to ask Connie and Louise,' Sylvie said. 'They don't have bonfires at home.'

Millie had heard that Louise's brother was engaged to a girl working in sales, and had given up hope that Sylvie's friendship with him would strengthen. She wanted her daughter to have more of a social life and that made her agree to have a little party, but she'd not intended to have all the staff until Albert Lancaster, who treated her more like a daughter than an employer, came to the lab one morning and said, 'I'm making some fireworks, are you going to have the usual bash? If you are, I'll bring them round and let them off in your place.'

'You'll have to take charge of any display of that sort,' Millie said.

'I know.' He patted her shoulder. She felt inveigled into inviting much the same crowd as Pete had last year.

They'd only started having fireworks again to celebrate the return of peace. It would not have been wise to cause even minor explosions in wartime. Fireworks were virtually unobtainable in the shops, so they had to make their own, but Pete and other members of the staff were either chemists or saw themselves as amateur chemists. Their home-made fireworks tended to be more blast than visual display but were part of the present make-do-and-mend culture, and were better than nothing on bonfire night.

Millie worried for a long time about whether she would invite Marcus and his side of the family but felt compelled to, as they'd no doubt hear of the party in the office. James said he didn't think he was well enough to stand about in the cold, but Marcus and Nigel accepted. Nigel said he would bring his wife.

'I'm glad Nigel and Marcus are coming,' Helen said. 'They used to be good company. We had marvellous holidays with them at Hafod when we were young.'

'Marcus was always in trouble,' Valerie remembered.

'Pete thought he was a little wild,' Millie said. She gave thanks that potatoes were not rationed and at this time of the year were plentiful. Valerie organised the buying of them, the scrubbing and the hour or so baking in the kitchen oven before they went out to the embers of the bonfire. Experience had told them they wouldn't bake through unless the kitchen oven played its part. Sylvie and Helen made toppings for them, begging scarce ingredients from whoever would part with them.

That morning, they went round the local butchers' shops and cleared them out of unrationed sausages. Millie would have liked to make a green salad to complete the meal but the lettuce had all died in the garden after a week of frost. She made a large pan of mushy peas as she had last year.

Sylvie was looking forward to the party though she knew her mother was on edge, afraid some disaster would occur. That afternoon she helped Simon and Kenny sweep the garden paths free of leaves and twigs, and hang the coloured Chinese lanterns that Dad had bought before the war on the trees and fences.

The boys had been given a broken chair and they tied the guy they'd made on to it, and managed to get it to balance on top of the bonfire. Everything was ready and they were keeping their fingers crossed that it wouldn't rain, because even a shower would mean more smoke than flames.

That evening Valerie and Roger were the first to arrive, and carried up their sleeping twins to Millie's bed. Sylvie had made up the old cot in the nursery for Helen's baby and wheeled it into her mother's room, so they'd all be together.

Val and Helen told Millie they were taking charge of the kitchen and she needn't worry about the food. Roger had brought the ingredients to make hot toddies and was making up two bowls of punch, mostly lemonade for the youngsters but with a little added strength for the older guests.

They had a lovely clear night for it, the sky sparkled with stars but it was very cold. Over the last week they'd been having hard frosts at night and it looked set to continue. Millie put extra chairs in the conservatory so that those who couldn't face the cold could see what was going on. She was dithering about when she should light the bonfire but Eric went out and did it fifteen minutes before the guests began to arrive.

Soon they were streaming in and Millie was kept busy greeting them. Nigel and his wife swept in together with Marcus. Dando had run them down. Sylvie was introduced to Clarissa and thought she looked glamorous.

Millie had insisted on inviting Denis, though Sylvie had asked her not to. Sylvie wanted to avoid him; he was too ready to spread gossip. She was watching for Connie and Louise, they'd promised to bring more wood from their gardens and a packing case or two, but when they arrived Denis was suddenly at her side. Connie liked him and got him to help toss their wood up on the bonfire. 'That's a smashing guy you've got on top,' he said.

Red embers were appearing in the fire and Eric and Roger were inserting potatoes into them with long fire tongs. One of the guests had brought some sparklers and was handing them round, and the party was beginning to hum.

Sylvie knew Denis would have latched on to them if she'd given him the slightest encouragement, but just as Connie was going to do that anyway Millie called out to him to help her serve the hot drinks.

There was Oxo for the kids, though Millie called it beef tea, and hot toddy for the adults. Sylvie collared three glasses of hot toddy for herself and her friends but after one taste, Louise said, 'I don't like this, it's all nutmeg and spices, and there's not much kick in it.' So they ditched it in the rhododendrons and went inside to get some Oxo.

Denis was carrying a tray of it from the kitchen to the table in the conservatory when Connie stopped him so they could take a mug each. As he turned to move on, his elbow caught Marcus's arm, his tray tilted, the mugs slipped and beef tea splashed everywhere.

'Look what you're doing you idiot,' Marcus barked in the same ferocious voice he used in the office. For once Sylvie felt sorry for Denis.

'Sorry, sir.' Denis's cheeks flamed.

Millie and Valerie came rushing in with cloths to mop up. 'Why do you have to overfill your house with this crowd?' Marcus shouted at Millie. 'Don't we see enough of our employees in the office?'

Sylvie was glad to see that his smart camel overcoat had caught a goodly amount of the splash and so had the turn-ups of his trousers.

'I think I'll go,' he said to Valerie. 'This isn't our sort of gathering. Come on, Nigel.' He held the conservatory door open for him, letting in an icy November blast. 'Are you and Clarissa coming?'

Nigel was talking to Tom Bedford and his wife. 'You'll need to call a taxi, Marcus,' he said. 'We'll stay a little longer. The bonfire has hardly got going.'

Marcus's face turned puce and without another word he went, slamming the conservatory door behind him with such force that a pane of glass fell out and splintered on the floor with a crash.

'Oh heavens!' Denis said. He apologised to Millie as Valerie rushed to get a dustpan and brush to sweep up the fragments.

'Don't worry about it,' Millie said. 'It wasn't your fault. Look after him, Connie. Get him a drink and go out and enjoy yourselves.'

'Marcus acted like a pig,' Valerie whispered. 'I asked Nigel and his wife round for supper the other night and they were both a bit toffee-nosed. He's changed too, no fun at all. I don't know how much we have in common any more.'

Connie put a full mug into Denis's hand and led him out to the garden. 'What a lovely smell of wood smoke,' she said.

The night was alive with the roar of flames and the crackle and spit of damp wood. Simon and Kenny were in charge of winding up the gramophone and putting on the records, but Millie was trying to choose the records they should play.

'Don't make the music too loud,' she said, but Kenny turned the sound up as soon as she went back indoors.

Roger raked the potatoes out of the fire and Helen cut them and handed out table napkins to hold them. They were so hot they still needed their gloves on, but they were soft and succulent and smelled delicious on the frosty air.

They could hear sounds of fireworks going off nearby and glimpse occasional streaks of colour flash in the night sky. Helen, still the schoolteacher at heart, told them that they were commemorating the true story of Guy Fawkes trying to blow up the Houses of Parliament. Tom Bedford was getting ready to let his own fireworks off and made them all stand back.

The bangs were enormous, 'Like heavy guns,' Millie said, pulling a face, but there were Catherine wheels and rockets too.

When the display finished, the older guests crowded back into the conservatory for another hot drink because the cold was beginning to bite. Connie and Louise were taken home by a relative. In the frosty semi-dark, with the bonfire dying away, Sylvie found herself alone with Denis. He said, 'Have I offended you? I get the feeling you're trying to avoid me. I'd like us to be friends.'

Offended her? He'd riled her! 'You told everybody about me,' she told him. 'You started the gossip about Dad not being my real father.'

He seemed horrified. 'No, I didn't!'

She hesitated. 'How else would everybody know? You heard what Uncle James and Marcus screamed at Mum in the lab and passed it round the whole factory.'

'No, Sylvie, I've said nothing about that to anyone.' He seemed hurt that she should think he had.

'But you overheard Marcus having a go at Mum, didn't you?'

'He was shouting, I couldn't help but hear.'

'Yes, and afterwards everybody was talking about us. Albert Lancaster sympathised with me about it.'

'Sylvie, a fight between the bosses will always cause gossip. You're getting some of the backwash, that's all. It's no secret that James and his sons resent your mother and therefore you too. I understand they're showing it all the time by trying to talk her down at staff meetings. Of course there's gossip about it but the staff are solidly on her side.'

'But all that talk about me being illegitimate was cruel.'

'It was Marcus who brought that up.'

'And now everybody knows.'

'Everybody has known for years,' he told her, 'that's not news. There are dozens of people working in the office and the factory who've worked there since before your mother started. When the boss took up with her it was the romance of the century, and they gossiped about every detail of it. They liked Peter Maynard, he was fair to everybody; he forgave their mistakes and looked after those in difficulties. If he wanted to marry your mother, they were all for it too.'

'But it was news to you?'

'No it wasn't. My mother was Arthur Knowles's daughter. He ran the lab for years.'

'My mother told me about him.'

'Grandpa helped bring me up. My father was killed in a road accident when I was small and when my grandmother died a few years later, it made sense that we move into Grandpa's house.'

'Mum says he taught her most of what she knows.'

'When I was still at school I remember my grandfather holding forth about it, about how happy their marriage turned out to be. Everybody talked about your mum and dad.'

'Yes, but I didn't know he wasn't my real father.'

'He treated you as though you were. Perhaps he wanted you to think he was.'

'It came as a shock to me.'

'I know it did, and it must be a shock to find out that the rest of us have always known.'

Sylvie felt somewhat comforted that he understood.

'It's all ancient history, nobody's thought of it for years, but yes, we knew the full story. Had Peter not died so suddenly, he would have told you in his own time and his own way, and you'd have accepted it and felt fine about it.'

Sylvie was heartened. That's exactly what Mum had said.

'Come on, we'd better go in,' Denis said. 'I think the party is over.'

Sylvie was sorry to hear the guests thanking her mum and taking their leave. She didn't want the party to end. Denis had been good company after all. 'Don't you go.' She put a hand on his arm. 'Mum will want you to stay and have supper with the family.'

The dining table had been extended to its limit and those remaining sat round to eat sausages and mushy peas with more baked potatoes. Sylvie was surprised to find Andrew Worthington was among those invited to stay.

When the party was finally over and the sleeping babies were being brought downstairs, Millie arranged a lift home for Denis with Helen and Eric as he lived in the same direction.

When Sylvie was seeing them off, Denis said to her, 'Will you come out with me on Saturday night, to the pictures or something?'

'Yes, I'd like to.' Sylvie felt a warm glow. Mum was right about him. Denis wasn't a bad sort.

It was late when the family went to bed that night and Sylvie couldn't sleep. Denis had stirred up deep memories of the man she'd thought was her father. She'd loved Peter Maynard, but it seemed everybody who knew him had loved him too. Denis had said he'd forgiven his employees their mistakes, so he'd surely forgive her for persuading him to put to sea in that storm.

They had to get up for an early breakfast the next morning because Millie had to take the boys to school on the way to work. They were in a rush and she was irritable.

'It was a good party,' Simon told her. Kenny chorused his approval.

'Marcus caused a bit of a scene,' Sylvie pointed out. 'There was a deathly silence for a few moments. All the chatter ceased.'

She could see her mother was frowning. 'It was the first party I've given since your dad died,' she said, clutching the steering wheel and staring straight ahead.

'It was a success,' Sylvie assured her. 'Lots of people said they enjoyed it. Nigel was being nice to us all.'

She saw her mother pull a face and knew she was upset. 'Nigel gave me a bit of a jolt too.'

'Was he nasty?'

'No, really he was trying rather too hard to be pleasant, but I went upstairs to the bathroom and found him and his wife in your bedroom, Kenny. He was showing her round the house and said, "I hope you don't mind, Millie, Clarissa wanted to see where my forebears used to live." Clarissa was all sweetness and light, and said, "His grandfather designed it and had it built, didn't he? It's part of Maynard history." '

'I hope he didn't touch my things.' Kenny was indignant.

'It won't be your toys they're after. Clarissa was admiring our house and leaking envy through every pore. I think she fancies it.'

'What a cheek they have,' Kenny and Simon chorused.

'What could be more normal than that Dad should will all his worldly goods to the family he loved?' Sylvie demanded. 'He'd want to know we had a house and enough to live on. It's what everybody does, isn't it?'

Chapter Eighteen

For Millie it was a quiet and restful morning and she was enjoying doing some of the routine work in the laboratory. But at eleven o'clock Billy Sankey, their buyer, came tearing angrily into the lab to see her.

'Millie,' he said, 'I can't be doing with James's boys, they've gone too far.'

She straightened up from her workbench with a sinking heart. 'What have they done now?'

'Marcus is trying to elbow me out of my job.'

'No, Billy, no. It's not your job he wants.'

'It is, Missus. He came to my office as bold as brass and said he'd be heading the buying team in future. That's got to mean I'm reduced to being his assistant. I'm not having that.'

'Billy, he can't do your work.' Millie was exasperated with Marcus.

'I know. No doubt he'll expect me to go on doing it all and he'll take the kudos.'

'Calm down. Come and sit down.' Billy could do neither, he was breathing flames.

'Denis, would you please make two cups of tea for us?' Millie asked.

She forced Billy into a chair but he raved on. 'He's got an ego the size of a house. Just because his family own this business he thinks he can walk straight in and do any job better than we can.'

'You do an excellent job.'

'I know but he thinks he can do it better. He thinks he can run the whole outfit, make it earn more money. I'm not staying to be put upon by him. I'll leave and get a job somewhere else. There's lots of jobs to be had these days.'

'Billy, we need you here. I don't want you to go, we can't manage without you. I'll talk to Marcus, leave him to me.'

He was still snorting with rage. 'He said I dressed like a scarecrow and was a disgrace to the firm.'

Millie giggled and failed to control it. She broke into a laugh and eventually Billy managed a wry smile. 'Well, you have to admit you are not our smartest dresser.' She laughed again.

He sighed. 'Perhaps it's time I ditched this suit.' The cuffs and pockets were fraying and it looked as though it hadn't ever been pressed during the years he'd worn it.

'If it makes you feel any better,' Millie said, 'I thought Marcus was trying to take over my job, and there's nothing else I can do.'

'You're good at it, Missus. He'd be hopeless.'

'Marcus doesn't know what he can do or where he fits in, that's his problem. How old are you now, Billy?'

'Fifty-nine and I've worked here since I was fourteen. Been round just about every department in that time, I have.'

'You know more about how we function than Marcus does, and he doesn't like that. You don't really want to leave us, do you? After all, another six years and you'll retire and draw your pension from us.'

'I'd rather stay, Missus, and that's the truth.' He took out his handkerchief and mopped his brow.

'Right, well, I'd better have a word with Marcus then.'

Millie got up with a sigh. She thought it better not to give Marcus any warning and went slowly up to the tower to see him. She felt full of dread, afraid he'd start another row. She hoped that James hadn't come in today because that would mean she'd have to argue with two of them. She rapped on the door and walked straight in and was relieved to find Marcus alone.

'Millie!' He lowered his cup to its saucer and put down a half-eaten biscuit beside it. There was another waiting untouched. 'To what do I owe this honour?'

'It's no honour,' she said. 'Marcus, I hate having to confront you like this, but you're always causing trouble of one sort or another.'

'Not again,' he sighed. 'What is it this time?'

'You've upset Billy Sankey. I know we've been through all this before, but couldn't you just take a quiet interest in what our buyer does? Ask him questions, look at his files and then when Billy retires in six years' time you'll understand what's required and be able to control the buying? Instead you're giving him the impression you know it all and that he knows nothing of value to us.'

'And that isn't right?'

'No. He's spent all his working life here, he knows what he's doing and he's got all the contacts. We wouldn't survive without him. So stop badgering him. Billy stays.'

Marcus was going puce with rage but before he could speak Millie strode from the room and ran down to the lab. Moments later Denis slid a cup of tea in front of her and disappeared again behind the high racks in the lab.

An hour later when she'd calmed down she went to speak to Billy. He wasn't his usual cheery self. 'I've had a word with Marcus,' she said, 'and I've told him we need you on the job. I've asked him to leave you alone. Don't worry about it. I won't let him push you out.'

He had a hangdog look. 'Thanks, Missus.'

'You keep out of his way, Billy. Just get on with your job.'

Sylvie was cross with herself. She'd agreed to go to the pictures with Denis on Saturday, having forgotten that she'd arranged to spend that afternoon and evening with Helen. Valerie had bought her a dress length of gorgeous blue and grey striped taffeta to reward her for babysitting the twins and Sylvie was eager to make herself a party dress for the Christmas season. Helen was very good at sewing and had offered to help her cut it out and show her how to make it up. Sylvie was keen to learn the basics of dressmaking because it stretched both money and coupons and meant she could have more clothes.

Helen had suggested she come on Saturday because Eric's company was holding a three monthly specialist sale of clocks and watches, and he generally didn't get home until seven o'clock on those days. Helen liked a bit of company, and Sylvie had spent similar Saturday afternoons with her and usually stayed on to have supper with them.

As her mother was parking the car outside the office, Sylvie saw Denis heading through the door ahead of them. The glow she'd felt for Denis's company had faded, and she'd made up her mind to call off her date with him as she wanted to get her party frock started. She said to her mother, 'I'll call in the lab on my way in,' and told her why.

Her mother frowned. 'You could get Helen to cut out your dress and then leave early and still go to the pictures with Denis.'

She was reluctant. 'I suppose I could,' she said.

'You do that.' Millie opened the lab door and Sylvie could see Denis fastening his white coat. 'If you've agreed to go out with him, you shouldn't back out. That wouldn't be kind.'

On Saturday, Sylvie felt she'd had a rewarding afternoon. She'd watched Helen lay out her paper pattern on the dress length and cut it out with expert ease. She'd given her the job of tacking some of the pieces together, then got out her sewing machine and showed her how to run up two of the main seams. Sylvie was pleased with the progress they were making and thrilled when Helen said, 'It's going to look very smart when it's finished.'

Eric rang up to say they were particularly busy and he'd be later getting home than he'd expected. Sylvie hadn't told her sister she would be leaving early until she'd arrived, and Helen had made a sponge cake for tea which was her favourite and had planned to make egg and chips when Eric came home. Baby Jenny was very good all afternoon, billing and cooing at them and wanting to play, and she knew Helen wanted her to stay.

When the time came for Sylvie to leave, rain was bucketing down and she had to borrow Helen's umbrella to run to the nearest bus stop. She was getting wet and cold and had to wait so long for a bus that she was afraid she'd be late for her meeting with Denis. She wished she hadn't allowed her mother to stop her calling this date off.

When finally the bus drew up at the stop, there was standing room only and it was all fogged up and smelled of wet macintoshes. It took her some time to realise someone was trying to attract her attention. It pleased her when she realised it was Denis. He was beaming at her and pushing through the other passengers to reach her.

'Sylvie, I'm so glad to see you, relieved really. What are you doing on this bus?'

'I've spent the afternoon with Helen.'

'I was afraid I was going to be late for our meeting. The last bus broke down and we had to wait for a replacement to come from the depot. Anyway, now we've met, I don't have to worry about that.'

Sylvie felt cheered. Denis looked quite handsome though

214

his hair was more than damp. When they got off in town, the rain had eased. He took her arm and threaded it through his.

'What would you like to do? *The Jolson Story* is showing at the Odeon or there's music hall at the Empire with George Formby topping the bill.'

'Oh, I'd like to see George Formby. He cheers everybody up, doesn't he? And Mum doesn't approve of him for my brothers so she won't take me there.'

'Not approve, why not?'

'It's his humour. The double innuendo, we children are too young.'

'It's pretty harmless, isn't it? A bit like Old Mother Riley.'

'Yes, and Mum takes us to see her. We all think she's great fun.'

Denis looked serious. 'Should we see George Formby if your mother doesn't approve?'

'That's exactly why we should.' Sylvie smiled. 'You don't always have to think of pleasing her.'

'I do because she's my boss – well, mostly I do, anyway.' He grinned at her. They went to the Empire and he bought chocolates for her.

'Marvellous,' she said, 'thank you very much. It's very generous of you to spend your sweet coupons on me.'

Sylvie loved the excitement of the theatre. The Sand Dancers were a supporting act and they laughed so much at their antics that Sylvie's sides ached. She couldn't help but notice that Denis spent almost as much time looking at her as he did watching the stage. He bought her an ice cream in the interval but Sylvie was getting hungry despite that, and her tummy was rumbling audibly. It was still only nine thirty when they came out but it was very dark. The rain had stopped, leaving a clean but cold blustery night.

'Let's walk down to the Pier Head,' he suggested. 'It's too

215

early to go home yet and there's always plenty of life down there.'

'And it's the bus terminus, so it's easy to get home when we want to.'

He put his arm round her waist and pulled her closer. Sylvie shivered as much from the thrill of that as from the cold. She decided her mother was right. Denis was a very nice person and it was great being escorted round by him.

The river seemed alive with lights glistening on the black water. A ferry boat was tying up ready to take passengers across the river. There were lights, too, on the fish and chip van parked on the front and the breeze was carrying the delicious scent to them.

'Would you like fish and chips?' he asked.

Sylvie laughed. 'I'd love some,' and she told him why she'd missed her supper. The fish had sold out but he bought them three pennyworth of chips each, and they leaned over the railings looking down on the landing stage to eat them. She'd never enjoyed chips more.

Sylvie was very aware of him standing closer to her than he ever had before. Suddenly, he pulled her even closer into a long, thrilling hug and bent to kiss her full on the lips. When he lifted his face from hers, he smiled and said, 'I've been hoping for a long time that you'd let me kiss you. Will you come out with me again?'

'Yes,' she said breathlessly.

'I've admired you from a distance for ages,' he said. 'I'd like you to be my girlfriend. Will you?'

Sylvie nodded, too overcome to speak.

'I'm afraid I'm not much of a catch for a girl like you.'

'Why not?' Sylvie was enjoying this.

'You're the most beautiful girl in the office. In all Liverpool really and just look at your family. I'm aiming high aren't I?'

To Sylvie it felt like balm. 'Not too high,' she said. 'I think we're well suited.'

He kissed her again and they spent the next half hour with their arms round each other battered by the blustery breeze. Denis began to worry that he was keeping her out too late and when her bus pulled into the terminus they both got on it.

'This is going a good bit out of your way,' she said. 'There was a bus waiting there that would have taken you straight home.'

'I'd like to see you safely home first,' he said. When they got off the bus he walked her along the road to her front gate. The lights were full on downstairs and radiating out into the garden. 'Your mother has waited up for you,' he said.

'It isn't that late.'

'I was told to deliver you home by ten thirty even though it is Saturday night.'

'Mum said that?' Sylvie wasn't sure she liked it. 'She must think I'm not old enough to look after myself.'

'Perhaps it's me she doesn't trust.' He kissed her again rather briskly, and pushed the gate open for her. 'Better if you go in now. I'll see you on Monday.'

Sylvie had expected another cuddle and more of a kiss than that after he'd come out of his way to see her home, but his hand was on her shoulder urging her through the gate. Mum was interfering and he was too much in her pocket. 'Goodnight,' she said, and used her key to let herself in.

Millie was crossing the hall, wearing her dressing gown. 'Hello, love,' she said. 'Have you had a good time?'

'It was all right. Mum, you've got to trust me to look after myself.'

'I do. Would you like a cup of cocoa? I'm just going to make some for myself.'

'No thank you,' she said icily. 'You're pulling the strings where Denis is concerned. I don't like you telling him to deliver me back to the door and at what time he has to do it.'

'Oh dear,' her mother said. 'It doesn't sound as though you've enjoyed yourself. You're a bit grumpy. That's a shame.'

Chapter Nineteen

Christmas was fast approaching and as this would be Millie's first without Pete, she was missing him more than ever and was thinking of him all the time. Tom Bedford procured a turkey for her as he had relatives who were farmers. Valerie had invited her and her children to have a midday Christmas dinner at her house and Helen was going to provide a cold supper and singing round the piano in the evening, so she handed the turkey over to them to feed the family.

Sylvie and the boys were invited to one or two pre-Christmas parties and at home they were busy making Christmas cards and additional decorations for the playroom. There was much whispering and secrecy about presents. The weekend before the holiday they brought down the tree and all the old decorations from the attic, and they had noisy fun hanging decorations and dressing the tree. As they'd used the same ones since before the war they remembered each one almost as though it was an old friend and exclaimed with delight as it came to light.

All the preparations reminded Millie that Uncle James had said he wanted to retire at the end of the year. In the past, whenever an employee retired, Pete had arranged some little ceremony and a parting gift to celebrate the occasion. When Marcus took over his office it was one of several tasks Millie had suggested he take over. Millie had had to step in for the last two men who had retired from the factory floor but now

James's retirement date was drawing closer and she felt it might cause resentment if she went ahead and organised something for him herself.

James hadn't come to the office for the last few weeks so she couldn't consult him, and as she'd heard no mention of any retirement arrangements, she climbed up to the room in the turret one morning to see Marcus.

He wasn't in, his desk was bare and his waste-paper basket empty. It was easy to see he hadn't come to work this morning. She felt a flush of anger; he and his brother had arrived saying that as family members they would step into Pete's shoes and run the company, but Marcus was following in his father's footsteps and rarely coming to work, and doing nothing when he was here. She thought he was a waste of time and money, a liability for the business.

Millie ran down to the boardroom to see Nigel. He had impeccable manners and leapt to his feet as she entered. She couldn't help complaining about Marcus and let him see her anger.

'What does he do with himself all day? He's supposed to be here in working hours, and he never gives any explanation or apology for his absence.'

Nigel backed her towards a chair. 'I'm sorry, I know Marcus isn't the easiest person to handle at the moment. He's got personal problems and we're all worried about him.'

'I suppose his absence is easier to take than having him here boxing Billy's ears and causing mayhem.' Millie relaxed and tried to smile. 'Straighten him out, Nigel. The business can't go on carrying him for ever.'

'I know. Father is losing patience with him too and I feel caught between them. Please give him another chance.'

Millie shrugged. 'What else can I do?'

'Why were you looking for him? Did you want him to do something?'

'Yes,' Millie explained. 'I wanted him to arrange something for your father's retirement. What would he like us to do? I can't ask him as he doesn't come in any more.'

Nigel sighed with exasperation. 'I don't know.'

'He'll want to come in and say goodbye to everybody, won't he? Make his retirement official.'

'Yes. Perhaps we could ask him to come in on his last day and give a little farewell speech. Then we could take him out for a celebratory dinner that evening.'

'But that will be New Year's Eve,' Millie pointed out, 'and everywhere gets booked up well ahead. We might have left it a bit late to book for a large number. Anyway, the staff may want to make their own arrangements for that night. Wouldn't it be better if we had it the week before? He could come in during the afternoon and make his farewell speech to the whole factory during their tea break. Then perhaps a dinner with the senior managers that evening.'

'I'll ask him,' Nigel said. 'Father has pretty fixed ideas about what he wants.'

'How is he?'

Nigel shook his head. 'Not well. No longer well enough to work. He couldn't cope with a full day's work now.'

'Nigel, it must be at least a decade since he worked a full day.'

'Yes, poor Father. I'll find out what he wants us to do.' Nigel smiled at her. 'I'm glad you remembered. We need to make a bit of a fuss of him.'

Millie went back to the lab shaking her head. It seemed both Nigel and Marcus had forgotten their father was about to retire. What were they thinking about?

The next morning Nigel came to the lab to see her. 'Father isn't feeling at all well,' he said. 'He says too many people round him exhaust him, and he doesn't feel he needs to speak to the whole staff. He'd prefer us to call a senior staff meeting on the last morning so he can say goodbye to them, and perhaps a lunch just for the family. He gets very tired towards evening and likes to stick to his usual routine.'

It sounded, Millie thought, as if James was failing more than she'd thought. 'Did you ask where he wanted to have this lunch?'

'The Adelphi.'

'Have you booked it?'

'Not yet, but I will.'

'At least he knows what he wants,' Millie said.

'Yes. There's one other thing.'

'Yes?' Millie thought he'd probably like a commemorative gift like a gold watch, that's what she'd done for other retirees. She could see Nigel was watching her closely.

'He believes a small bonus would be appropriate, a one-off payment to crown a lifetime's work.'

Millie felt suddenly sick. Alarm bells were ringing in her head. 'A small bonus? How much does he feel would be appropriate?'

'He said ten thousand at first, but I told him the company might find it difficult to meet that and persuaded him that you'd probably find five thousand a reasonable compromise.' He handed her an envelope. 'I asked him to put it in writing so we could authorise it and put the matter in hand. That's all right, isn't it?'

Millie froze. She felt she was being rushed into handing over a large amount of company money to James. Her house had had to be valued for probate and a figure of five and a half thousand had been put on it. So the amount proposed was hardly small. 'I'll have to think about it,' she said.

'Yes of course.' Nigel was smiling. 'Don't take too long. We should really present a bonus cheque to him on the day he retires.'

When the lab door closed behind him Millie went back

to her desk and slid limply on to her chair. The last thing she wanted was to pay James anything. But a bonus big enough to buy a substantial house when the company was struggling to supply its markets in this post-war era? She asked herself what Pete would do in these circumstances. She didn't think he'd want to do it either.

It took her a long time to tear open the envelope Nigel had given her and study the contents. It read, '*In accordance with the agreement made between me and my brother Peter on 3 August 1920, I request in writing a payment to be made to me from company funds as a bonus to reward a lifetime of hard work for the company.*'

There was the sum in black and white, £5,000. On the left-hand side it was signed by James and on the right-hand side was a line awaiting a signature, with the name Emily Jane Maynard typed underneath.

Millie took a couple of deep breaths before opening the bottom drawer of her desk. She wanted to see a copy of the agreement that had been drawn up in 1920. When Marcus had demanded the keys to Pete's desk she'd hurriedly cleared out everything that appeared to be of importance. She hoped to find it here.

She felt all thumbs and couldn't see what she was looking for, she needed to calm down. She lifted an armful of files and papers on top of her desk and started again more carefully but there was nothing like that here. She dropped them all back in again and closed the drawer with her foot. She didn't like the way Nigel and James had gone about this. They were trying to pressurise her into setting this up quickly. A small bonus indeed and the story about it being a compromise!

Another moment's thought and she sprang to her feet, snatched up the letter and went along to Andrew's office. She found him rifling through his file cabinet.

'While you're there,' she said, 'would you have a copy of

an agreement made between James and Peter in nineteen twenty?'

'Nineteen twenty? I don't think so. Would that be when their father handed the business over to them?' He came back to his desk.

'I don't know. No, it sounds more like a legal document drawn up to set out the rights of the partners, and possibly how the business was to be managed.' She pushed James's letter across to him and collapsed onto his visitor's chair. 'James is asking for a retirement bonus of five grand from company capital.'

He whistled through his teeth. 'Five grand?'

'It's a bit much, isn't it?'

Andrew was deep in thought. 'There's enough money to do it if that's what you want, over thirteen grand at the moment. Your solicitor should have a copy of the agreement and the best advice I can offer is, don't sign this until you've had a word with him and found out the legal position. It may be they need your goodwill for this, and you might decide it makes better economic sense to spend the money on other things.'

'I don't think he deserves a bonus.' Millie was cross that he'd even asked for it. 'We've been paying his salary for years and he hardly ever comes to work.'

She went back to her office and rang Mr Douglas. When his secretary answered, she asked if she might speak to him and was lucky enough to find he hadn't a client with him.

'Is something the matter, Mrs Maynard?' he asked, and when she told him he said, 'Bring the letter and come and see me this morning. I shall be free after eleven o'clock.'

She was impatient to have this sorted quickly but had to catch the bus because it was one of the days when she was running short of petrol. She found the quiet, formal atmosphere of Mr Douglas's office calming.

He had a document laid out in front of him. 'I looked out the agreement,' he said, 'and I've run my eye over it. You wanted to know what it lays down with regard to the payment of a bonus to your brother-in-law?'

His secretary placed a cup of tea in front of Millie. 'He's asking for one,' she said, sliding his letter across the desk to Mr Douglas. 'What I want to know is, does he have a legal right to this? Do I have to agree to him having it?'

'There's no mention of bonuses in this document,' he said, looking over his glasses at her, 'so the answer to that is no, he has no legal right to be paid a bonus, but that doesn't mean he can't have one.'

'I think the company will need cash soon. No maintenance has been done since before the war and our equipment will need to be brought up to date. I'd prefer to keep the money for that.'

'Very wise, my dear.' He took a sip from his own cup of tea. 'What this agreement lays down is that the profit accumulated by your business is jointly owned and therefore you must both agree as to how it is to be used. That is why you have to sign this if you want James to have a bonus.'

'I don't. He hasn't kept regular office hours for more than a decade. He hardly comes at all any more and I don't think he deserves it. He isn't well, you see. That's why he's decided to retire early.'

'Well, there is something here about retirement. Now where did I see that? Yes . . . "It is agreed that retirement can take place and a pension paid from the age of sixty-five. The pension being pro-rata . . ." etc. But he's retiring early, you said.'

'He'll be sixty-three on New Year's Day.'

'Ah yes, the younger brother.' Mr Douglas adjusted his glasses and went on in his pedantic manner, 'Then there is no legal requirement for his pension to be paid until he reaches

225

the age of sixty-five, unless you wish to pay it, of course.'

Millie allowed herself a little smile. 'Thank you.' Mr Douglas went on to explain the significance of the agreement to her and that gave her the confidence to make decisions. 'Could I have a copy of this agreement, d'you think?'

'By all means, I'll get my secretary to send you one.'

Millie wished him a Merry Christmas and travelled back to the lab with her mind made up. She would refuse to give James a bonus. She felt victorious, what she'd learned from Mr Douglas had given her an insight into what Nigel was trying to do and how she might get the better of him this time.

She'd been a fool to think he was easier to cope with than Marcus. He'd been friendly and agreed both sides of the family had to get along for the good of the company, but she could see now that that had been a façade. Nigel was no better than his father and brother. His methods were different, that was all, and it made him more dangerous.

It was almost lunchtime when Millie returned to the office. She was going upstairs to the lab when she met Andrew. 'How did you get on?' he asked.

'It was good advice you gave me, Mr Douglas has straightened me out.'

'Good. Have you brought sandwiches today? How about coming to my office to eat them? Come and tell me what he said.'

Millie was in good spirits, she felt she wanted to talk to somebody and who better than Andrew? He was doing his best to help her. Ten minutes later she was in his office biting into her bloater paste sandwiches and telling him what she'd found out.

'All three are determined to do me down,' she said. 'They thought they could get money out of the company this way and I'd feel unable to stop them. I bet Nigel would have persuaded his father to buy a house with it, either for him or Marcus.'

'He could buy them one each with that. They are beginning to build again, there's a new estate going up near us.'

'Not the sort of houses they aspire to. They keep on at me. It makes me wary, on edge, wondering what their next scheme will be.'

Andrew smiled. 'You've beaten them every time.'

'Yes, with help from you and Mr Douglas.'

'Millie, I'd avoid another fight with them. It just makes them more determined to have their own way.'

'I won't be able to avoid a fight. Not if I refuse Uncle James a bonus.'

'Well, be sure to work out your reasons first. Get your argument cut and dried and then say what you have to, quietly and calmly. Stay in control. Don't lose your temper even if Nigel does. Or . . .' He pondered for a moment. 'You could just return their document unsigned, with a letter giving your reasons.'

Millie was nervous, she hated having arguments with Pete's relatives and she was in no doubt this would cause one. If only Pete were here to handle this. Back in the lab, she gave Denis some work to do and then, with a pencil and paper in front of her, wrote out the reasons why she would not agree to this bonus. She'd decided to stay well away from Nigel and was drafting a letter explaining why she was refusing it when he came into the lab.

Her heart sank when she saw him. He pulled out the chair in front of her desk to sit down, and with great affability said, 'Have you had time to think about Father's bonus? We do need to move on this if we're to get it organised in time. Everything's closing down for Christmas.'

Millie could hear a brass band in the street below playing

'Hark, the herald angels sing'. She took a deep breath and pushed James's letter of request back to Nigel.

'I haven't signed it,' she said quietly. 'I don't think the company can afford to pay out such a bonus when we're trying to build it up and recover from the war.'

Nigel looked shocked. She could see he hadn't expected an outright refusal. 'But there are company profits amounting to thirteen thousand pounds that haven't been shared out.'

'Yes, I believe Pete and James agreed not to share out the profits for a year or two, and it has taken time and a lot of hard work to save that. I think we all understand that this building will need a lot spent on repairs as soon as materials are available. Nothing has been done since before the war.'

'Of course, but surely the bonus could be afforded?'

'Our machinery is old-fashioned and almost worn out. It would make economic sense to bring the factory up to date, and we are in dire need of a fleet of new delivery vans.'

'Yes, but—'

'I think your father and I should both keep our share of the profits in the company to spend in that way. We might even want to expand into new premises if the opportunity comes up. We wouldn't want shortage of cash to hold us back, would we?' Nigel was looking desperate. 'Of course,' she went on, 'if you feel your father must be rewarded with a bonus, he could take it out of his own half share of the accrued profit. I've discussed it with Mr Douglas. Why don't you do the same?'

'Perhaps I will.'

'But if my share of the profit is reinvested in the business – in new machines for instance – and James's is withdrawn, then my share of the business increases while his goes down, and I will eventually own the controlling share.'

'What?' He looked horrified.

'Well, it's obvious, isn't it?' Millie smiled. It hadn't been obvious to her until Mr Douglas had pointed it out. Like Nigel, she'd never given it any thought.

Nigel's face was flushed and angry. 'Are you trying to grab control of the company and ease us, the rightful owners, out?'

'No,' she said, trying to sound as superior as he did. 'I'm pointing out the legal position.' Thank goodness she'd found out the facts first. 'And also, in the same agreement you mention, the retirement age was fixed at sixty-five and Uncle James does not reach that age for another two years. There is no legal right for him to claim a pension now.'

Millie had never seen Nigel so irate and confused before. 'Are you telling me you'll deny him a pension too?'

'No, Nigel, I am not. I said he has no legal right to claim one from the company for another two years, but I am willing to allow him to draw it immediately. After all, he has been claiming a salary for nearly a decade and doing nothing for it, and the pension is lower so it will be to the company's advantage.'

Millie realised she was doing what Andrew had advised her not to, she was getting Nigel's back up.

He was so enraged he couldn't speak.

'What I'd like us to do,' she went on gently, 'is to concentrate on running the business as efficiently as we can. If we can keep the staff working contentedly, and we all work for the same goal, it will be to our mutual benefit.'

Nigel slammed out, leaving his father's letter requesting the bonus on her desk. It gave Millie great satisfaction to tear it into small pieces and drop them in her waste-paper basket.

Chapter Twenty

It was Christmas Eve, and Sylvie and the boys hung their stockings round the nursery fireplace as they always had. Once they'd gone to bed, Millie filled them with tangerines and nuts and small novelties that she'd been able to buy.

She was woken up early on Christmas morning by the sound of carols being played on the gramophone outside her room and the boys racing round the house in high good humour. Kenny appeared with a tray of morning tea, followed by Simon dragging a sleepy Sylvie and putting her in the double bed beside her.

They'd hardly had time to pour out their tea before the boys were back with their arms full of Christmas stockings and colourfully wrapped presents. They took turns to empty their stockings and open their gifts, cooing over the contents and spreading them across her eiderdown.

For her part, Millie enjoyed opening and exclaiming over the little gifts her children laid before her. With help from Helen, Sylvie had made her a blouse, Kenny had made home-made chocolate truffles, and Simon had bought her a new address book, of which she was very much in need. What she enjoyed most was seeing her children happy and excited.

When lunchtime drew near, she drove them to Valerie's house, with the boys singing carols on the back seat. Helen and her family were already there and the succulent scent of roasting turkey filled the house. The festive spirit was much in evidence, though they all talked of Pete and drank a toast to absent friends before they ate their Christmas dinner.

The evening spent at Helen's house playing games and singing round the piano was equally jolly, though Millie admitted to herself afterwards that without Pete it could never be as much fun as earlier Christmases.

It was the day of James's retirement ceremony, and the last time he would come to the office. As arranged, at eleven o'clock Millie and all the senior staff collected in the boardroom. There was an uneasy atmosphere, they didn't know whether to sit at the boardroom table as they usually did, or collect round Nigel's desk near the big window looking out over the Mersey. He and his father were already there. Coffee and biscuits were being served.

To Millie, it was only too obvious that James was cross, Nigel was agitated and the rest of the staff were growing increasingly on edge. 'Where is Marcus?' James kept asking. 'Where can he have got to? Has anybody seen him?'

He delayed his farewell speech for fifteen minutes. It was an uncomfortable delay and in the end he started before there was any sign of Marcus. By then, James was unable to concentrate on what he was saying, he kept losing the thread and his speech was neither clear nor coherent.

They were all relieved when Nigel suggested they make their way to the Adelphi Hotel. Andrew had already offered Millie a lift and he took Tom Bedford and Albert Lancashire as well on the back seat. When they arrived, they were surprised to find Marcus waiting for them at the front door, looking nervous.

'There you are,' Tom Bedford said. 'There's been a hue and cry out for you.'

'I think the plan was for you to join us earlier in the boardroom,' Millie said mildly.

Nigel and his father were on their heels. 'Where the hell have you been?' James demanded as soon as he saw his younger son.

'Sorry, Pa.' Marcus seemed to wilt. 'I was held up.'

'Held up? Where, for God's sake? You didn't sleep at home last night, where have you been? You knew this was a special occasion and you've disrupted everything.'

'Sorry, Pa,' he said again and scuttled off.

'Out all night?' Tom Bedford murmured to Millie. 'Has he been out on the tiles carousing? He doesn't look as though he's had much sleep.'

Millie thought he was right. Marcus looked both nervous and exhausted. His hair was still wet so he'd just had a bath to make himself presentable for this lunch.

'It's almost as though he has another job,' Andrew whispered, 'and he's putting more effort into that one than this.'

Millie had to agree, but she couldn't imagine what could have kept him up all night.

They were shown up to the private room Nigel had booked for them, and James was ushered to his place at the head of the table. Each place setting had a name in a silver holder. Millie found she was to sit next to James; she hadn't expected this. As a waiter pulled out the chair for her, she heard James say, 'Nigel, I wanted you on one side and Marcus on the other, that's only right.'

'That's where I put Marcus, Pa.'

Millie could see him pulling out a chair at the other end of the table. She thought he must have switched places with her. It didn't please her any, but what could he be up to? Perhaps he wanted to put distance between himself and his father. She thought the dining table very smart with its starched damask linen and sparkling glass. It was very elegant but then the Adelphi was reputed to be Liverpool's best hotel.

'The food here is said to be as good as it was in the middle of the war years,' James remarked. Millie wondered if he meant that as a joke, but he was in no mood to make jokes. She'd heard it said that hotel meals everywhere were becoming increasingly frugal as rations were reduced.

She decided she would make an effort to find out what Marcus was up to. She was puzzled and curious, and she could see that James was equally flummoxed. She wasn't sure what Nigel thought, he was very much in control of himself and didn't show his feelings. She was afraid the brothers were working on another scheme to get her out of the business. That was the only thing that made sense.

Chapter Twenty-One

Millie was getting on well with Andrew Worthington. He was friendly and she'd never been more in need of a friend. He'd become something of a confidant and she discussed business matters with him and got another viewpoint and good advice. She felt she was getting from him what Marcus and Nigel should have been providing.

Earlier that morning, Millie had been reading a trade paper at her desk when an advertisement caught her eye. A small local soap manufacturer was seeking another company in a similar line of business with a view to merging with them. She went along the corridor to show it to Andrew. 'We buy some of our raw soap from them, don't we?' she asked.

'We do. They might be a good fit for Maynard's.'

'I've no ambitions to merge with anyone but I'm wondering if it is the company owned by Elvira's family. I can't remember what her name was before she married Marcus.'

'Could it be Hampton?'

'It might, I'll have to ask Marcus. He might be in favour if it is.'

'He and Nigel have just gone out for lunch.'

'There's no hurry for this. Shall we go too?' He'd asked her if she'd have lunch with him today in Parker's Refreshment Rooms.

'Yes, we need to get to Parker's fairly early or all the best dishes go. It's the best food in the district.'

Millie had told him that Pete used to take her and Sylvie there regularly, and now he'd agreed she would pay her share, they went more often. As they went in and made their way to an empty table in the window, four diners stood up to leave from a nearby table.

'Why, hello.' One clapped Andrew on the shoulder and hovered beside them.

Andrew seemed pleased to see him and said to Millie, 'This is Jeffrey Willis, a friend I meet here a couple of times a month. We spent a lot of time together in the war. He's in the regular army.'

'Millie!' Willis had put out a hand to greet her, but now he bent to kiss her cheek as well. 'How are you?' He was a large rugged-looking man wearing the uniform of the Military Police with three sergeant's stripes on his arms.

'Of course,' Andrew said, 'you know each other. I should have remembered that you might.'

'We do.' Millie smiled. 'Jeff is a Maynard relative.'

'On the poor side of the family, a sort of third cousin,' he grinned, 'but Pete and I were good friends. I miss him, Millie.'

'I do too.' She wished she could say that more easily without having to fight off tears. 'You were Pete's favourite cousin.'

As they pulled out the chairs to sit down, Willis did too and went on, 'I thought at first my old mate Andrew had found himself a girlfriend.'

'Millie is my boss,' he protested awkwardly.

'I take it he's making the grade with you?' Jeff asked.

'Why yes.' Millie wondered what he meant by 'making the grade' and said, 'He's doing a good job for us.' She knew a flush was running up her cheeks.

'When Pete said his accountant was retiring and that he

needed to find a new one,' Jeff said, 'I recommended Andrew.'

'I didn't know that,' he retorted. 'When I was demobbed you threw me an advert torn from a newspaper and said I should apply.'

'Well, I couldn't guarantee Pete would take you on, could I?' he said. 'But I knew you both and thought you'd suit each other. And you needed to settle down in civilian life, didn't you?'

It was obvious that they'd forged a strong bond of friendship and trust during the war years. They began to talk about war surplus goods. She'd read an article in the newspaper this morning about the government being defrauded of much of the value.

'Does your work involve searching out fraudsters like that?' she wanted to know.

'No, worse luck,' Willis said, 'my job isn't nearly so interesting. I bring in the squaddies who get drunk and start fighting in pubs. Or it's petty crime, or car stealing.' He stood up. 'Right, it's back to the coal face for me. I'll see you next week, Andrew.' He smiled at Millie. 'Glad to see you looking better and I hope things continue to pick up for you. By the way, I recommend the rabbit stew. It was excellent today.'

Millie had hoped Sylvie was settling down at last. Andrew had assured her yet again that her daughter's behaviour was perfectly normal and her work well up to standard. Denis had taken her dancing on two consecutive Saturday nights and she'd come home in a happier frame of mind. But that evening she had a real flare-up at Kenny.

After supper had been cleared away, Millie was watching Kenny set up his train set on the nursery floor while Simon unearthed scenery and additional carriages from a collection of old boxes. Spread out everywhere were engines, rolling stock and station buildings once owned by their forebears, some of which were damaged or broken. It was Simon who asked Sylvie to help them set out the scenery round the track.

Millie liked to see them all playing together and it pleased her when Sylvie got down on the floor to join in, but she was more interested in the rolling stock than the scenery. She tried for some time to link up a long line of old coal trucks and cattle trucks to a newer engine.

'That won't work,' Kenny told her.

'It will, I've done it. It's a much longer train than yours.'

She set the engine to run and in less than two yards it had uncoupled from the trucks and went chugging away on its own. Kenny laughed and clapped his hands. 'I told you it wouldn't work,' he chortled.

Sylvie tried again. 'It's just a question of linking it on.'

'It won't,' he said. 'They're made by different makers. The coupling doesn't quite match.'

Sylvie leapt to her feet, kicking over the station in her haste. 'It's just old rubbish. I don't know why I waste my time doing this,' and ran upstairs in a storm of tears.

Kenny looked up at his mother in alarm. 'What have I said? What's the matter with her?'

'It's not you, love.' Millie put down her book and followed Sylvie upstairs to try and comfort her. She could see that her daughter was far from being back to normal, whatever others might tell her.

At work the next day, it occurred to Millie in the middle of doing a routine job in the lab that instead of waiting for Nigel and Marcus to think up another plan to do her down, there was no reason why she shouldn't go on the attack, get them on the run for a change. She picked up the internal phone and asked Andrew what he planned to do at lunchtime.

'Nothing special, I've brought my usual sandwich to eat here.'

'I need more of your advice,' she said. 'I'd like to join you.'

'I'll be very pleased to have your company,' he told her, 'but I hope you're not looking at trouble again.'

'Not exactly, it's different this time.'

When she went along to his office at half twelve, he'd arranged for a pot of tea to be brought up for them. 'Has Marcus had another swipe at you?' he asked.

'No, but I think he and Nigel must be working on something. Marcus is always going out, but what does he find to do? They must be up to something. It's like a weight hanging over my head, and I've heard attack is the best form of defence. What can I do to worry them?'

'What d'you mean?'

'You understand the legal set-up of companies and the money side better than I do, what can I do to upset them in the way they do me?'

'Ah, you want to go on the offensive. You can offer to buy them out.'

Millie laughed. 'I don't have that sort of money.'

'But they won't know that, will they?'

'They might, Alec Douglas could have told them what happened over Pete's will.'

'He won't have. Although Douglas acts for the company and James discusses company affairs with them, matters relating to Pete's will are strictly private between you and him.'

'You're sure?'

'Yes, that would be professional practice. Though now the will is settled anybody can read it in Somerset House, but that won't tell them what transpired between you and the solicitor handling it.'

Millie thought it was all very complicated. 'What else could I do?'

'You could merge with another similar company. We were talking about it the other day, weren't we? You saw an advert from a small soap manufacturer wanting to do that.'

'Yes, it's still on my desk.'

'If you did that, it would give you a smaller share in a bigger business, and as it would dilute management it could make things easier for you.'

Millie smiled. 'I could discuss that with them.'

'It's not a bad idea. To double the size of the firm brings an advantage in scale.'

'It would bring new managers, wouldn't it? What if I can't get on with them?'

'You would. Or you could set up on your own. You have the experience to do that.'

'That would take even more money. Heavens, Andrew, I'd never have the nerve. Think of all the things that could go wrong for me.'

'Most of the staff would follow you. It would leave your in-laws without experienced staff, working in an old building that needs maintenance, and using outdated machinery and equipment. That could be a recipe for disaster.' He laughed. 'You'd survive longer than them, and once they went under you'd pick up their trade. You might make your fortune that way.'

'And pigs might fly. What would you recommend I do?'

'Seriously?' He pulled a face. 'I don't think I'd recommend any of those things. I was just outlining the possibilities. Stay as you are, and continue to push production as hard as you can.'

Millie felt disappointed. 'Perhaps I'll just threaten, and not do anything.'

'Millie, can't you see that that will get their backs up just as much? Don't do anything like that. You should try to get on better terms with them or at the very least lie low for a while and wait and see what happens. Perhaps they'll give up sniping at you.'

Millie tried to take his advice. She had a long discussion with Nigel about the importance of increasing production, and he seemed to take it on board and said he would do his best. It didn't quieten her fears.

Sylvie and her friends often went out for a walk at lunchtime and ate their sandwiches at the Pier Head but it was a cold, grey January day with a heavy dark sky and they decided to eat round their desks in the typing pool. They were chatting about boyfriends when Sylvie told them Denis had invited her to meet his family and spend the evening at his home, Connie said, 'For a boyfriend to invite you to meet his mother means he's serious.'

'Denis is always serious.'

'Serious about you, you nut,' they chorused. 'He must love you.'

'Denis? He's just a friend.'

'Well, I wish he'd be my friend,' Connie said and they all laughed. 'You said he'd asked if you'd be his girlfriend, that's not just being a friend. Doesn't he kiss you?'

'Yes.'

'Well then, don't you like being taken out by a boy-friend?'

'Yes, of course I do.' Sylvie enjoyed going out with him but hadn't thought any further ahead.

'Don't you want to get married?'

She did, of course she did, but she was in no hurry. 'I'll

wait until somebody really romantic comes along before I go that far,' she said. 'It'll have to be somebody special.'

'Denis is special,' Connie told her. 'He's lovely. And he's made up his mind about you, hasn't he?'

'He is good-looking,' another girl said.

'Handsome,' she was corrected. 'He's well thought of here, he'll go far. Good husband material and I bet he can be romantic.'

'My mother's always singing his praises,' Sylvie sighed, 'but that's a bit off-putting, isn't it?'

'No, don't be daft,' they chorused. 'Your problems start if your parents don't like your boyfriend.'

Having learned that her friends approved of Denis, Sylvie started to look at him in a different light. Perhaps, as Connie had said, she didn't know a good thing when it was staring her in the face.

Millie was pleased to see Sylvie taking a real interest in dressmaking, she always seemed to be sewing some garment these days.

'Mum, I'd love to have a sewing machine,' she said, 'for my birthday if not before. I'm desperately in need of one. I'd be able to get my dresses finished in half the time.'

The best Millie could do in these times of shortage was to take her to the sewing room and show her the one that had been in the house for decades.

'That must have come out of the ark,' Sylvie said. 'It's too old-fashioned. I can't work that treadle. I'd like a new hand sewing machine like Helen's.'

Simon laughed at her. 'There's nothing the matter with this one,' he said. 'I'll show you how it works.'

'I could show you how it works too,' Kenny piped up. 'I've had a go.' He fetched his toy boats to show her. 'This schooner was Grandpa's and half the sails were missing and I wanted red sails on this yacht so we made all these on that machine.'

Simon said, 'Give me those two bits of your cloth.' He sat down at the machine and stitched them together in a moment. His stitching was neat and even. 'If we can make sails for boats on it, you'll have no trouble making dresses.'

Sylvie looked embarrassed to hear her young brothers say that. Millie blessed them for doing it but said, 'It's cold in here. Why don't we lift it into the playroom where Sylvie can use it in comfort?' Her children used the playroom quite a lot and there was a gas fire there.

Helen was Sylvie's mentor when it came to dressmaking, and they often spent time together sewing on Saturday afternoons. Denis was collecting her regularly from Helen's house to take her out on Saturday evenings.

Millie was pleased to see that at last her affair with Denis was blossoming and thought Sylvie's new contentment was mainly due to that. She could put Pete's accident out of her mind now she had other things in her life.

Marcus had done what Elvira had pressed him to do some time ago; he had rejoined the ring. Greg had welcomed him back with a good lunch and he'd met up with the ring in Leeds, Sheffield and Warrington and put in bids as instructed in rigged auctions. He'd ferried vehicles from one town to another and he'd been glad to have the money that it had generated. But today he'd met Greg at an auction in Manchester and he'd really put the fear of God into him.

'This afternoon, I want you to do something different,' he said. 'I'm going to drive you to a building estate where workmen are erecting prefabs. A lorry is due to deliver a load of white goods, refrigerators and cookers, that sort of thing. I want you to wait for it and stay out of sight of the workmen.' Marcus was primed with the make of the lorry and given several ignition keys and maps. 'The job is to drive it away from the site before it can be unloaded and take it to a warehouse in Leeds.'

Marcus gasped with shock but Greg ignored that and went on, 'I want you to take off that suit and put on this pullover and dungarees so you look like another workman. Make sure you know the quickest way out of the estate.'

Cold and frightened, Marcus tried to blend into the background as he waited for an hour. By that time he was shaking like a leaf but luck was on his side when the lorry drove on to the site. The driver jumped out with a clipboard of papers and went off, presumably to look for the foreman, leaving everything open for him. It was easier than he'd expected but it was the first job he'd done that was blatant theft and it terrified him.

When he'd delivered the loaded lorry to a garage six miles away, he was given the keys of a large Ford car that had just been re-sprayed, re-registered and given a new set of number plates, and asked to drive that back to a garage in Liverpool. It had been nearly two in the morning when he found the garage and, as he'd expected, it was closed. He'd been told to park in the street outside, push the documents and keys through the letter box and take himself off quietly.

The problem then was that his only means of getting home was shank's pony. Public transport stopped running early these days, and the fuel allowance that taxi drivers could claim was easily used up. He knew he was near the docks and closer to the factory than to his home. It made sense to go straight there.

He had keys to the office but needed to avoid the night-watchman. Using his torch he crept straight up to his room in the turret without showing much light. He hadn't eaten since lunchtime and was hungry, and he'd have loved a cup of tea but didn't know how to go about making it here. He found his gabardine mac hanging on his coat stand and, using it as a blanket, slumped on his chair and put his feet up on another. He managed to sleep fitfully until he heard the factory below him come to life.

Wearing the gabardine to cover his dungarees, he crept out of the office and caught a bus into town where he could get a taxi to take him home. He kept it waiting while he washed his face and changed into another suit and was back in the office showing himself to Nigel and several of the senior staff to get kudos for coming to work early. He'd never enjoyed tea more than the first cup that morning. He asked for biscuits but must have sounded disappointed when he heard they had none, because the woman in the kitchen made him a slice of toast with a scraping of jam on it.

It gave him satisfaction then to ring Greg and let him know he'd had no problems carrying out the tasks he'd been set. Greg promised him more work and said he'd be in touch.

Marcus was missing Elvira and wanted to persuade her to return as soon as possible. He rang her family home several times but it was the housekeeper who picked up the phone, and she said each time, 'Mrs Maynard is not at home this morning.'

When Marcus asked when she'd be back, she said she didn't know. He also wanted to retrieve his car. He needed it, so he could leave it in a convenient place to drive home when he did another job for Greg. He went home at lunchtime and fell asleep on his bed but that evening when he tried again to ring Elvira it was her brother, Cecil, who answered. He was always friendly, but the result was the same. Marcus was toying with the idea of ringing again and telling Cecil that he'd come over to collect his car, but he was too tired to think of doing that tonight.

Marcus now regretted leaving the ring nine months ago. If he'd kept his nerve and stayed, he'd have accumulated enough money to buy a house by now and Elvira would still be with him. Without her, he was feeling lost and near to the end of his tether.

One afternoon a week later, Millie was working quietly in the lab when she became aware of unusual noises not very far away. 'What's that?' she asked Denis. 'What's happening?'

'Sounds like a . . .'

Millie had already reached the lab door; as soon as she had it open she realised there was a skirmish going on in a nearby office. She shot down the corridor towards it with Denis at her heels, and stopped appalled at the open door of Billy Sankey's cubbyhole of an office.

Marcus was spreadeagled on the floor bleeding profusely, and Andrew Worthington who had got there before her was pulling Billy away from him.

'Have they been fighting?' she asked. Of course they had, a chair had been overturned and there were documents spread across the floor.

Half the people in the office had gathered in the corridor and were watching open-mouthed as Andrew helped Marcus to his feet. Billy was dancing with rage and shouted, 'He started this. He came to my office and waved his fists at me.'

Millie turned to Tom Bedford who appeared beside her. 'Please take Billy somewhere quiet and calm him down,' she said.

But Billy wasn't ready to leave yet. 'That man's a bloody maniac.'

Struggling for breath, Marcus glowered round at them all and dabbed gingerly at his nose which was bleeding. His shirt and tie had gleaming bright red stains.

'What was all that about?' Millie wanted to know.

'You said Billy was efficient,' Marcus sneered. 'Ten days

ago I asked him to get me some stationery and he still hasn't produced it. If I'm to work I have to have it.'

Billy was furious. 'You ordered three leatherbound notebooks,' he stormed at him. 'Everybody knows all that fancy stuff is going for export. I'd told him if he really wanted them I'd try. I've got somebody working on it, but tapping into the export trade can't be done overnight.'

'He was very rude.' Marcus was flushed with rage.

'He called me a lazy bastard,' Billy screamed. 'I'm not having that. I showed him our stock of ordinary notebooks but they aren't good enough for the likes of him. Leather covers are essential.'

'He's like a wild animal with his fists.'

Tom finally got Billy moving away. He called over his shoulder, 'He's all fighting words but he won't square up. You're a bloody coward, Mr Maynard.'

Millie raised her voice above the hubbub. 'It's all over now. Please all of you go back to your desks and get on with your work.'

She and Nigel half dragged Marcus into the boardroom and sat him down. He slumped back, struggling for breath.

'Don't ever do that again,' Millie ground out between clenched teeth. 'You're not in the army now. You've got to learn to handle people properly if you want to go on working here.'

'Billy Sankey went for me,' he puffed. 'He's a rough customer, an uncontrollable thug.'

'If you leave Billy alone, he'll do a good job,' Millie told him. 'They all do. You're upsetting people and disrupting the work here. There has never been a brawl in the office before, certainly not in the last eighteen years, and we're not going to have another.' She paused for breath. 'Is that understood?'

Marcus grunted which could have meant anything.

'I'll leave you to handle this,' she said to Nigel and went back to the peace of the lab.

It took her a long time to calm down enough to be able to get on with her work. She'd barely accomplished anything when she heard the lab door open and footsteps coming towards her. It was Nigel.

'I'm sorry, Millie,' he said. 'You'll have to forgive Marcus.'

She didn't feel ready to do that yet. 'He behaved out-rageously.'

'Make allowances for him, I mean. He's in a bit of a state.'

'I can see that.'

'I mean he has problems at home. Living with Father isn't easy, he says it's made Elvira ill. She's gone to visit her father just to get away. They're both desperate to have a place of their own. Marcus isn't himself at the moment.'

'Oh dear. But why does he have to fuss about having expensive notebooks? There's a paper shortage and we're allocated only so much and it isn't good quality, but if it was good enough for Pete to make notes on, it should be OK for Marcus. Leather covers indeed! We can't afford to buy fancy goods like that for the office. I take it the office has quietened down?'

'Yes, they're all back at their desks.'

'I do wonder whether Marcus wants to go on working here. He's tried it once before, I believe, and given up.'

'Yes, but it wouldn't help if he had to start job-hunting now. Give him another chance, Millie, please. I think he'll settle down eventually.'

She shrugged. 'Let's hope he does.'

At lunchtime, Millie met Marcus at the front door. His glance was malevolent and he looked uncomfortable as he said, 'I apologise, Millie, for my part in causing that fracas. I have already apologised to Billy Sankey.'

'In that case,' she said, 'I accept it and hope we don't have to mention this affair again.'

'Thank you,' he said stiffly.

Sylvie began to feel she was getting together enough new clothes to feel smart when she went out with Denis. The popularity of the New Look was spreading like wildfire across the country, and Sylvie and the girls in the office embraced it wholesale. It was so different from the old styles that it made last year's wardrobe almost unwearable. Women's magazines were full of ideas to lengthen skirts by six inches. Sylvie unpicked and remade several of her dresses.

But Princess Elizabeth was keeping to the old knee-length skirts and had even worn them on her honeymoon. The girls in the office thought she looked unfashionable and totally out of date, but Helen said she did it because the government had let it be known it considered the New Look to be a wicked waste of cloth in these difficult times and had berated women for following ephemeral fashions.

Sylvie had given up eating her lunchtime sandwiches with Connie and Louise, now she spent the time with Denis. Sometimes they went to the Pier Head and sometimes walked to a little park, with sooty shrubs and more bare earth than grass. If it was wet she joined him at his desk in the lab though she knew her mother was sometimes at her desk at the other end of the room hidden by high racks holding flasks, bottles and drums.

She felt she was really getting to know Denis and the more she saw of him, the better she liked him. He took her out every Saturday and every Sunday, and usually on one night in the week. Mum got iffy about her having late nights in the week so she couldn't see more of him. She'd told Sylvie she must not get too tired to do her work properly.

One Sunday, she'd been out with Denis all afternoon and

as he'd walked her home that night he'd said, 'I think I'm falling in love with you.'

Sylvie felt heat rush up her cheeks and was glad it was too dark for him to see. She reached up to kiss him. 'I'm so glad you love me, so happy.'

He was hesitant. 'Do you think you could love me?'

'Oh I do. I really do.'

His arm tightened round her waist. 'That's wonderful. Will you wait for me? I'll have to do my National Service soon, but after that . . .'

'Of course, for you I could wait for ever.'

She felt she was walking on air for a week or two after that. Denis loved her and she was head over heels in love with him. Her mother remarked on how much happier she seemed but she couldn't tell her the reason, it was a secret between her and Denis. She hugged it to her and he admitted he didn't want to talk about it to anybody else. Not yet.

Chapter Twenty-Two

Marcus had been doing several jobs each week for Greg Livingstone, and Nigel had asked him why he was never at his desk in the office, and that had scared him. He'd not arrived home last night from Barrow until after midnight and he felt tired out. He'd spent only an hour at his desk this morning when Greg Livingstone rang him.

He hadn't expected to hear from him again so soon and didn't feel ready to do another job for him, but he didn't want to put Greg off and instead of refusing he said, 'I'm shattered. I haven't recovered from the last job yet. I hope it's not another long drive.'

'It's a bit further than Barrow,' he replied. 'But do this job and if you prefer shorter trips I'll keep you in mind for them in future.'

Marcus had already decided his best plan was to work just long enough to get enough money to buy a house, and then distance himself from Greg and everybody in that ring.

'I want you to drive a van from Liverpool to Manchester tomorrow to be re-sprayed.'

'All right.'

'At the garage you deliver it to, they have a lorry on which they've done their work.'

'It'll be empty?'

'Yes, it'll look clean and there'll be a full set of documents for it. It's going for export, so it needs to be driven to the docks at Harwich. Then take the train back to Manchester and the same garage will give you a car to bring back to Liverpool.'

Marcus hesitated. 'It'll take hours to get to Harwich and back,' he said. He was nervous about absenting himself from the office for long periods when he was supposed to be working, but he agreed to do the job. At least he wouldn't have to steal these vehicles though he knew they'd all be stolen property.

He tried to ring Elvira, he wanted to tell her how much money he'd saved towards their house, but he got the housemaid again and had to put it off until evening when her family would be home. As soon as Pa went out that evening, he tried to phone Elvira again. It was Cecil who picked up the receiver. There had to be a few pleasantries but when Marcus asked to speak to Elvira, he said, 'She's moved out, didn't you know? She told us she was hoping to move into a place of her own.'

Marcus felt the strength drain from his legs. 'Where has she gone? Did she leave an address?'

'Only to Liverpool,' he said. 'She left her phone number and it's right here.'

Marcus took the little notebook from his breast pocket in which he recorded contact numbers, and Greg's instructions for the jobs he wanted done. He wrote down the number as Cecil dictated it and it seemed familiar. Why hadn't she told him she was looking for a place of her own in Liverpool? Why would she need it when she'd said she'd come back to live with him?

Once he'd put the phone down he flicked back the pages and compared the new phone number with the one on which he'd rung Greg Livingstone. They were one and the same.

It bowled him over and made him gulp with distress, but he'd long been suspicious of Elvira's relationship with Greg.

251

She'd threatened to work for him if he refused to do it, but he'd felt for a long time that there was more to it than that. Did this mean she was living with him? It sounded very much like it, but he had no idea where Greg lived, only that he had a Liverpool phone number. Marcus felt sick.

He reached for the phone book and flicked through it to find Greg's number because it also gave subscribers' addresses, but the number wasn't listed, it was ex-directory. He flung the book on the floor. Anyway, for all he knew, Greg could be using that as an office and be living somewhere else.

He felt in a flat spin. He had only the vaguest idea of what was expected of him in the family business. There was no point in pushing papers about his desk. He would go to the Sailor's Return and have a drink. Perhaps a whisky would clear his head.

An hour later he felt just as fuzzy. He went home and went to bed. If Elvira did not mean to return to him, he didn't know what he'd do. He needed her. He had to have somebody in his life. Pa was an irritation and Nigel had always been a pain.

He would do the job tomorrow in order to keep open the arrangements he'd made with Elvira, but he had to speak to her. He had to know what she meant to do, and whether she was prepared to return to live with him as his wife. If she wasn't, there was no point in him doing anything. He might as well give up.

Marcus lost his way twice when he was taking the lorry to the docks at Harwich, so the journey took even longer than he'd expected. But a dock worker showed him where he could get a meal and he managed to sleep on the train going back to Manchester. His head still felt woolly and he'd had a little weep, because he was afraid he might lose Elvira, but he was still coping, just.

When he'd picked up the car he was to take to Liverpool, he decided to drive straight home and sleep in his own bed. He'd get up early in the morning and deliver the car to the garage before going to work. He had no wish to spend another night on his office chair.

It was dark and getting late, and he got lost again when he was coming into Liverpool. It was a stupid thing to do because he'd spent most of his life here and prided himself on knowing his way around. He was tired again now, and the suburban streets were confusing, he needed to look at his street map.

He was passing a row of shops and over the post office he caught the name of the district; he was in Gateacre and knew he was not far from home. He slowed down, slid past a parked black Jaguar that reminded him of his own and pulled into the kerb in front of it. He shone his torch on the street map and found his route home; he'd have no problem now. He reached for the bag of caramels he'd bought earlier and looked again at the car behind him. He had a strange feeling about it.

One of the good things about the post-war world was that there were very few cars on the road and new ones were quite rare. He got out to stretch his legs and take a closer look at the car. One glance at the number plate told him it was indeed his own. His head began to reel and he had to lean against the car to stay upright. Elvira must be very near.

This was a good-class area, mostly houses built just before the war, but within yards was a rather grand block of flats. Had she found herself a place here? But Elvira didn't like flats, she wouldn't have chosen to live in one, would she? Greg Livingstone had separated from his wife some years ago, so he might live in a flat. Elvira must have moved in with him! That was what Marcus feared and wasn't this proof of exactly that?

His stomach was heaving and he knew he was going to be sick. He bent over the gutter to retch and retch, but little came up, his stomach was empty. He wiped his face on his handkerchief and looked at his watch. It was eleven o'clock and the streets were empty. He was angry now, really angry. Why wouldn't Elvira talk to him, tell him truthfully what she intended to do?

He tried all the car doors but they were locked. Frustration rose in him, the car was his and he wanted it. He'd believed Elvira only intended to keep it for a few days, and she'd more than had her share of driving it now. He had a spare set of keys but they were at home. He'd fetch them. He was trying to do two jobs at once and he'd never needed the car more.

Marcus walked up to the main entrance of the block of flats and wrote down the name Blackwood Court that he saw written in gold script on a plaque near the front door. Then he slowly drove the car he was delivering to the end of the road and wrote down the name, Bridlington Rise, that he saw there. Just to be sure, he marked the place on his street map. He meant to come back and get his car.

He went home as he'd planned, and before getting into bed he found his set of spare car keys and put them into his jacket pocket so as to be ready. He was desperately afraid Elvira had left him for good and hardly slept a wink that night, but he was up early and delivered the car to the garage just as it was opening, and asked the proprietor if he could give him a lift to Gateacre.

One of the garage hands got into the car he'd just delivered and drove him there. Marcus fingered the keys in his pocket feeling full of anticipation, he'd soon be sitting in his own car again and this job would be easier.

The place looked a little different in the cold light of morning and he couldn't at first see his car, but here he was in Bridlington Rise and there was Blackwood Court. He got out and gave the lad a tip for his trouble. Now where exactly was his car?

It took him a few moments to realise it had gone. He felt a huge void in his stomach as he walked past the block of flats, then to the end of the road and back. People were getting up to go to work. His car was definitely not here.

It was very bad news in one sense but did it mean Elvira had just been visiting? Maybe she'd spent the evening here; it had felt like the middle of the night to him but it had been before midnight. Marcus walked on until he came to a bus stop and shortly afterwards he caught a bus to the Pier Head and from there walked to the office. He rang Greg Livingstone to tell him he'd completed his tasks without incident and asked if he'd seen Elvira. 'No,' he said, 'not for some time.'

Marcus didn't believe him. 'She took my car and I can't manage without one. If you see her, tell her I really need to speak to her.'

There was a slight pause before Greg said, 'I can get you a car. There's a Morris Twelve coming up.'

Marcus sighed, knowing that would be a re-sprayed military vehicle bought cheaply at auction or one that had been stolen. Pa would have a fit if he thought he was parking a stolen car outside his front door. 'I suppose that'll have to do if I can't get another Jag.'

'OK,' Greg said easily. 'Let me know,' and went on to offer him several short trips around Lancashire and Cheshire.

The Jaguar that Elvira had taken had been bought new, and he'd had to pay well over the advertised price to get it, as most cars being made had to be exported. At the end of the war, all British car manufacturers had rushed back into production with their old pre-war models but Marcus knew Jaguar had been working on a brand new design that was said to be an absolute corker. He'd put his name down on the list to buy one as soon as it became available.

Now, he picked up his phone again and asked when it might be available and was surprised and delighted to hear it could be as soon as the end of the month. He confirmed he was ready to take delivery, having read in the press that due to scarcity, new models of the Jaguar XK120 were being resold on the open market at a big mark-up in price, though he meant to keep his.

'What colour do you want? There's a choice between oyster white or ice blue with a metallic finish.'

Marcus had never seen a metallic finish but it sounded exotic and very desirable. 'Ice blue,' he decided.

That lifted his mood. He needed a car and had the money to pay for it. Why worry that he'd have to work for Greg a little longer before he could buy a house? He deserved a treat after the trials of the last weeks.

Millie felt little had changed between her and her in-laws. Nigel was avoiding her, he'd settled into the grand boardroom office and she hoped he was taking over some of the duties of management. Marcus scowled at her if he met her about the corridors, though she saw very little of him. He'd caused no more fights but he'd become the centre of attention again because he'd come to work in a fantastic new car.

It was the sort of car that most people could only dream about, and nothing like it had been seen on the roads before. Its shape was pleasing and very different, and its engine was said to outclass everything else. It was capturing the export market in both Europe and America.

As soon as Marcus left it in the car park a crowd gathered round it to take a closer look. It caught the eye of sailors and workmen as they were walking along the road and they stood for a moment to admire it through the fence. A few even came inside. Tom Bedford and Albert Lancaster drooled with envy.

Millie wondered how he could suddenly afford it when Nigel had said he was unable to afford a house of his own. Was he earning money from somewhere else? He was so frequently absent from his desk in the office here that it seemed more than likely. Her curiosity was growing.

She thought Sylvie was much brighter than she used to be. She came in one Sunday evening and said, 'Denis has been asking me for ages if I'll go home with him. His mother thinks he should take me to be introduced. I've been invited to have a meal there on Wednesday evening and I said I would.'

That seemed to Millie an indication that the relationship was progressing favourably and that Denis was attaching importance to it. 'He was a bit worried about whether he should ask you too, but I told him no. You wouldn't think it wrong for me to go on my own.'

'No, but you mustn't be too late coming home because you'll both have to get up for work the next day.'

'I won't. Denis said to tell you that he'll see me safely home.'

Wednesday turned out to be a dark miserable morning, too cold to hang about at the bus stop, and as Millie had a few petrol coupons in hand she decided to drive to work. Today, Marcus was pulling into the car park just ahead of her, so for once he'd arrived on time.

She met Albert Lancaster on the front steps and he said, 'Come and see the talcum powder we made yesterday. It's as good as pre-war, a lovely soft slippery feel to it. You'll like it.'

She knew Billy Sankey had set up a new supplier of white magnesium silicate for them, as well as regular deliveries of powdered soapstone. She followed him into the factory to see it.

'A big improvement, we have to be pleased with that,' she said.

They were currently selling talc in stiff cardboard sprinkler cartons but Albert was hopeful that soon they'd be able to package it in tins as they had before the war.

'Billy Sankey assures me that he's found a firm who'll be able to make and supply the tins, so we need to decide on the shape and colour we want so he can negotiate a price.' Albert took her upstairs to his office and opened some of their old design books on his desk. 'What d'you reckon?'

Millie thought that perhaps they should go back to their old design, it sold well, but she took Albert and his pattern book along the corridor to Dan Quentin's office to hear what he thought would best help it to sell in the present market.

It was so cold that she leaned against the lukewarm radiator under the window that overlooked the car park while they decided to keep the old shape and the flower picture but have it against a pale cream background. Dan and Albert had got as far as discussing the wording for the logo they'd have printed on the tins when a movement outside caught Millie's attention.

It was less than an hour since she'd seen Marcus arrive but now he was heading back to his car. He got in and started the engine. Hastily she excused herself and ran down to the car park, meaning to follow him to see where he was going. She jumped in her car and as she drove out on to the road she could see he'd been held up at the traffic lights some hundred yards further along.

She blessed the fact that he'd acquired such a fancy car. He was easy to follow because traffic was light and most of the cars were black and of pre-war shape, as was her own. That allowed her to stay some distance behind him as she didn't want Marcus to see her. He was heading into the centre of Liverpool. She decided he must definitely be working for someone else and he didn't want her to know.

She found he'd parked his car near Exchange Station and was heading inside. He had no luggage so was he meeting somebody off a train? Hurriedly she parked her car well away from his and made her way into the station.

There were a lot of people about so it wasn't as easy to pick him out now, and she didn't want him to see her before she saw him. Yes, there he was buying a ticket, so where was he going? She hung back watching him from a distance. He bought a newpaper and then headed towards one of the platforms. She saw him get on the train that was waiting there. It would take him to Southport or any of the many stations on the way.

She went back to her car feeling she'd learned precious little. She couldn't imagine what he intended to do in Southport. It was definitely not the weather for a trip to the beach.

All morning it grew darker and the heavy cloud developed a yellowish tinge. Millie kept a watch on the car park but Marcus's car did not return. Immediately after lunch it began to snow, and as it was settling on the ground and building up on the roofs, Millie saw it as yet another problem. She rang the bus depot to see if the buses were continuing to run, because that was what Pete had done in the past. When she heard that they were still running but there was some doubt as to how long they could continue, she went to see Nigel and suggested they close the factory and office early and let the staff get off home.

'I agree,' he said, locking up his desk. 'It looks quite nasty. Better if we get off home while we can.' He made all haste to do that, leaving her to tell everybody else. Millie did so, going slowly along the corridor of offices occupied by their senior staff.

When she reached Andrew Worthington's office, she found Sylvie there taking dictation. He said, 'You go, Sylvie, there's nothing urgent amongst those letters.'

'Thanks, Mr Worthington.' She closed her notebook.

Millie said, 'You haven't chosen a good day to go home with Denis, the buses will stop running if this carries on.'

'Mum! Please don't stop me now.' Sylvie was keen to go. 'I'll be all right.'

Millie went to the window, it was snowing heavily and the sky was now pewter grey and leaden. 'It's not much after three o'clock and look at this. What will it be like by nightfall? What if you can't get home?' She glanced up to find Andrew's dark green eyes watching her sympathetically.

'I'll walk if I have to. What does Denis say?'

'Nothing to me, why would he?' Millie didn't want to discuss Sylvie with Denis. She felt what they did was their business and preferred to wait until she was told.

'I'll go and talk to him now. Goodnight, Mr Worthington.' Sylvie sped towards the lab while Millie followed at a more leisurely pace.

When she caught them up, Denis said, 'Please let her come, Mrs Maynard. My mother . . . Well, she was going to bake.'

Millie hesitated. 'She'll have gone to a lot of trouble, won't she?'

'I'll see her to your door, I promise.' He looked so intense, so full of hope that she knew she couldn't say no. 'I'll make sure she gets home safely.'

'All right, but early please. This isn't a night to be out late.'

'Thank you, thank you.' Both were all smiles now and went off together.

Millie slumped on to her desk chair. Moments later she heard footsteps coming up the lab.

'I take it you agreed?' It was Andrew. 'I saw them rushing off together in great excitement.'

'I hope I've done the right thing.'

'I'm sure you have. They're old enough to be responsible for what they do. You can't look after Sylvie for the rest of your life.'

'No, I hope I don't have to.'

'You'll be on your own at home tonight.'

She nodded. 'Yes.'

'That's what I thought, I'm glad I've caught you. Why don't you spend the evening with me? We'll have a drink and then a meal.'

Millie was taken aback. She hadn't been out with a man for years, not on a prearranged evening date. She was a grieving widow.

He said, 'I've been meaning to ask you for ages, and if you're to be alone tonight this seems a good time to do it. After all, I enjoyed your hospitality on bonfire night; you must allow me to ask you out in return.'

She smiled. 'Thank you, I'd like to go out with you.' For once she felt a bit shy of him but reminded herself that Andrew was a colleague, so it wasn't like a real date. 'It's not much fun waiting alone for a teenage daughter to return home.'

'Well, I've already arranged to have a drink with Jeff Willis at the Sailor's Return, across the road, so I'll need to take you there first. But you know him.'

'Yes, I like him, talking to him is always interesting.'

'Then you and I will go on for a meal afterwards.'

Millie went to the window. The snow was still swirling down. She could see the Sailor's Return on the other side of the shabby street, though she'd rarely been inside. At street level it had the usual rather noisy bar but upstairs was a large lounge where in cold weather an open fire roared up the chimney. Pete had occasionally had a drink there with one or other of the managers and said he thought the premises had been arranged to attract the local workforce. They certainly patronised it in large numbers.

'I need ten minutes to clear my desk and lock up for the night,' he said.

'So do I, but I won't be ready then, I told Tom Bedford I'd make sure the whole place was secured for the night.'

'OK. Give me ten minutes and I'll come back and walk round with you,' Andrew said. 'I ought to know how to lock the place up.'

For the first time, Millie really thought about Andrew. She'd been accepting his support and advice for some time and counted him a friend, but she knew virtually nothing about him. Pete had been impressed with his war service but she'd not asked, and he'd volunteered little. She should have shown more interest.

Chapter Twenty-Three

Andrew had been spending a lot of time thinking about Millie and felt he'd taken a great step forward in persuading her to spend the evening with him. By the time they were crossing the road, it was really dark and the snow was four inches deep. He took her arm as it was rutted and slippery. 'I hope this isn't going to stick on the streets for days,' he said.

The pub lounge was a warm and cheery place and he recognised some of the customers as Maynard's staff, despite being released to go home early on account of the weather. Andrew saw his friend waiting for him in front of the fire.

'Good, you've brought Millie with you.' Jeff beamed at her. 'Come and get a warm, Millie. How are you?' He settled her in the chair nearest the blaze and Andrew went to get their drinks.

It pleased him that they seemed to have plenty to say to each other but when he returned and put the glass of lemonade she'd asked for in her hand, it brought the flow to a halt.

Andrew said, 'I believe I owe my life to Jeff,' and that started Jeff telling her how they'd escaped from Singapore together when it fell to the Japanese. Andrew had not enjoyed the experience but Jeff had relished it and was happy to sit back and talk.

His huge bulk overhung the chair. Millie smiled at him. 'Pete told me about your wartime experiences, he was very impressed. I gather you had an exciting time.'

'I wouldn't describe it as exciting,' Jeff said drily. 'We were on the run from the Japanese for ten months. We had to go native and live on the beach.'

'I was terrified most of the time,' Andrew told her. 'I wouldn't have survived on my own.'

Jeff was beginning to hold forth. 'When the British surrendered, we decided we'd rather make a run for it than be rounded up and sent to Changi prison for the duration.'

'Yes, I and my friend Graham had made all sorts of preparations, drew out money from the bank, and packed a few clothes. We'd seen the European civilians scrambling to get out but we left it too late.'

'His friend Graham was killed.' Jeff's voice was matter-of-fact.

Millie looked appalled. 'That's terrible, how did it happen?'

'To start with we tried to get passages to a British port but the liners had all left by then, so had all the freighters, filled to capacity. We met up on our first night when we all hid in the same warehouse on the quay. Jeff speaks a little Malay and negotiated with several hundred cigarettes and treble the standard fare to get all three of us as deck passengers on a local junk bound for Jakarta.'

Jeff took up the tale. 'We cast off in a hail of shells and small-arms fire, but the master was determined that nothing would stop his vessel leaving. A bullet caught Graham in the back of his head and he collapsed at our feet, there was nothing we could do for him. He wasn't the only one, two other passengers and a sailor were also killed, and several were injured. Once out to sea the master ordered his crew to throw the bodies overboard.'

That had been the first time Andrew had been under fire

and experienced deadly danger. His neck had crawled with fear and he'd been very glad of Jeff's support. He felt sick as he remembered how he'd done his best to say a prayer over his friend before his body was committed to the sea. He'd had to write to Graham's parents after he'd got home and that had been painful too. Jeff had more stoicism, though they'd had little to say to each other that day. They didn't find out they both came from Liverpool for some time.

'It was not a luxury voyage,' Jeff said, sitting back with his glass of beer in his hand. 'There were twelve other deck passengers, mostly Malays and Chinese. At night it was cold and we lay down on deck to sleep under an old sail. During the day we were hot and sweaty and had nothing but a bucket of seawater to wash in and there was little shelter from the hot sun, but we had enough local food to avoid feeling hungry and we were evading capture. The boat made slow progress. Occasionally an enemy plane came over, circled to look at us but left us alone.'

'You must have been petrified,' Millie said.

'We were both pretty much on edge,' Jeff agreed, 'suffering from prickly heat, indigestion and more than a touch of gastro-enteritis. When we reached Jakarta we felt the same oppressive dread that the Japanese were approaching and would soon engulf the city. Shops and homes were already being abandoned. We took a room in a shabby hotel on the waterfront while we tried to find some way out of the place. We were aiming for Australia by then.

'We knew the Japanese were moving quickly but we no longer had access to a wireless and met nobody who could speak English, so we had no idea how near the enemy was. It took us a week or so to get on a junk heading for Bali. We intended to wait there until we could pick up a vessel to take us to Australia, but the Japanese were in control of the sea lanes so there was less shipping of any sort.

'It seemed safer to hire a canoe to take us to Lombok, a nearby island that was much less developed, because the Japanese tended to occupy the towns and didn't always penetrate the jungle areas beyond. Once there, we walked several miles out of the little town to live on the beach. The local fishermen fed us and showed us how to build a shelter and we spent our days helping them push their canoes into the waves and haul in their catch.'

Andrew met Millie's gaze. 'When I've told people that, they often say, "You must have enjoyed it. It would be like a long holiday, wouldn't it?" But as the months passed and we grew bored, it felt as though we'd be there for ever.'

'We spent hours telling each other about our homes and our families,' Jeff said.

Andrew felt, as things turned out, that he'd said far too much.

'We were both larger than the local men,' Jeff swept on, 'and stuck out like sore thumbs so we were scared of being picked up by the enemy. But we had no idea where they were, or whether that was likely or not until we met up with Hans, a Dutchman who came to the beach to barter his farm produce for fish. He spoke good English and as he also had a wireless he was able to tell us that the Dutch had surrendered and the Japanese now controlled Java and were advancing on through the islands of the Flores Sea towards New Guinea. We knew that by May, half of New Guinea had fallen to them. Hans was getting anxious about the safety of his wife and two small children.'

'How old were they?' Millie asked.

'Two and four. Then at last we had a stroke of luck. Hans heard that an Australian fishing boat had to put in to Lombok for repairs and would be heading back to Darwin. He arranged with the captain to take us there, together with his wife and children.'

'We were destitute,' Andrew said, 'but the Australian Army took care of us.' He remembered the enormous wave of relief he'd felt then. He'd lost a lot of weight and felt his physical endurance had been tested to the limit.

Jeff was very jovial. 'The first thing I did was to write to my wife to let her know I was safe. We were flown home on an Australian Air Force cargo flight.'

Jeff liked to talk about getting out of Asia; he saw it as a wartime adventure in his military career and he could give the tale a touch of drama. But then he'd returned home to a welcoming wife and family.

Andrew couldn't bear to think of it. He'd written to Annabel too but for him the tale didn't have a happy ending.

Just then he saw Marcus come into the pub with a sprinkling of snow on the shoulders of his overcoat. He took it off and sat down, and moments later the barman came with his drink. He hadn't noticed them yet but he was looking round and suddenly he leapt to his feet, snatched up the coat he'd taken off and rushed away, leaving his glass of whisky virtually untouched on the table before him.

Andrew wondered why, he'd seemed to be looking in their direction but surely catching sight of him and Millie here would not make him hare off and leave his drink? He guessed then that it was seeing Jeff that had made Marcus scarper. His uniform and booming voice made him stand out. Had Marcus not recognised Jeff Willis as his cousin, or had he not wanted to?

Later, before they left, Millie went to the ladies' cloakroom and Jeff said, 'I meant to ask you about Marcus Maynard. He belongs to the other side of the clan. How does he get on with Millie? Are they friendly? Do they pull together at work?'

'No, quite the opposite, he doesn't like her, doesn't think she's good enough to be a Maynard.'

Jeff laughed. 'We Willises aren't good enough for him either. He doesn't want to know us, but I gathered from Pete that even the true-blood Maynards have an occasional dust-up.'

'Funny you should mention Marcus. He came in here a short time ago and then went off in a hurry.'

'Well, it's near the business, isn't it?' They could see Millie coming back to join them and Jeff said, 'She's all right. You must bring her round to have a drink with us some time.'

It had stopped snowing, but four or five inches had settled on the road and was showing tyre ruts and footprints now. Andrew took Millie's arm to walk her back to the car park. 'We've got two cars,' she said. They had a covering of snow and were the only vehicles left.

'Safer to leave yours here tonight,' he said, trying the door handle to make sure it was locked. 'I'll run you home. Will you be able to get into work tomorrow? If the buses aren't running, ring me and I'll fetch you.'

He drove Millie slowly and carefully into town and they had dinner at the Stork Hotel in an almost empty dining room. Without Jeff's ready flow of boisterous conversation, Andrew was trying hard to find something to say. He should have paid more attention to her and not let Jeff take over the first part of the evening.

But sitting opposite Millie's smiling face cheered him up. This was what he'd wanted to do for a long time. She talked about her family and asked about his, but he couldn't bring himself to mention his personal difficulties. He felt on safer ground talking about the business.

She asked, 'What are you hearing about Nigel on the grapevine? Is it thought he's settling in and taking some responsibility for running the business?'

That made him smile. 'What they're saying is that you are doing that. It's you they go to when they've got a problem, not Nigel.'

'But does he do any useful work?'

'I don't know what he does. Better if you ask Tom or Arthur. I know they think Marcus is a complete waste of space. Mostly, when they have anything to say, it's to complain about him.'

'Yes, I'd like to sack Marcus but that would bring his father's wrath down on my head. I don't know what to do about him. What can you suggest?'

'I've absolutely no ideas to offer on that.' He laughed.

On the drive home she said, 'I'm sorry, I shouldn't bother you with these business problems. But I have nobody else who would understand and be able to help me.'

'Millie, it doesn't bother me in the least. In fact, I rather like it.'

At her garden gate she thanked him for what she called a very pleasant evening. He said, 'I'm afraid Jeff rather took over the early part.'

'That opened my eyes to how you spent the war. I don't suppose you would have told me half as much.'

She was right about that, he wouldn't have. He ached to take her in his arms, hug her and say, 'We've both had our losses and disappointments but let's put all that behind us. Together we could start afresh.'

But Millie gave no sign that she was interested in him, other than as a helpmate. She asked, 'Would you like to come in for a drink, a cup of tea? Or I do have cocoa.'

He wanted to say yes, he wanted to prolong this evening. But already she was looking away, her mind on other things. 'It doesn't look as though Sylvie is home yet.'

'Thank you but no,' he said. 'It's time I went home.'

He waited until her front door closed behind her and then drove off feeling he never would find anybody willing to share his life.

★ ★ ★

Denis's mother, Geraldine, welcomed Sylvie into the warmth of her home with a cup of tea and said, 'Denis's grandfather really took to your mother when she was a young apprentice like Denis is now. He said she was really interested in perfumes and seemed to retain everything he told her about them. Now she's done the same for Denis.'

Geraldine was a jolly person and had plenty to say; Sylvie liked her. What she said about times past in the lab reminded Sylvie that she had been born on her mother's eighteenth birthday. She decided she must be a slow starter because here she was at eighteen years of age having taken no interest in boys until now. Denis was her first boyfriend.

Savoury scents were coming from the kitchen making Sylvie's mouth water and later on she sat down to a meal of steak and kidney pie with roast potatoes and cabbage. At home, Sylvie refused to eat offal of any sort but felt she couldn't leave the kidney on her plate here, as Denis's mother might take it as an insult, especially in these times of shortage. She ate it and found it delicious. Perhaps she'd been wrong about that too.

At eight o'clock Denis opened the curtains to see what the weather was doing. 'It's stopped snowing,' he said, 'it's a lovely clear night now, but the snow's sticking.'

'Ring the bus depot,' his mother said, 'and find out if the buses are still running.'

The answer to that was no. 'I'll walk you home,' he said.

'Then you'd better start soon,' his mother said. 'It's some distance and you'll have to walk both ways. Why don't you phone your mother, Sylvie, and tell her you're setting out now? She could be worrying about you.'

Sylvie tried but her mother didn't pick up the phone. It rang and rang until she had to assume that she wasn't there. 'I wonder where she's gone on a night like this,' she said. 'She was worried about the snow.'

'Do you have a key?' Denis asked.

'Yes.'

'Then we'll make a start. She'll probably be there before we are.'

Geraldine insisted that Sylvie borrow her wellingtons and gave her a carrier bag to put her high-heeled court shoes in. She also provided extra socks and a warm scarf to wrap round her head. 'It'll be freezing hard by now.'

It was a lovely moonlit night and every roof and tree had its thick covering of crisp snow. There was almost no traffic and nobody about. Their footprints were the first on the pavements. It was a delight, the snow had transformed the mundane streets into a fairyland, but the wind was icy against Sylvie's cheeks and it was slippery underfoot.

'Take care,' Denis warned, and Sylvie felt his arm go round her waist to steady her. 'I've got to get you home in one piece, haven't I?' She smiled and he stopped to kiss her. She could see love, adoration almost, in his dark eyes. She shivered with delight and put up her face to be kissed again. Whatever had made her think Denis wasn't romantic?

Their progress was slow and it took more than an hour to reach her home. 'Mum's home now,' she said. The lights were on in the hall and as they watched they saw the light go on in the kitchen. Denis gathered Sylvie in his arms to kiss her a final goodnight, but she kept him with her for another half hour and by then they both felt very cold.

'Come on in,' she said, 'I could make you a hot drink to warm you up before you walk back.' She felt him hesitate. 'Come on,' she urged. 'Why not?'

Millie met them in the hall. 'Thank goodness you've got here. Denis, I rang your mother to tell you the buses had stopped running but she said you knew and had set out to walk home at eight o'clock. I was beginning to worry about you.'

'We're fine, Mum.'

'Denis, you aren't going to walk back again, are you?'

'I'm going to make him a hot drink first,' Sylvie said.

'It'll be midnight before you get home.' Sylvie had to stifle a giggle at that. It wasn't the walk that had taken so much time.

'I suggest you stay the night with us,' Millie went on. 'Why don't you ring your mother and tell her? We can make up a bed for you and you can come straight to work with us in the morning.'

Sylvie set about making three cups of cocoa while Millie found Denis a pair of slippers that had once been Pete's so he could take his wellingtons off, and she took him up to the old nursery where the gas fire was popping and giving out welcome heat.

Sylvie fell asleep that night thinking of Denis, and the love for her she'd seen in his eyes. To think of him sleeping downstairs gave her a lovely feeling of security.

Chapter Twenty-Four

When Andrew pulled up on the drive of his mother's house and walked to the front door, he remembered that other time years ago when he'd done this. It wasn't so much that he hated Jeff Willis retelling their Asian experiences but that it made the years roll back to 1942 and reminded him of how much he'd lost. He let himself in and found his mother had already gone to bed. He made haste to do the same.

He'd have been wiser to do what Annabel had asked of him in the first place, opt for the Pay Corps and the chance to stay in England with her. His life might have been different now if he had. How many times had he regretted that he hadn't? Thousands as he'd fled from the Japanese, but many more times since he'd returned to England. That had been one of the blackest days of his life.

As soon as the plane bringing him and Jeff home had landed, they tried to ring their wives but were told to try again later as the lines were still being repaired after a recent air raid.

A British Army colonel congratulated them on escaping from the Japanese and granted them a month's leave, telling them their salaries would be paid since the fall of Singapore. Andrew tried again to telephone Annabel but still no luck. Together he and Jeff boarded a train to Liverpool. Andrew thought of him now as a trustworthy friend; they'd parted in

Exchange Station with a handshake and a promise to keep in touch.

It was the evening rush hour; there was a queue to use the phone booths and no taxis. Andrew boarded a bus to Mossley Hill, bubbling with anticipation. The bomb damage shocked him. There were stark ruins, gaps where he remembered buildings, windows boarded up, holes in the road and piles of rubble everywhere. He couldn't wait to get home to Annabel and almost ran down the road to the semi-detached house they'd bought when they married.

Thank goodness these houses were undamaged but they looked shabbier than he remembered. The rose bushes he'd planted in the front garden were in full bloom and the little lawn neatly clipped; it gave him pleasure that Annabel had been taking care of things in his absence.

He dropped his bag on the doorstep to ring the bell, rattle the knocker and put his key in the lock. As soon as the door opened he caught the savoury scent of a good stew. His stomach rumbled in anticipation. How marvellous!

Annabel came rushing up the hall to meet him, her dark hair flying out round her beautiful face. He put out his arms to give her a welcoming hug but she stopped dead as soon as she saw him and her mouth fell open. 'Oh my God!' she gasped. 'I thought you were dead!'

The hall was spinning round him, he couldn't get his breath. Her shock was palpable and he knew beyond doubt that his return was unwelcome. The bottom was dropping out of his world.

He stared at her half paralysed but managed to choke out, 'Didn't you get my letter?' before he saw the man come to the dining-room door. They had been eating; their plates were still half full of stew.

'Darling,' he turned to Annabel, 'who is this?'

She looked numb and was unable to answer. For the first

time he noticed her thickening figure. 'You're pregnant?' He felt as though he'd been kicked. Scalding vomit was rising in his throat.

He couldn't stay here, couldn't look at her beautiful slanting brown eyes. He couldn't stop his fists clenching ready to punch the fellow who'd taken his place. He was older, taller, better looking, a civilian in a well-fitting suit. Andrew felt he was falling apart.

Annabel was weeping and trying to justify what she'd done. 'You went away. You left me. I haven't seen you for years. I couldn't manage on my own, Victor rescued me.'

Victor was calmer than either of them and took over. 'After the fall of Singapore, Annabel received a telegram saying you were missing believed killed. We really believed . . . I mean it's now August.' The official telegram was produced in evidence.

'You didn't write to let me know you were all right,' she accused, near to hysteria. 'What did you expect me to believe?'

'I wrote to you when I reached Darwin.' It was clear she'd never received it.

Andrew didn't know how he got out of the house he'd thought of as his own. He couldn't think. For an hour he walked the suburban streets not caring where he went. He still loved Annabel, still wanted her. He'd adored her, given her everything he could, but Annabel had rejected him. She'd turned her back on him, didn't want any more to do with him.

It began to rain, which made him shiver, he'd grown used to the jungle heat, but it brought him back to the present. It was after ten and dark and he had to find somewhere to spend the night.

He'd go to his mother's house. She was a widow and would be glad to see him, she always was. He hoped to see a phone box. He wanted to let her know he was coming. After his reception from Annabel, he was reluctant to walk in on her but he couldn't remember where the phone boxes were and neither could he think of her phone number. Once it had been his phone number, his mother hadn't moved from the family home. Well, not as far as he knew.

At least he knew the way. He'd been brought up in and around this district and had never moved far until he joined the army. He walked on until he came to his old home. He hesitated at the front gate, worried now about his mother. Did she still live here? Would she be coping after three years of war and widowhood?

No glimmer of light showed, there was no sign that anybody lived here, but a heavier flurry of rain drove him to the front door to ring the bell. He held his breath until he heard her coming to shoot the bolt off the door.

'Andy!' Her face lit up in a huge welcoming smile, she threw her arms round him. 'How marvellous to see you again.' She laughed with delight. 'Ugh, you're wet, like a drowned rat, come to the fire.'

Her welcome couldn't have been more different to Annabel's. That night, he'd pulled the blankets over his ears in his childhood bed. He'd had to tell his mother about Annabel, it had filled his mind and he'd broken down and wept. It was years since his mother had seen him cry and that had humiliated him further.

Even so, within an hour of entering his mother's house it was as though he'd never left. His mother said she was looking forward to having his company for the whole of his month's leave so he'd done the right thing by coming home.

But nothing could take away the raw hurt of Annabel's rejection. He'd believed she loved him and he'd trusted her. The last thing he'd expected was that she'd take another lover. Just to let that cross his mind cut him to ribbons. If his flight from the Japanese advance had taken all his physical stamina, Annabel's defection had delivered an emotional death blow. He couldn't look at life in the same way again. She'd changed him for ever. He felt finished, totally drained and exhausted.

When his leave was up he'd reported back to the army as ordered, and been posted to Catterick Camp in Yorkshire, where he'd put his head down and been a cog in the army financial service. For years, he'd done nothing about getting a divorce, it had seemed too hard. One part of him hoped Annabel would get fed up with Victor and return to him, but his mother thought he'd feel better if he was free of her and kept saying so.

At the end of the war in 1945, a flood of divorces had been reported in the newspapers and Andrew had finally got round to it. Victor bought his share of the house from him so his mother thought he was finally free of Annabel. He wasn't, he still thought of her, imagining things as they once were.

He met up with Jeff Willis every so often and had been introduced to his wife and three children. Jeff had survived their adventure in the Far East with less damage, but Andrew had always known he had a tough core. When the army no longer required Andrew's services in 1946, he'd returned to live with his mother and started job hunting. It was then that Jeff had handed him the advertisement torn from a newspaper. 'You'd be all right working for this fellow,' he'd said. 'Pete Maynard is a relative of mine. I reckon you'd get a fair deal from him.'

'William C. Maynard and Sons? They're quite a big Liverpool firm, I didn't realise you had relatives like that.'

'I come from the poor side of the family, though I count Pete a friend. I think you'll like him.'

Andrew had liked him and he'd got the job. All he'd wanted after that was a quiet life.

★ ★ ★

Millie was afraid the first anniversary of Pete's death would be difficult to get through and couldn't help thinking how different her life would be now if she still had him with her. It fell on a Sunday and Valerie invited all the family to lunch on that day. They were all looking forward to the birth of Helen's baby which was due in another ten days. She was sewing baby clothes and Valerie was crocheting a shawl, and Millie had helped by knitting a bonnet and matinee coat.

Late in the morning when Millie and her children had reached Valerie's house, Eric telephoned to say he was taking Helen into hospital, and could he bring baby Jenny over to stay a little earlier than he'd arranged?

That put them all on tenterhooks and they could talk of nothing else. Eric brought Jenny and ate a hasty lunch before returning to the hospital. Millie had thought it would be a sad day with them all talking about Pete and remembering how much he'd meant to them, but the imminent birth changed everything.

Sylvie played with baby Jenny, and eventually they went on to discuss the future, the party Val was planning for the twins who would soon have their fourth birthday, and Simon who was facing exams and a new school in September.

Valerie was putting the twins to bed that night and Millie was tucking Jenny into a cot in their bedroom when Eric phoned to say Helen had had a baby boy weighing seven and a half pounds and they wanted to call him Peter after her father. Millie had to wipe away a tear before she went downstairs to rejoin the rest of the family. Eric opened a bottle of wine to drink to the new baby's health and happiness, and then because they'd all enjoyed it so much, he opened another.

In future, this date would be remembered as baby Peter's birthday and not as the day of his grandfather's terrible accident. Millie knew she need never fear it again. She could see her family was ready to move forward and think of the future again, and she must try to do the same.

Sylvie began to dream of spending the future with Denis. She was quite sure he was the man for her. He could kiss her and bring her blood to the boil in a few moments. Every time she went out with him he brought her home, and they were spending longer and longer outside her front gate with their arms round each other, trying to say goodnight. But it was very cold, and darkness provided their only privacy. Sylvie thought longingly of the shed at the far end of their back garden. It would provide a lovely hidey-hole for them. One Tuesday she took the key to the shed door from the kitchen and looked inside. It was full of gardening equipment and furniture but nobody had been in since the end of the summer.

She decided it would suit them very well and pushed everything closer together to make more space. The cushions for the garden furniture had been packed away in a tea chest. She swept the floor and arranged them there in readiness. Then she oiled the catches on both the front gate and the side gate so Mum wouldn't hear them being opened. At work the next day, she felt quite excited about what was to come that evening.

Connie and her friends in the office had talked of an imaginary line drawn on the ground in front of them, which they were forbidden to cross until they were married. Sylvie knew her mother had crossed that line, and back in the old days when she was young it wasn't just a line, it was a great ditch with hedges that had to be climbed too. But the war had changed how many people felt about that. Loving Denis as she did, she could understand the thrills and temptations that had led Mum to do it and longed to experience love like that herself.

That evening, Denis took her to see Danny Kaye in *The Secret Life of Walter Mitty*, and it was such a laugh that she forgot everything else. When he took her home afterwards the night was cold and clear and the moon almost full. He tried to kiss her goodnight at the front gate, but she took his hand and led him silently across the front lawn and into the back garden, keeping well away from the light blazing out from the hall windows. Very little light came from the sitting-room windows at the back because the heavy curtains were drawn.

Inside the shed the dark seemed thick and black, but Sylvie had brought a torch and shone it round to show him. 'We'll be safe from prying eyes here,' she said.

'Won't your mother see the light and know you're here?'

'No, too many trees and bushes in between, and anyway once she's drawn the curtains she won't look out.'

He put his arms round her and kissed her and she urged him down on to the cushions. 'We might as well be comfortable,' she said. It was lovely to lie down with him and feel the weight of his body against hers. Sylvie undid the buttons on his coat, made him slip his arms out and used it to cover them instead. His kisses were eager and she returned them with equal joy. She wanted more and took off his tie and undid his shirt buttons, pushing her hand inside to stroke his warm smooth skin. She meant to encourage him to take a step further with his love-making.

Denis lifted himself up on his elbows. She knew he was smiling. 'Sylvie,' he said, 'you're leading me on. I think you're trying to seduce me.'

'Of course I am.' She laughed softly.

He kissed her again. 'I'm flattered, very flattered, but no. That must wait until we're married.'

Until we're married! His words thrilled her to the core. He hadn't mentioned marriage so far but he was thinking of it! She hugged him again. She'd already imagined walking down the aisle to him in a beautiful white gown. Now she knew he wanted the same thing.

'Yes.' He seemed suddenly shy. 'Would you be willing to wait? I really do want to marry you.'

'Oh yes,' she breathed and pulled him even closer. 'There's nothing I want more,' she had to smile. 'So it doesn't matter now if we do make love, we can go all the way.'

'Sylvie! No we can't. We need to stop now before things get out of hand.'

'Don't you want to?' She was suspicious.

'Of course I do. But we can't, not yet.'

'Come on, love me now.'

'What if I give you a baby?'

'Then we'd have to get married straight away, wouldn't we?'

He laughed. 'If only we could.'

'Why not?'

'Quite apart from everything else, I can't afford it yet. I'm an apprentice. I can't get married until I'm earning enough to support a wife and family.'

'Don't be a stodgy. This is the brave new world, isn't it? By September you'll be twenty-one and time served. Mum likes you, she'll not want you to leave. She'll give you a permanent job.'

'She can't, Sylvie,' he said gently. 'She knows I'll have to do my National Service. I'll be called up for that as soon as I'm out of my apprenticeship.'

Sylvie's mood plummeted, she'd forgotten about that. Everybody knew men had to do two years' National Service, either when they reached the age of eighteen or when they'd completed an apprenticeship or college course. Denis had spoken of it more than once and so had Mum, but her dreams of the future had been more real than life itself.

'That's why I asked if you'd wait. It'll be at least two and a half years. I can't marry you until I've done that. You will wait for me, won't you?'

Of course she would. 'Two and a half years will seem forever.'

'It will, but the war is over, so it's not as though I'm likely to be killed.'

'Come on, we can't wait all that time to find out about things like this.' She pulled him down again to kiss him.

She felt him pull away from her. 'Sylvie, I couldn't risk it. I couldn't go away and leave you on your own having a baby. I couldn't live with myself if I put you in that position.'

'Mum would look after me if that happened. She's already told me she would.'

Sylvie felt him straighten up with determination. 'You can't take risks like that and rely on other people to bail you out when you find you've got a problem. You have to learn to stand on your own feet.'

'It's only if the worst happened, and I know Mum would want to take care of me. I'd stay with her until you came home. For me there wouldn't be a problem. I don't need to wait until I'm twenty-one to do the things I want.'

'You do, Sylvie,' he said quietly. 'You've had a wonderful upbringing. Your family has given you all the love and care in the world, as well as everything else money could buy. They've also met every one of your passing whims, so you've received everything you thought you wanted. You've been too well protected, too well cared for. Adult life in the real world isn't like that. You have to face up to what it throws at you.'

Suddenly Sylvie felt like a spoilt child. Denis seemed much older and wiser than she was.

'Your dad spoilt you, even if he wasn't your real dad. Your mother spoils you too.' He stood up. 'If you were my wife, I might not be able to ease your difficulties in the same way. I've been trying not to say grow up because it sounds heartless, but I think you need another year or two to learn that you can't always have everything handed to you on a plate.'

She was indignant. 'I don't think you love me after all.'

'Sylvie, of course I do.' He pulled her to her feet. 'I love you, but I don't think you're ready for marriage yet. If you had a baby you'd have to take care of it and sometimes put the child's interests above your own.'

'I would,' she protested, 'of course I would.'

'No, Sylvie, I'm not sure you'd be able to. You always put your own needs first. It's always what your mother can do for you, not what you can do for her.' Denis went on, 'An adult knows other people have feelings too, which leads me to say that your mother would not approve of you bringing me here like this. Anyway, it's high time you went in. I expect she's already worried that you're later than usual.'

He felt on the floor for his coat and put it on. Sylvie felt she'd been found wanting. 'So I'm not ready for marriage yet? That's it then?'

'Where are you?' She knew he was feeling for her. His arms went round her and his lips found hers again. 'Please don't be upset. Whatever we feel we want, we'll have to wait another two and a half more years before we can have it, there's no way round that.'

Chapter Twenty-Five

Simon had done well in his exams and Millie was delighted when she received a large envelope from the headmaster of Liverpool College where she had applied for a place for him. She was informed that Simon could start in September.

Millie was given an appointment to take him to meet the headmaster and be shown round the school. Enclosed also were forms for her to fill in, and a uniform list.

'Mum,' Simon said, 'I don't want to be a boarder. Liverpool College is nearer than Heathfield, near enough for me to get there and back on the bus every day.'

'All your family have been boarders at that school,' she said. 'Your father was happy there and he wanted the same for you and Kenny.'

'Mum, everything has changed since the war. Dad can't be here with us now, but I know he'd let me live at home if I told him that was what I wanted.'

Millie had to laugh. 'Are you trying to get round me?'

'Say I can. I know they let boys do that these days.' He was looking at her with imploring eyes but really there was nothing Millie wanted more than to keep her children close.

'We'll have to see,' she said.

'What about me?' Kenny wailed. 'I don't want to be the only one boarding.'

'You'll be the only one at Heathfield anyway,' Simon retorted.

When Millie sat down to read the brochure for his new school she found they had opened a junior school in recent years, and she thought perhaps Kenny might prefer to go there as a day boy to sit the exam for the senior school. When she suggested it to him he was over the moon, so she telephoned the school secretary to find out if they had a place available for him. They had, so she wrote to the headmaster at Heathfield to tell him. It would be better for Kenny to stay close to his brother.

When she kept the appointment the headmaster had given her, she took both her boys with her, and spent most of the afternoon looking round both the junior and senior schools. Millie was delighted that she'd have her boys at home with her in future.

The summer holidays came and Millie took her children to Hafod for two weeks. Sylvie asked if Denis might come with them as he would be twenty-one at the end of September and could expect his call-up papers shortly after that. It took a lot of forward planning in the lab but he came and fitted in well with the family. The weather was warm and sunny so they could picnic on the beach and swim, and they had a lovely trip up Snowdon. They didn't go anywhere near the boat, nobody mentioned it, or suggested a fishing trip in one of the several boats advertising holiday trips.

For Millie, time seemed to fly past, and she thought things were getting easier too. At work, she was relying more and more on Andrew, he readily offered the sort of help that Nigel and Marcus should have provided. She sought his company too, but sometimes it gave them both uncomfortable moments.

Occasionally he asked her out for a drink or a meal which she enjoyed, but she felt somewhat embarrassed that he always insisted on paying. Ordinarily, she'd have repaid him by inviting him to meals at her house but he was now

Sylvie's boss and when she tried that, neither seemed at ease.

Andrew went striding to the lab one morning, pulled out the chair Millie kept for visitors and sat down. 'Will you come out and have dinner with me on Wednesday?' he asked. 'I have in mind the Adelphi Hotel.'

'Thank you, yes, I'd love to. The Adelphi sounds very extravagant. Is it a special occasion?'

'It's my birthday, I'll be thirty-eight. I'll book a table. Seven o'clock all right for you?'

Millie was smiling at him. She was a very attractive woman and very good company, and she certainly had plenty of guts. He couldn't help but admire how she'd stood up to Marcus and Nigel. She'd stood up for the staff too and fought their battles. It seemed she'd settled them down. Marcus was keeping a lower profile now and there had been peace in the office for the last few months. At the same time she was virtually running the business and it was making an increasing profit.

Andrew knew he loved Millie but felt she was wary of him. She wasn't encouraging him to show her any affection, and he didn't know whether she wasn't interested in men generally or whether it was just him. He'd told himself a dozen times that he must give her time, that she would still be grieving for Pete. But there was this additional problem that she was his boss. He'd seen her home and knew she had a higher standard of living than he could ever offer on his salary. It didn't make for an easy relationship.

On Wednesday evening, he picked her up in his car and was touched when she gave him a birthday card and a silk tie. 'You've even spared me some of your own clothing coupons,' he said.

'Just one, and there are strong rumours that clothes will be off ration soon.'

'I like it very much,' he said, 'exactly my sort of tie.' He undid the tie he was wearing and bundled it into the glove box, then put on the one she'd given him. 'How does it look?'

'Fine,' she told him.

When the soup came, Millie started to talk about Marcus. 'He bothers me. He's never in his office, and he doesn't appear to be doing much work. What does he do all day?'

'We've all noticed that he goes out a good deal and that he's very tense, nervous and sort of fidgety.'

'Nigel says his wife has left him, so I suppose he's upset, but I feel in my guts that's there's more to it. He's up to something.'

Andrew didn't want to talk about Marcus. He wanted to talk about Millie, he wanted to know more about her, she intrigued him.

There was casserole to follow. It was beautifully served and there was nothing the matter with it but his mother produced several casseroles each week. Nobody was going hungry but very little variety was available on the current rations. Millie told him the casserole was good but he longed for something different, pheasant or lobster would be marvellous.

He drove her home afterwards. When he pulled up outside her gate he got out of the car to go round and open the door for her but as usual she beat him to it. 'Thank you,' she said. 'I've really enjoyed your birthday outing. Would you like to come in for a nightcap?'

'Better not,' he said. 'It's getting late and it's a working day tomorrow.' He couldn't hold back the urge any longer. He took her into his arms and kissed her full on the mouth.

When he felt her struggle to pull away from him his toes curled with embarrassment. And, even worse, it made him feel rejected all over again. He should have had more sense than to do that.

Millie caught at his hand and said softly, 'I'm sorry, Andrew. I'm very grateful for all you do for me. You're a marvellous friend but I can't forget . . . Well, you know how it is.'

He did and it made him feel depressed.

Sylvie had had time to think about what Denis had said. He may not have said 'grow up' in so many words but that was what he'd meant, and she had to admit there might be some truth in it. He'd been right when he'd said she'd had a happy childhood, and perhaps Valerie and Helen had indulged her too, but that boat trip and Dad's accident had thrown a real whammy at her and changed her world. She hadn't stood up to that very well. She'd wailed and cried and felt sorry for herself. She'd seen problems everywhere and made others for herself and her mother. Her family had tried to comfort and help her. She'd taken all their support for granted.

She missed Dad terribly but Mum must miss him even more and Marcus was giving her problems at work as well, but Mum was making the best of what she still had and trying to help her too. Sylvie told herself she was no longer a child and must learn to take setbacks on the chin.

She knew that life with Denis would bring a whole new world to her feet. She loved him, and if she had to wait for two years while he did his National Service then she'd have to grin and bear it. She'd been searching for some time for a gift for Denis to mark his twenty-first birthday.

One evening she said to her mother, 'There's hardly anything in the shops to choose from. I saw a pair of second-hand cufflinks in a jeweller's shop window that were quite nice, but by the time I thought about them and went back, they'd been sold.'

'Sylvie, your father had several pairs of cufflinks, as well as

288

other pieces of jewellery. Why don't you give Denis something that belonged to him?'

'Would that be all right? I mean, it wouldn't really be from me, it would be handing on . . .'

'Of course it would be all right. You were talking about second-hand stuff a minute ago, what could be better than to give him something of Dad's? Why don't you come upstairs and see what there is?'

Her mother led her up to her bedroom and opened the top drawer of the tallboy where Pete had kept things like that. When Sylvie saw the collection of gold cufflinks, tie pins and the signet ring, she was bowled over. 'Denis would be thrilled with any one of these,' she said. 'Would you really let me give him something of Dad's?'

'Of course,' Millie said. 'What is it to be?'

'Denis doesn't use cufflinks that much, so the ring, I think. I remember Dad wearing that.'

'Take it then, you can get it polished up and wrapped.' Millie thought for a moment. 'Should I give him a pair of cufflinks, d'you think? After all, we've always got on well.'

'Why not?' Sylvie giggled. 'They're doing no good lying here. I like this pair best.' She picked them up and put them in her mother's hand.

For Millie, it was a peaceful morning and she'd pottered about the lab with Denis doing what she enjoyed most. She'd managed to buy a tin of instant coffee and at eleven o'clock Denis made them each a cup and they sat down at her desk to drink it.

She noticed that he stirred and stirred. 'Can I speak to you about something personal?' he asked. 'I've been meaning to for some time.'

'Of course, Denis. What is it?'

'I would like to ask your permission to marry Sylvie.'

Millie jerked her head up in surprise. Denis's face was scarlet. 'Well . . . Well, have you asked her?'

'Yes, yes, some time ago, but we wanted to keep it to ourselves for a while.'

'If it's what she wants, then I'd be very happy about it.'

'Oh good. Sylvie's only eighteen, you see, so she'd need your permission.'

Millie took a deep breath. 'When do you plan for this to take place?'

'Not yet, not until I've done my National Service, but I'd like us to be officially engaged, and I thought I'd better ask first.' His words were coming out in a rush now. 'I'd like to get her a ring before I go away.'

Millie said slowly, 'Sylvie's said nothing to me but I could see you were pairing off. I'm sure you'll be very good for her. I'm pleased, Denis, very pleased for you both.'

'It's my twenty-first birthday the week after next. I won't be having a proper party because it's so difficult to get extra food and drink, but my mother would like you and Sylvie to come round to tea on Sunday. It'll be just a family meal to—'

'I'd love to come and I'm sure Sylvie would too. Thank your mother. It's very kind of her.'

Millie had always liked Denis, he was serious, hardworking and reliable, and she'd known and admired his grandfather. She felt Sylvie had made a wise choice. It was bothering Millie that he would soon be called up, and as he was doing more and more of the work, she knew she was going to miss him in the lab.

'I need to find somebody to take your place when you go,' she told him. 'It won't be easy because you can do almost everything here now, but a pair of hands to do the basics would be better than nobody. If we found somebody now, you could show them what to do over the next few weeks. I don't suppose you know anybody who'd like the job?'

'Are you thinking of starting another apprentice like me?'

Millie sighed. 'I don't know. We took you on a full five-year apprenticeship because you were keen and your grandfather had taught me.' Denis had been their first real apprentice, Millie had been hired to wash and sterilise the equipment. It was only after she was married to Pete that a learning programme had been drawn up for her.

Denis crashed his cup down on the saucer. 'I know I'm looking a long time ahead, but when I finish my National Service I'd like to come back and work here. You see, there aren't many jobs like this around, and I don't want to move too far away from here. My mother is dreading being left on her own while I do my army service.'

The government had laid down that ex-servicemen and women must be offered their old jobs back after they were demobbed, should they want them, and Millie fully approved.

'We'd be delighted to have you back, Denis, though you're now qualified to do my job and with a bit more experience you could.'

'But you're doing more and more admin work now,' he told her. 'Everybody comes to you rather than . . .'

'It's a long time ahead but we're expanding quickly and I hope there'll be enough work for both of us by then. I'm glad you're thinking of a career here. We'll all welcome you back.'

'Thank you. Not another apprentice then?'

'I don't really have time to teach another school leaver from scratch. I think it would be easier for me to manage with basic help and bottle washing, so no, not another apprentice.'

'Then can I talk to you about my mother? She hasn't worked in a lab like this but now Grandpa has died and I'm leaving home, she needs something to fill her day and she'd love a real job. She could do the basics I'm sure, if I showed her what's needed. She knows a good deal already because Grandpa never stopped talking about his work. She's done secretarial work so she could help with the paperwork.'

Millie sat back in her chair and smiled. Why not? 'How old is she?'

'Fifty-three, too old for a normal apprenticeship.'

'Yes, ask her to come in and have chat with me. We could give her a try, couldn't we? What about next Monday? Would straight after lunch be a convenient time for her?'

'Yes, that's great. I could go home and bring her in.'

Sylvie had heard about it by the time they were going home that evening. 'I like his mother,' she said, 'and I think you will. She'll be more capable than an ordinary school leaver.'

The following Monday, Millie returned to the lab after eating her sandwiches in Andrew's office to find Denis waiting at the door for her.

'This is my mother, her name is Geraldine,' he said. She was sitting at Denis's desk in the far corner.

'Hello, I hope Denis has shown you round,' Millie said. 'Come down to my desk and we'll have a chat.' Geraldine was a big woman, tall as well as plump, with greying hair, but her face strongly resembled that of her father. She bustled rather than walked and looked very capable.

'I'm keen,' she said, 'to follow in the family footsteps and work in your laboratory.'

Millie thought she would be ideal.

Sylvie was getting excited. On Friday, Denis had said, 'Now our engagement is official, I want to buy you a ring. I don't know much about jewellery or what style you'd like, so I've been into that jewellery shop in Church Street and arranged it. Tomorrow I'm going to take you there and you can choose the ring you want.'

Sylvie was fizzing inside as he led her into the shop. Her feet sank into deep carpet and she was dazzled by glistening rings, necklaces and brooches displayed all around her in glass cases. Denis spoke to a salesman dressed in a very formal suit. He spread a black velvet cloth on the counter and ushered Sylvie into a chair in front of it.

'Up till now we've had to rely on a supply of second-hand jewellery,' he told her, 'but at last we've had a delivery of new rings that I can show you.'

Sylvie looked at the first tray he brought and thought they all looked beautiful. 'Denis,' she whispered, 'some of these rings could be very expensive and I don't want to put you in hock.'

'You won't,' he said, 'that's why I came in the other day. I can afford any of these he's showing you.'

'Trust you to do the right thing.' She smiled and gave herself up to deciding which one she liked best. She pointed out a three-stone diamond ring. The salesman was about to lift if from the tray but Denis's hand reached it first and he slid it on her finger. His touch sent thrills up her arm.

'I like that one too,' he told her.

'While you're here, you should try on some of the other rings,' the salesman said. 'This is a very nice sapphire,' it had a small diamond each side of it. 'Or there's this emerald in a similar design.'

Sylvie tried them on but came back to her original choice. 'You wouldn't prefer this solitaire diamond?' Denis asked. She shook her head. 'Then we'll have the three-diamond one,' he told the salesman.

'It fits you perfectly.' He smiled at her, and twisted it on her finger, 'Could have been made for you. Shall I wrap it up?' He produced a small leather box for it.

'Would you like to keep it on?' Denis asked her.

Sylvie looked at it sparking fire on her finger. 'Yes, I

think I would.' She'd chosen to spend the rest of her life with Denis and she couldn't have felt happier about it. She'd always wear this ring. Really they would be exchanging rings, but she'd wait until his birthday to give him his.

Outside on the pavement he took her arm and said, 'You thought of me in there, you didn't want me to spend more than I could afford. Did I get it all wrong?'

'No, you didn't get it wrong. I'm trying harder to grow up.'

Denis hugged her closer. 'On my birthday I'm going to take you to the Bear's Paw to celebrate. We'll have a slap-up supper and a dance. I'm told it's Liverpool's premier nightclub.'

Neither of them had been to a nightclub before, and Sylvie was delighted.

Denis came to work as usual on his birthday and Millie gave him a birthday card and the gift-wrapped cufflinks. 'Thank you,' he said. 'I'll feel very smart when I wear these.'

'They belonged to my husband,' she told him. 'They're better than anything I could see in the shops. He didn't wear them very often.'

'I shall think of him when I wear them,' Denis said. 'I'll take good care of them.'

To go out that evening, Sylvie wore the fashionable New Look blue and grey striped taffeta party dress that Helen had helped her make. She loved the feeling of long voluminous skirts rustling about her legs and was very pleased with the way it had turned out.

They went to first house at the Empire to see a variety show and then on to the Bear's Paw and were shown to a table on the edge of a tiny dance floor. 'Gosh, it's dark in here, isn't it?' Denis whispered.

Sylvie half wished there was more light so that her outfit could be appreciated. The other customers seemed older, some were in evening dress. Wine glasses were tinkling and soft dance music was playing. It seemed a very sophisticated place and Sylvie loved it. They were both hungry and ate the first two courses before she brought out her birthday gift to Denis. 'I hope you like it.'

He smiled. 'A signet ring. I'll treasure it.'

'It isn't new, it belonged to my dad.'

'Your mother said the same about these cufflinks. I'll wear them with pride, treasure them all the more.'

'Really, we're exchanging rings.'

Denis stretched across the table to kiss the tip of her nose. 'Very right and proper that we should, now we're engaged,' he said.

Chapter Twenty-Six

Marcus felt Elvira was doing her best to choke him off and he was getting brassed off with the treatment. He rang Greg's number one day and she picked up the phone. 'Are you living with him?' he barked.

'No, I'm working for Greg too, so we can get some money together for the house,' she said shortly. 'It's better if we both carry on earning the money while we can. After all, we know how painful it is to be short of a penny or two. We don't want to go back to that, do we?'

'But where are you living?'

'I'm staying with an old school friend. You've got hold of the wrong end of the stick. Greg has never been anything more than a friend.'

Marcus wanted to believe her but a few days later Greg said there were too many calls coming in on his number, it never stopped ringing, and it might attract the wrong sort of attention when it was supposed to be a residential number.

'In future, don't bother ringing in when the job has gone as expected, only do it if something goes wrong,' he told Marcus. 'It'll be safer that way.'

Marcus thought it was to stop him speaking to Elvira, but then something did go wrong. He'd been delivering a car to a garage in Barrow-in-Furness, only to find the place had been cordoned off by the police. That threw him into a panic but he saw it in time to drive on. He went round a few corners until he was well out of sight then pulled into the side of the road and sat back for a few minutes to calm his nerves. He was sweating but blessed the fact that he hadn't left his own car in that garage as he sometimes did, he'd been expecting to pick up another car from them to take back to Liverpool.

Greg sounded shocked when Marcus found a phone booth and rang him. 'Bring that car back to Liverpool,' he told him. 'I'll ring you tomorrow at work to let you know where you can deliver it.'

'I'm not doing that. I don't want it outside my office or my father's house.'

Greg tried to persuade him that it wouldn't attract attention in his office car park, but he wasn't having that. 'I could park it outside your flat,' he said, but finally Greg suggested another garage in Liverpool and as Marcus had been working for him for so long, he knew where to find all the bent garages.

Everything went quiet for a week after that, but it left him shaking in his shoes. When he rang Greg to find out what was happening, he told him that a man had been shot on the garage premises and had since died.

'It's caused a lot of trouble, of course. The police have arrested and charged a man with murder and it seems they found a cache of illegally held firearms on the premises so they're busy investigating that. That has nothing to do with us and it looks as though it will blow over, but in future,' Greg said, 'we will not be using that garage.'

Marcus knew he'd been lucky to avoid being caught up in any violence until now, but knowing it was there made him more fearful than ever. He carried on doing more jobs but the faces of the men in the ring were changing, some dropped out and new ones took their place. The atmosphere amongst them was changing too, they seemed less confident and, like him, more fearful.

Marcus was asked to collect a truck from a garage in Carlisle. He was having a pie and a cup of tea in a café next door when he recognised George, who had been a long-term member of the ring. He looked furtive and he spoke of his worries that the scam could not go on much longer without one or other of the members being caught. That terrified Marcus, the thought of being caught always had, though Greg did his best to talk that possibility down.

Marcus felt he'd reached the point when he couldn't stand much more and was coming to the conclusion that he'd have to stop. The job was playing havoc with his nerves, and besides, he'd done what he'd set out to do, he'd saved enough money to buy the house Elvira had set her heart on. It was time they got out.

He overslept the next morning and was an hour late getting to the office. He met Nigel as he was going in and he said impatiently, 'For goodness sake, Marcus, why can't you get here on time?'

That made him feel guilty and completely stressed out; it was Friday the thirteenth and even the date gave him collywobbles. He couldn't put it off any longer. The first thing he did when he reached his desk was to ring Greg and ask to speak to Elvira.

'I've got to see you,' he told her. 'I can't go on like this. I've done everything you asked of me and I want things to change. I want to know when we're going to get this house.'

He could hear her consulting Greg, then she said, 'Marcus, there's an auction of surplus equipment at that military establishment near Chester. Greg and I are both going but we need more people. Why don't you come too? You and I will have time to talk there.'

'All right,' he said, but he didn't like the fact that Greg

would be there too. 'I've not been there before, where is this place?' He took his little notebook from his breast pocket and opened it on his desk.

'It's Dale Barracks,' she said. 'Greg says to come by public transport so you can do some driving.' She went on to give him precise directions about how to get there and he wrote them down carefully.

Marcus wasn't pleased. She was staying too close to Greg who was using him like a lackey. He had to bring this situation to an end one way or another.

Over recent weekends, Millie had been having long sessions with the family turning out the attics and spare bedroom cupboards, and setting out all they found of value or interest in one room. Then, starting with their grandparents' jewellery and personal effects, she let each of them choose what they wanted to keep for themselves.

Millie thought her sons should keep what was left of the personal belongings, pocket watches, etc., that had belonged to their father and grandfather, but what fascinated them were the old train sets and tinplate toys. Helen brought Eric round to view the collection and advise on what would be worth putting in his saleroom. He recommended that Simon and Kenny keep their share of binoculars, pens and watches until they were grown up.

'By then,' he said, 'you may appreciate and want to use your grandfather's effects, and even if you don't they're likely to appreciate in value and be worth more.'

There were other pieces of jewellery that nobody wanted, several small pieces of furniture and a whole lot of ancient garden ornaments and furniture, and gardening equipment, outdated fishing tackle and cameras that Eric took away to sell. Millie had asked him to invest the proceeds and divide it between Pete's grandchildren. The whole process took some time because Eric had to wait for specialist sales to sell some things. But today, Sunday, he had told her he'd come round in the afternoon with all the figures.

While she was waiting for him to come she opened one of Eleanor's diaries at the roll-top desk in the study and started to read. She was so engrossed that she heard nothing until his footsteps were coming down the hall. She jerked to her feet and not wanting Eric to know about the diary, slammed it shut and put it on top of the other two that were on the desk.

'Hello, Millie,' Eric greeted her. 'Kenny let me in.' He pushed his briefcase onto her desk and added a cake tin he was returning. 'Helen said to thank Sylvie for the cake and tell her it was excellent. How are you?'

Suddenly there was a sound of sliding wood, and both Eric and Millie spun round to see that part of the ornamental beading along the back of the desk seemed to have collapsed. Eric said, 'Heavens, have I broken . . .?'

Millie whipped the things off the desk and piled them on the carpet. Together they peered at the damage. Eric bent nearer and lifted the beading back in position round the series of little drawers. He started to laugh. 'It's a secret drawer, did you know about it?'

'No.' Millie was amazed. 'What happened? What did you do?'

'I must have pushed my briefcase against something . . . See this flower in the carving? The drawer must open when it's pressed. Yes, look.' He pushed it closed to demonstrate the action. 'Secret drawers are not unusual in old furniture like this, and look, there's something in it.' Eric reached inside and brought out a notebook. He flicked through the pages before handing it to her. 'Just a notebook,' he said, but Millie had seen that it contained the same tiny, crabbed handwriting as the diaries. It was smaller than the others, and

300

she'd seen a lot of blank pages too. She cradled it in her hands like a hot potato.

Eric reached for his briefcase. 'I've brought you the figures. Shall we run through them?' He pulled up another chair to the desk and took out a file of documents. But Millie couldn't concentrate on what he was telling her. Her head was swimming. Why had this diary been hidden in a secret drawer instead of being kept with the other twelve? Did it contain something more important, even more secret than the truth about James's birth?

For the rest of the afternoon, Millie was on tenterhooks wanting to read the diary she had just found. As soon as Eric went home she snatched it from the study, ran up to her bedroom, and sat on her bed to open it. On the flyleaf she read: 'To our beloved son Peter. The truth cannot be told yet but I write all this down so that when you are grown up you will know the truth and understand.'

Millie was more intrigued than ever. She turned to the first page and it was dated 1886. So Peter would have been an infant when Eleanor had written this.

Freddie and I both come from large families but babies don't come for us. It's not for want of trying. I have just had my fifth miscarriage and Freddie and I both feel very low. We have not yet told Father-in-law as he will be as upset and disappointed as we are. I had four miscarriages in the first two years of marriage and we waited a whole year for me to regain my strength before trying again, but with the same result.

It now seems hopeless and Freddie thinks we should give up and resign ourselves to childlessness before repeated miscarriages ruin my health. He hasn't yet screwed himself up to tell his father. Poor Papa-in-law still lives in hope that we will give him grandsons to continue the Maynard line.

I was back on my feet again but at low ebb when on Sunday afternoon I went to visit my parents, meaning to tell them my bad news and have their sympathy. Before I had time to say anything, they were telling me how concerned they were about the health of my little sister Alice, only sixteen, and the youngest of the family.

'Suddenly, she seems to have outgrown her strength,' Mama said, wringing her hands. 'She's lethargic, eats little, and spends far too much time alone in her room lying on her bed.'

'Shall I go and fetch her down for tea?' I offered.

'I wish you would.'

Poor Alice did indeed look ill, drained and woebegone. She seemed pleased to see me and I persuaded her down to the sitting room. By then Mama had wheeled in the tea trolley, and when pressed to eat, Alice nibbled half-heartedly at a cucumber sandwich.

It seemed completely the wrong moment to add to their worries by telling them of my fifth miscarriage. I wanted to cheer Alice up and tried to interest her in a game of croquet after tea. Father, looking serious, said he'd ask the doctor to call, but Alice was adamant that she didn't need a doctor.

'I'm beginning to feel better,' she told them, though she was sucking on her upper lip and dragging it in over her teeth.

'A change of air might help,' Mama said. 'Could she spend a few days with you, Eleanor?'

'Of course,' I said, thinking it might do us both good. I turned to Alice and said, 'Why don't you come back with me this afternoon?'

She agreed with alacrity, and I went upstairs with her to help pack a few necessities. 'What's the matter?' I asked, as soon as we were alone. I could see that something was.

She shook her head, her eyes bright with unshed tears. 'Later,' she gulped, 'I'll tell you later,' inferring she wouldn't be able to hold back her tears if she talked about it before we got away.

Normally I drive myself over in the governess cart but Freddie had dropped me off en route to the golf club, as he thought me not sufficiently recovered to cope with the pony. We played a game of croquet as we had to wait for him to come back to pick us up.

'I'm glad you're coming to stay,' he told Alice, thinking she was coming to divert my thoughts from yet another miscarriage. 'It'll do Eleanor good to have a bit of company.'

Alice was very subdued on the way home and as Freddie could hear everything we said, I didn't press her to confide. Once we reached home, I asked Mrs Bowler, our housekeeper, to take Alice's bag up to our guest room and have the bed made up. I hurried her into the garden where nobody would hear us. 'Whatever is the matter?' I asked. The last time I'd seen her she'd seemed perfectly normal. 'What's happened?'

Alice grew agitated and burst into tears, she was clearly in a desperate state. It took promises of help and a lot of persuasion before she whispered that she was with child. It was a bombshell I wasn't expecting. I was shocked but at the same time envious, and said, 'I didn't know you even had a boyfriend!'

There is no sin so great as producing a child before gaining a husband. I didn't learn until the following day that the father was Robert Haskins, a 26-year-old distant cousin of ours several times removed, and a rakish young officer in the militia. He'd already been sent with his regiment to Abyssinia and didn't even know of the trouble he'd landed Alice in. His parents, General Sebastian Haskins and his lady wife, lived nearby and were revered by our parents. Alice had been meeting him without Father's consent or telling anybody.

'Did his parents know he was meeting you?'

'Robert doesn't get on with them,' Alice wept. 'He says they order him around as though he's still ten years old and expect instant obedience.' I couldn't believe Alice hadn't seen him as a dangerous friend before this had happened! 'You must swear to keep it a secret,' she implored.

'Alice, this isn't a secret that can be kept for long.'

'But for now, keep it from our parents and everybody else, please.'

'There's no way I can keep it from Freddie,' I told her, 'not while you're living in his house.'

She nodded, and eventually she let me tell him.

Freddie was horrified. 'Little Alice? Her reputation will be in ruins! Nay, not merely her reputation, this will ruin her whole life. No decent man will look at her, let alone marry her after this.'

I spent that night tossing and turning, pondering on why some girls who don't want babies have them forced on them, while wives like me, who long for them, try and try to produce them but fail. By morning, I knew what I wanted. I knew how to solve Alice's problem as well as my own, but it was much harder to persuade Freddie that it would be possible to do and keep the whole process a secret.

The next morning, before I let Freddie get out of bed to go to the factory, I said to him, 'We are desperate for a family, we could keep Alice's baby and pretend it's ours. The baby will be much in need of a home and, after all, it will be related to us. It would solve our difficulties, Alice's difficulties and please your father.'

'I don't see how we can possibly keep it a secret.'

'Yes, we can. For Alice's sake we have to. What a blessing we didn't tell anybody about this last miscarriage. Nobody knows. Nobody will question—'

'Dr Richards knows. He attended you so he'll certainly have questions if you try to pass the baby off as yours. And

304

what about Alice? She'll need a doctor when her time comes. It can't be done, not and be kept secret.'

'It has to be done, Freddie. Think of the gossip if we let this be known! Think of Alice's reputation. Think of your father's feelings as well as our own. I know you want a family and I certainly do. Really we'll be aunt and uncle to this baby, but where is the harm in bringing the child up as its parents? Alice can't do it, can she? There has to be a way to keep all the details between ourselves.'

I had been thinking of hiring a nurse, choosing a woman who had brought many babies into the world and hoping and praying that Alice wouldn't need the services of a doctor when her time came.

It took Freddie a little while to come round but eventually he said he'd been friendly at school with a man who was now a doctor. He was actually an orthopaedic surgeon working in the Royal Southern Hospital, but he'd ask his advice about dealing with Alice's predicament. He gave Freddie the name of a doctor who had rooms in Rodney Street and suggested that I make an appointment to take Alice to see him.

Alice, of course, was nervous and embarrassed, but he was very matter-of-fact and spoke more to me than to her. He checked her over and told us that the baby was developing normally, and that she could expect to be delivered about the end of March.

That shocked me because it was only four months off and there was little noticeable change in her figure. He said that was because she was very young and healthy. Alice enjoyed a daily walk and had played a lot of tennis in the summer. He booked her into the Tavistock Nursing Home where, he said, she would be well cared for when her time came.

I came out feeling relieved that all had been satisfactorily arranged. Alice had a big weep when I got her home and thanked me a dozen times. She also thanked Freddie and said *she was sorry he'd have to pay for it all. He laughed that off, of course, and the next day drove us round to find out exactly where this nursing home was.*

It was in Aigberth and conveniently close to home. It looked like an ordinary large Victorian house except for the board alongside the gate announcing its name, and the fact that it could provide luxury accommodation and treatment to patients suffering from many diseases.

That weekend, I went to visit my parents again and took Alice and Freddie with me. Mama holds open house on Sunday afternoons for our many siblings and their families, and teatime there is always well attended. The state of both my health and hers was asked for more than once. Alice told them she was feeling better and everybody agreed she was looking a little better. I told Papa that I would like Alice to stay with me for at least six months and that I meant to restore her to perfect health and give her a good time over the Christmas season.

Freddie told them that Alice would be company for me when my condition would make it difficult for me to get about. We received their blessing for our plan and Alice took me up to her room where we packed her clothes and belongings to take back with us.

'So far so good,' Freddie said, as he drove us home, 'but you both can't stay in purdah from now until the end of March. Soon the situation will become obvious.'

He was afraid of upsetting Alice's feelings by putting it bluntly but she understood only too well that shortly her condition would be noticeable, while I would remain relatively slim. I had my own ideas about overcoming that. I began to wear a little padding round the waist and abdomen while Alice took to wearing my clothes. She had been wand slim and I was a couple of inches wider round the waist. She fitted into them well enough and with the waist in the normal place looked only a little plumper. That enabled us to get through the many Christmas celebrations with our secret intact. Many wives withdraw from the social scene towards the end of pregnancy and we were planning to do the same.

Alas, we did not get away with it. In January, Mama came calling to see how we were getting on and took in the situation at a glance. She fainted and it took our combined smelling salts and care to bring her round.

'I'm horrified at your behaviour,' she told Alice and both were in tears. 'Think of the shame you bring to our family.' But she thought I had done the right thing and was supportive towards me. We knew we could trust her to keep the secret. She said even Papa must not be told.

It didn't end there. First our sister Mary came and then our sister Grace and her eldest daughter. They, too, were shocked and surprised but understood the need to keep it secret.

Alice went into labour in the afternoon of 29 March 1883 and I took her to the Tavistock Nursing Home in Aigberth. You were born that evening weighing six pounds twelve ounces, and given the name William Peter Maynard.

Millie put the diary down feeling exhausted and really quite shocked. In reality, the Maynard family had died out. Freddie had been the last of the line. It seemed Pete had been more Willis than Maynard.

Millie wondered if he'd known. She'd never heard him extol the superiority of the Maynard bloodline, and he'd always been careful to treat everybody according to their abilities. After much thought she decided that he probably had known. It seemed likely, as he had been brought up in this house and used the desk. Perhaps it was Pete who had hidden this last notebook in the secret drawer.

Millie turned over a few blank pages and found Eleanor had written a postscript almost two decades later.

June 1906

Dearest Peter, I can't tell you how much joy bringing you up gave me and Freddie. You were the most lovable of sons, kind to your younger brother and responsive to all your relatives, especially to me and Freddie. Everybody loves you and has tried to spoil you.

You were a great comfort to your grandfather, William Charles Maynard, in his old age. To the end of his days he rejoiced that you were a Maynard and hoped you'd marry and have a large family to carry it on. You became the centre of his life and he spent many happy hours in your nursery.

I'm sure you'll remember your Aunt Alice. She loved you dearly and came to see you often. She married Edgar Rowlands, a solicitor, when she was twenty-two and they now have three daughters and a son. Her plan was not to tell him the truth about your birth but I know that later she did.

She still came over to see us regularly, bringing her husband and their children – your half-siblings. I expect you remember them, Daisy, Rosa, Daphne and Charles. Daisy, the eldest, was born seven years after you and therefore you didn't play much together. I've always rejoiced that Alice was happy in her marriage.

Millie was bemused by what she'd learned from the diary and could think of nothing else for days. She wanted to tell Andrew and perhaps get him to read some of the diaries. She wanted to discuss all the ins and outs of it, but it still affected the living. She wanted Valerie and Helen to think of their family as they always had, and what about James and his sons? Millie felt she couldn't break a silence and tell family secrets that had been kept hidden for so many years.

Chapter Twenty-Seven

Andrew was away on his two weeks' annual holiday. 'I'm going to take my mother to Bournemouth,' he'd told Millie. 'She hasn't been too well recently. I'm hoping the change and the sea air will buck her up.'

Already Millie was missing him. At work these days she was doing more of the general administrative work and sometimes Andrew helped her with it. She sighed and looked again at the document Marcus had put on her desk. He was referring everything back to her as though she was his boss. Nigel, too, was inclined to do that. When they'd first started work here, she'd done it willingly to ease them in, but Marcus was making no progress.

Their annual bill for the company's insurances had come in and she'd asked him to check it and assess the cover held by the firm to decide whether it was adequate, before passing it on for payment.

Marcus had sent the file back to her asking if she thought the cover against accident and workmen's compensation was still adequate now they'd taken on another twenty-five workmen in the factory.

No, she scribbled on his letter, *increase pro-rata*. Also they'd increased their delivery vans from four to six and they were being billed only for four. It almost made her smile, Marcus had recently been involved in buying and insuring the vans, how could he forget their existence so quickly?

She got to her feet and was about to take the papers to Nigel's office to ask him to see to it as Marcus couldn't be trusted to do anything, but no, she decided this time she'd have a quiet word with him. Let him sort it out, he had little enough to do anyway.

She ran upstairs to the turret and stood at the door to his office. He was not there but she didn't think he'd gone far, there were papers all over his desk and one of his drawers was open. It was a circular room with small windows all the way round and had views in every direction. Magnificent views up and down the Mersey on a clear day. She crossed the room to the opposite side and looked down at the car park. Yes, Marcus was here, his car was down there looking large and elegant from above.

She went back to his desk, picked up his expensive gold-plated fountain pen and wrote across the insurance schedule, *Don't forget the two new delivery vans, Marcus. For some reason they've been left out*.

She was screwing the top back on his pen when she noticed the small notebook on his desk that he'd left open, and the words he'd written there under today's date: *Dale Barracks, military surplus auction. Twelve midday*. She stood staring down at it for a long moment. Was that the sort of place he went when he wasn't here? But it was half eleven now, he'd never get to Chester by twelve. She went back to the window. She'd not made a mistake, his car was still there.

She spun herself back to his desk and snatched up his little notebook to riffle through the pages. Manchester, Warrington, Barrow and even Harwich, Marcus had been to all these towns, some of them several times. There were telephone numbers and names of people and of garages; directions on how to get to these places and reasons for making the trips.

Millie felt the sweat break out on her forehead, she couldn't believe her eyes. She had always wondered what

Marcus got up to. Here it was, with dates and little ticks when he'd completed the jobs.

It looked very much as though he was lining his own pockets at the taxpayers' expense, but was she right? She didn't want to accuse him of breaking the law if he wasn't. She looked through his notebook again. Could there be an innocent explanation? She didn't think so, it looked like criminal activity. But what should she to do about it?

She slid the book into her pocket, closed his office door quietly, and ran back to the lab. She felt safer at her own desk with Denis clattering bottles at the back, but she still couldn't think. She wanted to talk to Andrew about it but he wasn't here. He was away in Bournemouth with his mother. She had to do something, but what? Take it straight to the police? But she didn't want any adverse publicity for the firm.

She could show it to Jeff Willis. He was a military police-man so this should be right up his street. Yes, he'd know exactly what should be done, though Marcus would see that as shopping him.

She paused, remembering that Jeff had told her he was involved only in minor crime, pub fights and suchlike, but it was one thing to keep mum about the lifetime secrets of Marcus's grandparents, and quite another to help hide what looked like criminal activity from the police.

But how to contact Jeff? If only Andrew were here, there'd be no problem. She'd have to look in his office. She'd seen him consult a flip-up telephone directory on his desk that contained the numbers he used most. She took a scrap of paper along to his office and turned up the name Willis. He had two contact numbers, one marked home, the other office.

Back in the lab she thought about it again. Was she doing the right thing? Yes, she had to do something. She lifted the phone and asked the operator to connect her to Jeff's office.

'I'm sorry, he's not here at the moment,' a female voice answered. 'Would you like to leave a message?'

'Yes,' she said. 'My name is Millie Maynard. Please let Mr Willis know I'd like him to get in touch with me as soon as possible, urgently. Tell him I'm worried.' She left her number.

She slid Marcus's little notebook into her desk drawer and hoped he wouldn't miss it any time soon. Then, nervously, she went to the window to see if his car was still there. It hadn't been moved.

An hour later Jeff rang her back and she tried to tell him what she wanted. 'I'll come over straight away,' he told her.

In less than fifteen minutes he was striding down the lab to her desk, and she handed over Marcus's notebook. 'I want your opinion,' she said, 'but please be discreet.' She watched him as he studied it, his large frame overhanging her visitor's chair. 'I think what he's written looks suspicious, but it's possible I've got it all wrong. I don't want this to go any further unless he's breaking the law.'

'Don't worry, I understand,' Jeff said. 'Is he in the building?'

'According to what he's written there, he was planning to go to Chester today, but his car is still down in the car park. It hasn't moved all morning.'

He looked up and smiled. 'It seems from this that he drives other vehicles, moves them on. This is very interesting.'

'Is he involved in war surplus fraud? I've heard there's a lot of that going on.'

'It looks pretty much like it.' Jeff was continuing to study the pages.

'But hunting down people doing this isn't the sort of work you do, is it?'

'It isn't, but I can pass it on to those who are engaged in it. They'll be more than interested. Can I see his office?'

Millie took him up to the turret and watched while he searched Marcus's desk drawers. He unearthed quite a collection of maps and street plans. 'These will be additional evidence.' He took a few away with him. 'Thank you,' he said, 'you can leave this to me. It is very useful information for us.'

Millie sank back at her desk, relieved that she'd dealt with the matter and it was now out of her hands. But Marcus wasn't going to be pleased.

Marcus got off the train in Chester and was heading towards the taxi rank when he met two men he recognised, Clive Armstrong and Paul Johns, fellow members of the ring. They shared a taxi to Dale Barracks where a crowd was collecting and Greg had arranged to meet them. Elvira was with him and she came forward to greet Marcus while Greg led away the other two.

Elvira's appearance shocked him. He'd not seen her for some time and she'd slimmed down and smartened up, she looked ten years younger. Wasn't that what women did when they had a new man in their life?

'I've had enough of this,' he told her. 'We need to get back together and buy our own house. You agreed we would sort this out if I came here today.'

'Yes,' she said, taking his arm, 'but the auction has started. You can buy me lunch at the Grosvenor Hotel afterwards and we'll talk about it then.'

She pushed him into position near the auctioneer, rammed a catalogue into his hand and told him to bid for the vehicles that they'd marked. The members of the ring spread through the crowd and gave no sign that they knew each other. An hour and a half later, between them they'd bought half a dozen heavy lorries at knock-down prices. Elvira came back to his side and steered him towards a field that was doing duty as a temporary car park. Marcus found himself sitting in the passenger seat of his old car while Elvira drove them into Chester.

'About the house,' he said. 'I have enough money to buy a good one now but I want you to choose it. I want you to be happy with it.'

'Good, I think the time has come to make a change. We need to get well away before this racket goes belly up.'

Marcus was delighted, there was nothing he wanted more. 'You're ready to give it up and have a quieter life?'

'Yes, these days there aren't many sales as big as today's. Greg thinks the services have more or less got rid of their surplus equipment.'

'The other jobs are worse,' Marcus said. Recently he'd been ferrying expensive, almost new cars from a nearby garage into one of the Liverpool docks. Sometimes he'd take three or four in a day. He'd seen the ship's derrick swinging a Jaguar like his up on the deck in a net. He knew the cars had been given new number plates and false documents and had probably been stolen to order. 'Jobs like that are more dangerous. They're making me nervous.'

'You always were nervous,' she retorted, 'nothing new in that, but I agree, I think soon we'll have to get out.' Elvira lifted her eyes from the road to give him a quick smile. She might look more like the woman he'd married but her attitude had toughened up.

'I'm glad to hear that. So we'll go ahead and buy a house now. Whereabouts do you want to live?'

'A long way away from your father,' she said. 'It might be better to get out of Liverpool altogether.'

Marcus agreed with that. 'I've had enough of Pa too, as well as his family business.' He thought of Millie and Billy Sankey and shuddered. 'It's not that easy getting on with the people running it. I'd be more than happy to leave all that to Nigel.'

Elvira parked the car and they went up the steps into the Grosvenor Hotel. 'A clean break then?' she said, as they were shown to a table in the dining room.

'Yes. Somewhere we have no connections. Bath perhaps or Cheltenham.' Marcus dropped his voice. 'Just in case the law decides to start looking for us some time in the future.'

'That has occurred to me. It's important then that you don't say anything about where we're going to your family. I certainly won't to mine.'

'Nor to Greg Livingstone,' he cautioned.

'No, we mustn't leave any clues.' He could see Elvira was pondering the options. 'What about getting a house down on the south coast? Portsmouth or Dover, somewhere where we could nip across the Channel if the worst happened. We need to give it some thought before we decide, but it's a good idea to have an escape route in case of emergency.'

Marcus thought it an excellent idea; it gave him a feeling of security. He was turning a corner; things were coming right for him at last.

'We can buy the house and get everything in place,' she said, 'then stay on with Greg for a bit while things are going well. We don't want to be troubled by shortage of money again, do we? Then we can retire altogether and disappear to the house we've bought.'

A waiter came to ask if they were ready to order. Marcus was running his finger down the wine menu, 'Let's have a bottle of wine,' he said. He felt he had something to celebrate.

'No, a glass each will be enough,' Elvira said. 'We've got to work this afternoon. Greg has a job for you.'

When the waiter moved away, she said, 'Greg is getting the paperwork for those heavy trucks in order. They're going to be exported to the Eastern Bloc and will have to be driven to Felixstowe. That's why he asked you to come here on public transport.'

'Oh.' Marcus hadn't been to Felixstowe before and wasn't keen on going now. 'It's straight to the docks then?'

'Yes.' Elvira took a sheet of paper from her handbag. 'You have to go to the Trimley Dock in Felixstowe. I've got the directions here. Do you want to scribble the road numbers down?'

Marcus slid his fingers into his breast pocket for his notebook and was shocked not to find it there. He groped for a second time, then searched round his other pockets and felt a rush of blood to his cheeks. He was always so careful with that book. What had happened to it?

'They're booked on a Russian ship with an unpronounceable name.' She was looking at him. 'Haven't you got anything to write with?' She handed him a pencil.

Marcus was suffused with panic. 'Thanks, thanks. Have you got a bit of paper too?'

She opened her handbag again and tore a sheet in half. 'You do tear up directions like these as soon as you've used them, don't you?'

'Yes,' he lied, 'I make sure I do. I burn them.'

'Well, this time you might not need directions as you'll be going down in convoy.'

'I'd better have them in case I get separated,' he said. Marcus felt he was going to pieces but he knew he mustn't show it. She mustn't guess. Could his notebook have been stolen? Were the police on to him? He had to force himself to swallow the food while all the time Elvira was saying how delicious it was.

Once he was in Elvira's car, heading back to the army barracks, he closed his eyes and tried to relax. He remembered using his notebook at his office desk this morning. Had he left it there? He'd have liked to go back and pick it up before driving down to Felixstowe, but with Greg making up a convoy of six trucks, that wouldn't be possible.

He was third in the convoy so he couldn't get left behind, and counted himself lucky just to be able to follow the truck in front. His head seemed addled. When the other drivers stopped for a meal at a pull-in, he ate too, but the loss of his notebook made him a bag of nerves.

Marcus went with the other five when they picked up a limousine in Felixstowe. They dropped one man in Manchester and the rest went back to Liverpool. Marcus was thankful he hadn't been asked to drive. The others were in a jolly mood with another successful job in the bag, but Marcus could think of nothing but his lost notebook. If that got into the wrong hands, it could sink them all.

They dropped him off at the office as dawn was breaking in the east. His car stood alone in the car park. His companions insisted on taking a closer look at it and they told him how lucky he was to have it. By then, Marcus felt emotionally drained and totally exhausted.

As soon as they left him, he let himself into the building and went up to his office in the turret. His first impression was that nothing had been moved, there were files and papers all over his desk, but though he searched through them he couldn't find his notebook. Had he left it here? Yes, he felt certain that he had. He could remember writing down the directions to Dale Barracks, but even worse were the countless directions, addresses, telephone numbers that he'd written previously.

His heart was pounding as he looked carefully through all the papers again in case it was hidden amongst them. It was essential that he found it. He searched the top drawers of his desk. He went round his room examining every surface where he might have put it down. He even looked on the floor in case he'd dropped it, but it wasn't here.

Somebody must have taken it. That could only mean that the person who'd taken it understood the meaning of what he'd written. It must mean that somebody was on to him. Could it have been Nigel? That would be the lesser evil, but even so, with sinking heart he put his head down on his desk and wept.

Soon it was full daylight and the factory beneath him was opening up for another day's work. He'd had very little sleep so perhaps it was as well he felt too much on edge to even think of it. He kept a safety razor and a comb in his desk drawer for occasions like this and went to the cloakroom and used them. When the office staff came in he rang the kitchen to ask for a cup of tea.

His night's work had left him feeling like a zombie and gave him plenty of time to think of the consequences this might have for Greg and the other members of the ring. Elvira would be furious. He was half dreading and half hoping that Nigel would come up to his room waving the notebook at him, demanding an explanation. At least then he'd have some hope of keeping it under wraps, but the office was eerily quiet. An hour passed but Nigel didn't come near.

He felt full of resentment for his brother. Nigel was getting on better with Pa than he was; everything was plain sailing for him, not only here in the office but with his wife who treated him with affection. He'd expected to find his father easier to live with once Elvira had gone, but he was as difficult as ever. He sighed as he remembered this was Saturday morning. It was a half day but he'd agreed to go out to lunch with Pa and the family.

Pa had said the club where he usually ate was invaded by hordes of youths at the weekends and that he and his cronies stayed away. So regularly at weekends Nigel and Clarissa invited Pa round to meals at their flat, and since Marcus was now alone, they invited him too. Occasionally, to repay them for their hospitality, Father asked them round for a drink and afterwards Dando would drive them all to a restaurant.

Marcus couldn't make up his mind to do anything. His hand hovered over the telephone, he wanted to speak to Elvira, he needed her, she'd know what he should do, but this might land her in trouble. He sent for more cups of tea, cleared his desk and waited, feeling half paralysed.

At mid-morning his internal phone rang. His hand shook as he picked it up. It was Nigel. 'I'll need a lift home with you, Marcus. Pa's taking us to lunch today. I've had to leave my car for Clarissa so she can join us. I'll see you in the car park at quarter to twelve, all right?'

'Yes,' Marcus managed, but that meant it wasn't Nigel who had taken his notebook.

'Don't forget.'

'I won't.'

There was only one thing he could do now and that was carry on as though there wasn't a time bomb out there that could explode in his face at any moment. Every nerve and every muscle in his body felt tight with tension.

As the appointed time drew near, he locked his desk and stood at the window taking deep breaths until he saw Nigel emerge from the building, then he went down to drive him home. He must appear to be his normal self and not let Nigel and Pa see that he was rattled.

They were shedding their coats in the hall of his father's house when the doorbell rang. Marcus turned round and answered it and was shocked to find two men on the step who introduced themselves as detectives and flashed their identification in front of his face. He didn't take in their names, only the horror that they were plainclothes detectives employed by the Liverpool Police Authority.

'Mr Marcus Maynard?' one asked. 'At one time Captain Marcus Maynard of the King's Own Regiment?'

'Yes.' Marcus felt the strength ebb from his knees.

'We're making inquires and would like to ask you a few questions. May we come in, sir?'

Marcus could only stare at him. Nigel took over. 'Yes of course, do step inside.' They didn't have to be invited twice. 'What sort of inquiries?' he asked.

'And you are, sir?'

Marcus pushed himself forward to say, 'My brother, Nigel Maynard.'

'It concerns only Mr Marcus Maynard, sir.' By now Pa had come into the hall.

'Come this way,' Marcus said hurriedly. He wanted privacy for this and was leading them towards the empty dining room.

But his father stepped forward. 'Bring them in here, Marcus, where it's warm,' he ordered. 'With this coal shortage we can have only one fire.'

They all went into the sitting room and Marcus had to follow. He felt in a state of near panic. His sister-in-law Clarissa was elegantly sipping a glass of sherry, and five pairs of expectant eyes stared at him.

One of the detectives took out a notebook. 'We would like to know if you are acquainted with a Major Gregory Livingstone?'

Marcus ran his tongue over his lips, his mouth was bone dry. 'Er – yes, I knew him in my army days.'

'When did you last see him?'

This was awful. 'Not since I was demobbed.'

'And when was that, sir?'

Marcus could feel the sweat standing out on his brow. 'Er … Last summer.'

His father as usual was impatient and answered for him. 'You came here with Elvira to live with me on the seventh of August, it's a date engraved on my mind if not on yours. So it was the sixth of August you were demobbed, wasn't it?'

'Last year?' asked the detective, with pencil poised.

Marcus swallowed hard. 'Yes, August the sixth, nineteen forty-seven.'

He'd been demobbed a year earlier but he'd misled his father to hide the year he'd been employed on nefarious duties involving war surplus. It had been a harmless fib then to prevent questions from his family but now he'd lied to a police officer. He was afraid that might cause trouble for him but what else could he say when Pa was listening? He was scared and could feel his hands shaking. He pushed them in his trouser pockets so they couldn't be seen.

'Did you know Captain Clive Edward Armstrong?'

'Yes, we served together – with Greg Livingstone.'

'When did you last see Clive Armstrong?'

Marcus shook his head. It had been this morning when he'd said goodbye to him. 'I think he might have been demobbed before me. I don't remember.'

'But not recently?'

'No.' Marcus wished this would end but it didn't. He was then asked if he knew several other people – civilians. He did but he denied it. Photographs were produced and he studied them to gain time to get his nerves under control. He was flustered and it didn't help.

'What have they done?' his father wanted to know.

'It's just a routine inquiry, sir,' the detective answered smoothly and turned back to Marcus, 'Thank you, sir,' he said. 'That's all for the moment.'

Marcus couldn't wait to show them out of the house. His mind was reduced to jelly, he couldn't think. Dando was taking some bottled beer into the sitting room and slowly Marcus followed him.

'What was all that about?' his father demanded.

'I've no idea,' Marcus said. His first glass of beer didn't touch the sides. Did they have his notebook? He'd written the name Greg in it and possibly Clive too. This was a disaster that could topple the whole ring. It had been a mistake to return home. It was the address he'd given the army; that must be how they'd traced him. He could have gone anywhere in England, found a job anywhere and the law might never have caught up with him. He'd been a fool to come home and try to work in the family business.

He'd tried it before and it hadn't worked then, it wasn't working now. Always there was somebody on his back and he didn't know what he was doing. What he ought to do was make a run for it now.

Chapter Twenty-Eight

Marcus sat through the restaurant lunch trembling with fear. He didn't know what to do, he couldn't think straight. He could hear Clarissa's pleasant piping voice and Pa's deep tones booming out but he wasn't taking in a word they said. A menu was put in front of him but he couldn't focus on it. He didn't hear what Nigel ordered but he said, 'I'll have the same.'

Once they returned home, Pa went upstairs to rest on his bed. Feeling absolutely exhausted, Marcus did the same. He hadn't had much sleep last night and thought half an hour's rest would help to clear his head.

He woke up slowly to find it was a clear, moonlit night. It puzzled him to find he was in bed with his clothes on until he remembered it was meant to be an after-lunch rest. He switched on his bedside light and found it was half past seven. He felt hungover and heavy but warm and secure lying here in his own bed.

There was a knock on his door and Dando's head came round. 'Your father's sent me up, sir, to see if you're coming down to supper. He's in the dining room waiting.'

Marcus wasn't hungry. 'I don't feel very well,' he said.

'Shall I bring you a little something up on a tray, sir?'

'Yes, Dando, please.' He felt quite woozy and totally devoid of energy, what he needed was more sleep. He'd overdone things going to Felixstowe. Doing two jobs was making him ill, it was too much for anyone.

Dando brought his tray. Marcus couldn't finish the soup but he enjoyed the apple pie and custard and felt a little better after that. He got up to clean his teeth and have a bath, then he got back into bed and fell sound asleep again.

He was woken the next morning by Dando bringing up Pa's breakfast tray. He lay still for a moment listening to the church bells, then turned over to look at his alarm clock. Pa was having a late breakfast, the bells were calling the congregation to the eleven o'clock service. Marcus's head felt clearer. He called out to Dando as he returned across the landing.

He came in and opened his curtains. 'Good morning, sir, I hope you're feeling better. Will you get up or would you like your breakfast up here?'

Memories of the previous day were flooding back to worry Marcus, the last thing he felt like was getting up. 'I don't want any breakfast, thank you, just tea this morning.'

Those two policemen had said, 'That's all for the moment,' which must mean they intended to come back. But it was Sunday, they wouldn't come back today. Or would they? He'd given a false date for his demob. If they checked that, they'd be on to him like terriers, turning up all sorts of evidence. He had to get away from here as soon as possible, but where could he go? Elvira would have to help him and so would Greg.

Greg! They could be on to him too! And Greg had told him many times that if there was any sign of trouble like this, he must be warned as soon as possible. But Greg would go berserk if he told him he'd written down all his instructions in a notebook and now he'd lost it. It could be used as evidence that he'd been involved in a whole range of thefts and other nefarious duties. Possibly it could be used as evidence against Greg and Elvira and others in the ring. Marcus writhed with fear as he thought of that but he ought to warn them.

At least he didn't need his notebook to call Greg, he could remember his number, but the only phone in the house was in the hall and he didn't want Dando to overhear what he was saying. He went through his pockets, collecting all his pennies. When he was dressed, he'd walk down to the nearest public phone box and ring from there.

The more Marcus thought about his situation, the more frightened he became. He had good reason to be anxious, he lay back against his pillows expecting every minute to hear a sharp ring on the doorbell and find those detectives had returned. Of course they could come back today. It wasn't as though it was just him, there were a goodly number of criminals involved, cheating the state out of thousands if not millions. He heard Pa lumbering along to the bathroom and a little later he came to his bedroom door.

'Nigel and Clarissa have invited both of us to Sunday lunch,' he said. 'It's time you were shaving and getting ready.'

Marcus groaned, he'd forgotten all about that. He couldn't go. He had things he must do. 'I don't feel well, Pa. Can you make my excuses?'

'What's the matter with you?' Pa was irritable. 'You've been acting strangely all weekend.'

'I've eaten something that's upset me. Must have been yesterday at that restaurant.'

'You hardly ate anything there.'

'I've vomited twice,' Marcus lied. He couldn't possibly go. 'The last thing I want is more food.'

'All right, but you'd better go to the doctor tomorrow if you aren't better.'

'I will,' he agreed, relieved to get rid of Pa. Then he lay back on his bed and listened. If Dando was going to drive Pa to Nigel's place, he'd have the house to himself and could ring Greg from here. He rehearsed the words he'd say. There must be no mention of the lost notebook, no mention of the names the police had asked about or his lie about his demob date. Just that they'd visited. Marcus sighed, knowing that wouldn't do; Greg would want to know exactly what they'd said, and what questions they'd asked.

He heard Pa and Dando go out, so the coast was now clear. He shaved and dressed and was ready to go downstairs when he heard the front door open. It made him jump and fear brought a lump to his throat. Had Dando returned? Of course he had, why had he never questioned what he did between dropping and collecting Pa from his various appointments? No matter, he'd walk down to the phone box.

It was a cold day though fine and clear, but he was acutely anxious about what Greg was going to say. He slid his four pennies into the apparatus and gave the operator the number. He could hear it ringing and ringing until the girl came back to him. 'There's no answer, I'm afraid. Try again later.'

He was filled with frustration, he'd worked himself up to warn Greg and now he was out. He strode on down the hill for five minutes, looked in some shop windows before returning to the phone box to try again, but the result was the same. He felt desperate, he had to warn Greg. Time was going on, if he didn't speak to him soon, he'd have to tell him the policeman had come this lunchtime, not yesterday.

He wanted to get right away from Liverpool before the police came back. He rushed home and began to pack. That done, he took two suitcases down to his car and locked them in the boot, then drove to the phone box to try Greg's number again.

He couldn't believe his good fortune when Elvira picked up the receiver. 'You've got to help me,' he said, 'the police are on to me.' He told her about the two detectives who had called on him at lunchtime, inferring it was today.

He heard her sharp intake of breath and knew the news

frightened her. 'There's been nobody round here. What did they want to know?'

'Did I drive a truck to Felixstowe on Friday, and have I ever taken vehicles to Harwich.' Marcus wanted them to know how serious it was but he didn't want the finger of blame pointed at him.

'Oh my God! What did you say?'

'I denied everything, what else could I do?'

'Did they ask about the auctions? Did you say anything to make them suspicious?'

'No, nothing, I'm not daft. The auctions were not mentioned, but I can't stay at Pa's place. The police could be back at any moment. I've packed a couple of bags, I'll come over.'

'No, Marcus, you can't come here,' she said sharply.

He shivered. It felt as though she'd thrown a bucket of cold water over him, she didn't want him. 'You've got to help me,' he implored.

'I will, don't worry.'

'Is Greg there?'

'No, he's out at the moment but he won't be long.'

'Are you living with him in that flat?'

'No, I've told you, but don't come here. Not under any circumstances.'

'Why not?' he demanded.

'They could be watching you, you might be followed.' That scared him even more. He didn't dare tell her that they'd already asked about Greg and Clive.

'Then what am I to do? I'm almost out of my mind.'

'That's only too obvious. Calm down and let me think.'

Marcus was at screaming point. 'It's a dire emergency. I've got to get away.'

'Don't panic,' she said coldly. 'Of course we'll help you, it won't help any of us if you get arrested and grilled by the police. Look, I need to alert the others. I'll ring you back,

Marcus, when Greg comes in and we've had time to think. Don't worry about the police, I doubt they'll be back today.'

'I'm afraid they will, I'm worried stiff. You've got to …' He heard the money run out and the phone go dead.

Another wave of panic ran through him. He had no more pennies but Elvira had said she'd ring him and she knew where to contact him. He took a couple of deep breaths, there was nothing for it; he'd have to go back to his father's house.

All was quiet when he let himself in. Pa was home again, his coat and trilby were in the cloakroom; he'd be having his rest now. Marcus went up to his room but left the door open so he'd be sure to hear the phone ring in the hall below.

He'd never felt further from sleep but he lay down on his bed to wait and at last he heard the phone ring. He scrambled off the bed and rushed downstairs in his stockinged feet. Dando had already answered it. 'It's your wife, sir, she'd like a word.'

He whispered into the phone, 'Hello, I can't say much now, I could be overheard.'

'You don't need to say anything, we've got the picture.' Elvira's voice was forceful. 'Listen carefully, Marcus. Get yourself down to Dover. Book yourself into the White Cliffs Hotel for a few nights, that'll give you time to fix yourself up with something more permanent. It's a small place two streets back from the harbour. Greg and I will meet you there. Have you got that?'

He assured her he had.

'Don't tell anybody where you're going. You mustn't leave a path that can be followed. That's very important, Marcus.'

'I know.' He shuddered. At least Elvira and Greg understood his problem. They were as keen as he was to keep him out of the hands of the police.

Suddenly it was Greg's voice speaking to him. 'Marcus,

you must have done something that's attracted police attention.'

'No, I haven't,' he wailed.

'Then it's that car of yours, it sticks out like a sore thumb. If that was seen anywhere suspicious, it would be child's play to follow you. Get rid of it tomorrow. Stapleton's garage on the Dock Road will take it off you for cash. You'll even gain money on the deal because of the long waiting list for new Jaguars. Get yourself a Morris Eight. No, on second thoughts, it would be safer for you to travel by public transport for a time.'

'Yes,' he said faintly. He was suddenly aware that his father was coming downstairs. He lumbered past him and went into the sitting room. Moments later Dando emerged from the kitchen with a tea tray. Marcus missed something of what Greg had been saying.

'. . . you can't just disappear,' he was going on. 'You must spin a story to your family to explain your absence. We don't want your father to report you as a missing person as that could start a hue and cry for you. We don't want the police to speculate about your movements and it would look very suspicious if your father told them you had disappeared.'

'All right.'

'We'll all lie low for a while and see if it blows over, but we might have to jettison everything. We need to see how things go.'

'Lie low? But I can't ever come back here. I wouldn't want to.'

'Marcus, tomorrow morning take the train down to Dover. Be sure to have your passport with you, in case we have to skip over to France. We'll see you in the hotel.'

'What was the name of it again?'

He heard Greg's tongue click with irritation. 'The White Cliffs, two streets back from the harbour. You can't miss it.'

Marcus went back to his room and threw himself on the

329

bed to think. He'd not taken any holiday since he'd started in the office. He'd been half afraid that in his absence Nigel would get his feet further under the table and he'd be elbowed out. He would tell everybody he wanted his holiday now and that he was going to see Elvira in Rochdale, they'd understand why.

Marcus went down to join his father for tea in the sitting room and spin him the story about needing a holiday now. He gave Elvira as his reason, and went on, 'I haven't had a break since I started last summer. I feel I need a rest and it'll help me get over this stomach upset.'

Then he rang Nigel and gave him the same story. 'Two weeks' holiday starting tomorrow? For goodness sake, Marcus,' he said, 'you don't give us much notice. Did you finish drawing up those tables I asked you to do?'

Marcus couldn't remember agreeing to do anything for Nigel. 'Er . . Not quite finished,' he said.

Nigel sighed impatiently. 'Well, it won't take you long to drive to Rochdale. Could you come into the office first and bring me what you've done? I'll finish the job while you're away. And be sure to tell Millie that you're going to see Elvira. Please don't give her any more grounds for complaint.'

'All right.' He'd have to make time for that. What he needed to do now was to find out the times of the trains to Dover. He drove his car down to Lime Street Station and found there were two possibilities between eleven and midday, one train involving a change at Euston the other ran via through Birmingham. Neither would be easy, he'd have to wait three hours in Birmingham for a connection, or he'd have to take a taxi to cross London.

Chapter Twenty-Nine

Marcus didn't sleep too well but he was up early on Monday morning. He'd been making his own breakfast since Elvira had left, and as he would be on the train at lunchtime and most didn't have restaurant cars these days, he needed a substantial one. He found two eggs in the kitchen as well as sausages, and he fried them all. This was not the moment to think of rations.

He switched on the wireless to listen to the news while he ate. His fork stayed poised between his plate and his mouth when he heard the announcer say, 'Four pilots have been arrested and charged with flying stolen aircraft out of the country. It is understood the planes were sold to Eastern Bloc countries. The thefts occurred between March and May last year and the arrests were made possible by liaison between Interpol, the Air Force Police, and British civilian police forces. More arrests are expected to follow.'

Marcus was so shocked he allowed egg yolk to drip on his tie. He'd heard Greg Livingstone laugh about the effrontery shown by those pilots and he was a great friend of ex-Flying Officer Gilbert Robertson who was dangerously reckless. Marcus was ready to bet Greg had had a hand in making the arrangements and he was in no doubt now that the net was closing in on them all.

He couldn't eat another mouthful. Dropping his knife and fork on his plate, he switched off the wireless and shot upstairs, in the grip of abject terror. He felt pursued by a thousand fears as he remembered seeing a military policeman in the Sailors' Return holding forth to Millie on that snowy afternoon; he was afraid she already knew he was caught up in a web of criminal activity.

He was very tempted to drive straight down to Stapleton's garage, ditch the car and get them to take him straight to the station. But no, it would be safer to stick to what he'd told Pa and Nigel he was going to do. He needed to have the police sent off on a wild goose chase if they did return.

He knew he had to keep his wits about him and stay calm. He put on his coat and went out to his car, but as he drove he was writhing in emotional turmoil. He went up to his office in the turret but couldn't remember what he'd come here to do. He phoned down to the kitchen to get a cup of tea.

It took him the best part of an hour to find the file Nigel had asked for. He'd done very little of the job and couldn't face his brother while he was shaking like this. Instead, he took it to the typing pool and asked the nearest girl to deliver it to Nigel in the boardroom.

Marcus wouldn't have gone anywhere near Millie but she was talking to the sales manager at the head of the stairs as he retraced his steps. She broke off and said, 'Can I have a word with you, Marcus? There's something I'd like to show you.'

What could he do but follow her through the lab to her desk? She pushed a trade periodical in front of him. The print danced before his eyes. He had to ask, 'What's this?'

'It's a company advertising for another to merge with. The name is Arthur Hampton and Sons.' She sat down. 'Do you know them?' He stared blankly down at her. 'I've had a word with Andrew Worthington about it and he says we buy raw soap from them, and their business might be a fit with ours.'

'Merge with them? Why?' Marcus tried to focus on what she was saying; his mouth was dry and his tongue felt too big. There was no way he could get his head round merger problems now, he couldn't care less. Was she making a play to gain more shares or more power in their business? He didn't care about that either. His head was reeling. The lab was beginning to spin slowly round him.

Millie was staring up at him. 'Does this business belong to your wife's family? I'm afraid I don't remember her maiden name.'

Elvira's maiden name? He couldn't remember it either. He pushed her periodical back at her. 'It isn't this. It's nothing to do with her.'

'Still, it might be an idea to discuss a merger with Nigel. What d'you think?'

He couldn't grapple with this. He said, 'I saw you with a military policeman. In the pub across the road that day it was snowing. What was he saying to you?'

Her face, confused and shocked, eddied past him. 'What's he got to do with this?'

'Was he talking about me? He was, wasn't he?' Millie had been tormenting him for ages and he was going to let her have it. He lunged for her throat and he heard her scream. For once he had the upper hand. She was trying to fight him off but he was twice her weight. Suddenly, she jerked her knee up to his groin with all her might. He gasped and the pain almost made him let go. He caught a glimpse of her face, there was terror in her eyes, she was frightened of him. Good, he wasn't going to let her get the better of him, not this time.

She screamed at him, 'Marcus, what the hell d'you think you're doing?'

He swung her office chair round and got her head down on her desk but she was screaming and screaming. He took a firmer grasp on her neck and banged her head twice. He hated her, she thought she was so clever and she'd made him feel a fool.

Suddenly, something that felt like an animal pounced on him from behind the racks of jars and demijohns. It weighed a ton and knocked him off balance. Not an animal, he was being hauled away from Millie. He fell back, catching a glimpse of a white coat before he cracked his head on the desk. Marcus struggled upright, gasping for breath, his head was reeling and it hurt. He felt dizzy, and now there were two white coats swinging round him. It was the new woman they had working in the lab, she looked as ferocious as her son. He had to get away.

He tried to turn but tripped and fell against her desk. He pulled himself upright again and hurtled down the lab. In the corridor, men were coming towards him with arms outstretched, trying to stop him. 'Out of my way,' he roared.

A familiar face yelled at him, 'For God's sake stop.'

Marcus aimed a punch at his nose that hurt his knuckles and skidded on down the stairs at breakneck pace. He had to get to his car. He banged his shoulder on the front door but he was through it and outside. Cold, wet rain blew in his face; he'd left his raincoat in his office but, no matter, his keys were in his jacket pocket.

He almost fell into the driving seat and started the engine, but men were streaming across the car park after him. He locked his car door and headed it towards the exit. Albert Lancaster was standing in front of him and waving him down. Marcus jerked on the steering wheel to avoid him and scraped along the wing of an Austin 12, before he rolled out on to the street and turned down-river towards the Pier Head. His lovely car would be damaged but he had to sell it anyway.

He couldn't see very well, something was blinding him. He wiped his eyes with the back of his hand and saw it was coated with blood. He squinted at a heavy dray coming towards him being pulled by two carthorses. The driver was staring at him with his mouth open, looking shocked. Marcus whizzed passed with inches to spare.

At least he'd got away from all those people who were chasing him. He was on course for the garage, all he had to do now was to sell his car and get the 11.42 train to Dover. He drove another couple of miles but he couldn't see again. He switched on the windscreen wipers but it didn't help much.

Blood was dripping into his eyes and he caught a glimpse of a large truck chugging towards him. He knew he was too far over to the right on the road, and tried to correct it as he felt in his pocket for his handkerchief. The crash when it came wrenched the steering wheel out of his hand. The screech of metal scraping on metal was deafening, somebody was screaming. His head crashed against the steering wheel and was then flung painfully backwards and a searing pain shot up his leg.

Chapter Thirty

Nigel was in the boardroom dictating letters to his secretary Louise Lambert when his concentration was broken by the noise outside in the corridor.

'What's that?' he barked, but he knew because he'd heard something similar before. Was Marcus having another fight with Billy Sankey? Horrified, Nigel rushed to the door to find out. Pandemonium raged in the corridors, every office door was open and desks were being deserted.

Nigel stood back and roared, 'What is the matter? What is going on?'

Frightened faces turned towards him. 'It's Marcus,' he heard from several lips. 'He's tried to strangle Millie.'

Nigel's jaw dropped, he felt sick. Had Marcus taken leave of his senses? He pushed through the crowd to the lab.

Millie was coughing and spluttering. Her desk was surrounded. Her screams had brought others running from nearby offices. Denis was trying to explain what had happened and they were all firing questions.

'Marcus attacked Millie? What did he do?'

'Millie, how d'you feel?'

She was coughing so much she found it hard to get the words out. 'I can't get my breath, he's hurt my throat.'

'You sound hoarse.'

'Where is he?'

'He's gone, he ran away like a scalded cat.'

'Heavens, Millie.' Billy Sankey pushed himself over to her and lifted her head up to look at her neck. 'He tried to strangle you. We should get you to a doctor.'

'I'll be all right.'

Billy said, 'I was afraid he might turn on you. You took my part against him.'

'Mum!' Sylvie came and threw her arms round her. 'I told you Marcus was going mad, now d'you believe me? He's out of his mind. What did he do to you?'

'He grabbed my throat.' Millie coughed. 'My head hurts too. He banged it on my desk.'

'We should get the doctor.'

'I'm all right now.'

A glass of water appeared in front of her. Millie could see Nigel had come and was looking down at her, and the story had to be told again from the beginning.

'I can't believe it.' He sounded shocked.

'It's true enough,' Billy Sankey assured him. 'Look at his finger marks on her neck. He must have put some force behind them to do that. I think the police should be informed, this is serious bodily harm.'

'No,' Nigel said, 'I don't think we should, it would be bad publicity for the business. We should all calm down.'

Sylvie said furiously, 'Who cares about the publicity? He would have killed Mum if Denis hadn't stopped him. He saved her life.'

Billy said, 'I'm going to ring the police straight away. The man's damn dangerous. He shouldn't be allowed to get away with this. First me and now you, missus. Who knows who he'll go for next? He could kill somebody.'

'No, wait,' Nigel protested. 'Let's think carefully before . . .'

Billy pushed past him and others sided with him. 'This is

a police matter. He shouldn't be allowed to go on working here.'

'He never did much work.'

'Where's he gone?'

Tom Bedford had just joined them. 'He came rushing downstairs as if he was being chased, almost knocked me over.'

'But where's he gone?'

'Mum, I'll take you home,' Sylvie said. 'You won't feel like work now.'

'Millie shouldn't drive after that. She should see a doctor.'

Sylvie said, 'We came on the bus this morning.'

'Millie, I'll drive you home,' Nigel offered.

'I'm all right now,' Millie put in. 'Don't make so much fuss. I think I should stay here if Billy's calling the police in. They'll want to talk to me.'

'The colour is coming back into your face,' Geraldine agreed. 'You're sure you're all right?'

'I'll be fine. I just need to sit here quietly for a while.'

Tom Bedford began to herd his colleagues out. 'Give her space. Millie needs air.'

'What can I do that will help?' Sylvie wanted to know.

'A cup of tea,' Millie coughed. 'I'd love a cup of tea.'

She felt as though she'd been mangled and was glad to be left alone to recover. Her neck was sore and her heart was still thumping, she'd really believed for an awful minute that Marcus was going to kill her.

In the past, she'd occasionally caught him looking at her with such fixed intensity that it made her feel uncomfortable, and she'd often been nervous when she was alone with him, but nothing had prepared her for an attack like that. She'd really thought her end was coming and she'd been terrified. She'd seen black hate for her on his face. But why had he asked about the military policeman at the pub? Did he know she'd spoken to Jeff Wills and put the police on his trail?

Nigel was furious with his brother. Recently he'd been acting queerly and he was nervous about what Millie was going to tell police. He didn't want Marcus to get into more trouble and this was the second time he'd caused a fracas in the office. He was making their side of the family look like dangerous fools. Things were going very wrong.

He went out to the car park, meaning to drive over to see his father. He had to involve him or he'd be upset and angry when he found out later. He had difficulty reaching his car, the car park was heaving with their employees. All were excited, aghast even, at the scratches Marcus had inflicted on several cars as he'd driven recklessly out.

'He was like a mad thing,' they shouted. 'Look what he's done to the gatepost!'

Nigel had to raise his voice above the noise they were making. 'Go back to work, all of you,' he bellowed. His hand shook as he opened the door of his car. He was shaking with fury as he edged his way out of the car park and drove upriver towards Maplethorpe. He arrived as his father was coming downstairs, and Dando was taking his morning coffee to the sitting room. 'Shall I bring you a cup, sir?' he asked.

'No, I don't want coffee.' Nigel threw himself down on the sofa. 'Pa, Marcus has attacked Millie.'

His father didn't seem to hear, he was already angry with Marcus. 'I don't know what Marcus is playing at, wanting his holiday on the spur of the moment, wanting to go chasing off after that wife of his. Do you know what he did this morning? He cooked all our rations, all the food we had in the house, for his own breakfast and then he didn't eat it. Dando found a plateful of fried eggs congealing on the kitchen table. You can guess what my breakfast had to be,

Dando had to warm up the food Marcus had left to make a sandwich for me. There was nothing else to eat in the house.'

'Pa, he tried to strangle Millie. He caused an uproar in the office and then shot off like a bat out of hell.'

'Strangle Millie? I've often felt like doing that myself. I'd like to strangle both of them.'

'Please be serious, Pa. How can we run the business when he's causing mayhem? I'm sick of him, he's out of control.'

'Well, there's not much I can do about that,' his father said. 'I blame Elvira. Perhaps he'll be better when he's had his holiday.'

Nigel did not hold out much hope of that. He was no sooner back at his desk than Miss Lambert came in to let him know that two uniformed policemen had arrived. 'Show them in,' he said, thankful that the staff were now back at their desks and the office quiet.

The officers introduced themselves and showed him their identity cards. One took out a notebook.

The more senior of the two said, 'We received a phone call from a member of your staff saying that your brother went berserk and showed extreme violence towards a Mrs Millie Maynard and would have killed her if another member of staff hadn't intervened.'

Nigel played down the events as much as he could to protect his brother and avoid bad publicity for the business. The officers asked to speak to Billy so Nigel sent Miss Lambert to get him.

Billy appeared, looking dishevelled and angry. He was sweating and too agitated to tell the story clearly, swearing and stumbling over his words and showing his personal hatred of Marcus. He didn't come over well.

They turned to Nigel and said, 'And following this episode your brother ran out of the building and disappeared? Do you know where he could have gone?'

'He'd arranged to take a fortnight's holiday starting today and said he was going to see his wife.' They asked for Elvira's address. 'She's staying with her parents in Rochdale.' He gave them the address. Then they wanted to talk to Millie so Nigel led them along the corridor to the lab.

Millie looked unusually white-faced and she still had vivid red marks on her neck. She made no fuss about what had happened and simply recounted what had taken place. Nigel was glad to see there wasn't much the matter with her. As he was seeing the policemen out, it occurred to him that they had shown more concern for Millie than he had. To remedy that he said, 'Perhaps I should ask the doctor to check her over, make sure she's all right.'

'I would,' the senior one said.

As soon as he'd seen them off the premises, Nigel went back to his office to ring the doctor the company used for medicals and accidents. He practised on his own from a surgery at the end of the road and his wife acted as his receptionist.

She picked up the receiver. 'He's already on his way,' she said. 'A Mr Denis Knowles asked him to call and see Millie.'

That made Nigel scowl but he hoped the matter would now blow over, and as it was lunchtime he put on his coat and set off to the Sailor's Return for a whisky to settle his nerves. However, as he was crossing the car park another police car pulled in and two different officers got out. Nigel's first thought was that the police had started to hassle him. He strode up to them and said with icy politeness, 'Can I help you?'

'We've come about a Mr Marcus Maynard,' he was told. 'We understand he has relatives working in this business.'

'Yes, I am his brother,' he said shortly, worried now about what else Marcus had done.

'Could we go inside? Somewhere—'

'No,' he was impatient, 'I'm just on my way out.'

'Oh. I'm afraid we have some bad news for you, Mr Maynard. Your brother has had an accident.'

He snorted with contempt; after what Marcus had done, he might have guessed. 'I suppose he's crashed his car.'

'Yes, I'm afraid so, a bad accident.'

'And he's hurt?'

'I'm sorry to tell you, Mr Maynard, that it was a fatal crash.'

Suddenly, Nigel was aware of the strength ebbing from his knees, he felt near to collapse. 'What? He's dead?' He found that hard to believe. 'Are you sure it's him?' The police officer put out a hand to steady him. 'What's happened?'

'Yes, we're sure it is him. He had his passport on him and there were documents in the car showing this firm's letter heading.'

'My brother was going to Rochdale. Why would he need his passport?'

'We don't know, sir, but it was in his pocket. To make quite sure, we would like you to identify him, but as I said, there isn't much doubt.'

'Right, then I might as well do that now,' Nigel said.

'Well, we thought tomorrow morning, sir. He's only just been taken to the morgue.'

Nigel shuddered, he didn't want to think about that; the inference was that they didn't want him to see Marcus yet because he needed to be cleaned up and made presentable. 'So where did this accident happen?'

'In Regent Road in Bootle, some three miles or so from here. Do you know it?'

'No, not really. Is it near the docks?'

'Yes, near Huskisson Dock.'

'Could you take me to see the place?'

The police officer was showing reluctance. 'Well, we don't really advise it.'

'Take me please,' he ordered.

The traffic was quite heavy but before long Nigel could see the large six-wheeler truck slewed across the road. The roof of the car was half under the front of the truck, squashed almost flat; the truck's momentum had carried it several yards. The ice-blue paintwork or what was left of it was unmistakable, it was definitely Marcus's Jaguar.

Nigel felt sick, hot acid rushed into his throat. 'Was anybody else hurt?'

'Not badly hurt, but the truck driver was taken to hospital. He was badly shocked. The officer opened his notebook and read: 'The driver was shouting, "The bugger came straight for me. There was nothing I could do." '

Nigel closed his eyes and swallowed hard. 'Oh God! Poor Marcus.'

Millie was feeling a little better by the time Geraldine brought the doctor to her desk. 'Hello,' she said. She knew him as she'd had dealings with him over the years. 'I think I'll be all right, there was no need to call you out.'

'Well, as I'm here I might as well take a look at you,' he told her. He shone a torch down her throat and examined her neck. 'I think you're right, Mrs Maynard. Your throat will be sore and your neck will look bruised for a while, but there's no great damage done and nature will heal it.'

'I tried to tell them,' Millie said.

'Take frequent hot drinks and a couple of aspirin to ease the pain.'

'I think you should go home.' Billy Sankey had not gone away. 'You can't possibly settle to work after that. I'll take you. You've had enough for one day. Sylvie should come too to look after you.'

'I don't need looking after,' Millie said. But she allowed him to drive her and Sylvie home. It had been an awful day, everybody had rallied round but she'd really missed Andrew and wished he'd been at work.

Nigel was back working in the office when his father rang him. 'The police are here asking questions about Marcus,' he said. 'They want to speak to you too. Can you come here now?'

This irritated Nigel. 'For goodness sake! Marcus is dead, why can't they leave us in peace?'

'You'd better come,' James told him, his voice serious. 'It seems Marcus was up to all sorts of tricks. They think you and I could be involved too.'

'What nonsense. What sort of tricks?'

'Worse than anything I thought possible. I asked the police not to go to the office to question you, we don't want this talked about. You had better come here.'

Nigel was angry. 'They have no business to keep on at us like this,' he retorted.

'Come home now,' James ordered.

Nigel went.

'What is it?' he asked when his father opened the front door to him.

'Elvira has been arrested and is being questioned in the police station.'

Nigel was truly shocked when he heard what the police had to tell them and though he protested his innocence, he went voluntarily to the police station to be interrogated.

Chapter Thirty-One

The day following Marcus's death was Denis's last day at work. A few days after his twenty-first birthday he'd received his call-up papers. Sylvie told herself the fun was over and now she had to be brave. He'd been for his medical examination and been graded A1. He was told he'd be sent to Taunton to do his basic training.

'Such a long way,' Sylvie mourned to the girls at work. 'I won't be able to see him all the time he's there.'

'It'll only be for six weeks,' Connie told her briskly, 'then he'll be posted somewhere else. At least the war's over and you don't have to worry about him being injured or killed.'

A few weeks ago, Millie had asked Sylvie to help her buy a pewter tankard and have it engraved as a gift from William C. Maynard and Sons, and she had ready a certificate duly signed to prove he'd completed an apprenticeship with them.

Having decided it would be too dangerous to have a crowd in the lab, she'd asked Nigel if they might open up the boardroom during the afternoon tea break so the twenty-four office staff and the half dozen or so in the factory whose work brought them into contact with Denis, could say goodbye to him. She'd ordered three dozen assorted fancy cakes from Sayers to be delivered today, and sent out a general invitation.

Millie's throat still hurt when she swallowed and her neck now looked worse than it had yesterday because the bruising had come out. Everybody was in a subdued frame of mind. Nobody was in any mood to enjoy a party. 'But we'll do it,' Millie said, 'we have to.'

They gathered in the boardroom at three o'clock, all looking rather glum, and Millie made her farewell speech to Denis, though she had to break off twice to clear her throat and take a mouthful of water. She made the presentation, wished him well on his National Service, and told him the company would welcome him back.

Only twenty of the cakes were eaten. Millie told the younger staff members to take the rest of them home.

On his first day back, Andrew had been in his office for only ten minutes and was thinking of going to the lab to see Millie when the door opened and she was there smiling diffidently at him. 'Such a lot has happened while you've been away,' she said. 'I must bring you up to date. I really missed you last week.'

He had hoped she might be pleased to see him, but what she told him was a catalogue of work-related disasters. She hadn't missed him in the way he'd missed her.

'I was trying to talk to Marcus about that merger we discussed and he suddenly went berserk.'

'Berserk? What d'you mean? He didn't attack you?'

'Yes, I thought he was going to kill me.'

'Heavens, Millie, he's dangerous! You can't let him go on working here.'

She looked numb. 'Marcus is dead,' she said.

'Dead?' Andrew was astounded and he listened speechlessly as Millie told him how it had come about and all the harrowing details.

'The staff can talk of nothing else. They're all shocked at

what has happened. I gave everybody time off to go to his funeral if they wanted to. When I saw Nigel and his father there, they both looked shattered, and Uncle James had visibly aged.'

Andrew felt shocked too. 'We must put all that behind us now,' he said, 'and look to the future.' It had all happened without him and had changed for ever the dynamics in the office.

'Have you had a good holiday?' she asked eventually.

'Yes, restful. My mother is getting on in years and as you know she hasn't been well. She enjoyed Bournemouth, and I think it's done her good.'

'What did you do?'

'Nothing exciting, we strolled along the prom, sat in deckchairs listening to the band, and read. In the evenings we saw the shows on the pier.' He'd have preferred to be out on the Downs hiking, or on the beach swimming. He'd wanted to be with Millie.

Millie was more beautiful than he remembered and he could hardly drag his gaze away. She had on a dress he hadn't seen before, it was the colour of the sun. He wanted now to tell her how much he loved her, but that wasn't what she wanted to hear. He pushed his hands deeper into his pockets so they wouldn't reach out to touch her.

'I've got to go,' she said, 'work is pressing.' But she agreed to come back to eat her lunchtime sandwich with him, and he had to be satisfied with what little of her company he could get.

That afternoon Jeff Willis rang him and said, 'Had a good holiday? I've got news for you. Could you bring Millie Maynard and come over to the Sailor's Return for a drink at five o'clock? She asked me to do something for her.'

'So she told me. What sort of news?'

'Good news. She'll be pleased.'

'That's a change. The news is bad here. OK, we'll see you at five.'

Millie had not been in the lounge of the Sailor's Return since that snowy day in the winter. Today it seemed dusty and close in the warmth of September.

She'd been disappointed in Andrew's attitude earlier that morning, she'd really been looking forward to his return from holiday and she'd tried to tell him so, but he hadn't seemed that interested.

When he'd come striding down the lab during the afternoon, she'd wondered if he'd had a change of heart. It turned out he had not, but all the same, she was intrigued when he told her about Jeff's request.

Jeff's presence seemed to fill the room, he always seemed larger than life. 'I want to thank you, Millie.' He shook her hand and patted her shoulder at the same time. 'The information in that notebook of Marcus's has proved invaluable in several ways. It has done wonders for my career. I've been given a much more interesting job. No longer do I have to round up drunken military personnel in the pubs and bars. I'm now a detective, rounding up real criminals, and you're about to see a whole circle of fraudsters brought to justice. In future, the government will be able to get the true worth of any war surplus goods it still has to sell.'

'That's marvellous news,' she said.

'What about a drink to celebrate?' Andrew suggested.

'I've already tried,' Jeff laughed. 'Gin is off, whisky is off and the only beer is mild,' his voice dropped an octave, 'and I think that has been watered.'

A few days later, Millie had barely sat down at her desk when Tom Bedford, who was staid and never rushed, shot in with two newspapers folded to a story on the front page. 'Millie,' he said, putting them on her desk, 'you ought to read these, all the national newspapers are carrying the story. Trust Marcus, this is going to throw a spanner in the works,' and he hurried off.

She pulled the first newspaper in front of her. 'Civilian and military police join forces to break large criminal ring,' she read, and was immediately gripped by the story. It appeared that a large gang had been systematically stealing, or buying up at fraudulent giveaway prices, government war surplus equipment and selling it on to unfriendly foreign countries. 'One of the accused, Marcus Maynard, was recently killed in a traffic accident. He was a member of the prominent Maynard family and Managing Director of William C. Maynard and Sons, a reputable Liverpool business established on 1870, making luxury toilet products. Fifteen other people have been charged, including Marcus Maynard's wife, and are expected to appear in court today.'

A list of names followed that included Gregory Livingstone and Captain Clive Edward Armstrong and gave potted histories of each.

Millie straightened up in her chair. She was horrified but it did explain what Marcus had been doing when he wasn't in the office. She read the other newspaper article and it said much the same thing. She leapt to her feet and headed for the boardroom. The corridors were full and the door to the general office was wide open.

Millie could see the staff gossiping in little groups and heard the whispered name of Marcus Maynard.

'Is it true?' she was asked.

'I don't know.'

Nigel had only just arrived and was opening his briefcase.

'Have you seen this?' she demanded, tossing the newspapers on his desk.

He wouldn't meet her gaze and seemed mightily embarrassed. 'Yes,' he grunted.

'What d'you make of it? Is it true?'

'I'm afraid it is,' he said through tight lips.

'How long have you known about it? This is appallingly bad publicity for the company. Couldn't be worse.'

'Yes, I know, I'm sorry.'

That surprised her, Nigel always seemed to believe that his side of the family could do little wrong. 'What are we going to do about it?' she asked.

'What can we do? I've had enough. I shall hand in my notice and leave.'

Millie gasped. 'Good gracious! But you'll need to look for another job.'

'No, Clarissa and I are returning to Calcutta. We've both had enough of austerity England, and she's been keen to go back for some time. Her father wrote telling me of an international paper-making company that has just opened up a new factory in Calcutta. They advertised here for administrative staff, so I applied and I heard this morning that I've been given a post.

'I should have told you what I was doing, but all this publicity about Marcus means I can't possibly stay anyway. It tars me with the same brush. I'm sorry if this means you're left in the lurch again to see to everything. Father says he'll try and come back to work for a few days a week to tide you over.'

'Nigel, you mustn't let him come,' Millie said quickly. 'I'll be able to struggle through with the help of the managers. They're a good bunch, and very efficient.'

'Are you sure?'

'Yes. Uncle James isn't well enough to come back, and we none of us want his general health to suffer.'

'Good, I'm sure he'll be relieved.'

'Don't worry, Nigel,' she said, 'we'll manage. I hope things work out for you in Calcutta.'

★ ★ ★

To Millie, it felt as though a tornado had blown through the business and it left her feeling very much on edge. Everything seemed to have changed almost overnight. She immediately called the senior managers to the boardroom for a meeting. Marcus's dramatic death had caused considerable unrest and she needed to let them talk about that and settle down.

She started by saying, 'I have to tell you that Nigel has given in his notice. He doesn't want to go on working for us after what has happened.'

Billy Sankey was very outspoken as usual. 'Good riddance to both of them, I say. They did damn all work and caused maximum trouble. We'll be better off without them.'

'Nigel did try,' she said. 'He's planning to return to India, he doesn't like life in this country. That does leave us short-handed at management level and I think we'll have to recruit someone to take Nigel's place.'

'You can do it,' Albert Lancaster said. 'You've been doing it since Pete died.'

'But I can't do everything and Denis Knowles has gone too, which gives me more work in the lab. I need to think this over but I thought I'd let you know how things stood first.'

'We want to help you,' Tom Bedford told her. 'We'll all keep our own departments running as smoothly as we can.'

'I'm not all that hard pressed at the moment,' Dan Quentin, the sales manager, said. 'Everything the factory makes is flying off the shelves. The population has been starved of luxuries for so long they can't get enough of them now. So if there's anything I can do to help, Millie, I have time and I'd be glad to.'

'Well, there is. I'd like you to give some thought to our Christmas market, while it's still some time ahead. Actually, as you know what sells, there's no one better than you to do it.

351

We'll need new packaging or, better still, new products, but nothing that's expensive or will disrupt our standard lines.'

'Right,' he said, 'I'll give it some thought.'

Millie gave it more thought too. She'd expected more help from Nigel than he'd ever delivered though he had done some work and had seemed to be improving. Marcus had always been more a liability than a help, so their departure had removed some of her problems.

But suddenly she was in sole charge and feeling the responsibility and her workload was growing, not least in the lab now that Denis had gone. She was surprised at how much his mother Geraldine had picked up in the few weeks she'd been with them, and knew she was better than any school leaver could be, but with the best will in the world she couldn't do as much as Denis had.

Millie missed his cheerful presence but she could see his mother and Sylvie missed him even more. Every morning, a letter from him came through the letter box for Sylvie, and she knew she was writing regularly to him. Both she and his mother gave her snippets of information about how he was faring, but they were all finding the first weeks difficult.

One morning a few weeks later, they were having breakfast when Sylvie looked up from the letter she'd just received to shout with pleasure. 'Denis has nearly completed his basic training. When he does, he'll be given a forty-eight-hour pass.'

At work Geraldine was equally excited by the news and they were both making big plans for his visit. He came a few days later but Millie caught only glimpses of him. He laughed as he told her, 'As soon as I mentioned I'd served a five-year apprenticeship in a perfume laboratory, I was given a posting to work in a hospital laboratory.'

'He's going to Netley Hospital near Southampton,' Sylvie added. 'Such a long way.'

'Yes, I'm going straight there after my leave. I tried to tell them that it wasn't that sort of a lab and I knew nothing about medical work, but I was told I'd be taught what I needed to know.'

His first visit seemed quickly over and everything settled back to an even tenor. He would now receive regular leave of forty-eight hours at a time. Sylvie mourned the fact that a large proportion of it had to be spent travelling, but his flying visits became part of her life.

Millie thought she was growing up fast and had at last put Pete's accident behind her. She was taking more responsibility about the house, as well as doing more with the boys. They had soon settled down in their new school and Millie was enjoying having them living at home.

For them all, time was flying ever faster. Millie wanted to continue the family traditions and once again held open house on Guy Fawkes' night. Uncle James said he'd come. He looked very frail when he arrived and Dando had to help him into an armchair in the conservatory. She heard James say to him, 'Wait in the car outside, don't go away.'

By then Valerie was talking to James, so Millie said, 'There's no need for you to wait outside in the cold, stay here and join in.'

'Thank you, madam,' he said. 'I don't think Mr Maynard will want to stay very long.'

Later, when Millie gave James a glass of whisky, he said, 'I came to congratulate you on producing growing profits from the business. You've done very well.'

'Thank you.' She was pleased that he, too, wanted to put their earlier conflicts behind them. 'How is Nigel?'

'He says all is well, but I don't know whether he's settling in his new job.'

Uncle James stayed only for half an hour and it saddened Millie that the other side of the family was not as happy as hers.

353

Chapter Thirty-Two

At Christmas, Dan Quentin's designs for the seasonal trade proved to be outstanding and gave them their most profitable Christmas ever. Millie enjoyed another family-orientated Christmas and a very jolly New Year's Eve.

They were all back at work again and she was decanting perfumes in the lab when Valerie rang her. She was surprised, as the family didn't usually contact her during working hours.

'Millie,' she said, 'I've just had a phone call from Nigel. He says his father had a stroke the night before last and died in hospital. He said—'

'Good gracious! What a shock, but he did look ill the last time we saw him. Did Nigel phone you? Is he back home?'

'No, he phoned long distance, radio telephone. He's still in Calcutta. He's coming home for the funeral so that won't be until January the twelfth. Nigel hopes to get here by the eleventh and wants me to liaise with the vicar about the arrangements for the funeral service.'

'Are you all right with that?'

'Yes, yes of course, just surprised he didn't ask you to do it.'

Millie was too. James might have forgiven her but clearly Nigel hadn't. 'He hasn't recovered from working with me, we didn't always see eye to eye,' she said.

'The funeral refreshments are to be held in his house, Dando will take care of all that.'

'What else did he say?'

'Well, it seems he and Clarissa aren't planning to return to Calcutta after the funeral. He'll be in touch when he gets home.'

'Thanks, Val, for letting me know.'

Millie sat back to muse on this latest twist of fate. She'd always thought James had played up his ill health to avoid doing his share of the work, but perhaps she'd misjudged him. Perhaps she hadn't appreciated how ill he was. He'd certainly died young. It dismayed her that Nigel hadn't managed to settle in his new job in Calcutta. Clarissa had been looking forward to returning to India.

Millie asked all her family to accompany her to the funeral, as she expected nobody else apart from Nigel and Clarissa to be there. But on the day, she was surprised to see a large number of elderly gentlemen in the church.

'They're Pa's friends,' Nigel told her. 'He had a wide circle of friends and acquaintances, knew almost everybody in Mossley Hill. He went to a club every evening. Millie, I'd like to talk to you about the business.'

'Of course, but you won't want to do that today surely?'

'Tomorrow then. There's something I'd like to settle.' His manner was brisk. 'I'll come to the office, shall I? After lunch, about two o'clock. Is that all right for you?'

Later that afternoon, when they were back in the office, Andrew said, 'Nigel isn't wasting much time. He expects to inherit the other half of this company from his father and I bet he wants you to buy it from him.'

'That's the first thing I thought of,' Millie said. 'Quite a turnaround for him if we're right. Would it be a good thing for me to buy it?'

'Yes, a very good thing, because then you'll own it all. It'll give you a free hand and be up to you how it is managed.

Well,' he paused to think, 'it'll be a good thing as long as you don't pay over the odds.'

'Perhaps you should start figuring out what would be a reasonable price to pay.'

'Nigel will probably employ a firm of accountants to do the same thing. You'd better be prepared to negotiate hard.'

'Yes, I'll need your help with that. But it isn't his yet.'

'No, you're right, first he'll have to have it valued for probate and that usually means a conservative figure.' Andrew's green eyes smiled into hers. 'This isn't the best time for him to sell. He should hang on to it for a year or so.'

'Perhaps he wants the money, though he'll have Uncle James's house to sell too.' Millie frowned. 'D'you know, I had no idea Uncle James had a social life and all those friends. Really, I hardly knew him.'

By lunchtime Andrew had given her two figures. 'If you can get it for the lower one, you'll be doing reasonably well.'

'Will it be fair to him?'

'It'll be fair to both of you. But before you settle on a figure, you need to know what it was valued at for probate. Be sure to ask him for that. And whatever figure you eventually settle on, get him to agree that you pay him half now and the other half in a year's time. On no account agree to pay more than the higher figure.'

'Can I buy this out of company funds?'

'Half the company funds belonged to James, and you'll have to pay them over to Nigel if you buy. The other half belongs to you and you can use the money in any way you want.'

'Aren't I lucky to have someone as canny with accounting as you are?'

She was waiting for Nigel at two o'clock and had arranged that Geraldine would make them some tea. He didn't look well and less than confident when he arrived. There was no sign of his previous bombastic manner.

She was sympathetic. One way and another, Nigel had had a hard time of it. 'Terrible thing to have to rush home to bury your father,' she said. 'I gather you didn't manage to settle in Calcutta.'

'No, the political situation in India has changed completely.'

'I'm sorry, that must be unsettling.'

'Very. Now they have self-government, the top jobs are not being reserved for Europeans and they're all leaving. Even Clarissa's father is retiring early so I gave in my notice too.'

'How is Clarissa?' Millie asked.

'Well, upset at the way things have turned out. We'd like to get settled somewhere more peaceful before we start our family.'

'Do you have somewhere in mind?'

'Yes, that's why I've come to talk to you. I wanted to ask if you'll buy Father's half share of this business once it's mine.'

Millie sucked her lip. 'In theory,' she said, 'I'll be happy to buy it, but we can't make any concrete arrangements now. It'll have to be valued for probate and I'll need to know that figure before we can agree on a price.'

'Yes,' Nigel sighed, 'it will all take time, but I need to know where I'm heading. You see, Clarissa's brother owns a business making shoes in Northampton but it's in need of more capital. He's happy to take me in as a partner but I'll have to invest money in the company.'

'I see.'

'Clarissa's family think that my experience working here will be a great help to them.'

Millie doubted that; as she saw it, Nigel was unlikely to

find a job that really suited him and settle down. But she took the opportunity to outline Andrew's other conditions and confirmed that she would buy if the price was right.

'There's another thing, Millie. I discovered from Pa's will that he owned half of Hafod and that will be mine too. Would you be prepared to buy that from me as well?'

'I was half expecting that,' Millie said. 'Won't you be interested in keeping it? It's a good place for weekends and holidays, especially for children.'

'No, I don't think Clarissa and I are interested in holidays like that.'

'It needs to stay in the family, of course,' Millie said. 'When it's been valued, let me know. If it costs too much for me I think Helen and Eric might be interested.'

The even tenor of Millie's life was resumed. In the months that followed, they spent many weekends and holidays at Hafod. Val and Roger had the boat checked over and repainted, and she and Sylvie had been out in it again, but neither really enjoyed it in the way they once had.

Helen's baby was thriving. Sylvie had always been particularly close to Helen and she was often round at her house helping with the children. Millie, too, made a point of seeing Jenny and baby Peter every weekend. His first birthday came and Helen and Eric had a little celebration with the older members of the family.

It was also the second anniversary of Pete's accident. Valerie spoke of him, remembering some of the good times she'd spent with him, and Helen, Sylvie and the boys joined in. Millie remembered him with love and gratitude and felt that the passage of time had eased the pain and anguish for all of them.

Several more months passed before James's will was settled and Nigel was able to sell to Millie. He and Clarissa had gone down to Northampton so that he could start work at the shoe factory and learn the ropes. He wrote to tell her that the half share of William C. Maynard and Sons had been valued at a little less than Andrew's lower figure, and he offered it to Millie at the probate value.

'Jump at it,' Andrew said. 'It's something you'll never regret buying.'

'Would it be doing him down?' She was frowning. 'You said it was worth more.'

'Millie! Don't tell me you feel sorry for him after what he did to you?'

'A bit. I can't see him being a roaring success in the shoe industry. I'd be willing to pay him your lower figure,' she said, 'if you're sure I'd not be paying too much.'

Andrew smiled. 'That price is fair to you both.'

Nigel came up to Merseyside to tie everything up, and called in the office. 'How are you finding Northampton?' Millie asked.

'It's not all that easy,' he admitted. 'I have so much to learn and we're still living in cramped conditions. But I have a buyer for Pa's house, so we'll be able to get something better now. And once I'm a partner, we'll have a little more income. Things will improve.'

'I hope they do,' she said. 'Andrew has worked out that this is a fair price to pay for your half share.' She pushed some papers across her desk to him.

Nigel smiled. 'That's very kind of you. Pa said you were doing well here.'

'Yes,' she said, 'we all work very hard. Helen tells me you and Eric have agreed a price for your half share of Hafod.'

'Yes, he drives a harder bargain than you.'

Millie had been getting more help from Andrew since Nigel had ceased to be employed, and though they were coping, the business was growing and she knew before long she

359

would have to have more help. At home in bed, Millie had considered advertising for an executive manager to run the company, but after her experience with Nigel she knew finding the right man would not be easy.

Recently, she'd been feeling closer to Andrew and thinking more and more about him. He had attractive dark green eyes that frequently showed his concern for her, and a quirky smile that lit up his face. She'd always valued his companionship and when he'd been away on holiday during her dark hours of need, she'd really missed him. It made her realise just how much she relied on him for advice and support, but it took almost another year of quiet routine to see that he had also woken her from the trance she'd been in since Pete's accident. She knew now that it was love she felt for Andrew, and she wanted much more of his company.

It took Millie a long time to make up her mind about how best to run the business, but she'd finally decided the way that would bring her most satisfaction would be to find another accountant to take over some of Andrew's work so that he could do more on the management side. She didn't doubt he would be capable. She knew he'd fit in well with the other managers, they'd all taken to him, but she didn't know whether he'd want to spend less time on accounting and take on wider responsibilities.

Somehow their relationship had always had an awkward edge to it. For a long time, Andrew had seemed to be reaching out to her, wanting more than friendship, and she was beginning to think she'd been a fool to push him away when he'd tried to kiss her.

Pete would be the first to say, 'It's no good hankering after me, I'm history now. It's time you got on with life. I want you to enjoy it. If you feel you'll be happy with Andrew, tell him so and go for it.'

Perhaps she was dreaming of a rosy future for them,

happily married and working together to make the business a real success. Perhaps she'd left it too late for them to get together, perhaps she'd pushed him away once too often and he no longer wanted that. Perhaps he wouldn't want to take on management duties. His ideas about the future could be very different from hers, but she knew there was only one way to find out. If she wanted things settled, she would have to ask him. She would have to lay all her cards on the table and openly discuss all her ideas with him.

The next morning, as soon as she'd made sure that all was under control in the lab, she went along to Andrew's office. It was easy enough to talk about the business side and ask if he wanted to help her run the company. Business was what they usually talked about in his office. She started to outline her plans.

His dark eyes beamed at her. 'You're offering me a wonderful opportunity,' he said, 'and I'm thrilled you want me to help you. You and I work well together. It's a splendid idea.'

They spent all that day and most of the next getting an advertisement into several newspapers for a young qualified accountant to take on some of Andrew's work, and deciding how the duties and responsibilities of the business should be divided up between them. Millie shared his enthusiasm, excitement sparked between them and when his hand happened to brush against hers, she thought they both felt the thrill. She hoped he'd speak of it. She was certain now that it was love she felt for him, she wanted more, but hesitated before taking the last step.

It was only when they'd drafted everything out on paper and given it to Sylvie to type that their excitement calmed down. Millie regretted that she'd given no indication of what she felt for him, said nothing about love or marriage, so that part of her plan was still up in the air.

361

What she'd intended to do was propose marriage to a man who had said nothing about his feelings for her. It was a subject they'd never discussed and she was finding it difficult now. The very thought made her nervous because she was afraid she might have read signs she thought she'd seen all wrong. She went home and worried about it all night, but she knew if that was what she wanted, she'd have to propose to him.

Sylvie and Geraldine were in high spirits, looking forward to seeing Denis again. Millie decided his visit would provide an opportunity to have a private talk with Andrew. She would invite him to have supper with her at home. Sylvie would be tied up with Denis and though the boys would be there, when she sent them off to do their homework she could rely on them doing exactly that.

When she invited Andrew, his smile was dazzling. 'Supper at your house tomorrow evening? I'll look forward to that. Thank you. At what time?'

'Straight from work,' Millie said, heartened by his response. 'It'll be nothing special, I'm afraid, an informal meal with the boys. In fact, Sylvie's going out to dinner so you'll be eating her ration.' Millie planned to make the stew tonight so it would only need warming up tomorrow.

'That sounds great,' he said, 'excellent.'

All the same, when she went along to his office at five o'clock the following day, she was feeling a little on edge and he was quieter than usual. He drove them home, parked on her drive and presented her with a bottle of red wine. She took him to the kitchen where she lit one gas under the stew pan, and another under the pan of potatoes. Then she filled the kettle and gave him a bottle opener for the wine.

From the window, she could see the boys in the garden kicking a ball about. Millie tapped on the glass, signalling for them to come in. She'd set the table this morning and made everything ready and she'd agreed with the boys that they should take over the job of cooking the potatoes and cabbage.

'Hello, Mum.' They came in looking hot and untidy.

'Wash your hands before you do anything,' she said hastily, and when they came back she added, 'This is our accountant, Andrew Worthington. Sylvie is his secretary.'

Simon offered him a damp hand and assumed a formal grown-up manner. 'How d'you do?' She could see Andrew was not at ease.

'We know you, don't we?' Kenny said, peering up at him. 'You came to our bonfire night party.'

'Yes,' Simon said, 'and Sylvie talks about you sometimes.'

Kenny added, 'She said working for you was better than working for Cousin Marcus.'

Millie pulled a face, and picked up the wine and two glasses. 'Call me when everything's ready.'

She took Andrew up to the playroom where she lit the gas fire. It popped and spluttered and, seated one on each side of it, she knew the time had come to say her piece. But Andrew was sitting straight and stiff on the edge of the armchair, staring at the glass in his hand.

That gave her cold feet and she decided to put it off until they'd eaten and the wine had had time to take effect. He talked about the new arrangements in the office until Kenny came running up to tell them that Simon was dishing up the dinner.

The food was passable, just, the boiled potatoes and cabbage were overcooked but the wine was good and by then their inhibitions were melting. The boys chatted about school and it was quite a relaxed meal. Sylvie had made queen of puddings for them which was excellent and the boys made a cup of tea. Afterwards they cleared the table between them and dealt with the washing-up.

Millie sent the boys to do their homework and took

Andrew into the sitting room. The room felt a little chilly though Simon had put a match to the fire she'd laid ready when he'd come home from school. The time had come, and she couldn't put it off any longer.

She took a deep breath and said what she'd rehearsed. 'Andrew, there's something I have to say to you. I feel in a way I've used you. I've accepted all your kindnesses and advice and shown you little regard in return.'

'No, no,' he protested, 'nonsense, you've just promoted me.'

She shook her head. 'I don't mean that. I've pushed you away when you were trying to . . .'

'Kiss you?' He came nearer to sit beside her on the sofa. 'I'm sorry. I was showing no understanding of your feelings.'

'What I'm trying to say,' Millie stumbled on, 'is that I'm over Pete and . . .'

His arms went round her in an exuberant hug, 'Millie, I was afraid I'd never hear you say that. I love you. I have for ages. I'm absolutely thrilled.' His lips came down on hers. 'I've known almost since I first saw you that I wanted you in my life,' he told her.

They stayed on the sofa with their arms round each other and had the heart-to-heart talk Millie thought they should have had sooner. She knew she hadn't yet made clear what she wanted and said, 'Dare I ask what your thoughts are about marriage?'

'I'm all for it.' His eyes looked into hers for a long moment. 'To you? Are you asking me if . . .?'

'Yes. I haven't always been kind . . .'

'My darling Millie,' he laughed. 'Marry you? You must know I'd jump at the chance. I was afraid the only thing you wanted from me was help with the job. I was prepared to settle for that if it was all you could give.'

'I'm sorry. I choked you off, didn't I?'

'I should have been more patient,' Andrew was saying when Kenny came down in his pyjamas.

'We've got ourselves bathed and ready for bed,' he said. 'We've done everything you said we must. We haven't been a nuisance, have we?'

'No, love, you've both been very good,' Millie said. 'Come on, we'll both come up to tuck you in and say goodnight.'

As they were coming downstairs afterwards, Andrew said, 'I feel very lucky to be gaining a family as well as a wife. My lonely days are over.'

'You haven't told me very much about yourself,' she said. 'Compared with me, you're really quite shy.'

He told her then about his first marriage and asked about Sylvie's father.

'I was in love with him when I was seventeen,' she said, 'but he left me in the lurch when I was pregnant. Pete rescued me, but not until after Sylvie was born. I had no idea how I was going to cope. I agonised long and hard about it and promised myself then that I'd never allow myself to be in that position again.'

'Quite right,' he said.

'But it's left me with a hang-up. I can't sleep with you until we're married. Apart from that, it would be setting a bad example to my children.'

'I do understand,' he said. 'I promise to respect your wishes. I feel everything is in reach now.'

It was late when Denis brought Sylvie home that night.

'I'd better be off,' Andrew said. 'We all have to go to work tomorrow. Can I offer you a lift home, Denis?'

'Yes please,' he said, 'though I don't have to be up early.'

Millie thought her evening ended rather abruptly, but she was very happy and more confident about the future than she had been for a long time.

Chapter Thirty-Three

Millie still felt on cloud nine when she arrived in the lab the next morning. She knew Andrew was already here, she'd seen his car in the car park, and a few minutes later he came to see her, but Geraldine was chatting about Denis and Sylvie. Millie caught his eye and he indicated that he'd like them to go to his office, where they could talk in private.

He hurried her down the corridor, pushed the door shut behind them and caught both her hands in his. 'Millie, I hardly slept a wink last night, I couldn't stop thinking about you.' His eyes were shining, 'I can't believe you really want to marry me.' He pulled her into his arms and kissed her.

'There's nothing I want more,' she said, 'and afterwards I want you to come and live in our house, we've loads of room.'

The phone on his desk rang, and clucking with impatience he broke off to answer some routine query. When he'd put it down he smiled across his desk at her and said, 'We haven't talked about what sort of a wedding you want or all the hundred and one other arrangements we'll have to make.'

'I've been thinking about it. I'd like to get married quickly with no fuss.'

'So would I.'

'But then there are my children. I think it would be better if we gave the boys time to get to know you.'

'It might, they'll need time to get used to the idea of a new father, won't they?'

Millie nodded. 'Yes, I want us to be a happy family.'

'Perhaps we should be engaged for a while.'

'Yes. They've lost their father. I don't want them to think I'm deserting them for you.'

'But you'd still be there with them.'

'Yes, but I want ours to be a proper marriage so a lot of my attention will be on you.'

Andrew came round and took her into his arms again. 'Millie, I do love you.'

She whispered, 'Pete said that he'd told his daughters he wanted to marry me before he proposed to me. He said it was obvious they wouldn't see me as a replacement for their mother, but he wanted them to be happy too. It turned out very well for us all and I'd like that for my sons.'

'Then we must do it that way. What about Sylvie?'

'She has Denis now, so I think she'll have less trouble than the boys.'

'But she's my secretary and soon she'll be my stepdaughter.'

'I know, but she'll get used to the idea.'

He laughed. 'Millie, I was thinking of myself. How do I treat her? I mean, I'd have a different relationship with my secretary than I would with my stepdaughter, wouldn't I?'

'That is something you'll have to work for yourself. But we can ask her if she wants to carry on working for you, or whether she'd prefer to change to someone else. Let's start by telling the children. Come round again for dinner . . .'

'No, let me take you all out together to have a slap-up meal. We can tell them it's by way of celebration.'

'I'd like them to make up their own minds about it being a good idea. Sylvie says she likes you but I want the boys to like you too. Better to start on a lower key, take them out on a day trip, and tell them we plan to get married over tea and cakes. Just let it sink in slowly.'

'Whatever you think best,' Andrew agreed. 'You know them better than I do.'

'Right, then to start with, we'll just tell Sylvie and the boys and Pete's daughters and let them know it's a family secret. We'll leave it a week or two before we say anything here at work.'

'I need to tell my mother straight away,' Andrew said. 'It'll mean big changes for her and I don't think she'll welcome them. I'll take you to meet her.'

'Yes, and you must bring her to meet the children and see where you'll be living. Everyone will accept it, if we give them time.'

The following day over their lunchtime sandwich, Andrew said, 'I told my mother about you last night.'

Millie smiled. 'What did she say?'

'That she was glad I'd found somebody at last. She kept asking questions about you and wanted to know if you'd be coming to live with us. Afterwards she looked very sad. She'd told me ages ago that when my father died and I was away during the war, she felt lonely and frightened.'

Millie was concerned. 'How old is she?'

'Seventy-six but she hasn't been too well recently.'

'She doesn't like the idea of being left on her own?'

'She doesn't say that, but I'm sure you're right. Come home with me this afternoon and have a cup of tea with her. She needs to get to know you.'

'Andrew, I need to get to know her and the sooner the better. Sylvie can go home on the bus today and I'll come with you.'

'Good, as you say, the sooner the better. I don't think she likes change.'

'Does anybody at her age? It's Friday, let's leave early, say four o'clock, so I can spend a bit of time with her. I don't want to seem rushed.'

Millie followed Andrew's car through pleasant suburban roads and saw him pull into the drive of a smart, semi-detached house. It had been freshly painted and the garden was well cared for, but she found Elsie Worthington looked very frail and thin, and walked with the aid of a stick.

'Just a touch of rheumatics,' she told Millie. 'It's beginning to catch up with me now but I still enjoy pottering round the house and garden. I don't let it stop me doing things.' She had a tray set with her best cups and saucers and the kettle filled in readiness. 'I was so pleased when Andrew phoned to say you were coming for tea. Though I'm afraid I have no cake to offer you.'

'Don't worry, Mum,' Andrew said from the kitchen, 'I've got the kettle on and I'm just getting a few plates. I told Sylvie I had to provide an afternoon tea for her mother and got her to nip round to the Refreshment rooms. She managed to get three cream slices and borrow a packet of ginger nuts from the kitchen at work, though she told me I'd have to replace that.' He brought them into the living room.

Millie laughed, and Andrew's mother said, 'Resourceful as ever.'

She had plenty of small talk and asked about Millie's children. Millie invited her to come and meet them on Sunday afternoon.

She drove home pondering on Andrew's present situation. Clearly he was doing much of the housework and his mother would not relish being left on her own. She knew what she had to do. All those years ago Pete had taken over responsibility for her mother and she was in the position to sort the problem out for Andrew now. He would not be happy if his mother was left on her own.

★ ★ ★

By Sunday afternoon Millie had finalised her plans. She was watching for Andrew's arrival and went out to his car when she saw him pull up on her drive. Elsie Worthington seemed stiff and fragile as she helped her into the house and through to the conservatory. Millie had decided they'd have their afternoon tea here because although the sun was shining, there was too sharp a breeze to have it in the garden.

'What a lovely house you have. So big and bright.'

Millie introduced her to her children. 'Sylvie baked the Victoria sponge this morning and the boys made the scones and the gingerbread men,' she said as she poured out the tea. The children handed round the food and Elsie praised everything.

'If Andrew comes to live here, he won't know he's born. Home-made cakes too.'

'I hope he will come,' Millie smiled at him. But she thought her guests were not entirely at ease and when they'd finished their tea, she said, 'The children have promised to clear away and wash up, so while they're doing that let me show you more of my house. Andrew hasn't seen it all yet. Can you manage the stairs?'

'Yes, no problem,' Elsie said cheerfully but it took her a long time to get up.

Millie had spent a couple of hours spring-cleaning the room that Hattie had used, and took them there now. It had two big windows with views over the garden and a gas fire fitted into the grate. Two small armchairs were pulled up to it and there was a bookcase and a small table. On the other side of the room was a single bed and two wardrobes. Once it had been the main bedroom of the house and for Hattie the adjoining dressing-room had been turned into a bathroom.

'This is a magnificent room,' Elsie said, 'a bed sitting-room.'

'Would you be happy living here?' Millie asked. 'I'd want

you to spend most of your time downstairs with us, but if the boys get too boisterous for you, you can come up here and find peace. I've asked Andrew to make this his home when we're married, but we'd both be worried about leaving you on your own, so I'm inviting you to come too.'

'Oh Millie you are so kind! Are you sure?' Elsie was blinking back tears of emotion. 'I'm so pleased. I didn't dare hope … You are so thoughtful. I know Andrew will be happy with you. Did he put you up to this?'

'No,' Andrew said, 'it's entirely Millie's idea. Thank you.' Andrew's eyes too were glistening with unshed tears. He put an arm round Millie's waist and kissed her cheek. 'I told you she was one in a million.'

Millie had started holding monthly senior staff meetings again so they all knew what was going on in the company. Four months later, she and Andrew announced their engagement at one of them. They received hearty congratulations and several said they'd make a good team. They were all happy to see the business settling into the new regime and continuing to increase its profits. The office had settled down and everyone was pulling their weight. They'd all recovered from a bad patch.

Millie felt equally happy about how things were going at home. Andrew was developing an interest in the city of Liverpool, its history and how it had grown and developed. He'd found books about how the slave trade had been carried on in the old days, and gave them to Simon and Kenny to read. He took the whole family on expeditions to see places of interest in the city, and swept Valerie and Helen and their families along too.

Sylvie, too, seemed to be on an even keel. 'I've decided it would be better if I didn't work for you,' she told Andrew. 'The other secretaries are saying it's a very cushy number for me as you'd have to make excuses for any mistakes I make.'

Millie asked Miss Franklin to switch her to someone else. She became Tom Bedford's secretary, while Andrew was allotted Connie Grey's services in her stead. Sylvie was living in a fever of anticipation and continuing to write to Denis every day and it seemed they were making plans for a big wedding.

Millie was more than content with the way things were turning out but she was longing to be married and have her own affairs settled.

One Sunday, Andrew took all the family out on a visit to Speke Hall and they returned home tired and hungry after a long day out to yet another pre-cooked casserole. Andrew had stayed to eat supper with them before going home, and afterwards Sylvie had sent them out on to the terrace to enjoy the last of the sun while she and the boys washed up.

Stretched out in the garden chair, Millie said, 'Andrew, you've practically made yourself one of the family, I don't think we need to wait any longer for our wedding.'

He jerked upright in his chair and felt for her hand. 'That's wonderful. It can't come soon enough for me. I've had to make a big effort to be patient.'

'I know you have and so have I. Let's go ahead and set the date.' Millie felt a thrill of anticipation akin to what Sylvie was showing. 'It's time we thought of ourselves and what we want.'

He pulled her to her feet. 'I want to kiss you but I can't show any passion here, we're too near this family of yours. Let's walk round the garden, find a more private spot.'

Millie had to laugh as he led her behind the bushes. 'Fancy having to do this at our age.'

They'd had plenty of time to discuss and agree on what they wanted. It was to be a quiet church wedding, with just the immediate family on both sides. Valerie had offered to put on the wedding breakfast and had been collecting items of food for that for some time. Simon, as the man of the family, was to walk her down the aisle and give her away, and there was to be as little fuss as possible.

'No,' Sylvie objected, when she heard what was planned, 'you can't do that, it would be too quiet. I want to be your bridesmaid and wear a long frock. I want you to look like a bride in a white gown.'

'Hold on,' Millie told her, 'you can be my bridesmaid but I can't wear a white gown.'

'Yes, you can, clothes rationing finished long ago.'

'No,' Millie insisted, 'absolutely not. I'm past all that. I'm a widow marrying for the second time, I've had three children and we're all going to wear ordinary clothes.'

'Not too ordinary,' Helen said. 'Let me make your outfit, it can be my wedding present to you. You need a really stunning dress, it's got to be New Look at the very least.'

Since it had first burst on the fashion scene the style had become somewhat modified, the waist was not quite so cinched, the skirt not quite so full and long, but it was still radically different to wartime fashions and more people were wearing it. It had changed women's wear for good.

'But first,' Helen went on, 'I'm going to take you out to choose a hat that suits you and fits the occasion. Then we can choose a pattern for the dress and look for the right material.'

Millie took an afternoon off the following week to go shopping with her, and chose a blue hat.

'No,' Helen said, 'it suits you but it's too plain and service-able.' They went to another shop where Millie tried on a dozen hats. Helen picked out one in a soft peach organza with a wide floppy brim. 'This is more a wedding hat, try it on.'

Millie looked at herself in the mirror and thought the hat was a revelation. It added a warm tint to her face. 'I love it,' she said. 'How clever of you to know it would suit me.'

'The pattern next,' Helen said, and it took Millie a long time to decide on that. 'Now we need some filmy material in the same shade as your hat, georgette or chiffon, I think.' Helen was not satisfied until she had an exact match in soft silk chiffon.

'That's terribly extravagant,' Millie protested, 'especially as it will need lining.'

Helen was already buying taffeta in a similar shade, 'It can't be too extravagant for a wedding dress. What about Sylvie? She must have a dress that tones with yours, and as she'll be making it up herself, it needs to be easier material to manage than silk chiffon.'

They eventually bought Sylvie a dress length of fine cotton cambric, with a flower pattern on a peach background.

'Once I've cut your dress out I can adjust the pattern to Sylvie's size so you'll look like a bride and bridesmaid.'

'I love the full skirt,' Millie told Helen when she tried it on during a later weekend visit, 'and I'll be a very fashionable bride.'

Helen stood back to view her handiwork. 'The material drapes beautifully across this narrow bodice.'

'I shall be able to wear my dress for parties afterwards,' Sylvie said. 'I love it.'

Valerie had come upstairs to help. 'You'll both look very elegant and summery,' she told them.

They were still discussing the dress when they rejoined the family downstairs. 'What about me?' Kenny wailed. 'I don't want to be left out of this wedding. What can I do?'

'You could be a page,' Sylvie suggested.

Kenny was suspicious. 'Would I have to dress up in silly clothes?'

'Yes, of course,' Sylvie told him. 'A white satin shirt and velvet breeches.'

'No, I'm too old for all that, it's baby stuff. I want to wear a smart new suit.'

'That won't do,' Sylvie was scornful, 'you wouldn't look anything like a page.'

Kenny looked hurt. 'What does a page have to do?' he asked.

Andrew smiled at Millie and said, 'Kenny, I need to find a best man. Do you feel you could manage that? You'd have to stand at the front of the church with me, and look after the wedding ring until the vicar says it's time to put it on your mother's finger.'

'You could do that in a smart new suit,' Millie agreed.

His face screwed up with delight. 'Yes, I'd like that,' he said. 'Is it a more important job than Simon's?'

Millie chose to be married in the Maynard family church in Mossley Hill. She told the vicar that she wanted a quiet, simple wedding but he thought that with her Maynard connections she should have the organ and the choir.

The guest list was growing beyond her first estimate as Millie remembered friends and distant relatives, so the venue for the wedding breakfast was changed to Helen's house, because it was nearer to the church and a more suitable size to hold a large party. After all the planning and the waiting, the day seemed suddenly to be on them.

At eleven o'clock on a sunny June morning, it all began to take place as Millie had planned. Dressed in her finery, Millie felt strangely nervous and half afraid something might go wrong to spoil the occasion, but she felt heady with excitement too.

She arrived at the church on time with Simon who suddenly seemed almost grown up. It calmed the butterflies in her stomach to see Sylvie, her bridesmaid, looking very elegant, waiting in the porch for her. They paused until the music changed before Simon led her forward. The congregation stood and all the way down the aisle friendly faces were turning to smile at her. She was surprised to find the church almost full although Andrew had predicted it would be, because all those working in the business had been told they could take time off in order to come if they wanted to.

When she saw Andrew waiting for her, smiling encouragingly and looking handsome and his usual confident self, she had no doubts that she was doing the right thing and they would both be happy. She was able to give her attention to the age-old traditional service after that, knowing she was making her promises with all her friends and family round her, and they would be kept.

Coming out of church into the bright sunlight with her wedding entourage crowding behind her, there were the photographs to be taken. After that Millie led the way across the churchyard to the Maynard family grave, where she wanted to leave her flowers. She'd found it impossible not to think of Pete, but she knew he'd approve of her new husband. He'd wish her well if he could. She was touched when Sylvie laid down her little nosegay of flowers too, and all his family followed suit, laying down the flowers they'd worn.

Then Valerie and Helen were leading the bridal pair to Eric's car, decorated with white satin ribbons. He drove them to his home so that they could stand beside the steps leading to their front door to greet their guests who were walking the two hundred yards or so along the pavement. Hattie and her sister had come and Jeff Willis and his wife. Denis had managed to get leave and brought his mother, and of course the four managers who ran the company had been invited with their wives.

Later that afternoon, the bridal couple drove to Hafod for

their honeymoon. Millie felt supremely happy; as far as she was concerned, she had everything the world had to offer.

Fifteen months later, Denis was demobbed from the army, having completed his National Service. Sylvie had been looking forward to this moment for a long time and had been growing increasingly excited. She'd been building up a bottom drawer, making herself a whole new wardrobe, and was also planning a honeymoon at Hafod.

On his first evening home, she'd brought Denis round to see Millie. She thought his shoulders had broadened, his skin was tanned and he'd matured into a handsome young man. She kissed him. 'Welcome home,' she said.

'I've come to ask if my job is still open,' he told her. 'Sylvie and I want to get married and I have to be able to support her.'

'Of course it is.' Millie smiled. 'I've been half afraid you'd decide you preferred working in a hospital laboratory.'

'No, perfumes are in my blood.'

'Good, business is burgeoning here, we really need you.'

Denis started work in the lab almost immediately and preparations for their wedding went into top gear.

'He'll need six months to get back into the routine,' Millie said to Andrew, 'and then I'll move out and hand responsibility for the lab over to him.'

'And will you make your office in the boardroom then?' he asked. Andrew had moved into the turret when they'd taken on another accountant.

'It's the only available space.' She laughed. 'Such a grand room, but it'll have to be there. Fancy me having that as my office.'

'Why not? You've been running this business very successfully for years, and you own it too. Pete would be proud of what you've achieved. And by the way,' Andrew dropped a kiss on her forehead, 'I'm proud of what you've achieved too.'

'I think it's time I started bringing the boys in during their school holidays,' she said. 'They're old enough to start learning what we do here. I'd like them to carry the firm on in their turn.'

'Spoken like a true Maynard.' Andrew laughed. Millie laughed with him, she'd never told him that there were no Maynards left. Eleanor's last notebook was back in its hiding place in her roll-top desk. It was a secret she intended to keep for the time being. Perhaps she'd tell her boys when they were old enough.

By the time Denis had been working for six months, he and Sylvie had found a small house being built on a nearby estate. They proposed to buy it on a mortgage and start their married life there.

Sylvie walked down the aisle in a white lace bridal gown. She had asked Andrew, as her stepfather, to give her away, and had insisted that he, and all the other gentlemen in the wedding party, wear full morning dress. Andrew gave a very apt and amusing speech at the hotel reception that Geraldine had arranged.

As the clapping died away, he sat down next to Millie. 'I do love you,' he whispered. 'I hope they'll be as happy as we are.'

'There's something I need to tell you that might make you even happier,' she said. 'We're going to have a baby. Let's keep it a secret for now, as I wouldn't want to steal Sylvie's thunder today.'

As Andrew hugged her, Millie felt truly blessed to see her entire family so happy in the present, and with so much to look forward to in the future.